SAMUEL DEKSIS

and the Castle of the Kings

J. R. Roberts

First published in the Great Britain in 2009 by Adhurst Press

ISBN 978-0-9561550-0-9

Printed and bound in Great Britain

Adhurst Press
71 Marchmont Street
London WC1N 1AP

CONTENTS:

Dedicated to the memory of my mother, Valerie Ruth Roberts

1953 – 2005

Who would have loved Mole

-- CHAPTER ONE --

The Secrets of Pebble Lane

Pebble Lane stood forgotten among the brambles and thorns, its centre covered in moss and grass as it had not been used for many years. The lane and the surrounding area was not a pleasant topic for polite conversation in the small rural village of Little Tunlings nearby. The village was itself a dreary and forgotten little place, so far from anything, that time thought it not worth its while to exist there. The quiet rural community was quite satisfied with its sleepy existence, although whether anyone had ever considered change was questionable in itself.

Society was filled with all the little comings and goings that townsfolk find quite unremarkable, but which strikes a spark in the mind of thrifty country gossips. Take for example the talk about Mrs. Potts and her weight problem. Several animated discussions had been held about it in the dingy, beer soaked haze that was The Black Hen, the only local drinking haunt around. Marion Monroe, from the lofty perch of her barstool, declared that she was quite convinced it was comfort eating by a broody wife. Mr. Fletcher, owner of the establishment weighed in. Mr. Potts the station master was, on his account, a moody old grump and that had to be the reason.

The truth was that Mr. Potts was nothing of the sort. He was instead a keen and loving man, happy to keep the local railway station as spick and span as possible and stay away from the evils of idle talk such as that which was spun at length in The Black Hen. Few trains came, and few trains went. After all, this was Little Tunlings, the end of the line.

Geraldine Potts, for her part, was of course carrying excess weight. The burden of running a poorly frequented post office and sweet shop had taken its toll heavily. And furthermore, what none of the gossips at The Black Hen knew was that Mrs. Potts was pregnant with her first child.

The Black Hen, when it had turned from talk of the Potts, came to discussing the 'vicar problem' as it had been labelled. The only church in Little Tunlings was St. Quains and it had been lacking a vicar since the death of its elderly Reverend Hector Grey. With a replacement imminent, all were itching to speculate. Whatever each might have to say the new Reverend would be revealed at the Christmas Day service this year come what may. A little late some felt but the new vicar had been laid up after slipping on some ice apparently; at least that was what Mrs. Monroe's mother had heard.

Idle though talk in The Black Hen might be, there were some topics to which discussion never strayed. To the villagers, Pebble Lane was a dark place of dark deeds from the past and best forgotten as soon as possible. Each mother would forbid her children to venture near it; not that any ever wanted to. It was only later that Pebble Lane was to come to the full attention of the villagers of Little Tunlings in a way that meant it could never again simply be ignored. It was the McGill boys who were about to discovered its most dark secret.

Late on a Christmas Eve night, several years ago, the countryside lay frozen; smothered beneath a thick blanket of crisp icy snow. The snow lay in deep drifts along country lanes and against hedges, lighting a world nearing midnight with a white glow as it reflected the light of the moon. The moon was full; a large misty swirl of glowing light against the dark, clear Christmas Eve sky.

The McGills were an old farming family who had lived in the same farm house, doing the same sort of things for literally centuries. They had two sons, Eraill and Daniel who were inquisitive and quite ready for the adventures that life was sure to throw at them.

The oldest boy, Daniel, had gone out to check the sheep with his father as they always did, every evening. During this cold spell the sheep were staying in the cattle shed overnight practically through choice, but they could normally stay outside for most of the year. Daniel had been complaining of the cold but his father had seemed unperturbed, telling his son that 'the cold did no sensible man any harm.' They removed the loose panel of protective winter shuttering from the cattle shed and climbed over the low wall which separated the pens from the field outside. The sheep then had to be counted by torchlight, but on this occasion the usual sixty seven sheep had become sixty six, a fact which irritated both father and son as neither wanted the bother of having to find a lost sheep on Christmas Eve. Daniel knew his father had important things to sort out in the house and the sheep had only been let out in the sheltered lower fields during the day. A lost sheep would either find shelter or wander back to the cattle shed and wait to be let in. As they left, Mr. McGill replaced the loose panel of shuttering securely behind them. With no snow forecast for the next couple of days at least they were both unconcerned, but mindful to check all was well later on.

Daniel and Eraill had later slunk out of the farmhouse for a midnight walk and, pulling their thick coats tightly around them, they had set off over the scattered layer of frozen snow.

About half an hour into the walk they noticed a thick cloud cover the moon that had been their guide, blocking out the light altogether. About fifteen minutes later it began to snow; slowly at first, then with a strong head wind it began to drive in the way only a blizzard can do. Disorientated, and with pocket torches fading, they sought shelter at the side of the track, half hidden from the raging wind, though it still clawed at them through the hawthorn's bare patches. They huddled together for warmth, transferring whatever body heat they could to one another, half blinded by the fast moving snow flakes and chilled by the relentless wind which howled and mourned around them like some dying banshee.

The boys were on a part of the road which they did not recognise. Great trees hung low overhead but their bare, twiggy arms provided little protection against either the wind or the snow. Struggling on, they found that the track was disappearing beneath the snow very quickly, making it more difficult to follow. The thick blanket of snow weighed down the skeletal structures of wintering undergrowth, causing dips at the edges of the road to become hidden and treacherous, and the snow began clinging to their boots as though it was deliberately trying to slow down their progress.

A large, flat, irregular stone stood upright at one side of the road. Unable to walk any further without rest they made for its protection and led their weary, frozen heads against it. It was as Eraill was bordering on becoming unconscious that Daniel began fumbling with the uncomfortable piece of rock behind him. He could dimly feel regular engravings; letters and then words. He numbly scrabbled for his pocket torch. The scrawled writing was dimly readable in the fading light –

"Here is the final resting place of Jonoway Deksis..."

The rest of the inscription was hidden beneath the snow and Daniel felt a sudden urgency to read the rest of the inscription but, in his haste, a section of the ancient stone crumbled, making part of the inscription unreadable. What he could read struck fear into his heart.

"...a fallen prince among the pale ghosts of Pebble Lane"

PEBBLE LANE! The place they had been brought up to fear! In their delirium they must have taken a wrong turning, for he was certain they were the first to have entered this area in many years. Amidst the panic that ensued, the fact that Eraill had turned pale blue went unnoticed, as did the moment shortly afterwards when he departed from life. Pebble Lane had silently claimed its first victim.

Daniel's first thought was to set off and be away from this dreadful place. He dragged his cold limbs into motion and began trudging forward as quickly as possible, only realising that Eraill was missing as he was almost out of sight of the stone. He started to run back to get him, but the snow was so thick that idea of carrying him was difficult to entertain; better then to go by himself and return with help.

Putting his indecision behind him, Daniel trudged through a narrow opening in the trees and down a slender path created by the action of a stream which now lay frozen beneath his feet. It was with a heavy and fearful heart that he travelled over open fields, now completely covered again with the new heavy fall of snow. Relief flooded through him as he spotted their father's cattle shed in the distance. It was easy to recognise because the McGills held the only major livestock in the local area. Perhaps largely infertile land was a reason for the under development of Little Tunlings.

The chill of the air bit at Daniel's limbs as he made his way closer to the cattle shed, little by little, ploughing on through the snow that was in places knee deep, although at least the snow and wind were now starting to ease somewhat. At the cattle shed he briefly rested to give himself a chance to catch his breath and recover from the exertion of the journey. A momentary pause was sufficient for this purpose, but just as he started to move on towards the farmhouse he felt his foot catch under something. A panel of winter shuttering was lying near the surface of the fresh snowfall. Looking back at the cattle shed, Daniel could see that it was the one which was kept loose to provide entry. It must have been left unsecured when his father had replaced it after the earlier check on the sheep. Daniel moved back to the opening. Cautiously, he reached over the low wall to touch some of the cold, dead bodies of what were formally some of the best sixty six sheep in the country. His father came running from the house, flashlight in hand, when he heard Daniel's wild cries of distress. Mr. McGill stood rooted to the spot beside the cattle shed and swore with his head held in his hands as it became apparent what had happened to their sheep.

On Christmas Day morning, Little Tunlings was more sleepy than usual. At St. Quains a young and nervous Reverend Philip Knock awaited the first arrivals for the Christmas service. He had consulted several times the stash of scruffy notes he had been given to double check that the service was supposed to have commenced at ten. Ten o' clock had come and gone and a full half hour had passed without a sign of anyone. Reverend Knock sighed heavily. This parish was going to be more of a challenge than he had imagined. This was the final outpost of the church. He would be living on the frontier... he was fighting the greatest battle. It did not take long before such noble thoughts were crushed by the heavy gloom that settled in his heart. No wonder he had ended up here – it was obviously because no one else had wanted to come.

A wailing drew him from his pondering, as up the pathway staggered a sobbing woman dressed in black. With a distinct Scottish lilt she told a heart rendering story. Her two children dead, the cattle dead. Mrs. Potts had miscarried, Mr. Fletcher's boy dead and he even lived abroad apparently. All children, she wailed, all dead. For Reverend Knock her grief was quite beyond his emotional capability so he stood frozen, ashen and uncomprehending as she continued to weep in terrible distress. The curse of Pebble Lane had cast its long bleak shadow over the village.

Some hours earlier, far away in a bedroom of a terraced house amid the urban sprawl of the inner city, a child was lying in bed, barely awake, but half listening, half wanting to hear a sound of footsteps. Not the footsteps of some Father Christmas, but the footsteps of his elderly guardian.

Where she was, he did not know; he had been left in the house alone all day since she had failed to return from the shops yesterday evening. At barely eight years old, it was surprising how well he had coped. Now, as he led half awake, there was one thing he feared more that anything. That she should not return. He knew he could cope for a while, but his money would run out eventually, and then after much wrangling he would be returned to his father. This would mean a return to a world which he could escape from every winter, a world which offered for him very little hope or excitement. For now, the only sound which he could hear was the unnatural call of birdsong as the glow of the streetlamp outside his window confused the birds into a premature dawn chorus. He saw a tiny flutter against the orange glow that spread its penetrating hands through his curtains and smiled – he loved how the city was alive even at night.

And the name of this boy? It was by birth Samuel Deksis. A boy about whom the only remarkable thing was his unusual surname. Perhaps it is strange, that this one unusual feature would mould his destiny for the rest of his life. But for the time being its burden was not upon him, for he had been known for as long as he could remember as Samuel Hawkins.

Samuel was so desperate to stay here in the city. Away from his father's house in Little Tunlings; away from the boring rural existence of home education (which had only ever involved him reading books) and waiting. Samuel had always been waiting; what for he did not know, but something deep inside him told him that he was different. Considering his home education, he was remarkably well spoken and knowledgeable, displaying a quick and fertile mind, although his skills were always repressed by his father. And this is what he had put this waiting down to; a repressed existence, longing for change. The winter months which he spent here with his Aunt Mulltasch were different. Full of fun and freedom, he often laughed so much at her silly jokes and songs that he honestly thought he might die.

There were foot steps, heavy but clear, causing Samuel to stir and awaken. He called out: 'Aunt Mulltasch?'

'Oh, Samuel, where oh where are you?'

'Here, here …' he cried, suddenly wide awake, throwing himself out of bed and racing to the landing. And there she was. His Aunt Mulltasch. Glasses askew, nose bloodied and clothes filthy.

'What on earth happened to you?'

'Oh I don't know - I don't know, they took me and threatened me, if I didn't tell them where I lived. They must have wanted to rob me.'

'Who are they? Did you tell them?'

'Oh, no, no, I did not, but they hurt me, and I am aching all over.'

So he sat her down and helped to tend to her wounds, although he was glad to find that her mental wounds and anxieties were in need of the greatest attention. She told Samuel that she had been returning from the shops when she had heard the sound of loud music – a Christmas holiday fancy dress party. As she had turned to come down the narrow alley she had passed some of the revellers who had been drinking outside. Then, right in the dark in front of her in the dim light, this Red Indian had grabbed her, feathers waving, muscles flexing, and pulled her through a doorway into a darkened room. A man had spoken to her there; asked who she was and where she lived, but she had remained silent. The man had left her for a while, and then he had returned, bringing some food. She must have fallen asleep on the floor at some point because when she had woken she could see that it was daylight outside, visible through the cracks around the door. The man had kicked her about a bit and drilled her with a few more questions. There had been a commotion and some talking which she couldn't understand. After a bit of waiting the man had pulled her up and roughly pushed her out of the door. She had made her way back home as quickly as she could. After telling her story in full once, and shuddering as she went, Aunt Mulltasch seemed to have expended the worst of her anxieties and they both went to bed before long.

Our story really begins almost exactly four years later, in a cramped but comfortably furnished room in an old and rambling stone walled house in the village of Little Tunlings. A warm fire was roaring in a magnificent, marble lined grate and issuing violent explosions of white hot sparks which were dancing gaily in the air at one end of the square room. There was no back wall to the fire place; instead, visible beyond it was a second room, accessible only by a short, low passageway to the right of the fire.

It was a strange place, almost as strange as the brightly patterned carpet underfoot, but that paled in comparison to the collection of bizarre objects which lined the pale apricot walls and white bay window. On a rusty metal shelf there was a device that appeared as though it was made of a red coloured metal which shone with unusual lustre considering the many cobwebs which were hanging from its numerous extremities. Next to it there was a collection of unusual utensils, each appearing more warped and twisted than the previous one and, in a far corner, a big bookcase held a large collection of ancient scripts and books, several of which were whispering and quivering quietly as though they had many secrets they wished to share.

The room overall had a rustic appearance with great gnarled oak beams stretching across the ceiling, several sagging armchairs centred around the grate and thick oak tables pilled unreasonably high with ancient, dusty books and yellowing maps. Where there were spaces on the walls between the many long shelves, photographs were displayed, mainly depicting old buildings and street scenes. There were also several old oil paintings, showing images of what one would presume must have been austere relations, as not one of the images showed a smiling or relaxed face, and yet each person depicted shared similar features; either a pointed nose or thin streaky hair. Overhead, a simplistic chandelier was hanging slightly askew and the burning candles it held were casting moving shadows around the room which seemed long and menacing. Quite how the chandelier was suspended appeared a mystery as there was no obvious means displayed that would account for it hanging from the ceiling in such a manner.

In the corner nearest to the open fire there sat a man apparently oblivious to the fact that sparks were singeing his long grey trousers and thick woollen jumper. He rested his head in his hands so that his long silver-grey hair drooped down, covering his face. Occasionally he was reaching up with his hand to part his long hair, revealing two beady, black eyes beneath two bushy ginger eyebrows. It appeared that for several years his eyebrows had decided not to follow the decline in hair colour that had resulted in his long silvery-grey locks. This gave his face the strange appearance that the eyebrows were rather detached and independent facial features. An agitated shouting from the room beyond the fire heralded the interruption of an unwelcome distraction.

'Albert, do you want your tea brought to you at six this evening like usually? It's just that Mrs. McGill from the farm has been a little unwell over the weekend and I promised her that I would pop round to see her'

'I still want it at six Marion' replied Albert curtly, 'And I have told you before about calling me Albert. In future you shall address me properly.'

'Yes, my apologies Mr. Hawkins'

'Mrs. McGill can wait. I still haven't forgiven the old crab for telling me she wasn't coming to my Christmas party last year, and then deciding to turn up at the last minute.

When she marched in I was halfway through a drunken rendition of *'Ye Vilest Vulture'* with that hideous Geraldine Potts who was simultaneously participating, as the only contestant, in a 'mince pies in a minute' competition. Beat her personal best of forty-two I daresay. Come to think of it, that Potts is rather bird like; ungainly on her feet and with such a crooked nose you might take her for a podgy witch. And that McGill woman dared say we were a *'cutie wee pair!'* and in that highly irritating accent of hers. I certainly don't owe someone like that any favours.'

'Very well Albert. While I remember, your shopping bill came in over budget so I need more money from you.'

'Marion, every shopping budget for the last few years has been over budget. Either you're siphoning off the money or that thieving brat is overeating,' he said, stabbing an accusing finger beyond the fire place.

'One small thing before I go then. I need my payment for this months cleaning soon please because my mother is not well as I believe you are already aware and she has been off work recently so perhaps you might be able to... well you know... bring forward the payment a little bit.'

'Most certainly not Marion! Your mother had plenty of family heir looms located around her neck and on her fingers last time she was here. Perhaps you should remind Phyllis of that the next time you see her and also of the fact that objects, such as the exquisite emerald ring she wears, can be surgically removed if she has fallen upon hard times.'

With that a thin, sour faced woman came down the passage way and, collecting her blue coat and a violently pink feathered hat from the coat peg on the wall, found her way through the messy jumble of tables and objects. She left the room without as much as another word. Several moments of heated silence followed before a younger voice broke the silence from the room beyond the fire.

'It's so unfair that you still shout at me like I am about three years old. For goodness sake father, I am twelve years old with a mind of my own. You might as well tell me what the matter is otherwise I am going to have to endure your impatience all evening and I am simply no longer prepared to put up with that.'

'Isn't it obvious what the matter is?' shouted an aggravated Albert, savagely kicking out at the table nearby, 'It grieves me that you even have to take it upon yourself to ask. I would have expected you to have had some greater foresight seeing that I am "*your father*." When your mother was alive she always said to me that you had proved to be the greatest disappointment in her life. Come around here Samuel and then I will have to talk to you.'

Sulky and sullen faced, a dark haired boy stormed down the passage, brown eyes wild and indignant. The conversation resumed as the boy stood, arms clasped behind his back and head staring at the floor.

'There are so many things I have not got around to telling you young Samuel. So many harsh lessons I have not had the chance to teach you and so many punishments I have not had the opportunity to enact. With each day that passes I feel weaker and my old strength seems to just ebb away. I am what they call an old man, but not so old that I have forgotten what it was like to be young.'

'But father...'

'Don't interrupt Samuel!' snarled Albert. 'Time is short, I see it as a tiny quantity of sand slipping through my clenched and gnarled fingers,' he proceeded to demonstrate with his long sharp fingers in a menacing fashion, 'I hope, but sadly doubt, you have the intelligence to understand that even if I could be sustained I would still ultimately be heading towards oblivion.'

'And I assume by that you mean you are going to die?' interjected Samuel.

'Yes boy, I am heading towards the one thing none of us can control. It is the ultimate switching off of the light, the snuffing out of the candle, the faltering, and failing of the flame. I would have tried to explain what I am about to tell you when you would have come of age at seventeen, but time being what it is, I have no option other that to start setting down the basics right here, right now. Do you remember your mother when you were a child? Initially she was weak and placid. I spent years building her up, before she did me the ultimate honour of leaving me forever.'

He breathed the last words with a deep sense of self satisfaction. Albert continued as though he felt there was no need to pause for thought, perhaps as he already suspected the boy was unable to keep up.

'Now don't get me wrong, your mother was of good blood, but she married unwisely.'

'She married you?' questioned Samuel in a bored and tired voice.

'Not me you stupid boy, not me! The Hawkins family are very well connected. Extremely well in fact, now I come to think of it. But that is beside the point because you can't possibly understand the importance. Now where was I? Ah yes, She married badly because she married a certain Harold Deksis; handsome but a dim wit in my eyes and from a relatively poor background. Not a piece of family silver to their name as I recall, and that really does show a lack of class and prosperity. I don't think I knew of a Deksis who was interested in either gold or silver. A very strange lot and a bad bunch. Now tell me Samuel have you ever heard of a Deksis?'

'No father, it is an extremely unusual surname.'

'Precisely; it is no normal surname, and I have never spoken of it with you before. But now, back to your mother. The silly bitch was intoxicated with him. Could not get enough of him, and then one day they both disappeared. Neither hide nor hair was seen of them for several years. Then one foggy February morning they found your mother ragged and bleeding with a baby wrapped in blankets. She was cold and, apart from the baby, completely alone. When they took her away for questioning they found her to be rendered dumb. They said it was shock or something similar. Eventually she disclosed that her husband had been taken away, although she had no recollection of who had taken him, or where they had been for the past few years. She was declared mad and the child was taken away from her and it died in an orphanage from pneumonia several months later.

'Poor little mite,' shuddered Samuel under his breath.

'Boy, that child was your brother!'

A stunned silence cut across the room. For several stinging seconds neither person moved a muscle. Samuel stared at his father in disbelief.

'My brother, how could he be, only my half brother surely!'

'No boy, he was your brother.'

'Then that makes you…'

'…Well, not your father at least. It makes me your ruddy guardian. If I had known she was pregnant with his second ruddy child there is no way that I would have taken her in and cared for her.'

'But you didn't do it for love did you? You told me that you were never happy with mum from the first day you met her.'

'Right you are. I did it because I needed to get in with a Deksis. Night after night during your life time I have pondered over my family collection of old books and scrolls. It just so happened that I had reached a point in my studies where I realised that a Deksis would hold the key to everything.'

Albert was sitting bolt upright in his chair now, more alert than ever before and eyes staring with a new found intensity.

'Where is that red bound book? I am sure I put it somewhere nearby,' Wondered Albert out loud, to himself more than anyone else.

Samuel lifted his head slowly to stare at the tyrant he now knew to be his step father.

'But she was not a Deksis was she? She was only by marriage to a deceased husband.'

'Yes boy, but she knew. Somewhere within that clamped up store of memories there lay the secrets of the Deksis family. I realised that if only I could find some way to get at them that I would finally understand all the pieces of the jigsaw that intrigued me so… I had that wretched book out yesterday, but I can't find it in this pile of books… but alas I am no magician, and I could not get into her memories of the time they had shared together, however hard I tried. She could only remember so far and then it was just like walking straight into a brick wall. As time passed her mentor became her lover. I believed that only through marriage could I overcome the barriers and unlock the secrets her mind contained.'

Albert's eyes continued searching the room for the book, evidently distracted by its disappearance. Samuel was also glancing around, his eyes coming to rest on a dark red volume stored in the bookcase which was marginally less dusty than its neighbours. He leaned forward slowly to reach it.

'Samuel, you clumsy great clot! Get your hands off my bookcase at once. Stop touching my things because you know you will only end up damaging something, you useless article.'

Standing up from the chair Albert strode forwards flinging Samuel backwards so that his head made contact with one of the tables. A trickle of falling documents suddenly became a torrent as teetering piles on the table came raining down on top of Samuel. Albert fumed with irritation but in a bid to maintain focus he paid little attention to what had happened, continuing to speak as he plied the red book carefully out of the bookcase and returned to his seat. He immediately continued, so Samuel listened while lying on the floor, surrounded by a sea of papers.

'So we were married. Both ending up hating each other pretty quickly, but not before I had discovered everything I needed to know. At the same time you were being brought up as my own wretched child. Your mother ended up hating you too. The sight reminded her of her late husband, the reason why I had forced her to marry me, and the reason why her life was hell. She was so desperate to dispose of you. Several times I had to persuade her against knifing you to death in your sleep. And as she realised there was no escape she ran off and disappeared. Not like the time with her first wretched husband, because there were sightings of her in nearby towns which reached me. And then I was left with you, the indelible stain upon my life, the cause of so much anger and hatred. I hate you still because you remind me of her and what she did to me. But I am no fool. I am a learned man in my field and through my investigations and research, through painstaking hours of reading, I know of the strange protection placed over you. I cannot harm you without evoking certain penalties upon myself, penalties that I am unwilling to accept. That said I can still make your life boring, pitiful and wasted. I think in that I have at least succeeded. Tell me that boy, and give me my last bit of pleasure.'

Samuel remained silent, unwilling to co-operate with any unnecessary demands. He simply nodded slowly with contempt written upon his face.

'As I can no longer provide for you, I have arranged for you to go to stay with the people at the farm soon. They are the only people who will take you. How quickly you leave here depends on the speed of decline in my health, and how long you stay with them depends when you are required. I do not have the power to re-write destiny, history, or ritual. And what is more I have already explained enough for tonight.'

Albert did not speak another word to Samuel for the rest of the evening, leaving him to digest all he had been told. Mrs. Monroe returned and provided an embittered dinner of sorts and set Albert to bed before leaving.

That night, when the house was quiet, Samuel sat and pondered his fate by the dying embers of the fire. He often came back into the main room once Albert was in bed. This was the only existence he had ever known during the summer, being locked away in the house with Albert, or perhaps he should call him his father as he would have done up to a couple of hours ago.

During the winter, on the other hand, things were usually different. He would catch the weekly train out of dreary Little Tunlings and make the journey to stay with his Aunt Mulltasch. She lived in a quiet corner of suburbia and he had no idea if she was really his aunt, although he rather doubted it. She was of German origin, and he had no knowledge of anyone in his background that was German.

Aunt Mulltasch liked to talk. It was the only thing in life which she had ever seemed to enjoy with a passion. She would talk about everything and anything; the news in the newspaper, the family next door, and what the postman really got up to. Not that any of these things were of any interest to Samuel. He had always rather enjoyed his time there, and Aunt Mulltasch was always good to him in her own way, or at least considerably kinder than his 'father.'

He could remember one Christmas when she had forced him to stand outside in the freezing air to put a standing stone back into its upright position. She told him it was a 'skyscraper to the dwarfs'.

That was the only trouble with Aunt Mulltasch, she was a little bit eccentric and as a result a bit of an embarrassment in public. Ever since she had enrolled him at First Avenue Primary she would meet him at the gate come rain or shine wearing some outrageous flowery outfit. Samuel had always been quite a popular boy at First Avenue although his summerly disappearances thwarted his desire to become captain of the school cricket team. It was customary at First Avenue for last year's captain to choose his successor, and a sneering Jack Watson had told him that he was looking for someone with true commitment who didn't slink off for the best part of half the year.

But the days of spending the winter months with Aunt Mulltasch were now long gone. The last time he had seen her house it was up for sale, looking forsaken and blackened with its windows boarded up. The doctors had found that Aunt Mulltasch was suffering from a degenerative disease, which accounted for her accelerating forgetfulness. Not that it had been the disease which killed her. Samuel had been at school one cold January morning when he was taken out of lessons and informed gently that Mrs. Mulltasch had perished in blaze at her home. It later transpired that the fire started when she forgot to turn the gas stove off while cooking. So her memory loss had killed her really, just a symptom of the real problem, yet still fatal.

That all happened last winter, so this would be his first here in Little Tunlings. He could not honestly say he had been looking forward to it very much, although there was so much change ahead now which he had not counted on that perhaps this winter would turn out more interesting than he had been anticipating.

A sudden flurry of sparks in the grate caused him to jump a little. A few sprayed into a mug that had been left beside the fire and fizzled out in the liquid. Albert must have forgotten to put it away. Samuel formed the intention to take the mug out to the kitchen, but the thought was displaced almost as soon as it had formed. He tried to picture his real father's face in his mind's eye but somehow in his imagination he seemed unable to create anything that resembled a complete person.

If only he could remember more of his mother. He could remember only a couple of words that she had spoken and he could remember one night when she had tucked him into bed, and had sat for hours crying. Did she really do that? Come to think of it he was quite unsure whether he was remembering her doing that, or whether it was something Albert had told him. The fact that Albert was not really his father made him feel sort of warm inside. It was a nice thought that the embittered old man was not a part of his own personality. It was something he had been wishing for all his life, although it was not until now that he realised it.

Whilst he was glad to hear most of what he had been told, (the fact that Albert was going to die soon was a real unexpected bonus), the only trouble was that now he had thousands of questions he wanted answers to. It felt as though they were burning a hole in his brain because, for the time being, they would have to be left unanswered. There were so many more pressing practical concerns.

Although he had heard the McGills mentioned some time in the past he knew nothing of them except that they owned the only farm for miles around. Samuel knew little of the village folk because Albert never took him out to meet anyone and few people ever called. News filtered through mouthy Marion. Apart from her he only knew Mr. Potts who waved Samuel off cheerily from the station each time he caught the train to visit Aunt Mulltasch. The thought of staying with complete strangers suddenly seemed rather daunting, although he quickly reminded himself that anything would be better than staying here in the house with Albert. He tried to remember everything that had been said about the McGills. Marion was always mentioning people from the village which she occasionally went to visit. Samuel had never got on with Mrs. Marion Monroe. Come to think of it he aught to have an awful lot in common with her. She likewise was as downtrodden by Albert as he was. Yet she was a bitter person too which made him take an instant dislike. Her visits to people nearby were usually prompted by jealousy at their many possessions. She was always one for that Marion, always one for sizing people up. Samuel had no idea how she had come to work for Mr. Hawkins, as she was instructed to call him. Perhaps she had come there after mum had died. He certainly could not recall Albert ever doing anything practical in the way of housework.

Anyway, the McGills were his main current concern he decided. The fact that they had a farm was probably the only thing that made them stand out in his mind. Just today Marion had been saying she was to visit Mrs. McGill because she was unwell. He had a sudden image in his mind of a beautiful young woman staring up into his face with tender eyes. He stopped himself before his mind wandered any further. Samuel wondered if they had any children. Perhaps there would be some his age. That would be the first time in his life he had ever had anyone his own age around him at home.

How different things would have been if his brother had lived. By now he would be his big brother; perhaps he would be just like his father. There were just so many things to dream about, not least the mystery of where his mother and father went for those lost years. Perhaps they had simply run away together to live somewhere else and perhaps, perhaps…

Samuel had failed to notice how heavy his eyelids felt, and suddenly his head felt heavy too. But his feet were cold. It was time to head once again to a cold, hard bed, but he would not have to do this forever, he reminded himself. There was a real blend of hope and change on the horizon.

As sleep grasped him, Samuel thought he heard something rustle past the door to his room. He rolled over, confused, and switched on the bedside lamp. All was quiet once again and Samuel was content that the creaky old house was playing its usual tricks. He turned the dimmer control on the bedside lamp down so that it glowed with a gentle, peaceful light and fixed his eyes on a heavy oil painting mounted on the wall in front of his bed, which featured an old and weary woman. She looked as weary as Samuel felt, he thought, as sleep dissolved sight and consciousness led into the fluid world of dreams.

The following morning dawned bright and beautiful. From the inadequate narrow window in his room Samuel could see the great mountains in the distance, looking vast and tinged with the pinkie-red hue of the light of the morning sunshine. As he undid the catch the air which flowed in through the open window was crisp and clear, as though it had descended from high in the atmosphere and had been chilled and cleansed on the way down. The ground that was visible below seemed to have been covered in an icy glaze of frost, by the same hand which had created the glistening holly bush in the distance and the shimmering frosted tree branches hanging above the lane. He could just make out a thin distant figure coming up it. Mrs. Monroe often came early. There was no time in the day quite like this Samuel thought to himself as, feeling refreshed, he closed the window and made his way back to his uncomfortable bed. This room in which he slept was reasonably small and tidy, although a lack of natural light made it appear rather dark and gloomy. The painting at the foot of his bed which he had stared at so attentively in his sleepy haze still loomed miserably in its usual position; the woman depicted was perhaps a little more sour than usual with her eyes just as dark. The gloomy light also hid the damp and prevented it showing up in the corners of the walls. It did the same for the deep, draughty cracks which were to be found here and there on the walls and between the floorboards. It was in this hovel that Samuel had spent all of his earthly existence to date. He slumped back into bed, feeling sleep pouring over him in great waves. He was fully expectant that Albert would be shouting up before long, and the smell of cooked breakfast would drift up to his nostrils. This morning that call never came.

Samuel slept on until he heard the rasping knock of Mrs. Monroe on his door. Stirring from his deep sleep he rolled over, confused to see his watch pointing to twelve o' clock. He was so confused that he tried turning it upside down; just to check he was looking at it the right way up. Samuel could not recall an occasion when he had been left to sleep on for this long.

The rasping knock on the door occurred once again, accompanied with Marion's shrill instruction to make himself decent, so he called for her to come in, ensuring his naked body was covered completely by the thick blankets on his bed. He looked up expectedly at her entrance, although he could discern little from her facial appearance. She began to speak very quickly after some initial hesitation, as though she simply wanted to get it over and done with as quickly as possible in one burst.

'Samuel, your step-father passed away during the night. I found him this morning and he had already died. I had previously been informed by him that you are to move out straight away. Pack your things, bring them down to the hallway and wait by the front door. I have been told that someone is coming to pick you up.' She said the last words rather stiffly, with a slight hint of what Samuel took to be disproval. She then turned and marched out of sight.

He led back down on his bed for a couple of minutes studying the ceiling very carefully, deeply engrossed in the slow acrobatics performed by several wintering spiders. He felt strangely empty and hollow. It was so strange and almost unimaginable to picture a future without the bullying influence of Albert Hawkins.

Samuel felt suddenly unnerved. He never imagined that Albert was going to die quite as quickly as this. He had pictured in his head that in about a month he would have to consider change. Now all of a sudden an event that played out in his imagination was to become a reality, today. Mrs. Monroe was waiting in the hallway when Samuel arrived. He had struggled to find something in which he could place his few belongings; having never been away from the house except to visit Aunt Mulltasch, (where she had provided almost everything he would need), he was not exactly used to packing up all his things. He had managed to stuff his property into a black holdall which he now carried at his side. It was almost impossible to imagine that he may never return to this house. Mrs. Monroe went bustling off when he arrived, saying she had things to attend to before the funeral undertakers arrived. Samuel stood there staring through the small window set into the hall out into the tiny court yard outside. He could dimly remember in his younger years when he had been allowed to play outside. His mother must have still been with them at that time, he thought to himself sighing. Behind him was the sitting room and fire place. He saw the mug which he had spotted and intended to take to the kitchen last night. It was lying on its side; knocked over by a hasty Mrs. Monroe he had no doubt. He shook off fear of Albert's reaction at the stain on the carpet which was clearly visible even from where he was standing. No doubt he would have got the blame.

A confident knock at the front door interrupted his thoughts, and put him in an immediate dilemma. He had never been allowed to answer the door in the past. That had always been something Albert had done. With a sudden feeling of increased power he walked to the door. Slowly and carefully he unbolted it and then proceeded to unlock it using the keys on the wall as he had seen Albert do many times in the past. Albert had always said gruffly that security was his number one concern, and had insisted that the door was both locked and bolted even when Mrs. Monroe was in the house. Samuel seemed to remember that the issue had been the cause of several fiery exchanges between the pair in the past. Very few days had gone by without some bust up between Albert and Mrs. Monroe. It was a wonder she had kept on working for him.

Opening the door, Samuel saw with some surprise a tall man next to a relatively short woman. Both looked middle aged, and the woman had her hair covered by a red silk shawl. There were a few of seconds of rather uncomfortable silence before the man began to speak.

'Good morning, you must be Samuel. I am Henry McGill, pleasure to meet you.'

'Morning' replied Samuel.

'This is my wife Mirabella.'

'Nice to meet you Samuel.'

Behind him, Samuel could here the sound of Mrs. Monroe approaching.

'Morning Henry, Mirabella, best not to come in. I am expecting the undertaker as I explained in my message. Samuel is ready to go with you now.'

Samuel felt her slowly, but forcefully pushing him out of the door. When he turned around the door was already closing behind him. He felt rather guilty for not saying goodbye, not that Mrs. Monroe would have appreciated it much.

With a rather heavy heart Samuel turned to see his new guardians. They had both begun to walk away through the stone archway leading to the world outside. Mrs. McGill turned back expectantly. Samuel stepped forwards to join her.

'Good morning wee Samuel.'

'Good morning,' replied Samuel, rather taken aback by the Scottish lilt in her voice.

'It is a great pleasure to have you with us today and I hope that you are going to be very, very happy. I'll take that holdall from you?'

'Ok, well, thank you' said Samuel awkwardly.

'We are both very, very sorry to hear your sad news my dear, if it can be any consolation to you. We had better get going right now so come along wee Samuel and we can talk along the way.'

Samuel made his way alongside the pair. The conversation was not initially as forthcoming as he had anticipated, but secretly he was glad to remain wrapped up in his own thoughts for a little while.

They soon passed down the road from the house and there was a really biting chill in the air. Winter was definitely on its way and the last dregs of autumn would abate before long. They reached the fork in the road. Samuel would usually go right, which would lead him downhill to the centre of Little Tunlings and hence down to the railway station.

It felt strange to choose the road to the left. It was not really much more than a track, but it was evidently quite well used. Samuel was amazed at the view from the crest of the hill. Whilst Little Tunlings was tucked away in the hollow out of sight, the old house he had lived in with Albert seemed huge. He had never realised quite how large it must look even from this distance away.

The banks began to rise up steeply on both sides of the track and Mrs. McGill began to enquire about Albert. Samuel had never felt able to talk much about Albert and the way he had treated him. However nasty Albert had been, it was done now. He had never even told Aunt Mulltasch about Albert, although he sensed that she would have been able to do little for him. Albert was such a strong person that if he found Samuel had been prattling to someone about him, he would come down on Samuel himself even harder. That was certainly how Samuel saw it. He was therefore relieved when Mrs. McGill said she was sorry to have brought up the topic and understood that he did not want to talk about it.

Perhaps she thought it was a 'wee' bit too nasty for him, thought Samuel to himself. He was beginning to find her particular Scottish accent rather annoying. He felt like she was continually treating him like a three year old child.

They arrived at the house with little fanfare, and Samuel was rather surprised to see how run down the place was looking. He had always imagined it would be a farm in peak production, but the reality of the place was that it looked past its prime. In the fields, rusting farm machinery stood with its paint peeling and the roof of the farm house looked decidedly dilapidated.

Inside, the farmhouse seemed comfy and homely; Mrs McGill took Samuel straight to his new room once she had collected the keys from the Kitchen. She revealed that she had just cleaned out his room this morning, her face turning slightly red as she said this. Samuel felt a bit awkward that the woman had not had more notice of his impending arrival. He thanked her for everything she had done, and once she unlocked his door, he reclaimed his holdall from her and settled down on his new bed.

At least he had a decent window, he thought to himself. Sitting up slightly, he could see out of it while still lying on the bed. At least he could not see his old home from here. It reminded him so much of Albert, as though with it in sight he would never really be able to escape from the dismal weight and indifferent control that had loomed over him there. At least he would not have to spend this Christmas with Albert. Perhaps his life was going to be better here after all. Perhaps!

-- CHAPTER TWO --

Life with the McGills

In some ways the next few months were both the hardest and easiest of Samuel's life. That apparent paradox can be understood because the McGills provided everything he could possible need. He now had two sane guardians who were extremely protective over him.

The problem was that at the same time the McGills presented Samuel with a big obstacle. He suddenly found that he had no choice other than to respond to the kind actions of this lonely couple. Yet he did not know the slightest thing about either of them. They both lavished him with praise, used what money they had (which it turned out was quite considerable) to buy him anything they thought he might need. They tried to teach him at home and he felt he had to try and pay attention. He dared not break the spell which they seemed to be bound by.

Meal times had always been difficult from the moment he arrived, and for some reason they never seemed to become an awful lot easier. Firstly there was the issue of whether he ought to speak or whether he should just sit there quietly. Then, if he did decide to say anything, what should he say?

With the McGills one topic always seemed closed. That topic was the past. The couple seemed to have a shared desire to avoid the topic at all lengths, and whether it was from the knowing glance between them or the sudden coughing fits, Samuel got the message loud and clear that they were not willing to talk about their lives before he had arrived.

Sometimes, when Samuel was feeling somewhat downhearted during those dark winter months, he wondered why Albert Hawkins had chosen to send him here. Had he dreamt this up as some sort of eternal punishment? Was there some deep rooted reason why he had chosen the McGills? They certainly did not seem taken aback that Samuel was now with them. They instead seemed totally overjoyed. Too overjoyed Samuel thought. In his mind there seemed to be something which was not ringing true.

He had not realised how much he was missing Aunt Mulltasch. He had never before realised how close he was to that woman. She might have been totally barmy but she was the closest thing to a true friend he had ever known.

There was one event that Samuel was dreading more that any other. Christmas. Every time he thought about it his stomach gave a sudden lurch. The thought of Mrs. McGill lavishing her 'precious wee boy' with presents was positively sickening. Yet what choice did he have other than to act out his part like some pawn in a giant game of chess? He seemed to have no control over his future. That was all in the hands of the McGills.

The McGills expected little from Samuel in return for their total and undivided devotion, yet Samuel felt he had to do something, so he decided to help Mr. McGill with the livestock. At least that got him outdoors and away from Mrs. McGill. Samuel found Mr. McGill to be a more palatable person. Quite what he had ever seen in Mrs. McGill Samuel could never understand. Together they worked at improving the farm. They replaced the roof on the large hay barn and scrapped some of the old machinery. Samuel enjoyed this work, despite the fact that it was physically very demanding and often tiring. From the hay barn there was a pleasant view down the grassy valley to St. Quains which Samuel would take time to admire. The only problem with working hard on the farm was that it seemed to have the effect of making Mrs. McGill even more besotted with him, one reason that was good enough to almost stop him helping out on the farm anymore.

Yet life on the farm was just about bearable for Samuel. Some of the deep scars left by Mr. Hawkins and his bullying seemed to be lifting. A new, more confident Samuel was emerging.

With Christmas approaching fast, Mrs. McGill began going on an endless stream of shopping trips to Little Tunlings and sometimes even further away. Samuel of course was barred from going with her as she said it might spoil her 'wee surprise' for him.

Before Samuel was aware of how fast the days were sliding by it was the day before Christmas Eve. One thing that had struck Samuel as odd from the first day he had arrived was the fact that no one seemed to come to the house to visit the McGills much. He had seen Mrs. Monroe only a handful of times and she had never stayed very long. Perhaps there was an underlying reason why the couple seemed to be so friendless and unpopular.

There was another strange thing about the farm house. Several rooms had stayed locked from the day he had set foot in there, and quite what they hid he had not the faintest idea. From outside it was clear to see the curtains to the rooms remained continually closed. Samuel had taken the time to examine the locks on the doors. They seemed like they had been there quite a while, but were perfectly strong, and not likely to give way easily. There had been one or two occasions when Samuel had thought that he had seen Mrs. McGill coming out of the rooms, but he had never been certain.

An unexpected opportunity presented itself to Samuel that afternoon. It was one of the few occasions when he had been left in the farm house completely on his own. Mrs. McGill was out on one of her infamous shopping trips and it was impossible that she was going to be returning quickly. Mr. McGill was working near the hay barn in the furthest field, far away from the farm house, so to Samuel it seemed the coast was clear. It was not in his nature to just sit around. He had learnt to be an opportunist whilst he was living with Albert Hawkins. The opportunity which now presented itself involved doing some exploration of his own and the temptation was simply too much for Samuel to resist. Samuel knew that the keys to the house were usually found down in the kitchen, so he made his way there first.

The bunch of keys to the house was hanging on a key hook set into the kitchen wall. Samuel could see that there was little point trying them since they were all polished and looked very new; more up-to-date than the locks upstairs at least.

Presently Samuel found himself down in the cellar. He had the vaguest instinct that he might find something useful down there. It was another area he had never had a good look around. Once he had pushed his way through the tangle of cob webs it became evident that there were no keys to be found there.

A thought struck Samuel. The keys hanging in the kitchen were used to unlock his own room on the day he arrived. Assuming that lock on his room was similar in age to those on the other doors, perhaps they were just a new set of keys. He could recall how rusted the lock on his door was since he had recently brushed past it causing the rust to leave a stain on his T-Shirt.

A burst of inspiration caught hold of Samuel and provided some conformation of his theory. He cursed himself for discounting the keys in the kitchen so quickly. That was a new secondary set, and Mr. McGill had the originals on him, because Samuel had seen him using them.

Quickly picking them up, Samuel made his way out of the kitchen via the spiral stone stairs and on down the corridor to the locked doors. His fingers were trembling slightly as he tried one key, followed by another. He could feel his heart in his mouth as he heard the lock click open. As he pushed the handle, the door swung backwards.

The sight which was now before his eyes left him slightly dazed. The room appeared as if it was still lived in, although the thick veneer of dust, which coated almost everything in sight, showed that the room had not been used for many years. A book lay open on the floor and a collection of toys was strewn around the room. Judging by the blue colour of the wall paper, this had been a boy's room. A collection of toy soldiers and tanks were arranged in a battle formation in one corner. It was as though the room had been vacated in a hurry, and it had been left exactly as it had been then. Samuel felt an overwhelming sense of sadness. So many toys, and yet no one left to play with them. There was a picture frame on the wall, but the picture was missing, and upon the floor was a model aeroplane. A thousand questions seemed to be jostling for attention in his mind. Who was the person who had once inhabited the room, and what on earth had happened to them?

Samuel looked around for a couple more seconds. He knew he must leave the room untouched because Mrs. McGill would easily see if the dust had been disturbed. He was just about to leave when he thought he heard something moving downstairs. He froze, rooted to the spot, with his heart thumping and adrenalin pumping through his veins.

He turned to leave, swayed slightly, stumbling. It was too late. There were ominous footsteps on the stairs. From the sound of the footsteps it was Mrs. McGill. She must have come home very early.

'Samuel?'

It was the muffled voice of Mrs. Monroe.

'Samuel, is that you? I need to speak to you.'

Samuel, who had regained his balance, closed the door hastily and was just locking it up when Mrs. Monroe came into sight. Today she was dressed all in green, the only exception being the scarlet feathers exploding out of her leaf green hat. She had wrapped her face in a thick green scarf so that only her upper nose and eyes were visible.

'Oh, has Mrs. McGill let you in that room?'

'Well no, not exactly… no.'

'I was going to say… I would have been quite surprised if she had. Mirabella has never taken me in there,' said she with a sniff of irritation, 'At least you live here I suppose '

'— I was just looking quickly, but I didn't touch anything,' interrupted Samuel, keen to explain his actions before any interpretation of the situation could otherwise be made.

'Perhaps you can tell me what …'

Samuel trailed to a nervous halt. Mrs. Monroe seemed to accept his explanation without question, as though her mind was on other things. Following a short silence, she proposed that they went into his room so that they could talk in comfort. Rather reluctantly, Samuel led her into his room and offered her a chair.

'I am sorry about all the secrecy Samuel, but I have to ensure we won't be interrupted. I won't take off my disguise in case I need to make a hasty exit. It would not do for Mrs. McGill to find me here at the moment. Now I know this is going to be a lot to take in, but I want you to do your best.'

Quite how Mrs. Monroe could convince herself that wrapping her mouth in a vivid green scarf counted as a disguise was a complete mystery to Samuel. He had to make an effort not to laugh at her, sitting there with the usual flamboyant hat perched on her head.

'I have just received word this morning that they are coming for you Samuel. They will —'

'— Who, who are …*they*?'

'Well...yes of course, do be patient please. They are... well perhaps I should say that they come from... under the mountain. Once or twice in my life...but then they do have other ways in and out you see...'

But Samuel did not see. He could not understand anything about this. What was this nonsense Mrs. Monroe talking about?

Mrs. Monroe continued to talk, but Samuel was barely listening. Something deep inside him was awakening. A shiver ran through his body, a deep shiver of nervous, tingling excitement. When Samuel came to his senses, Mrs. Monroe had stopped talking and her eyes looked inquiringly at him, as though desiring a response. Samuel was surprised to see her hands trembling slightly and the red feathers in her hat were positively bobbing. As no response was forthcoming she ventured to continue what she had been saying.

'I have not informed your guardians yet. I am not responsible for that task thank goodness. Your future is most certainly assured Samuel. A prediction has been made by the Lampmaker that the first King of the city of Grat who is brought from the world outside will reunite the once great city to its surrounding kingdom,' She paused for breath,

'In a coming day you are going to be a Sovereign, perhaps even a great one. Best of luck, the very best of luck to you. You will be told what to do tomorrow evening at about nine o' clock.'

Later that evening, Samuel was sitting, once again, on his bed. It had been a dreadful afternoon. All the excitement this morning, then Mrs. Monroe, insisting upon his secrecy, had abruptly left. He felt a golden opportunity had been missed to find out more about the mysterious empty bedroom. Mrs. Monroe had given him no opportunity to enquire further about it. It had been an afternoon of wondering, scarcely believing any of it, and struggling to grasp that he was not dreaming.

Mrs. McGill had returned from her shopping trip at around tea time. She had been intercepted on the way and had been told that Samuel had to leave tomorrow. Tears had flowed, loving fondles had been given, followed by yet more tears and a lot of talking. Hysterical hardly described it. Mr. McGill reacted differently to his wife. A certain look of resignation emanated from his eyes, and he was a lot more accepting that Mrs. McGill, although Samuel did observe that he looked a bit numb and quite listless.

Samuel, for his part, was silently relieved that he was leaving. Whilst his courage had increased greatly here, he found the level of attention to himself to be quite stifling. The sincerity of the love he had been given was, however, impossible to doubt. He was certainly grateful for it. The truth was that the prospect of a new adventure was far more enticing than the prospect of staying here with the McGills. Hope and excitement filled him as he hurtled up the stairs to pack his black holdall once again, struggling to hide his secret excitement from the McGills.

Christmas Eve was very strange. Initially the McGills seemed very uncertain whether the Christmas preparations should continue. Mrs. McGill decided to give Samuel his 'presents' this evening, and that the Christmas preparations should be hurried so a Christmas meal of sorts could be enjoyed later in the evening, after the present giving. Samuel was drafted in to help as much as possible, because Mrs. McGill had to go out in the early afternoon, for some 'mysterious presents' as she put it.

At six o' clock the McGills both joined Samuel in the living room. On the floor were three parcels, each wrapped in shining paper and finished off with a cherry rosette.

Samuel kneeled down to open the first present. His face was flushed with embarrassment. Aunt Mulltasch had bought him presents, but they had never been expensive. She had never had the money to spend. Usually they were something bought cheap at the local cash and carry. He began to read the label. It read:

'To our dear Samuel. Lots of love from Mirabella and Henry McGill.

Samuel glanced towards Mrs. McGill. Her bright eyes were shining with tears. Slowly he unwrapped the parcel and looked inside. At first he thought it contained only a selection of sweets and chocolate, but then beneath the confectionary packing and wrappers, emerged a beautiful gold picture frame. The style of the frame was unrecognisable, and the strange carvings were very unusual. The photograph contained in the frame was one of Henry and Mirabella. Both looked younger and their hair was less grey. Samuel turned to them and murmured his thanks, before he was ushered on to open his next present. Inside was a small painting. It was a painting of the old farmhouse with the great hills in the distance. It was undoubtedly very pleasant.

The final gift was the most surprising. Samuel opened the parcel as quickly as he could, and inside was a large hourglass. But there was no sand. Once again Samuel turned to the McGills this time expecting an explanation, but none followed. He thanked them once again, conscious that he was being carefully studied by both.

The late Christmas tea was uneventfully quiet and a rather sober affair. Mrs. McGill, thankfully a little more composed, seemed to be finding it difficult to make conversation. Samuel offered to help wash up after the meal, as he normally did, but it was insisted that he went to his room to pack. He had only to pack his new presents in reality, so at least this gave him some time to reflect in his bedroom. Thankfully the presents he had been given all slotted in to the remaining space in his black holdall perfectly.

He thought all of the presents had been rather curious. The painting and photograph were understandable, each a little something for him to remember them by, but that frame with its strange engravings? He pulled it from the top of the holdall and examined it further, feeling the rough wood under his fingers. There were strange creatures shown, winged beasts with large fangs and many other creatures in what seemed to be a great battle. At the bottom centre of the frame the fighting seemed to intensify and at the very centre was an empty hang-mans noose.

Samuel decided to go downstairs and wait. He put the framed photograph back in the holdall and zipped it up. The tension up here was getting unbearable. A quick glance around the room ensured everything was packed, and he began to make his way down the corridor. Suddenly he backtracked. The door to the strange room was standing open. There was a light on inside. Everything appeared the same as this morning. Well almost, but something was different. There was gap on the wall where the picture frame had been hanging yesterday.

His picture frame? Could they be one of the same? It seemed plausible. Perhaps that was where Mrs. McGill had gone this afternoon – to have the frame carved. Samuel was uncertain as to whether the carving had been on the frame yesterday. He certainly could not remember it standing out particularly, but with the curtains draw it had been pretty dark. He would have to look at the caving on his frame once again to see if it appeared fresh.

It was about quarter past six when Samuel got downstairs. At six thirty the heavens opened. The rain fell in heavy sheets against the windows. Samuel sat upon one of the kitchen chairs opposite Mr. McGill, whose face was a deadly white. The shock and strain of the last twenty four hours was etched deeply into his face.

If Samuel had been expecting to be well looked after during the remainder of his last evening he would have been much mistaken. Mr. McGill was locked into his private world of mourning and neither more food, or conversation, was to prove forthcoming.

At nine o' clock the kitchen clock chimed loudly, piercing the silence. Somewhere outside a cat was mewing. It must have been drenched in the rain. As the chimes finished, silence settled in the farm house once again. Five minutes past nine. The time was passing ever so slowly. Samuel felt numb in his seat and felt the urge to stretch. He managed to resist, and as a result began to feel distinctly uncomfortable, having sat on the hard wooden chair for such a long time.

Ten past nine. Only five minutes to go. Were they coming at all? 'They have to be', murmured Samuel, 'they have to be'. At nine fourteen, time seemed to stand still. Just as Samuel witnessed the small hand complete its revolution there was a rap at the window. Mr. McGill rose slowly but steadily from his seat and made for the front door. He opened it in the same movement and before him stood a tall young man with a bowler hat on his head.

'The McGill residence I believe?'

'Most certainly. We have been expecting you. Please come in. This is my wife and our Samuel is over here.'

Samuel found it difficult not to gaze at the man. His bowler hat was perched at such a jaunty angle that it gave the appearance that his body was lop-sided, but that the hat was in the right place.

'Good evening Samuel,' said he, bowing low, 'I trust I will be of good service to you.'

Straightening up, he looked around with bright, keen eyes. His face was clean shaven and he had a slight twitch in his left eye as Samuel observed.

'I bring you instructions Samuel. At 10.05 this evening you are to catch a Dark Train at Little Tunlings. You should be the only person to get on it —'

'— So you are saying it will not be a scheduled train?'

'Yes I am saying that Mr. McGill. Little Tunlings is normally the end of the track, but this train will be going beyond Little Tunlings.' he gave a short pause.

'How is that possible?' enquired Mr McGill.

'We will be taking the old track, the one that once lead under the mountain. While I remember, you need a key for the train door, best collect it at the station because I seem to have misplaced it, someone will be waiting to give it to you.'

'Are you really sure that the old line is safe?'

'Mrs. McGill! We would never put the life of someone as important as Samuel in danger! Since we have used the old track several times during the last... I should not be telling you that. That is enough talking from me before I say too much. So, just get him there on time, but don't walk there. The lanes will be crawling tonight. Well, goodnight everyone. At least this rain will provide good cover. Goodbye and good luck to you.' With one final pointed look at Samuel he turned and left, a cat which no one had noticed following in his wake.

They left the house together at nine thirty five. It had been decided after much debate, that they would have to walk despite the warning they had been given. As a precaution they were each to dress in black and wear thick scarves to keep most of their faces covered. If they were stopped, then no one was to speak except Mr. McGill. They were going to keep in the shadows as much as possible and would hope not to be stopped at all.

Mr. McGill carried his holdall for him, as Samuel ventured out with his guardians into the wet, bleak night. Umbrellas could not be used because of the attention they might draw, so they were each wearing thick, waterproof jackets. People of the countryside don't use umbrellas anyway.

The lanes passed by slowly, each running with excess water. Little Tunlings was not far off when out of the shadows there stepped a person.

'McGill is that you?'

'Alfred Beavitch, yes of course it is me'

'Could not make any of you out in all that getup. And you must be Samuel,' said Alfred in a husky whisper,

'A great pleasure for me, a truly great pleasure.'

'Can't hang around Alfred. Need to get this little one on his way.'

'Of course, of course. They have stationed me here to keep an eye on movement. Had quite a lot of activity around Pebble Lane. Seem to think we would take him that way for some reason. I'm to take his holdall and bring it with me later. Anyway best of luck.'

Samuel handed over his black holdall.

'See you then.'

'Oh, blast headed bullfrogs, forgot the key. Here take it McGill.'

The Station at Little Tunlings was as dreary as the rest of the place. It was a shabby, run down affair despite the efforts of Mr. Potts, and most certainly empty at this time of night. The three of them waited together, and as five past ten approached the chill in the air seemed to deepen. From out of the silence an ear shattering noise erupted, and the black train screamed its arrival from nowhere.

Final goodbyes were said, and the key was handed over.

'My father knew of this strange Dark Train as I seem to recall,' said Mr. McGill, keen to reassure Samuel, 'So they must have been up and running for years. Take care now. And remember, we are always going to think of you and be here for you if ever you need us.'

Samuel thanked them for all their kindness and endured a final round of silent sobs from Mrs. McGill before walking over to the train.

At first Samuel could not make out any door on the train. Upon closer inspection there seemed to be a door just to his left, so nervously he felt for any lock upon it. After a few seconds he found one, and gingerly inserted the key. Its most unusual shape, like a large talon, caught his attention only momentarily. It fitted. He turned it left. Nothing. He tried again. It resisted his pressure. He turned it back to the right, pushing hard. He heard the lock turn over and the odd talon-like key vanished away to nothing in his hands; the door began to swing automatically towards him so that he had to dodge it to avoid getting hit in the face.

Samuel took one last look behind him at his waving Guardians. He could feel an invisible hand grabbing at him from inside the train. As much as he tried to resist, it kept pulling him further and further inside. Samuel was about to shout out when he felt himself tumble forwards into the interior compartment. Before he could even work out where he was, he could hear the door closing behind him and the Dark Train screaming as it began to hurtle out of Little Tunlings station.

-- CHAPTER THREE --

A Journey to Somewhere Impossible

Samuel slowly pulled himself up from the thick carpeted floor. The interior of the Dark Train took his breath away. Strangely there were no windows at all, but the detail in the carved wooden panels that adorned the walls was astonishing, and whole battle scenes seemed to come alive in the light of the great candelabras which shone, rocking with each jolt of the train, from the ceiling overhead. Pairs of seats were arranged along each side of the train, and, steadying himself, Samuel made for an empty seat in the first pair on the side of the entrance. If the décor of the train had amazed him, nothing could prepare him to meet the people who were on it.

Beside Samuel, near the entrance, an old man was sitting. He had a large moustache which seemed to have a life of its own. The man was eating a peculiar purple pie and every now and again, as he swallowed a particularly satisfying chunk, his moustache would flick to life at each end and wipe around his mouth for him. To Samuel's left, across the isle, a plump woman was sitting by herself in the further seat. She had long silvery hair, rosy red cheeks, and silver spectacles and was completely absorbed in a newspaper, although it was quite unlike any newspaper Samuel had seen before. Every few minutes, miniature people would pop up out of the page and from their grand gestures Samuel assumed they were each making some sort of speech, which he could not hear. The woman seemed to have no such problem as she was periodically nodding in delight or shaking her head in disgust as each speaker aired their views. Samuel was so mesmerised by the sight of the women and the newspaper that he almost forgot about the other people on the train.

Glancing behind he could see all the way to the back. It was strange that there were no carriages; the train seemed to just consist of one compartment. There were about ten rows of empty seats at the back of the train, and only the two rows behind him were occupied on the side he was sitting. Directly behind him sat a small, pug-nosed man with a bright yellow beard and watery yellow eyes. His fingers were the most extraordinary thing about him, each one thick, and each fingernail curling and tapering to a sharp point. Every few seconds he would breathe out heavily and from his nose a sickly odour would waft. It had seemed rude to turn around to look at the oddly proportioned man but Samuel could justify doing so in light of the man's bad breath.

There were several other people on the train. A row behind Samuel and across the isle sat an elderly woman clutching an empty cage and, beside her, a young boy was playing with a tiny green bird in his hands. There were also a couple of men spread out in the rows further back on the other side of the train, several of them asleep and several only half awake, with eyes occasionally flickering open.

Everyone on the train seemed to be settled for a long journey, so Samuel assumed he should try and settle in the same way. He could feel breath on the back of his neck and the smell was starting to make him quite nauseous. Samuel glanced down towards the newspaper which was spread out in the lap of the plump woman across the isle from him to take his mind off the smell. A series of characters had now assembled, apparently performers, seeing that several were performing somersaults and other acrobatics. Smiling, the woman folded up the newspaper, and noticed Samuel staring at her.

Samuel slowly got up and made his way over to the vacant seat, glad to move further away from the man with the bad breath. The man with the bad breath, from the row behind quickly moved forward to take his place. It was only when he walked that Samuel could see just how short he was. He was only about half of Samuel's height.

Samuel's attention was drawn back to the woman sitting next to him.

'Well, um, hello, nice to meet you,' he managed to stumble out. He had to speak quite loudly so that his words were not drowned out by the noise of the train.

'Well, my dear, it is yet more of an honour for me to meet you at last,' she glanced away shyly, 'they told us you would be on here tonight, but I was not so sure if I believed them.'

'Well, what do you mean?' enquired Samuel.

'Oh, they tell you anything these days, all so secretive. Security is such a problem for them; often they use decoys and such, so…you might not be the real thing.'

'I can… I can assure you I am real!'

'Well, that's good isn't it dear? It's always a good thing to be real.'

She turned her head away from his gaze and fell silent for a moment. She appeared about to speak again, when the lights suddenly flickered and died, plunging the train into complete blackness. Several passengers groaned loudly. Apparently this was a frequent occurrence. Samuel could feel the train coming to halt. Everything became still and silent. For some reason his heart began beating faster. He thought he felt something catch on his cheek and then an abrupt shout rang out through the blackness. For a few seconds a searing scream tore through the carriage like a violent gale, leaving stillness and foreboding silence in its wake.

The lights flickered back on as quickly as they had died a few moments before. Samuel blinked. In front of him, sprawled on the floor was the little man with bad breath. His face was a bright purple and his throat was terribly bruised. He was still, silent and total drained of life.

All around him other passengers were stirring. Samuel's companion to his left seemed as dazed as he was. He enquired if she was alright. The sound of his voice seemed to move her to action. Pandemonium was breaking out in the carriage as people were rushing forward to look at the man on the floor. Samuel had no idea what to do. The terrified chatter seemed to flood over him in a wave. Beside him the newspaper was frantically re-emerging and the woman was feverishly leafing through it.

'Health, health, health, where is he? Dr. Felecia, no Dr Filixia come on, come on, ah Dr. Flint, got you!'

'Can I help…at all?' enquired Samuel

'Best just to keep out of the way,' muttered the woman leaning forward from her seat and crouching over the body of the man, 'Just surprised no one has come to help us yet.'

The confused babble in the carriage was continuing. People, so repulsed by the sight of the body of the man, were beginning to retreat to the back of the carriage, white, confused, and frightened.

In front of Samuel, the woman had pulled the man into a more comfortable position and had produced, from her pocket, a bottle, the contents of which she was now administering to the man. Having done this, she stood up and resumed her seat, apparently at the limit of her medical expertise.

'I have done what I can for him, but I don't know how successful it will be.'

'Why on earth do you think he was attacked?' Enquired Samuel –

'He hadn't provoked anyone.'

'Oh no,' replied the woman 'I think we can be sure that they did not mean to get Gredric. They wanted to kill you.'

'Why would anyone want to kill me?'

'Because very soon you are going to be King Samuel'

'How do you know my name?'

Before the woman could answer, in the midst of the carriage there was a brilliant white flash of dazzling luminosity, so intense that Samuel could almost see through the body on the floor. Three men appeared, each flustered and out of breath.

'Calm down everyone, sorry we did not get here as quickly as we would have liked to. Where is Samuel?'

He made eye contacted with them and nodded his head.

'Perhaps if you would step this way Sir?'

Samuel was led by the three men to a corner at the front of the train. He recognised the man who had spoken because he was wearing the same bowler hat he had been wearing when he met Samuel at the McGills earlier in the evening. In low voices the man began to talk to him.

'So sorry we were not able to get to you sooner. Some sort of shield had been placed over the train to delay us being transported in here. Perhaps you can tell us exactly what happened.'

'Well,' stammered Samuel, 'The lights went off and I heard a scream in the darkness –'

'– excuse me, but there is a lot more to it than that!'

The woman who had been sitting next to Samuel had risen from her seat and was making her way past the body on the floor and over to the three men and Samuel.

'Perhaps you would sit down madam, while Samuel tells us what happened.'

'Most certainly not! How dare you! I am Lady Flint, wife of the Royal Physician. If he hears his wife has been treated rudely by someone as disposable as you… need I say more?'

'Oh, Mrs. Flint...'

She stood staring straight up at the man, whose face gained the slightest hint of redness.

'Do continue to indulge us Mrs. Flint, pray, do!'

His words, although without the slightest hint of anger, seemed to be laced with poison.

'Might I enquire as to your names, young men?'

Lady Flint turned to address all three of them.

'I am William, William Sorrow.'

'Horace Ledbury'

'And I am Mr. Harbury'

'Well, Mr. Harbury, since you seem to be in charge of this band of merry men, I suggest you get these young gentlemen to see to Mr. Gredric, whom you have yet to even show the least concern for. And you, Mr. Harbury, will go and fetch someone more senior to investigate this most serious breach of security.'

'Well of course My Lady, we most graciously accept your wisdom and direction. I must of course make the final decision over what has to be done. In this instance I would remind you that you are yourself as much of a suspect as anyone else.'

'Nonsense. If this was an attempt upon Samuel's life, as is the initial conclusion we seem to have already reached, then why would I, being the person who Samuel moved to sit next to, possibly make the mistake of killing a dwarf sitting over the isle from me?'

'Well, Samuel… are the words of this Lady true?'

'I moved to sit next to her, if that's what you mean?'

Lady Flint interjected once again.

'– Mr. Harbury, might I remind you that still no one has looked at Gredric!'

‘Oh, well yes, of course. Men, perhaps you would see to the floor-bound dwarf.’

‘With every second that passes, Mr. Harbury, we are at yet greater risk of another attack. We must keep moving.’

‘In that case, and to such ends, we had better get everyone off the train. They won’t be making the journey in tonight.’

And so it was that, once Mr. Harbury unlocked the door and allowed it to swing upwards, the occupants of the carriage began to slowly troop of the Dark Train, all quiet, confused and more than a little dazed, until finally Samuel was alone with Lady Flint and the mysterious men. Gredric was still lying motionless on the floor. Mr. Harbury continued to look flustered, but slowly began to gather himself together.

‘Now with the gracious permission of all those present, ahem, I would like the men to take the dwarf with them. He probably needs major treatment I would have thought –’

Lady Flint sniffed sharply,

‘– See to it then men, get on with it.’

The men who had identified themselves as Horace Ledbury and William Sorrow moved forwards and, after they had sorted themselves out, disappeared in a brilliant flare of white light.

‘Now to you Samuel,’ Said Mr. Harbury,

‘We are just inside the mouth of the tunnel. It must be about four hours walk from here through the tunnel, to the shafts. You should be accompanied of course, but I have to stay here, and Lady Flint is not accustomed to walking in general, I would say.’

‘I beg your pardon?’

‘Merely the truth My Lady, a person of your position is not so well acquainted to circumstances that require physical effort with respect to one’s legs.’

‘End your nonsense Mr. Harbury! If our future King can walk a tunnel, I daresay you and I can do it as well.’

‘Well, if you insist Mrs. Flint, if you insist then I will have no choice but to allow you to continue.’

‘Ignore him Samuel; come this way with me, not a moment to lose.’

Lady Flint skirted Mr. Harbury and walked through the open carriage door without as much as a second glance at him. Samuel trailed alongside her, although it seemed madness to him to be setting off into a pitch black tunnel with no torch, no light source at all in fact.

It was hard walking because the surface was rough beside the track, and Samuel could hardly make out where he was going. Lady Flint stopped for a moment when they had just passed the end of the Dark Train.

‘They won’t all be like that to you, you know. And it was only because I was there, anyway. Senior Cresta’s like Mr. Harbury can’t resist a dig at me, even if it jeopardises the most important person in our world. Mr. Harbury is a fool. As the old rhyme says, ‘folly made him and folly kept him until the day death slowly crept in’. There – at least I have let off a bit of steam. Now perhaps we should see about some light for us. But how? With this of course, dear. The flute will call them to light our way.’

Lady Flint produced from about her person a tiny flute which Samuel, in the darkness, couldn’t see. But he could soon hear it. It was a beautiful sound, which bounced and resonated tunefully from the tunnel walls. After a few minutes she stopped playing the instrument.

‘That should do it. Just wait a few minutes.’

After a few minutes had gone by, Samuel’s legs began to ache. He began to wonder if the woman was mad, but soon he could hear a flutter of wings far off in the darkness. Slowly they came into view; five vast, bat-like birds of large wing span, each casting out a green, shimmering light.

'Dumb beasts of course,' Said Lady Flint, laughing, 'But these Igni are pretty unusual to you I imagine – yes – well, I can assure you, this is just the beginning!'

It had been cold when Samuel had walked to the station with his guardians in the snow, but amid all the excitement it had gone unnoticed. Now, as he moved deeper underground, the tempestuous, chilly gusts of winter were replaced with air that provided a sustained and unavoidable chill. Samuel was forced to spend a good deal of the time shivering uncontrollably. At least this spurred him on to move in a bid to keep his body temperature up. But alas progress proved to be tortuously slow, as they were moving over such uneven terrain and his feet were soon killing him. The Igni swooped overhead, illuminating the track which glinted to their right. Conversation, however, was to prove remarkably well sustained along this most arduous journey.

To Samuel nothing was making sense. Why had they left the train if he was in so much danger? He put the question to Lady Flint as they walked along.

'Well dear, I had a bad feeling as soon as those men appeared, particularly Mr. Harbury. You might have noticed that I am not a very big fan of him. I cannot say the same for William and Horace. They are two of the most brilliant young men I have ever met to tell you the truth. I am quite certain that normally they would have dashed to help Gredric but instead they seemed very subdued. The first thing in my mind was to get as far away from the Dark Train and Mr. Harbury as possible. He claimed he was coming to aid you, but in fact I believe he was coming to cause you trouble.'

'So Mr. Harbury was real, but his two companions were not?'

'Yes, I believe so. You will have to take my word that there are ways to take on the appearance of another. The result is usually blank stooge which would enable Mr. Harbury to take control of them both. Just the sort of thing he might do, in my opinion.'

Lady Flint went on to tell Samuel quite a bit about herself and her husband, who was the Royal Physician, the best of all Royal Physicians according to her. Great man she said, great man, but no good at all at organising the kitchen.

He was just about to ask her more about Mr. Harbury when the Igni overhead give out shrill and piercing squawks and out of the darkness ahead of them stepped two men. Samuel recognised them immediately as Mr. Sorrow and Mr. Ledbury, who had transported onto the Dark Train.

'At last! My Lady Flint, so glad it is you! And Samuel, is he safe?'

They both turned to look at him, nodding, and smiling. Samuel returned with a nervous grin. It was hard to precisely read their facial expressions in the ever-changing glow cast by the Igni overhead, but from what Samuel could deduce, the two men were genuinely pleased to see him.

'We had no idea what was going on. All lines of communication went down about an hour ago. We were told the Dark Train was just about to enter the tunnel and then…silence.'

'But we had been told to stay here at out post whatever happened. Where is the train then?'

'Perhaps we had better keep moving'

'Of course, My Lady, please, let us get moving at once. Tell us everything along the way.'

So Lady Flint began to elaborate on events and Samuel gradually allowed his mind wander. It appeared that the William and Horace on the train had been dummies, duplicates. Identical in all but knowledge and personality.

A terrific blast suddenly cut through the air, rudely awakening his senses. It was so almighty that Samuel thought for a moment that his eardrums might burst. Once the blast had passed the tunnel still shook with small tremors, and the company looked at each other in the light, wide eyed, and shaken. From the direction they had come, a low rumble was gathering. It was as though day light was reaching right into the very heart of the tunnel. But this was not daylight. The red glow was one of a fire ball hurtling towards them. There was little time to prepare. The two men dragged Samuel to the far side of the tunnel, pushing him into a position where, between them, they could shield him with their bodies.

The fire ball seemed to hit them almost instantly. Samuel felt its burning hot fury pass over him and he cried out, but luckily the most intense region of the flames seemed to veer away from him. Like a serpent retracting its tongue, the fire suddenly died out. The moments which followed were panicky. The tunnel was plunged into terrifying, inky blackness which flooded over Samuel like a great rip tide. There was a smell of burning, smouldering material in the air.

Mr. Sorrow was first to move. Groaning, he reached into his pocket and produced a small light. Samuel could now see the men properly. Each was covered in soot, their clothes burnt. They seemed, luckily, to have survived without terrible burns to their bodies. Samuel looked around for Lady Flint but she was nowhere to be found. Deep panic took hold of him once again and he shouted her name. He was answered only by the echoes of his own voice.

'Samuel, get up, we need to get on!'

Before he knew it, he had been pulled to his feet.

'Lady Flint, where is she?'

Mr. Sorrow moved his light to illuminate the surrounding area of the tunnel.

'She must have made it.'

'Made it! How…?'

'The Igni have gone. They must have carried her.'

Samuel felt uncertain, but it was true that there was no sign of roasted Igni on the floor.

Under the influence of the two men Samuel pressed on. They were all subdued and shocked, but evidently there was a great urgency to make progress. In silence they walked for about another half an hour before the light showed the tunnel was narrowing, still large enough to allow a train to pass through it, but narrow enough to force them to walk between the tracks. Mr. Sorrow was taking the lead with Samuel following closely behind and Mr. Ledbury taking the rear. Mr. Sorrow suddenly stopped so sharply that Samuel almost stumbled into his back.

'Samuel, I know this will sound a bit strange, but we are about to pass from your world into ours. Up ahead are two large sets of double doors which mark the boundaries of a chamber which is a transition place between worlds. Normally they open up automatically as the Dark Train approaches them, but in this instance I shall open them by hand. It is said that there are sights inside the transition chamber that no man alive has been allowed to see and live. For that reason the Dark Train has no windows. We will each have to put on blindfolds before I open the doors, but I have to warn you it will be quite an unpleasant experience because we are not inside the Dark Train.'

Samuel ventured to ask when the last person had made the journey by foot. He received no reply and so decided not to press the matter further.

Mr. Sorrow made a blindfold for each of them out of his shirt before turning to a round steel wheel set into the wall of the tunnel at this point. Ahead Samuel could see two heavy metal doors, just before he blindfolded himself. He could hear Mr. Sorrow straining to turn the wheel set in the wall and eventually the grating noise of the large doors sliding apart with sombre moaning.

'Samuel, just feel your way along the wall at your right hand side and don't allow your mind to wander. You will find this place has a habit of making you do that, so stay close behind me and keep up all the way. It should only take a couple of minutes to get across the void.'

The company stumbled on slowly. Samuel felt moist, damp air hit his face. His balance seemed a little weakened; in fact he sometimes felt like the world was revolving around him. He felt a desperate desire to rip the blindfold from his eyes. With every moment that passed this urge was becoming harder to resist. His foot must have caught in part of the track because he felt himself stumble and twist his ankle. The pain was agonising.

Suddenly Samuel felt a wave of guilt wash over him. He felt bad about himself. Who was he and what had he ever done with his life? He felt for the wall to steady himself. It was still there. He moved forward again, urging himself to focus on reaching the other side, despite the fact that he had no idea how far away the other side was. He was feeling sick and there was a lump in his throat. He was sweating profusely, aching, and shaking. There was a moment when he thought he was not going to make it. The desire to rip off the blindfold had become too great. Samuel took three final steps forward and ripped the blindfold from his head. Thankfully, the second set of double doors was already shutting behind him, cutting off the place of transition between worlds.

Samuel looked around for his two companions and found them both out of breath nearby. After they had rested for a few minutes Mr. Sorrow began to speak.

'Well done Samuel. We all knew that was not going to be easy. Welcome to our world.'

'We have about a half hour walk from here to the end of the line. That brings us to the five passages and the Lampmaker's Cottage. From there we must proceed down Fable's Passage and about an hour later we will reach the lift chamber. It will be a long trek, so I am sorry for you Samuel. I hope you can forgive us for this most unceremonious welcome, but as you have experienced all is not well in this world.'

Once the group had recovered they set off again, and in his mind Samuel traced out the line of the track in front of him. It was vaguely visible in the light of the torch, but somehow it seemed faint and unreal. Samuel hurriedly shook off these dark notions, and turned his mind to unravelling the situation that he was in, and the events that had just occurred. Most people in his situation would have longed for some known companion to talk to, but a life of consistent solitude had enabled Samuel to function as an individual, in a manner that was well beyond his years.

The so called 'Lady Flint' kept surfacing in his mind. He trusted her, for what he knew of her, but deep down he felt uneasy. There was something about her which did not quite tie up. She had been so domineering over all those around, especially Mr. Harbury. Whether her dislike and distrust of him would prove to be well grounded was a matter for future resolution.

Half an hour must have passed because the group had reached the end of the line. There were two large buffers, situated in a large open cavern. The cavern was not huge, but considerably larger than the tunnel itself had been.

The men asked Samuel if he would like to rest, but when he shook his head, they looked delighted by his decision and appeared just as eager to push on.

A light was visible at a corner of the cavern, and as Samuel moved closer it became evident that it radiated from a window which was cut into the stone wall. Next to it there was a door. A large green door.

'Better check if the Lampmaker is in?'

'Well, he could hardly be out could he?'

There was a swift exchange of smiles between the two men.

'Better to be safe. Nowhere is safer than in the Lampmaker's Cottage –'

Turning to Samuel,

'– Get ready Samuel, I think we are in for an unscheduled warm welcome!'

There was large knocker on the door and, as Mr. Sorrow knocked it, the noise was deep, and rumbled around the cavern. But the noise of the knocker was nothing compared to the noise which emanated from the being that lived inside it.

'COME IN!!'

The command was loud but warm and not unfriendly. Cautiously, the men opened the door, pushing Samuel in before them and quickly closing it behind them.

'Well, well well, I say, bless my soul, I can't believe it! He does look so like his father! Come and sit by the fire Samuel, don't be frightened.'

Cautiously Samuel moved forward. There, in front of him, slouched in a chair was the most colossal man he could imagine. Easily three times the height of the doorway if he had been standing up, and with a bright red beard as large as a bush, it was hard not to be impressed by the 'Lampmaker.' And nor was this the 'cottage' Samuel had imagined from the connotations of the word. This was a vast chamber which was part of a warren of foundries. There were fires burning at the end of passages in the distance, and the Lampmaker, apparently the only occupant, sat in front of a great fire himself, surrounded by all manner of peculiar instruments and machinery.

Mr. Sorrow whispered into Samuel's ear, 'He is one of the greatest thinkers in our world. Years ago, the Lampmaker made a prophecy that the first king who was born outside our world and brought into it via the route under the mountain would unite the city of Grat with the countries it once ruled. Many believe that you are going to be that king.'

'What an unexpected surprise but pleasant surprise that you should have decided to call in to see me.'

He let out a bellow of laughter that shook the floor, and left him gulping for breath a few seconds later. The exertion of laughter had made his huge face grow a deep red. Slowly he leant forward a little in his chair to peer down at Samuel. Yet his glance and his voice were far gentler than Samuel would have expected.

'I know of difficulties ahead for you, my King; greater difficulties than those you have left behind. But those clouds are coming in the distant years –' he winked,

'– Make the most of these happy times, for little ones rarely notice them until they are over.'

He stopped speaking for a moment, staring into the huge fire in front of him. It was so bright that it hurt Samuel's eyes, although the waves of heat that washed over him were a welcome change from the cold, damp air that he had experienced for the last few hours. The Lampmaker seemed to recollect the visitors a few moments later.

'I had better be giving you my present! Before you go wandering off again! It must be somewhere around here!'

The Lampmaker leant to his left and reached for a grubby, elongated parcel, which he handed to Samuel, whose mind first jumped to the hourglass in his bag. When he received the parcel, and was told to unwrap it, he was surprised by just how light it was. The wrapping slid off, to reveal a glowing orb set into the top of an ornate, burnished gold handle. Samuel waited for an explanation of the object, and this time at least he was not entirely left disappointed.

'That is the finest lamp I have. Fit for a handsome king like you, I dare say!'

The Lampmaker's face was once again flushed with pleasure.

'I trust it will be a helpful guide to you! It is bound to come in useful! Remember my warnings to you of the future; best to hurry now, through Fable's Passage, and on your way…'

The Lampmaker was speaking now as much to the two men as to Samuel. Each bid him a cheery farewell, before shrinking with remorse from the delightful fire, out through the doorway and back into the main chamber at the end of the tunnel.

'What is it, the gift that he gave me?' Enquired an eager Samuel as soon as he was outside

'– What does it do?'

Mr. Sorrow was the first to reply, in a slightly awed voice; 'Very rare, that is, very rare, I have never seen a lamp like that one. So rare that I don't know what it does, or what it can be used to do beyond acting as a beacon, but if the Lampmaker himself gave it to you, I think we can be sure that he knew what he was doing.'

Samuel could think of very little to say to this. The lamp was carried by Samuel, since it helped to light his way through the entrance to Fable's Passage. There were indeed five passages leading off from the main chamber, and Fable's Passage as it appeared to be known, was the furthest passage to the right. The word 'passage' was perhaps a little too generous, since it really was just barely passable in size, and each member of the trio had to stoop at the entrance, although the height of the roof increased a little way inside.

The group made their way in silence, as water dripped down on each of their heads. Sound was muffled down here, and the air felt mustier than it had in the main tunnel. The passage beckoned them forwards, along a maze-like twisting route. Time seemed to slip by ever so slowly down here, and it seemed like an age before at last Mr. Sorrow stopped, so that Samuel almost slammed into him again.

'Right. I imagine we could be there in five minutes. Any time now really I would think. If things had gone according to plan the shafts would have been a hive of activity, but the way things have turned out, I imagine people will have been called away to attend to other things. We might have to wait a while for the lifts to be lowered.

It was almost within that same minute that Fable's Passage opened onto the lift shaft. It was a medium sized chamber, lit by about fifty large chandeliers, which were hanging from the roof of the cavern far above. It was quite strange to see something so unnatural, deep in the bowels of the earth.

As had been predicted, they did have to wait. Mr. Ledbury told Samuel to leave the lamp which he had been given in a small alcove to one side. He said it would be brought into the city of Grat later. The smaller torch which he had should be able to light the rest of the way. The carriages were at last lowered, four in total, down four different shafts. Since there were only three people to be taken up, the group made their way to one of the carriages. They were unusual, rather like mining cages, although a little larger, and comprised mainly of wood. Where they differed was in their motion. Samuel had to be strapped against the wall, as did each of the two men. Then, with a sudden groaning lurch, the cages shot upwards. Samuel felt his stomach drop away beneath him, as the carriages gained speed, and the cold air rushed past his face. This felt impossibly fast, dangerously fast. The vibration of the carriage shook Samuel's head violently, and he was glad when at last he felt the carriage slowing down and his vision becoming less blurred.

At the top, another chamber was reached, as dark as the first, or so Samuel thought at first. The men un-strapped themselves, and then helped Samuel out of his harness.
Each looked a little shaken and unsteady as they walked from the shafts. The trio made their way onward, with only Mr. Ledbury's small torch for guidance. Slowly, they rounded a corner and found themselves walking down a paved corridor which still had walls of rock and stone on both sides and overhead.

Slowly they rounded a bend in this new passage. And what a very strange sight met Samuel's eyes. Cut into the tunnel wall were several tiny, circular windows, through which Samuel could see into a chamber of lighted rooms. It was the people who resided in them that surprised him most. Around a long table sat a motley collection of people, a number of dwarfs, with their bright yellow beards and sharp clawed hands, each drinking and chortling so loudly that Samuel could hear them quite clearly. There were others with them, several beautiful women, with flowing blond hair and bright blue eyes and what appeared to be several squirrels acting as waitresses, each wearing a white frilled piny, much larger than normal squirrels – at least two thirds the height of a human perhaps.

'What is this place?' murmured Samuel.

'These are the Warren Kitchens.'

'Can we go in?'

'Well, we had better check if Lady Flint passed by I suppose. '

'Would the Igni have brought her all this way?'

'Oh no, of course not. Just to the shaft I would imagine, what do you reckon Horace?' (Mr. Ledbury nodded, in agreement.) 'Better go in and then quickly get on our way. We have to get to Grat by nightfall.'

Within a moment they came upon another door, black this time and with a round port-hole window in the top. This, it appeared, was the entrance to the Warren Kitchens.

As Mr. Ledbury opened the door, Samuel followed him in, with Mr. Sorrow behind him. The noise and laugher from inside became immediately much louder, but died away quite soon when the arrivals were noticed.

'Sir, and Sir and Master! Have we not been waiting for you many a long hour; hoping and hoping for an audience with you – well, I say we have – we all have. And are we not all very honoured to have you with us.' Her voice was quite high pitched, but not unpleasant to listen to.

'What news squirrel, of the Lady by the name of Rose?'

'That I can tell you, Sir. She sends you all her warmest regards and wishes to inform you that she has gone on ahead to…'

There was the sound of loud shushing from an approaching squirrel behind her, so she continued in a quieter voice.

'…To prepare a place for you at her residence. Do you need directions or, or an address…?'

'No, oh, don't trouble yourself; our collective knowledge of the city is such that I have no concern about finding her abode once we arrive.'

'And yes of course – where was I? – you must indeed be on your way, but perhaps, perhaps before you would seek to leave, you would be so gracious as to sample one of our home made specialities here at the Warren Kitchens. You would? Oh well do come this way, all of you. You can be assured of the heartiest welcome from all of your well wishers that have gathered here, the squirrels included.'

As the squirrel turned around a large springy tail swept up behind her. She was beautiful, of that Samuel had no doubt. And how could a squirrel ever be beautiful? Precisely because she was not just a squirrel, but more a person.

'Do you have a name?' he enquired quietly as she led them. She stopped to look back at Samuel, and then bowed to him.

'Martharnia at your service.' Then she gave him a tiny smile, just a small one, but it was the first squirrel smile Samuel had ever seen, and it amazed him. This whole place was amazing. Talking animals, all underground! What was a squirrel doing so far underground anyway? The name 'Warren kitchens' would be more suitable if the place was inhabited by rabbits. Alas there was no time for further thought.

Martharnia called to another squirrel in one of the rooms.

'Peaks, scamper to Messy and ask for some of the nut cake if you would,' and turning to the others, 'Perhaps you would prefer to make yourselves comfortable next door? And then I can send in your well wishers one by one.'

She smiled again, and this time Samuel smiled back. The company made themselves comfortable in a little annex room, quite empty aside from them, fitted with a long table with benches either side and containing a window which Samuel had first spotted when walking up the passage outside – if you could call that outside.

Samuel was most intrigued by the squirrels and why they inhabited this place, so took advantage of asking Mr. Sorrow.

'They would be offended if I talked of the rabbits in front of them, but briefly, they built this place, but a very bad business occurred in which they all died. The Warren Kitchens was put up for sale and the squirrels jumped at it. Said it was nice and cosy and that it had good custom too. Although I don't imagine people walk all the way up here from the city now. This place relies on passing trade. Must be why the squirrels kept trading under the same name.'

They had been sitting for only a moment when the cake arrived. It was a magnificent hazelnut cake, topped with the juiciest, ripest, and most delicious hazel nuts that Samuel had ever tasted.

Once the company had finished eating it was time for them to meet the well wishers. When the company of dwarfs appeared before Samuel, it was evident that elocution was not their most developed attribute.

'We.. have come 'ere today to.. wish the very best to.. our new King, and represent the support of the.. Eloth Gold Mines. We trust.. that you will accept our humble.. best wishes, and will support the rights of dwarfs and their families.'

'With pleasure,' replied Samuel, smiling.

Next came the squirrels, Martharnia not included. They said much the same, wished Samuel every success, said they hoped he would return to the Warren Kitchens one day and that was about it.

The final group who came into the room were the beautiful women Samuel had noticed through the window earlier.

'We are the spirits of the woodland. Our gift to you today is our forests, which stand and fall at your command. We will sacrifice the oldest of our number for building and construction which you may wish to undertake, with the greatest pleasure.'

'Well, thank you, um, yes that is very kind,' was all that Samuel could think to say.

And then the company had to be off straight away. Samuel thanked all the squirrels for their kind hospitality. Each lined the hallway, and bowed to him, smiling and cheerful. Martharnia agreed to come with them to the entrance. She scampered out through the door and up the paved corridor to the right, away from the direction they had come. The tunnel seemed to get darker rather than lighter as they proceeded down it.

At last there was brighter light up ahead; Martharnia was tugging open a heavy door to reveal the way out but on the inside, to one corner, the light revealed another contraption – A wooden cart.

'We brought the cart here to provide cover for you. No one could suspect that we would use this!'

'No indeed, It was a stroke of genius. It is so unsophisticated.'

'And we have put some sacking in the back. Samuel could cover himself with that, and you could pull the cart by hand, it is not that big or heavy, I think you will find – not between you anyway.'

'Samuel! Get in the back now quickly. Mr. Ledbury and I will pull the cart, come on now, and hurry please. We stayed longer than I had imagined. The sun is setting outside. That's it; keep all your body covered unless we tell you to uncover yourself.'

Samuel was just able to curl up beneath the sacking, on a straw lining. The position was not exactly comfortable, but it would have to suffice. The cart began to move; it was a rough, jolting ride, although not quite as bad as the lift had been. The men walked on in silence for what felt like ages to Samuel. His leg was cramping up badly and he was beginning to get desperate for some fresh air.

'Should be fine here Samuel, come on, out you get. Come and admire the view here.' Samuel pulled the sacking off himself. It took a minute or so for his eyes to adjust to the bright light around him.

In the far distance a large, setting sun haloed a vast mountain range. Several warm rays of dying sunlight still cut through the crisp evening air, being simultaneously both blinding and brilliant. And yet beyond the glare of the sun, and far below, each of miniscule size and viewed across a distance immeasurably large, were thousands of glowing lights, creating a sight quite incomparable with any Samuel had ever seen before. These grew from tiny clusters to a large nucleus, where the lights intensified and shone the brightest through a misty, glowing haze. Off to the right hand side there arose several magnificent towers and spires, apparently part of the same structure. The tallest towers were capped with crenellations, and hundreds upon hundreds of window panes, which were set into the tower walls, shone and twinkled in the sunlight that hit them, or else were lit from inside, Samuel could not make out which.

Samuel's two companions motioned to Samuel to fully uncover himself, and slowly he came to stand in a position where he could better appreciate the view. Deep in his heart a feeling of pride was welling. So this was it. The fabled city. At least it did not disappoint. He was so intent on studying the land spread out before him that he did not at first notice his companions fall back. Eventually when he came to break his gaze and turn around he found them both kneeled at his feet, heads bowed before him.

'Dear Prince, at last we welcome you to our land. It is our privilege-'

'– Our great privilege,'

'– To swear our allegiance to you. Our lives our families, our kinsmen are all surrendered unto you.'

'To you we dedicate our lives and our souls'

'Upon your command our families will pour out their blood like water for your sake.'

'Lead us well, prince, when you become our king.'

There were tears in their eyes, tears of joy that at last their hope had come to the land of which they were so proud. And there were tears in the eyes of Samuel too. His heart had melted to see these great men, who had hours ago risked their lives for his sake, who, in their poverty, were so ready to give all that they had to serve him. He turned away. He could say nothing.

Samuel made his way back to the cart and covered himself once again. The journey continued in silence. It seemed to get darker under the sacking as time passed by, and Samuel assumed that twilight, and ultimately night, was approaching. The sounds that Samuel could here were also changing with the light. He could hear the hoot of an owl in the distance, mingled with other melancholy calls of the night.

A considerable time passed until the cart stopped and Horace Ledbury leant over to rearrange the sacking. He quietly informed Samuel they were within a few minutes of the main gates to the city so he should take additional care to keep himself covered. Samuel was warned to remain still and silent.

They moved on again for a few minutes, and then Samuel felt the cart stop. A voice rang out in the silence, shrill with officialdom.

'You are ordered to stop by the High Council of the Gate Keepers of the city of Grat. Under the Opate Declaration, subsection seventy, beings or persons unnamed must explain their reason for entering the city by foot so that it may be recorded as permanent evidence of their activity. State your reasons and titles!'

'We go by the names of MR. WILLIAM SORROW and MR. HORACE LEDBURY. We request leave to enter the city as members of the Cresta, to be given due leave to enter by rights of our education.'

'You have stated provision twelve of the afore mentioned subsection providing for entry of Cresta graduates. No record of your graduation from the Longwhey Institute can be found.'

'Pardon?'

'You claim to be of the Cresta, but this is a false claim. We have no record of your involvement.'

'But that is impossible; IMPOSSIBLE! I entered this gate two days ago.'

'You have quoted provision ten of the afore mentioned subsection which provides that if persons have had leave to pass in the last ten days, they shall have leave to pass now also. This claim has been verified. You may pass through the gates.'

'THANK YOU, at last!'

Samuel felt the cart move off again and gather some pace. It was pitch black now beneath the sacking, as dark as it was in the tunnel and caves.

He could hear voices, but they were quiet and confusing. Tiredness and exhaustion swept over him. This was a desire for sleep stronger than any resistance in him. So he closed his eyes, caring little about the jolting motion which he was becoming used to. His mind began to wander into a world of dreams where dwarfs lived in trees, trains kept breaking down and exploding squirrels swarmed in large caves.

Samuel awoke with a start. Where was he? The rocking motion had stopped, and all felt still and silent, but there were some faint voices. Did he dare pull back the sacking? He was aching from the position in which he had slept. He pulled the sacking from his face very slowly.

It was not totally dark outside. There was a moon out. No, there were actually two moons? How could that be? And those voices, where did they come from? Everything was coming flooding back to Samuel. He could make out Mr. Sorrow and Mr. Ledbury. Beside them was a woman, bespectacled and with silver haired; it was Lady Flint!

Samuel did not like to shout out to the group, so he got off the cart and walked quietly towards them.

'Lady Flint, look who has woken up!'

'It is dear Samuel, Come here dear! Not long now until I get you into a proper bed! That will be good won't it? Yes. Yes. Come along with me straight away. This is Larkin.'

Samuel looked to where she was pointing, just able to make out a large man, smoking a pipe and sitting on a chair outside a doorway. Lady Flint spoke again.

'My landlord Samuel, come and introduce yourself – Larkin, look who is staying with us tonight!'

'Bless my soul! If it isn't! I should have cleaned the porch a little more thoroughly if I knew this little mite was staying in my apartment for the night – You will look after him well Lady Flint?'

'We will certainly do our best,' said Lady Flint, smiling to herself in the darkness:

'Come on Samuel, your holdall has been taken up already, so just follow me.'

Samuel went with Lady Flint and left behind the two men that had brought him all this way. They made their way up a narrow twisting staircase until they were on the top floor. When Samuel reached the landing, Lady Flint had already opened the door, and switched the light on in the hallway. She explained to Samuel that for a number of years now she and her husband had rented this reasonably small, dark, and dusty apartment. Lady Flint was keen to make Samuel feel at home as soon as possible.

Samuel's legs felt like lead as a he was taken by lady Flint into a small room which she declared was his. Gratefully, he sank down on the bed, and after a murmured goodnight fell into a deep sleep.

-- CHAPTER FOUR --

Moving at Midnight

The abode of Lady Flint could be described as modest at best. When Samuel had been allotted his room the night before, he had been too tired to notice the layout of the whole apartment.

It was getting towards early evening before Samuel made his way into the kitchen. Lady Flint was at the sink, apron on, busily instructing a tiny girl how to peel what looked like blue carrots. It was immediately evident that Lady Flint enjoyed taking upon herself a motherly role.

'Well done dear, a fine cut as always Minty! You do the Flint family proud, especially when we have important visitors like Samuel here.'

'But Samuel is the only important visitor we have ever had here!'

'Don't you remember the time, Minty, when Mr. Flint came home!'

'But Mr. Flint hardly ever comes home.'

'Yes, yes dear, times are difficult. We all know that. You keep on peeling these …while I speak to Samuel.'

Samuel was bursting to find out more about queer little Minty.

'Who is Minty, Lady Flint?'

'Oh, my dear Samuel, I have scarcely had a moment to talk to you today, but of course you have so much to learn about tradition in the great city of Grat. My daughter, Rose, will tell you all about Minty. Rose, where are you, love?'

Rose Flint scrambled hastily from her room at the shrill sound of her mothers call.

'Yes mum, coming now!'

Samuel waited for Rose to come into the room, but Lady Flint insisted that he should go into the living room and wait for her there. Samuel made his way into the living room and just as he had settled into the armchair, Rose came rushing into the room, her flowing brown hair trailing behind her rosy red cheeks. She sat down. Then she looked up, smiling at Samuel.

'You wanted to know about Minty'

'Well, yes I asked Lady Flint… your mother, and she said I should speak to you.'

'Well, she is one of about three hundred wood elves who have a strong relationship with an old family. Mum is a Lady because her father was knighted, you see.

When mum married we kept the older family name because the Flint family go back, ooh, too long to recount. My grandfather took care of Minty, well of course she wasn't Minty then, but I will explain that later. Mum was Lord Flint's only child, so naturally, when mum and dad got married or cratased as we would call it, we inherited the Flint family wood elf. I call her an elf but of course that is not strictly true. She is more like a spirit of a tree. The Olwock tree is native to a valley south of the city of Grat, and every autumn the wood elves leave their families and make the journey back to their individual tree. They climb up and fall asleep on one of the branches. Their constitution is such that they are absorbed into the bark and the next spring they re-emerge a different wood elf from before, but still attached to the same family. They do carry some of the characteristics of their predecessors. Minty has a particularly sharp nose…'

'...I noticed…'

'Yes well, I think Gambie before her had a similar sort of nose.'

'So a year ago, Minty was Gambie?'

'Correct, and you will find that our years are longer here: six hundred and thirty two and a third days in a year to be exact.'

'Not the most simple of numbers!'

'Not half as simple as many of the people who live here, that I can tell you!'

Each chuckled heartily. For Samuel, it felt good to relax after the stressful experience of the day before.

'I ought to say don't have a go at mum if she is a bit abrupt today. She was expecting Alfred Beavitch…'

'– I think I recognise that name'

'– He gave you your key to the Dark Train I think. Yes, as I was saying she expected him to call last night but he never arrived. A search party was sent out but there has been no sign of him yet. So mum is understandably stressed and worried. She has a soft spot for dear Alfred.

A few moments later came a call from Mrs. Flint.

'Rose! I need you to put an extra peneochli in the oven dear!'

Rose turned to Samuel and explained that Larkin was coming to dinner with them. Then she left the room. Samuel let his eyes wander around the sitting area, and finally came to rest on a newspaper. It looked the same as the newspaper the Mrs. Flint had been looking at on the Dark Train yesterday. Samuel leant over to pick it up. Nothing happened at first. Without warning a silver chariot erupted out of the page. It was pulled by a row of silver horses, whose panting flanks shifted like flowing mercury.

Seated in the chariot itself, holding the reins, was what appeared to be a mouse. As the carriage drew to a stop, it opened its mouth and started singing:

'With every salutation –'

(The mouse removed its hat)

'There is a price to pay...
But you can have the Chariot
For quite a nutty price today!
No other broadsheet's good enough
To bring you so much thrilling stuff...
Though some still say that we're full of air
And others say they just despair!'

(The mouse strutted around the carriage making a mock cut throat gesture)

'Four peks and a ponis is our price,
We trust you will think it rather nice
And it will, a sale, to you, entice'

(The mouse pointed a finger at Samuel in quite a provocative manner)

Also available in elvish and goblish!

Samuel heard footsteps entering the room, and quickly closed the paper before he was noticed, or so he thought.

'Liked *The Chariot* then?'

'Well, I hope you don't mind, I was just…'

'– no, of course not, I will get mum to pay for you to register, and then you can have one of your own. How much is it?'

'Four…something or other, I can't quite remember.'

'Not to worry, I'm certain mum will know. MUM!'

It took a minute for Lady Flint to reach the room from the kitchen. Samuel felt embarrassed that Rose had called her on his behalf, especially to accept the money of strangers. Lady Flint clattered into the room, and looked enquiringly at Rose.

'Ah, *The chariot* is it Samuel? Well I, I, I…'

'What is it, mum?'

'Quiet, quiet, look!'

The mouse on the chariot was quivering and the whole construction melted away into a globule, suspended in the air above the page. Then, like metal in a mould, it was transformed into a man and a woman.

'Oh, my! My, My, My!'

'MUM! What in the name of Grat is the matter?'

The two characters were moving, smiling. They mesmerised Samuel.

'I am afraid this quite changes everything!'

'Tell me now, clearly what is happening!'

'They say it's a miracle. Unbelievable, quite totally unexpected.'

'What is?'

'She is.'

'Who is she?'

'That is the Queen of Grat! And next to her was our King!'

'That means that they are your mother and father Samuel!'

Samuel stayed silent for a moment then swallowed.

'I know.'

'But mum! Tell me what has happened.'

'She is alive. They found her today!'

Samuel's head was hurting. His mother. Alive! How could this be? Had he not been told by Albert Hawkins that she was dead? And his father... 'was he alive too?'

'Oh, no, no. King Harold Deksis died a good few years ago. Before Rose can even remember.'

Rose nodded at Samuel.

'So this was it then, a twist of fate–' thought Samuel, '– He had come to his 'kingdom', and ironically, at the same time his life outside was also to be restored.' Samuel was unsure whether he could really believe his mother was alive until he saw her and even then, memories of her which he could recall, were so vague that he could never be certain this person really was his mother.

'Rose, dear, please can you go and help Minty with laying the table, I need to let Samuel know exactly what is happening.'

Rose left the room once again.

'Look dear, it has all been a bit of a mess really, so I don't know quite where to start! To begin with, you were supposed to be taken straight to the Royal Palace for your coronation. Evidently, that has not happened due to… unforeseen events. It was always going to be difficult to get you here unnoticed, and I am afraid to say we failed miserably on that front. But you are safe here, I assure you, they don't know where you are. We think it is best to keep you here for ten days, then the cart can be used, and we can smuggle you into the Royal Palace by the back door; none of the media attention until you are ready for it. How does that sound?'

'Fine, but what about my mother?'

'Well, I can only tell you as much as I know. I have heard that she is to be waiting at the Royal Palace to watch your coronation, and that she will meet you afterwards. She can't come here because that would lead them straight to you.'

'How is she?'

‘Well, I don’t know really. I haven’t heard anything remotely convincing that acts as an explanation for her absence from this world for so many years.’

‘Why did she turn up now?’

‘Oh, um, I think she turned up because you turned up. I think somehow the two events are intrinsically linked: but that is only my opinion, and I can claim to be no expert upon the matter, my dear. But I can tell you that you will still become King, and your mother’s role as Queen will not be regained, so no need to worry there. She has been absent for too long, and your father made it clear who was to become King after his death.’

So she would just walk back into his life, this person who said she was his mother. Just like that, and take up the reins. This just could not be true.

The meal that night was a strange affair. Larkin was a man of leisure and pleasure, fond of the bottle and even fonder of his tenants. Yet how could such a merry man exist alongside a worried and withdrawn Lady Flint, and a deeply disturbed Samuel?

That was the first night Samuel tried drinking alcohol. On this first occasion he kept his consumption to such a minimum that he could feel no ill effects. Samuel was glad when the meal came to an end and he could be persuaded to take rest in the lounge once again. Larkin drank rather too much, and was in a mood too buoyant, too aggressive and too loud to be sustained.

The evening passed as slowly as it could and Samuel returned to his room later in the night, worried and confused.

The next day passed without any drama, but the following day there was more activity. Lady Flint had decided Samuel needed some new clothes. The hot weather of Grat was best suited to those wearing long flowing tunics, so following a few measurements, Lady Flint left the apartment to stock up on robes and garments for Samuel. Rose and Minty sat with Samuel while lady Flint was out.

‘Samuel, I though you ought to know that there has been no news on Alfred.’

‘I am sorry to hear that for your mother’s sake, Rose.’

‘So am I. Mum has been finding it quite difficult at the moment and I can’t help but feel worried about her.’

‘I think Lady Flint is the bravest, one of the bravest people in the world,’ piped up Minty in her chirpy little voice.

Rose looked away before saying ‘even mum can’t carry on with dad being away for such a long time, and you know it Minty.’

Lady Flint arrived back a little later in the afternoon. Her trip had amassed quite an array of clothes and so a fitting session had to follow with lots of fussing from Lady Flint, and lots of moaning from a bored Minty and Samuel. At last he had an appropriate outfit, which even he had to confess suited the climate. The heat in the apartment had been close to insufferable during the daytime. Having been in the apartment now for a couple of days, Samuel still knew little about the world outside, since he was not allowed to move near the windows for fear of his being seen from outside by a passer by. Lady Flint was insistent that security and secrecy were paramount. Yet, despite all her very best efforts, she was to find that her trust had been placed in one who could not really be trusted to say the right things, but instead had a reputation for saying rather too much.

News of the blunder reached Lady Flint by the means of a caller at the door. Thankfully it was a friendly one but the news that William Sorrow was to bring, was anything but.

Larkin had been out drinking that night at a tavern at the end of the road. It was there that he had acquired his reputation for regularly propping up the bar. His drinking antics this time had lead him into deep trouble. A game of boasts had lead him to reveal the presence of Samuel in one of his apartments to the whole of the room.

Lady Flint invited Mr. Sorrow in, but he said he had to go. Once he had left, Samuel was surprised to see Lady Flint burst into tears. Minty ran to fetch tissues, but made the mistake of bring towels, which made everyone laugh, even the tearful Lady Flint.

'I am sorry Samuel! I was just thinking of what a terrible couple of days it has been. What with Alfred and now this. I was waiting for something to go terribly wrong again and now it has. I feel terrible for telling Larkin you were here. I even had him to dinner with you. What an idiot I have been. What a fool!'

'That is enough mum! You must not be too hard on yourself. Mr. Larkin and his big gob is the one to blame.'

'ROSE! How many times have I told you not to use rude words like that in my apartment! But you are right…'

The little conference was interrupted by yet another knock at the door. When Lady Flint opened in this time it revealed a red eyed and shaking Larkin, who was shabbily dressed and looked rather neurotic.

'Oh Lady, Lady F-F-Flint. I am such an idiot. I'm sorry. A burden I know. A hag-headed fool if-if-if every there was one. Oh, Oh, Oh, and I had to come in and come here and come to say sorry. And and since I have been the cause of your problems I am so, so, also determined to be a part of the solution to the terrible situation.'

'Calm down now Larkin! You were drunk at the time. Come in and sit down. I think a cup of brew might steady your nerves and get you talking straight. Then you can tell us your entire plan to get Samuel out of this pickle.'

Minty went to put the kettle on and everyone sat down. Larkin was able to dry his eyes and gradually return from the brink of hysterics.

'So Larkin, tell us your plan then, and take it slowly.'

'Well, well I, well I don't really know where to begin. This fine wood elf here, how much does she weigh?'

'My goodness! Larkin, that could be taken the wrong way. Well, not much I suppose. Minty is pretty skinny.'

'Then I declare Minny here shall lead the way!'

'Lead the way where precisely?'

'I will come to that now! That tavern was the source of all my ills. I want to see it in the plan of salvation for Samuel here. How many nights have I spent there, drinking and talking? Always talking. And when you talk you often listen. And I have often been listening. I have been listening to what they say about the ghosts in the tavern, about the things that used to happen in the past. And when I was listening to this I have often heard talk of the cellar beneath the tavern, and though I have never been down there, I have heard so very many times of a tunnel that runs from there and comes up just inside the Royal Palace.'

'Well Larkin, I can see what you are saying, but I can already see two holes in your plan. Firstly, we can't risk taking Samuel out of here because they will probably be watching for him, and secondly, we don't know if this tunnel exists, or if it is usable.'

'Lady Flint, I have solutions to both of your objections. In the first instance, I know the tunnel definitely exists and, secondly, I know of a way in which Samuel need never even venture outside to reach it.'

'What is this way precisely?'

'The attic. We must use the attic. The attics run all the way along the street, until you get above the tavern at the end. The top room there is unused, and the staircase leads down to the Tavern itself, and is never used since it goes no where other than to the disused room.'

'But are there no walls separating the attics?-' enquired Samuel.

'No, there are none at all. Of that I am sure. But we can be absolutely certain of this very soon because Minny here is going first. She is going to test the route for you. It has to be her because she is the lightest and will thus be the quietest. Those old beams in the attic are not too strong and I say we only risk it once with you, Samuel after that.'

'I say Larkin, what about the people in the tavern, can't they see the stairs, and how can Samuel get from the stairs to the cellar unseen?' Enquired Rose.

'Well now, again I have thought of this, and we can test it with Minny. After midnight there is usually the barman with me in the tavern. Didn't I tell you I like to talk? I only have to distract him while you get to the trap door of the cellar, which the barman has opened so he can fetch the empty barrels ready for the morning. You see! It's genius, it can't go wrong. Minny can go down into the tunnel by herself, once she finds it. She can test the air, test the walls, and then let me know everything is fine. Then I can let you lot here know that all is fine, and then you send Samuel down, while I return to the bar to distract the barman again.'

'What makes you so sure *Minty* will be able to find the tunnel in the cellar?'

'Minny will find what she is meant to find I am sure. We know it has to be there, and she can tell me how Samuel is to find it. If it is very hard to get to, Minty can come back and get Samuel and go with her through the attics again.'

'Thinking about it Larkin, that would be a much better idea, I have no doubt. I don't like the idea of Samuel up in the attics without anyone to look after him.'

'Well in that case Minny can do that can't she?'

Larkin was beaming and exasperated at the same time – exasperated that the others did not immediately leap at the plan. But nor did they rubbish it, and slowly Lady Flint could see that the plan made sense. If Minty could not find the passage then Samuel was still as safe as ever in the apartment, and yet if the route was clear then he might be able to get to the Royal Palace. Larkin started to speak again.

'Now Miss Flint, I need you to play a part as well. The Royal Palace need to know where to meet Samuel and how to get him ready for his coronation. He can wear his basic robes when he leaves here, but the finishing touches must be added at the Palace.'

'Fine Larkin! There is no problem there. But before I dash off, I must advise against using the beams in the attic to walk upon. I have been up there and they will not take Samuel's weight, even for one trip.'

There was a disappointed silence in the room and then very slowly and with gathering certainly Lady Flint began to speak.

'Larkin, I think you are forgetting the carpet.'

'The carpet?'

'Yes, the one my husband was given by the Grand Visril Chang of Ling.'

'You mean, you mean the hovering carpet?'

'Yes, yes, the very same.'

'Well indeed that would be rather dangerous in quite a confined space, and it takes a year to learn how to fly the thing.'

'I think Gambie mastered it last year, perhaps Minty has maintained the skill. We won't know until she tries it.'

'In that case Lady Flint, I must ask you to get it for her so she can practice.'

Lady Flint hastened away to another room and for several minutes a mighty tussle could be heard as she waded through deep wardrobes of clothes and packages until at last she came upon the carpet. She brought it back to the lounge and immediately started untying the string binding it.

The string came undone quite easily, and Lady Flint let the carpet fall elegantly towards the ground. It unfolded by itself and then gracefully came to rest, hovering several inches above the floor. The carpet quivered as it waited. Minty hopped deftly on board, and Lady Flint stood nearby, telling Minty loudly and clearly what to do.

'Cross your legs Minty, that's right, like that. Exactly right, then sit upright. Now lean backward.'

The carpet shot backwards and flew from under Minty completely, hit the wall, and then landed in a graceless pile on the floor.

'Not so much next time Minty, a little less leaning I think. Lean forwards this time, and try to lean to your left a little so as to turn you in a circle. But only do it ever so slightly – it really is very sensitive.'

Minty continued to practice as Samuel watched. He longed to have a go himself, but did not dare to ask Lady Flint in case he hit into something in her apartment. About half an hour later it was declared that Minty could fly the carpet well enough, and Rose was dispatched to send the news of Samuel's imminent arrival at the Royal Palace via the old tunnel from the tavern.

Larkin was kept busy sorting out the ladder to the loft, which was jammed, and Minty carried on her practice with the carpet. Samuel sat helplessly waiting. At last Samuel was glad to hear Larkin shout that he was ready for Minty to go up into the attic above the apartment. It was decided that it was better for Minty to crawl along the rafters this time because she was so light.

Samuel and Lady Flint watched from the landing as Minty, carrying a small torch, used her skinny arms and legs to climb the ladder up to the attic. Larkin pulled her up inside from the only safe beam up there, conveniently located by the hatch. Lady Flint winced as Larkin lowered himself through the narrow hole, and made his way back down the ladder.

'On her own now is Minny,' he declared.

'And you, Larkin had better be on your way to the tavern, to distract that barman of yours.'

And so Samuel was left alone in the apartment with Lady Flint. He ventured to ask about his mother – 'had there been any news of her?' He enquired. Lady Flint unfolded The Chariot from the table. Out of it erupted a miniature merchant stall, selling what looked to Samuel like eggs. Lady Flint smiled.

'The Borrow Ways have reached their trading peak for this year with a record fifty thousand transactions in the last two days. It seems that things are finally picking up in the economic heartland of Grat. It must be because you have arrived Samuel. We haven't seen sales of these mock Tahriha Dynasty goblets reach into the thousands for the last ten years at least.'

'But what about my mother…' murmured Samuel.

'Nothing on that yet dear, it must have been the breaking news so we will have to wait for that to come back around again. It will be here shortly.'

'Lady Flint, I want to ask you something which has been bothering me…if this…if this really is a different world from the one I lived in, why do we speak the same language and understand each other so clearly?'

'Oh, what a question! Showing such insight! I can't say I am not impressed, and I hope you will find my answer satisfactory. The reason everyone you have met understands you is because everyone you have met have been travellers. All of us have been in your world and here, in and out. We were all taught at an early age, how to fit in, in your world, how to understand your culture, and how to speak your language. But your language is never *our* language. Gratians traditionally speak *Tire*, a language creolised from *Old Davish* and *Old Telfon*.'

Lady Flint pushed the Newspaper down the table away from her and turned to look at Samuel.

'This is going to be a strange couple of months for you, dear. But don't despair. Things will settle down soon, I promise you. My husband will see to that. I wish you could speak to him right now so that he could put your mind at rest. But alas, he is detained on business once again. But I have no doubt at all in my mind that he will meet you at the Royal Palace. When you do speak to him, you must tell him that I send my very best regards to him, and look forward desperately to seeing him again soon. You will do that for me, my dear, won't you?'

'But of course, Lady Flint. It will be my pleasure. It has been so kind of you to look after me here during these difficult days, it is really the least I can do.'

'Oh, thank you, thank you. Now I feel so much calmer. Lets have a drink and wait shall we?'

And so they did just that. Sat and waited for a knock at the door from Minty and Larkin. Lady Flint called out with a sigh to Samuel to tell him it was almost eleven o' clock. They had been waiting at least an hour and a half.

At last there was a knock and Lady Flint let in an exhausted Minty and a slightly tipsy Larkin. The group of four sat down together to discuss how things had gone. Larkin told his story first.

He had made his way quickly to the tavern, and had met up with a couple of old friends inside. Thankfully they had been just about to leave and he managed to hurry them away as quickly as he could. He had then sat down to have a drink and calm his nerves, and had begun to talk with the barman. So busy had Larkin been with his talking that both he and the barman had failed to see 'Minny' slip past. At one point Larkin had thought he could hear something move in the cellar beneath him, but the barman had not heard a thing. The only difficulty had been when the barman decided he needed to go to the cellar to find a cloth he had apparently left down there the day before. Larkin had thankfully managed to distract him, and Minty had emerged from the cellar behind his back, made her way to the door, and quietly slipped out. Larkin had made the excuse that he had just remembered leaving his newspaper by the fire and had said he was worried it might catch alight if he did not check immediately, so he had taken his leave, met 'Minny' outside and walked with her back to the abode of Lady Flint.

Now it was Minty's turn to tell her story. She had proceeded along the rafters very carefully, picking her way across the weak joists. The only problem occurred when she ran into a family of rodents, who apparently failed to make her very welcome. Apart from that she had made her way without significant difficulty to the attic space above the Tavern. Thankfully, the trap door was not bolted. Minty had been able to use her sharp nails to prise it up, and had then dropped down into the space below. Thankfully a dirty old bed was directly beneath and had provided quite a soft landing.

She had struggled opening the swollen door out of the spare room, but had managed it eventually, and had left it slightly open for the next time around. The stairs had been navigated uneventfully, and slipping past the barman to the open trap door to the cellar had been easy. That hardest part, as everyone had expected, was finding the tunnel. First off, Minty had thought she had found the passage, but it had turned out to be an additional storage area which led nowhere. She had even less success in moving a couple of the barrels, and had knocked one onto the floor – resulting in the noise heard by Larkin in the tavern, above. Finally she located the passage behind a canvas on the wall, and had walked some way in. Beyond the cobwebs she said that it was not too bad, and although the air was certainly musty it was not dangerously so.

Lady Flint declared that once Samuel had changed into his basic robes, both Minty and Samuel were to rest until she and Larkin had raised the height at which the carpet hovered. This was to be achieved, she said, by stretching the carpet itself, and after quite a tussle, sufficient ground clearance was achieved. Larkin was instructed to climb the ladder to the attic with the carpet and unroll it up there ready for the two riders. Minty then went up first and got in position. Lady Flint made sure Samuel was alright, assuring him that his belongings would arrive at the Royal Palace later on. She said this would be her personal duty. Then Samuel had to climb the ladder. It was a strange ladder at best. All he had to do was to stand on the rung, and then it pushed him upwards towards the attic so that he rose gently upwards. Larkin pulled him through the hole, and up onto the one safe beam. From there he was able to steady himself, and then step onto the carpet. He wobbled slightly and then sank to his knees behind little Minty. It was a strange feeling being on the carpet, a bit like sitting on a bag filled with water.

'Ready?' That was Larkin checking they were both fine before he made his way back down the ladder. Minty slowly and carefully leant forwards, and Samuel felt the carpet slowly accelerate beneath him, pulling him forwards. It was dark up in the attic space, and Samuel could see very little apart from the outline of the odd dark beam that shot past them as they accelerated forwards. The air was very hot and, as they flew on, Samuel could feel it warming his cheeks. There was a light in the floor up ahead which Samuel assumed was the opening leading down into the disused room. Minty brought the carpet to a halt just to the left of the opening, and gestured for Samuel to swing himself around so that his legs were dangling down through the hole. It was difficult getting off the carpet, but Samuel managed to shuffle off it gradually, and once he was sitting at the edge of the hole he could clearly see the bed in the room beneath which Minty had described earlier. Samuel was keen not to hang around too long. He counted down in his head, 'Three, two…one!'

He pushed himself forwards and felt himself falling through the air. He hit the bed feet first and was sent bouncing onto his back. The springs groaned under the weight of the impact, but the bedclothes masked the sound. A moment later, Samuel was able to gather himself together and pull himself off the bed to clear the way for Minty. She took a moment to roll up the carpet, and then dropped from the hole in the ceiling. She landed in much the same way, and was soon standing next to Samuel on the floor. The floor itself was uncarpeted and so they were both walking on bare floorboards.

Both Samuel and Minty were careful to ensure they did not creek too loudly. Both felt that the crash of falling onto the bed was the biggest risk they could afford to take. It was lucky that the old floor was so thick that the chances of anything being heard downstairs were remote.

Minty led the way to the door and Samuel followed behind her. The door was slightly open as Minty had left it the first time around. The doorway led onto the landing. The spiral staircase in front of them was made of stone, thankfully strong and intact. They both made their way forwards and down it, around and around, until Minty came to a halt and turned to face Samuel, indicating with a finger on her lips that they were both to be very quiet. The sound of talking and laughter was getting quite loud and, as they crept onward, the bar of the Tavern came into view. There was the barman talking to Larkin, who thankfully was now the only person there. If Larkin had spotted them, he certainly did not show it. Minty scuttled forward while the barman had his back to them, and Samuel followed closely on her heels. Minty then stood aside to allow Samuel to get through the trap door, but just as his feet were on the first rung of the ladder leading below things took a turn for the worse. The barman had stopped talking, and his footsteps indicated he was walking towards them. Minty panicked and whispered 'Go!' to Samuel pushed him down the ladder, and shutting the trap door closed behind him. The Barman had seen her, but had he seen Samuel?

'A wood ELF! At my Bar! And what do you think you are doing! You THIEF! You thieving little bag of wood! Get out of this tavern! LEAVE and don't you DARE ever come back!'

Minty was then forced to leave the tavern, but Larkin remained seated, and showed no visible sign of recognising her. Meanwhile in the cellar Samuel was struggling to find the old passage. After he had hurriedly gathered his senses he had tried to follow Minty's directions to find the canvas. The only light down there was that which came through the gaps in the floor boards of the tavern above. Samuel had heard the sound of shouting, which made him all the more determined to find the tunnel quickly. At last he found the canvas and pulling it aside he could see the tunnel. He switched on his torch and entered. Samuel was confident there would be no cobwebs down here because Minty would have broken them all when she explored the tunnel earlier. WRONG! He had overlooked her lack of height. She might have broken cobwebs that were lower down, but high ones at the height of his face had been left intact. Samuel spent the next five minutes pulling cobwebs apart in front of him before moving onwards. He began to feel the passage sloping downwards and before long he could feel water underfoot. Samuel kept on walking for what must have been about three quarters of an hour. His feet were soaked from wading through the stagnant water that had flooded the ageing passage. Thankfully the passage was intact throughout and there had been no roof falls.

The air was getting warmer and fresher, and the tunnel appeared to change up ahead. Samuel could just make out the first step of a stone staircase. Soon Samuel found himself slowly ascending a flight of stone steps. Light flooded in ahead and Samuel emerged into a huge hallway. The walls were supported by mighty pillars that reminded Samuel of the columns of a huge cathedral. In front of him was a woman, dressed in white robes and with platted white hair. She turned to him smiling.

'At last. Welcome to the Royal Palace, Samuel. Thank goodness Lady Flint had the foresight to make you wear your basic robes over here. Saves time as they are all waiting for you in there,' she pointed in front of him at a set of golden double doors so high that Samuel could hardly see the top of them. They stood just slightly ajar, towering upwards.

'You should come this way, Samuel. Into the annex room to get ready.'

The lady in white robes led the way through a small archway nearby and into a room where a splendid golden gown had been laid out in readiness. The Lady turned to Samuel and explained the formalities of the coronation while she helped him to put on the gown over his basic robes. A man would be holding the King's Crown near the throne when Samuel arrived in the main hall. He was to wait by the throne until he was told to be seated.

After this, the lady led Samuel back out of the annex and into the reception chamber. After wishing him luck, she pointed to the doors and indicated that he should open them and go inside.

Cautiously and with a degree of uncertainty, he moved forward slowly, gently pushing the huge doors open. They required scarcely any pressure and both swung open with gathering pace to reveal the throne room within. Samuel was completely overawed. The space inside was majestic beyond belief. Great pillars towered upwards, twisting beyond sight and thought. And on either side of the room a few hundred people were standing, heads bowed, respectfully silent, showing reverence, and submission to the person who was about to become their Sovereign. At the end of the isle a man stood, holding a crown, as Samuel had been told to expect.

This was it. He waited his cue, and the herald of trumpets provided it. Cautiously, he began to walk forwards, pacing himself slowly so that his strides were approximately equal. He noticed that a troop of mice had begun to follow behind him. They held what he thought were cameras to their tiny eyes, the first flashes of which, proved his suspicions to be correct. They might be from The Chariot itself, he thought with a smile. Perhaps the next time Lady Flint opened her newspaper she would see King Samuel at his coronation. What a strange thought.

The throne itself was now quite close. Samuel stopped, lining himself up with the edge of the light from a huge chandelier overhead. He waited. No one moved. Then slowly the man with the crown turned his head to Samuel.

'BE SEATED!'

His mighty voice echoed into silence.

'I CROWN YOU KING SAMUEL!'

-- CHAPTER FIVE --

In the First Light of Morning

The Ceremony was over quicker than anyone, particularly Samuel, had expected. Once he had been crowned, and the necessary had been conducted, Samuel was lead away from the sea of faces and taken back to the annex room where he had changed. The Lady in white robes who had helped when he arrived was waiting there. He noticed she had been crying as she helped him out of his robe. He caught sight of her eyes and they met his in a moment of time. She was just at the point of turning away when, in a sudden impulse, she leant towards Samuel and hugged him. He could smell her hair; fresh and calming. And then ever, ever so quietly she whispered in his ear: 'Well done, my son.'

There was a lot of hugging that went on that morning. Dawn had long arrived by the time Samuel and his mother made there way out of the annex room and into the main complex of the palace. The exchange between son and mother had been deep and heartfelt, although Samuel still felt his mother had been too evasive in her answers and, despite their long talk, he was still none the wiser about exactly where she had been and what she had been doing all this time. There had been a moment when she looked at him so sadly and said 'You don't even know my name, do you?' and he had to shake his head. With tears glistening in her eyes, she told him her name was 'Saffie Deksis.' It sounded like a perfect name to him. Samuel was happy to accept the offer of an extensive tour of the Royal Palace, conducted by His mother.

Saffie Deksis pulled aside a tapestry and led the way into a narrow passage, lit by burning candles which were placed in alcoves at the side of the walls. They cast an odd, ever-changing light into the surrounding area.

Something was strange but for a moment Samuel could not make out what it was. There was a soft scraping sound, a sort of quiet whoosh, and a very faint spotlight seemed to surround him. He looked to his mother who had turned around smiling. She pointed upwards. Above Samuel was a large chandelier similar to the ones he had seen elsewhere in this world. The sound had gone now, but as Samuel ventured forwards he heard it again, and looking upwards was amazed to see the chandelier gliding along after him. He heard his mother break into a soft laugh before she spoke.

'The Royal Magician has been re-bewitching that for days! It does wear off after a few months, but I think you have to agree that the effect is quite splendid when it all works well. If you keep walking up to the next chandelier, that one takes over and follows you along a set path. Quite amazing! And look at the Oro-fices.'

Saffie pointed to the lit alcoves.

'Lit by everlasting candles and just you put your head in there! That will give Your Majesty surprise I have no doubt.'

This intrigued Samuel, and it surprised him – what purpose could such an alcove have other than to light up the corridor. With his mother watching, Samuel moved towards the one nearest to him and started to put his head inside. It was surprisingly deep, and the candles gave off no heat so he became less cautious of him burning himself. All of a sudden, out of the flames erupted a human size head so that the eyes were blinking straight into Samuels. Samuel recoiled in horror and cracked his head hard against the roof of the Oro-fice. Samuel could see stars for a moment. Looking back at the Oro-fice it was plain to see that the head had disappeared as quickly as it had come.

'W-What was that!' stammered Samuel.

'That was a memory. The richest people of this city paid to have the memory of themselves preserved as talking heads here in the Royal Palace so that they could continue to look after the city after their death. The most recent Oro-fice to be built was that of your father, and I think it is somewhere near the Fiftieth-Floor Meeting Room, but I would have to check' – she looked at him – 'They are just memories, just reflections of the people they were. But if you ever need to talk something through with any ancestor of yours, with any ancient king who had some knowledge of some obscure topic which your require, then all you have to do is search for the Oro-fice and put your head into it. Now come along Your Majesty! I think you have had quite enough excitement and public exposure for one day, and you must be exhausted having lost a whole night of sleep. We shall keep to the quieter passageways and only glance into some of the rooms.

The passage led on for quite a distance, then quickly widened. Samuel's mother informed him that the kitchens were up ahead. A doorway was open, and she led Samuel to it to look inside. All he could see were rows upon rows of tables, and the whole hall was surrounded by fireplaces and cooking pots. This was catering on a Royal industrial scale. Samuel felt a burning question rise to his mind.

'Who does the cooking in here then?'

'Who? Well all humans of course! Many have worked here all their lives.'

'No squirrels then?'

'Squirrels? No, definitely not! I don't think there has ever been even a wood elf in here, so only humans. This is a Royal palace for Humans you see.'

Samuel was a little disappointed. He had imagined that all sorts of unusual creatures would inhabit the Royal palace itself.

'Follow me, your majesty. I want you to see the Grand Dining Hall.'

She led him up the passage a little way and then stopped in front of a slightly larger Oro-fice. She then proceeded to put her head into it, and re-emerged moments later.

'We have to know the password, but I have forgotten it already. Hang on a minute. They said they would be changing it today. Ah yes, I've just remembered! The password is 'Crowned' of course! To celebrate your coronation your majesty. So CROWNED it is!'

As she clearly spoke the word, the wall containing the Oro-fice issued a grating noise and revolved around a central point, giving the pair entry to a corridor with deep red carpet and carved wooden flooring beyond the carpet at either side. They came to a pair of doors at the end which Samuel's mother pushed open.

'Just a peep now! It had all been laid out for you top have a meal following your Coronation, but when everything went wrong it was deemed too dangerous for you to be in a room with so many people at once. They didn't have the time to sort it all out and make it secure so they abandoned the attempt.'

The doors were open just wide enough for Samuel to see inside. Although not as vast as the hall in which he had been crowned, this was still very impressive. The beautiful vaulted ceiling gave way to elaborate roof supports that twisted like the trunks of giant, gnarled trees. On the floor there were rows of tables stretching away into the distance for almost as far as Samuel could see.

His mother soon wanted to move on, so they left the Dining Hall far behind them and followed a maze of passages until they reached a small spiral staircase. Samuel's mother announced that the Royal Library was situated on the floor above. It contained a copy of every Gratian document in existence, every law, every novel, every contract. They trooped upstairs together, Samuel following closely at his mother's heels. The stairs seemed to go on forever, and at last they emerged onto a balcony. From here they had a view over much of the Library, although the book lined walls at each side of the room carried on upwards out of sight. Below them were shelves upon shelves upon which books of every colour and shape were in storage. Samuel thought he could make out a group of people sitting, reading in one corner.

His eye was drawn to a beautiful stained glass window which was set into the wall, but surrounded by shelves in such way that the wall was almost invisible. It depicted a boat caught in a storm on a lake. There were huge waves rolling and really breaking in the picture. On board the boat there was a man, standing. He occasionally moved his arms, and looked at Samuel.

'What is that image?'

'That? That is a stained glass window depicting a scene from our folk law tales. I don't suppose you know the tale of '*The folly on Moon-Water Lake*'? It is quite a long tale but perhaps I can cut it down it for you. It is about time Your Majesty started absorbing the culture and history of his subjects.

The City of Grat is actually built around what remains of 'Moon-water Lake.' That is not its true name in the language of Tire, but that is a rough translation of what it means. The large expanse of water is fed by a stream which flows from a spring that starts high up, near the summit of the North Mountain – You would have seen that upon your approach to the city, I think it is the very highest mountain in the country. The lake was thought to have been named by the first King of Grat as he fled from his usurped castle after a revolt by the citizens of the city.

Being such a vain man, he had valued his gold and silver above anything else and fled in too much of a hurry, overloading his small boat. He then rowed out across the lake, alone. The old boat started to let in water; gradually it seeped inside and the boat became lower and lower in the water. The citizens stood in the shallows of the lake shaking their fists at him; for though many were very brave, none dared to venture out into 'The Deeps'. For there were older stories of people who had swum out and never returned to shore, and others of people who did return, but who lost the power of speech for the rest of their lives.

You will hear of the first King referred to as 'King Krinked'- Krinked means 'fool' in *Tire*, but I believe amongst the people of your world he was popularly known as 'Krinked the Foolish.'

'So the name of the first King was Krinked?'

'No, that was just improvised I think; his real name was lost as the tale was handed down from generation to generation.

As the boat began to sink, King Krinked stood on deck and screamed back to shore – 'long may the moon shine on my gold', and with that he jumped from the boat and sank down into the terrible watery world below. This glass window was commissioned to remind all subjects and rulers that humility opposes vanity; life is about more than physical belongings alone.'

Samuel looked back at the man in the stained glass window. Now he could make out the gold piled high on the deck of the boat. At first he had through it was a furled sail. He was just pondering if the man looked vain when he was caught by surprise and let out an almighty yawn.

'History not quite your thing, Your Majesty?'

'Oh no! It was…reasonably interesting. I just feel totally drained and exhausted. '

'King Samuel! Your Majesty! I do apologise and you are quite right. It is wicked of me to drag you around on a tour like this when really all you need is rest. I was going to show you the Grand Debating Chamber, but that can easily wait.'

Despite Samuel's protestations, his mother insisted that she took him straight to the Royal Bed Chamber. Samuel had to eventually agree, for he did feel tired and, from what his mother said, it sounded like quite a walk from here anyway.

She led the way back onto the spiral staircase, down a couple of turns and through a doorway Samuel had not noticed on the way up. They carried on across a large gallery, with chandeliers moving overhead to light the way. Another labyrinth of passages had to be navigated before they reached another massive hall. His mother indicated the direction of the staircase they now had to climb.

Samuel was speechless. The first curving step in front of him was easily a mile long; he could scarcely see the hand rail on either side. His mother hastened him upwards, step after step, after step. The blood red carpet underfoot was spotless and immaculate, punctuated only by thin golden stair rods. As they continued to climb, Samuel could see that each step was narrowing. The ornate, carved ivory handrail on either side was gradually closing in.

They paused for breath and Samuel was able to look back at the void they had left behind. From this position the stairs looked just as impressive, just as overwhelmingly grand.

The stairs began to turn to the left and twist around them self, spiralling upwards. The pair began to pass landing after landing. They saw only a couple of people here; first, a tall lady dressed in a long orange gown who curtsied to King Samuel and avoided any contact with his eyes as they walked past. Samuel knew the attention which the position of 'King Samuel' attracted, was going to be hard to get used to, but he felt that, in time, he might quite like it. He was starting to enjoy the level of respect which the position evidently afforded. They also passed a group of men who, from a distance, had appeared to be arguing, but this abated as king Samuel approached.

'I think we are nearly there now your majesty. The Royal Bedroom waits! -' declared Samuels mother.

The Stairs, which were by now relatively narrow, continued upwards, but Samuel was led off them and onto one of the higher landing by his mother. They still had to navigate several corridors before finally they arrived outside a door. It was a carved, wooden door, and Samuel was told by his mother that he was the only person in the Palace, or outside it, that could open it.

Samuel found that he could turn the knob easily and the pair presently found themselves inside the Royal Bedroom. It was undoubtedly the least ostentatious of all the rooms Samuel had seen in the palace to date, although it was by no means plain. There could be no doubt that it was indeed fit for a King. Its plainer undertones had an immediate calming effect.

Samuel's mother pointed to an open archway, which led out onto a large balcony. Together, they walked outside and, before him, Samuel could admire a similar view to the one that had first astounded him upon his arrival in Grat, just as he had left the Warren Kitchens – albeit from a different angle and lit by an early morning, not an evening, sun. The rest of the mighty Royal Palace was spread out before them, and from this position its size could be truly appreciated. Samuel could make out areas of parkland surrounding the Palace, but it was too far away to see much at all.

'Although we call this the Royal Palace now, Your Majesty might be interested to know that this place was once called 'Cresta de Kain' which translates to 'Castle of the Kings.' I think it's a much better title don't you think? And this really is a place fit for a King.'

Samuel's mother left him alone in his room for a rest and Samuel was glad of the chance to relax. He had found his black holdall that Alfred Beavitch brought into Grat for him, beside the lamp which the Lampmaker had given him, at the far side of the bed. Samuel pushed the lamp under the bed itself and opened the holdall up. The carved frame of the photograph of the McGills was still on top, just as he had placed it. Samuel took it out and placed it on the table at the side of the bed. It was a comfort to see the McGills for a while. Whilst Samuel had not felt tired during the night the exertion and tension of the journey here and the Coronation had really taken its toll, and now had truly caught up with him. The large empty hour glass was also taking up a lot of space in the holdall. He could imagine no possible use for it so Samuel also placed it under the bed, beside the lamp, for safekeeping. When Samuel awoke in his four poster bed he found it hard to believe he was in a Palace. He was brought from his slumber by a gentle knocking on the door, and pulling his robes back on, he made the long walk to the door to open it.

'A very good late morning to Your Majesty. Firstly, my most sincere apologies for waking you from your sleep; it was most reckless of me. I am the Royal Physician, Dr. Flint.'

'My pleasure to meet you, Dr. Flint! I believe I have met your wife and your daughter.'

'My wife and Rose; I understand you were staying with them: no longer a secret now that you are safely here!'

'Yes that is correct. Minty was there as well.'

'Ah! Minty, yes, plucky little elf! Can get in the way a bit, but my wife likes her… yes, yes she does.'

'Please do pass on my thanks to your wife…'

'No, No! Not at all! Our pleasure, our pleasure. Now, I don't intend to…how you would say it…beat around the tree.'

'Beat around the bush?'

'Yes, yes that's it. I have for you an important proposal-'

Samuel did not much like the sound of this!

'– There is an option available to us, thanks to the advanced chemical knowledge of this world to immerse you more deeply in this world… and to ensure you are ready to take on the role of King as one who has been brought up to understand the values of this world.'

'And how exactly are you going to do that?'

Dr Flint reached inside a pocket in his orange robes, producing a small bottle. It appeared to be cut glass containing a quantity of a purple liquid. In the top of the bottle was a quivering plug.

'Consumption of the contents of this bottle will result in a depreciation of your age over the period of one night. You will become a baby once again.'

Samuel looked a bit pale. This was not the sort of thing he had had in mind. He was in complete quandary and wanted to know more; Dr. Flint was only too willing to explain.

'The bottle contains an age reversing agent which stops your cells multiplying for growth and reverses the trend. Non reproducing cells, such as brain cells, are re-written, and any depletion since birth is cancelled out via a biological calculation. The extent of this process is limited by the contents of the bottle. Over consumption would reduce a person to a foetal state. In terms of memories, since the existing brain cells are overwritten and not replaced, the memories held now are retained but inaccessible. They would require a trigger to be re-awoken; something as strong as leaving the world of Grat and returning to the world outside. In that event old memories would be likely to come flooding back, but here in Grat it was unlikely that Samuel would be able to remember any of his past.'

Dr. Flint went on to warn against having pictures of the McGills, related so directly to his past, out on show.

It took a while for Samuel to allow everything to sink in. He started to rationalise things. This was going to be a complete gamble. He had to trust in the people of this new world, and in the existence of this new world. Then he had to trust in a process, which Dr. Flint assured him was almost risk free, and thinking about it, it would have to be low risk for them to want to do this to their King – unless they wanted to get rid of him? The thought of leaving behind his past was strange but not unappealing. How often had Samuel complained of how bored and unhappy he was with it? How long had he hated Albert and his life there? The only good times had been with Aunt Mulltasch, and she was dead now, so there was nothing very profitable to be gained from retaining those memories. Here was a chance to gain a whole new childhood, void only of a father, but placated by the presence of a mother who claimed to love him dearly. He knew it was a dangerous, perhaps even reckless, decision but he also knew he was ready to grasp this opportunity.

'Fine, Dr. Flint. Just tell me what I have to do.'

'The contents of this bottle should be consumed as you get into bed, assuming you turn the light out straight away and start to prepare for sleep. The potion won't permeate the lining of the stomach until it is in a relaxed sleep induced state. The bottle is here – take it and put it next to your bed, Your Majesty. And I will take your bag away with at photograph as well. You won't need these items from the past now that you have come home. I will dispose of them.

Might I, at this point, take the opportunity to settle some other outstanding business? Yes? Very well. Whilst your mother is of course intending to take a most full role in your new upbringing after your re-birth, but it is felt among the Palace Staff that there should be an appointment of a designated nurse. I have a number of excellent people lined up in my mind, all of whom will be delighted... no, even overjoyed, to be bestowed the honour, so if you would let me make that decision on your behalf –'

'That is...that is most kind of you Dr. Flint, but perhaps I might decide that myself.'

Disappointment was etched into Dr. Flints face, but he did his uttermost not to show it.

'Well...uh...who do you have in mind exactly?'

'My choice – and it might seem a bit unconventional, is a person by the name of Martharnia.'

'Martharnia, an unusual name, might I enquire how Your Majesty came to be acquainted with this... Martharnia'

'Martharnia is a squirrel I met at the Warren Kitchens when I made the journey here.'

'A squirrel!'

A look of growing horror was etched into Dr. Flint's face. He swallowed hard and looked about to object, when he remembered perhaps his position and gathered his emotions and response.

'Well of course Your Majesty is perfectly at liberty to make such a choice, and there can be no objections upon any grounds, although it would not have been my personal choice...'

Dr. Flint allowed his voice to trail off into silence. Samuel was not too sure if he should say anything, so eventually ventured to ask, 'Will it be made possible for her to be contacted today?'

'Yes, of course, we will summon her here, but perhaps she won't arrive until tonight. Your majesty required proper food before tonight; a small supper is what I would advise, yes? In that case I shall have something tasty dropped in around sunset. Until then... relax.'

Dr. Flint bowed, and turned away, closing the door behind him. Samuel took the bottle that he held in his hand over to the ivory table beside his bed. He placed it down and observed that it had left a silvery stain upon his hand. His mind began to flood with thoughts again. Why had he chosen Martharnia? It had seemed the most natural thing to do. He had trusted her immediately upon meeting her, and why put your eggs in one wee basket as Mrs. McGill would have said? If at first you don't trust humans, get another type of person involved, it just so happens that this time it's a talking Squirrel. He had yet to unravel why there were only humans here, but he felt certain that there was some reason which he had not been told. Perhaps it was simply custom, or perhaps not. Reflecting upon his decision Samuel felt decidedly happy with it.

Samuel decided to take the advice of Dr. Flint and relax. He wandered out onto the massive balcony and leant on the balustrade, staring down into the heart of the city of Grat, his city, and watching it for several hours until it started to get dark.

Dinner, when it arrived, was quite splendid. An array of small dishes, all unusual but quite palatable and without the side effect of really filling him up. Once dinner was dispensed with, Samuel had only the impending arrival of Martharnia to look forward to. The sun had well and truly set and it was getting colder in the room. Samuel was staring to get sleepy and nod off again, when there was another knock at his door. He opened it and it was his mother.

'Your majesty, Might I speak a moment? Firstly I have some night robes here which you can borrow and secondly I have news of Martharnia. She wasn't able to make it down the mountain and through the city gates before they were closed. She's staying with a friend just outside of the city, so I am told, but will arrive here tomorrow instead of today.'

Samuel nodded. It was annoying, but it sounded like not much could be done. His mother wished him a good night, and winked at him. The bottle on the side table by his bed was quivering hard, desperate to be opened. A little while after his mother had left, Samuel gave in. The bottle had been vibrating even more violently, and he felt the time had come. He undressed and got into bed, took one last look around then uncorked the cut-glass bottle. He looked at the contents swirling around. Now was not a time for second thoughts. He downed it in one, leaving a sugary residue in his mouth. He placed the bottle back, and as he led back the candles in the room dimmed instantly. Sleep flooded over him, as he rearranged the bed sheets to make himself comfortable. This was it. A final night for his old life.

About a dozen cream veils in the huge, long windows were rippling and gently fluttering in a silent early morning breeze. It was as if the world itself was breathing and dreaming, refreshed from the restful night that had preceded the morning. The large room was quietly lit with the warm, silky light of day break. Gone was any trace of teenage boy, who just the day before had arrived in this great Palace. Lying, fast asleep in the vast four poster bed, was, a new born baby, King Samuel IV of Grat.

And it was on this fresh morning that his mother rose first from her bed to tend to her child. She sat nearby and watched him sleeping ever so peacefully. Her heart was turning, moving, resolving that this time her care for her son would not diminish over time. She would not be dragged away from her precious son this time.

Martharnia arrived at the Royal Palace later that morning quite overawed and overjoyed simultaneously by the position to which she had been appointed. She remarked how beautiful Samuel was when she saw him, how very, very beautiful.

The early childhood of Samuel Deksis in the city of Grat was marked by all the usual adventures of childhood. Many could fill entire books by themselves and here is no place to do them justice. We must content ourselves with the knowledge that Samuel grew up in a very privileged society and a loving environment, where a caring mother and nurse made him as happy as any future King could be. He was left free from the trappings of official business that would one day rest upon his shoulders. Martharnia was good to her word and cared well for Samuel, but it was the bond between mother and son that was to grow the strongest, as it naturally should. Samuel was attended throughout his childhood by an aging Dr. Flint, who eventually relinquished the role due to ill health. Where this relationship faltered, others sprang up. Samuel got to know Rose Flint a little better; at times she was like a big older sister to the young King.

The strongest friendship to develop came via a different contact. Jack Sorrow was the son of Mr. William Sorrow, one of the men who brought Samuel to Grat. It was with Jack that Samuel was able to take some time away from the Royal Palace as he grew older. They knew how to slip out of the Palace unnoticed through an old side entrance. As long as they kept to the quieter backstreets, much of the city was accessible to them without Samuel running the risk of being recognised. Jack knew the quiet areas well, and often their trips out would be full of surprises. This was the case on one warm, memorable afternoon. The pair had wandered down to a quiet part of the marshy area known as the Borrow Ways.

'I've brought you here in the hope of meeting some friends,' announced Jack suddenly.

'Are they expecting us?' enquired Samuel, somewhat unsure whether this chance meeting was going to be a pleasant surprise.

'Come on Samuel!'

In front of them, emerging from behind the reeds, was a most unusual vessel. On board, what appeared to be a small, black, hairy creature was punting with a long wooden pole. When Samuel looked a little closer he could make out a pale snout and the bulging patchy green waistcoat which the little fellow was wearing. He was humming to himself, quite oblivious to the two watchers.

'Mole! I've brought him at last!'

'Master Jack, good to be seeings you 'ere! And young Master Samuel, Your Majeshty! Shabbers, come out, come out we 'aves Royalty about!'

A shabby looking man, quite suited to his name, emerged from the interior of the vessel and bowed with reverence to Samuel. Mole was buzzing with excitement and bowed beside him so vigorously that he almost fell off the boat in his enthusiasm.

Samuel and Jack talked with the pair for a while with Mole doing almost all of the talking. It was evident that Jack was very fond of Mole and the little creature had so many ideas, opinions and jokes which he expressed in his own odd way that it was impossible not to warm to him.

As Samuel advanced in years, meetings with such interesting characters became more fleeting. Before Samuel could take on the formal duties of the King of Grat, some formal education was required. Samuel's mother was insistent that he should attend the Longwhey Institute in Grat, especially given its international reputation for excellence. By the time Samuel reached the age of sixteen, Martharnia and a variety of tutors had taught him all that they could. Martharnia was to leave her role as his nurse and insisted that she would happily return to work at the Warren Kitchens. It was a sad parting, but Samuel promised to come and see her again as soon as he could.

There was one benefit for Samuel in starting at the Longwhey Institute. Despite the need to leave his mother and Martharnia behind, Jack was also going to be starting at Longwhey at the same time. The coming months would be a time for making friends and forming an alliance with those who were to become very powerful people in the city of Grat in the future. This was the time to weave a web of contacts. This was a time for personal politics.

-- CHAPTER SIX --

The Longwhey Institute

'So tell me Jack, what is Longwhey going to be like exactly?'

'Well, you have seen the place out on Moonwater, yes?'

'You mean the building out on the island in Moonwater Lake?

'Yeah, that's it. Well, it's centuries old, and they only let down the drawbridge to let the students out twice every year; it's down over Summer-retreat and at Winterville. Dad told me there's a staircase in there that goes up forever; you can go up as far as you want but you never reach the top!'

'Do you believe him?'

'Well…it would take some pretty powerful magic to pull off something like that, but dad said he knew an old lecturer who went a bit mad, and when one of his classes put up a poster of him dressed in a unicorn outfit he stormed off up the stairs, and only came back down about two years later. Unfortunately no one recognised him at first and he died soon after so no one found out how far he went up.'

'Must have been a bit nuts! – to have kept going up and up for that long, I mean.'

'Nutty as a fruitcake I would imagine.'

The pair laughed. They had been discussing the impending move to the '*Longwhey Institute*' for a couple of months now and although they would both be starting in just a couple of days it still felt a long way off. Jack leant back on his elbows, enjoying lying in the grassy grounds surrounding the Royal Palace. Samuel would be the first to admit that his childhood at the Royal Palace had been very secluded. The attention he would receive outside was the reason he rarely went into the city. Jack was one of the few people of his own age who regularly came in to see him, and it was Jack who kept him sane and stable. Behind the laughter and gossip about Longwhey there was real tension and nerves for both. It was to be the first step for each of them out into the big wide city of Grat and the world beyond it.

'How much do you know about Timelore Jack?'

'Only a little bit, to be honest. It is the speciality of Longwhey and involves an advanced knowledge of the many secrets of time and how to control them. It is the art which students go there to learn.'

'I think you said before that the art of Timelore has made Grat a famous city?'

'Certainly Grat profits greatly from the knowledge which it has. I'm sure we'll see how it all makes sense when we get there. It's the exams I'm dreading. You can bet they will be hard. They won't give you anything unless you work very hard for it at Longwhey. My sister, Kleveris, worked her backside off and only got a low grade. Mum was totally gutted. They had a big row on results day and mum ended up sending Kleveris on an exchange to Ling for a month to get her out of the house.'

'But Ling is miles from Grat! Miles to the East! Your sister must have hated it!'

'She did… but I wouldn't mind. Think about it – a break from mum and dad, a whole new country and the International Levish Championships every summer! – It's not all bad! Typical of girls to say a place like Ling is unhygienic and uneducated!'

Samuel smiled. He was quite used to Jack recounting stories of his squabbles with his pushy mother. He had heard Jack speak before about Levish too. From what he could gather it was a dangerous carpet race that was held in Ling from time to time.

'I have to go now Samuel; see you at midweek, early at Moonside by the drawbridge then! Remember to bring thick robes with you – they say Longwhey is freezing around Winterville!'

It was a crystal clear morning and the sky was as blue as it could have been. Samuel's mother had woken him at the crack of dawn, and had arranged for a servant to carry Samuels' bags for him. They had trooped down the grand staircase together, and out through the long passage, into the Orangery and on, into the grounds. It had taken a long time to make their way down the drive and out into the centre of the city of Grat. The city was just awakening from its slumber and there were signs of growing activity as they hurried down narrow streets and alleyways. The servant had brought some additional security with him for the King, and the extra people skirted around the group. King Samuel was quite used to ignoring them, and he did so this time as well. Moonwater Lake was soon visible at the end of an alleyway and the very long drawbridge was clearly down.

The entourage proceeded out onto Moonside, the name given to the area along the front. There was already a large group of prospective students gathered in the area.

Samuel thought he could make out Jack with his parents in the distance, but before he could look again he was accosted. At his feet, a group of mice were assembled, squeakily requesting an interview with His Majesty. They said they were from 'The Chariot' and were preparing an exclusive article upon the arrival of the King at Longwhey at the beginning of his formal education. Samuel turned to one of the minders, and asked that the mice be removed from the area. Today was not a day for interviews: there was too much going on for that.

The mice were hurried away, squeaking something about freedom of speech and rights of access to the king.

'It was always like this when he went out,' sighed Samuel, longing for one moment to be able to move around the city unnoticed and unrecognised.

He turned his attention to finding Jack in the throng of people and children. Somewhere in the distance someone was shouting, and Samuel thought he heard his name. The crowd of people fell silent and separated as they recognised the arrival of their Monarch. The mothers curtsied, fathers bowed and children blatantly stared, open mouthed as the group made its way closer to the entrance of the drawbridge. At last Samuel could clearly make out Jack. They smiled at each other, and Samuel brought the group to a halt nearby. His mother was whispering something in his ear about having to be the first student to walk over the drawbridge, but Samuel was only half listening. He had seen someone in the crowd. Only for an instant, but something inside him was awaking. His head was hurting and his hands were trembling. The scene in front of him disappeared and for an instant he was on a train, and in front of him stood a man, staring directly at him with piercing black eyes. Samuel heard himself breathe a name- 'Mr. Harbury.'

In an instant the vision was over. Samuel was doubled up, feeling dizzy and winded. His mother was at his side, nervously asking him what was wrong. Samuel slowly drew himself into a standing position, panting heavily. He must have looked shaken, but he denied that there was anything wrong. Inside, he knew it had been a flash back, which Dr. Flint had long ago warned him of. The trigger had been the man in the crowd. He was the spitting image of the man in the flash back. The two must be the same. Samuel had no time to gather his thoughts because his mother was speaking to him again.

'Nearly ready now, Your Majesty. When the trumpets sound you have to make your way across the drawbridge. You have to carry your own bags across – PORTER… bring them here.'

Samuel could feel a handle being thrust into his hand. Jack was at his side.

'Ready?' he enquired?

'Not really-' replied Samuel, 'but it looks like I have to be. This place is going to be home for the next three years.'

He looked up ahead to the gloomy structure that was known as the *Longwhey Institute.* It looked more foreboding and gloomy than ever.

The trumpets heralded the return of the students for a new term. Samuel slowly moved forwards and made his first step onto the drawbridge. It creaked ever so slightly. He gathered his pace, and could hear the sound of footsteps following behind him. He thought he heard his mother shout goodbye, but he couldn't look around yet. The drawbridge was ridiculously long, and Samuel soon realised it was going to take a good fifteen minutes to walk its full length. The pounding of feet behind him was just as strong, if not stronger, than it had been earlier. He could look back now, at a trail of students making their way across the drawbridge and, in the very far distance, back at Moonside, Samuel could make out his mother waving. He waved back. It was a good job he could not see her clearly, because he knew that if he saw her crying, he would end up crying himself.

The end of the drawbridge gradually edged closer and the weight of Samuel's bag seemed to increase. He could just make out a black dot looming in the distance. At first he thought it might be a rock but as he edged closer it became evident that it was moving. Still, it seemed too low for a normal human being, but yet it had two stout legs, he was sure of it. At last Samuel reached the final boards of the drawbridge. The black lump seemed more human like now; a short human being bent completely double with its back hunched in almost hideous deformity. From under the thick black cloak that was shrouded in all manner of shawls there reached a twisted and wrinkled hand. In the stiff sea breeze which had arisen the frilled black cloak billowed around the edge of what must be its hood and pulled it back just a little to show the wizened brow and protruding nose of an old woman. Her chin was somewhat askew as though it had been knocked out of position in some long forgotten vicious sport. She gestured again to Samuel with her hand so he drew closer to her on the island and made to listen as she croaked.

'Maj'sty, welcome to Longwhey. Dame Leria, keeper o' the place. Let me feel your face...'

She pushed her hand up Samuels' chest and onto his chin.

''Ansome,' she mused, 'Like father war. I 'member when I met 'im. Step inside now. We shall obs'rve.'

She coughed loudly in a manner as if her lungs might issue from her mouth at any moment, then turned and shuffled towards a tunnel cut, like a piercing eye, into the ancient looking fortress structure behind her. Dame Leria walked with evident difficulty, effort being required to swing each twisted leg in its socket so that she could step forward. At the same time attention had to be given to her centre of gravity, thrown off position by her hunched back and twisted spine. In the tunnel she turned left and led the way slowly up a twisting spiral staircase and out onto a dark and cobwebbed landing. In front of them a narrow slit window gave a view back over the drawbridge which Samuel had walked across.

Straining to look out of the narrow window it was clear that the group of people who had made it onto the island was gradually swelling in size, and Samuel was at last able to make out the end of the snake of people making their way across. As the final dregs of stragglers traipsed into the crowd beneath the window there was a great moaning and creaking sound. The drawbridge started to coil itself up at the Moonside end and as it rolled closer to the island its coiled tip began to glide upwards into the air, cutting them off from the shore completely. Samuel suddenly felt extremely anxious and alone. The drawbridge continued to rise up yet higher out of sight from his windowed vantage point, up to a forty-five degree angle, where it halted for a moment before completing the lift and coming to a fully vertical coiled position. The view to the shore at Moonside was replaced with the coiled mess of planks and boards that made up the odd drawbridge. From Moonside it must have been as if there had never been a route across to the island at all. It was such a distance away that none of the noise from the people left there could be heard at all.

Samuel had been so mesmerised by the view from the window of the coiled drawbridge and the crowd beneath it that he had quite forgotten about old Dame Leria. Another spasm of severe coughing and croaking on her behalf alerted Samuel to her new position by a rusty looking metal door at the far side of the dusty landing. She was fumbling in some obscure pocket for a bunch of keys and then proceeded to sort through them amid mutterings and curses until she found what she was looking for. The door final creaked open and she beckoned for Samuel to follow her. Inside she shuffled to some rough looking wooden pews and made to sit awkwardly down on them. She puffed and panted for a few moments before beadily eyeing Samuel and giving him a cracked smile from within her dark hood. Samuel sat beside the queer old woman, aghast at the dusty cloud which he caused to rise all around him in the process. No wonder Dame Leria was coughing if she lived in a place with air like this all of the time.

'I'm keeper, see,' she panted,

'Only one who stays in 'olidays. Keep it clean as I can. 'ave a big task on 'ands with this place. The 'elp you get ain't up to much either. Marlow, 'e's more trouble than worth it.'

'Where are we?'

'Royal Box, Maj'sty. Not used since father war 'ere.'

Now she said it, Samuel could see he was in a small balcony-like gallery space looking over a dark circular room which was spread out below them.

'Leave bag 'ere and it be took on.'

She pointed to a space by the door through which they had entered and Samuel lifted the bag he had dumped in a cramped fashion at his feet and gladly placed it as he had been directed.

'Don't 'ave to be in Royal Box of'en Maj'sty but we like to adhere to custom, specially on formals'.

She sniffed awkwardly. Hardly a bundle of laughs he thought. Looking down Samuel could see people filing into the round room. They sat on chairs which had been laid out, all facing inwards towards a central area. Samuel was pleased with the view he had of it, far better than most which could be attained from the floor below. While he was here at Longwhey Samuel had hoped he would be treated a bit less like a king than back in the heart of the city. All this talk of a Royal Box seemed to trash such a hope, but at least old Dame Leria had said that he would not be here often. Hopefully he wouldn't have to spend much of his time with her, either.

Below, everyone had filed in and Samuel heard a door closing behind the group at last. It slammed shut, and the noise echoed around the room making many of the more nervous students jump. It took several minutes for it to become quiet and for the general hubbub and chatter to die down.

There was a grating sound and the floor slid apart in the space at the centre of the room. Upwards there rose a man on a grey slab with his back to Samuel. Hardly a gracious entry, to be faced away like that, he thought. When the slab came to rest level with the floor around it there was a dull clapping from a small portion of the crowd. Silence followed later. A crisp voice rang out around the round room all business like.

'Welcome to the Longwhey Institute. To those of you, who are returning to be with us again, welcome back. To those who have arrived with us afresh-'

He turned to face a different portion of the crowd below,

'- just…welcome.'

Samuel jerked upright and gave a shudder. It was Mr. Harbury! He stood dressed in a shiny black velvet suit which seemed to Samuel quite revolting. He looked like some ugly black beetle.

'For those just embarking on your study of Timelore with us, this is a day of great anticipation, no doubt. You will have the finest and most gifted teachers of their art at your disposal. Might I congratulate each and every one of you upon having made it to this stage, for I know our selection process is one of the toughest, so well done.'

There was a ripple of applause through the audience once again. Mr. Harbury turned around to face the main body of older students once more.

'As you are all aware, this is my first year here, but I am sure we can all work together to make this the most successful year yet, in the life of the Longwhey Institute. My congratulations to you all once again!'

The formal address seemed to be over and after a few minutes people below began to slowly file out of the round room. Mr. Harbury wandered away from sight.

'E's new so said. Don't like 'im. Straight from Cresta to education at Longwhey. It stinks Maj'sty, least I think so.'

Dame Leria rose to stand and urged Samuel out of the Royal Box and back onto the landing. Her crooked claw like hand pointed to the left. They headed together down a flight of stairs and into a maze of passages. The sounds of student chatter seemed to rise louder with every step they took.

'I leave now Maj'sty. Right then left again.'

Dame Leria hobbled off in a different direction and Samuel made his way down the passage in front of him. Presently he came upon a large mass of students crowded into a small hall.

Everyone seemed to have congregated by what looked at first to Samuel like a giant wooden piano. He was, of course, quite wrong. Although the shape was not dissimilar, there were no keys, and in the top section a wedge shaped segment had been cut out. Inside it was an image of a face which Samuel did not recognise. He would have looked further at the strange contraption, but his attention was caught by the shrieks of several younger students. What had caused the commotion was at first unclear, but this did not remain the case for long. Through the wall came gliding a pale figure, dressed in long translucent robes. His lock of silver hair shimmered in the light. The youngest students shrank back, but the older students remained exactly where they were and looked rather unimpressed by the unusual entrant.

'Ghost!' Whispered Jack in Samuels' ear. Samuel smiled at his friend, glad to be reunited. There was no time for talk now with such an interesting spectacle in front of them. And it did indeed appear that this was a 'ghost.' Its body was entirely translucent, it could move through solid walls, and solid people, judging by the way in which it was gliding through an older girl at this very moment. Samuel felt Jack give a shudder next to him, but this was no time to be afraid; the figure was making straight towards Samuel.

'Your majesty… Marlow at your service. I am… I am to be… so they tell me… your Royal Butler. '

Samuel heard Jack give a gasp; 'Marlow! Is it true what they say… about you having been locked in an asylum?'

'*They* know very little about me! Anyway, I got locked in there by mistake-'

He looked suddenly fierce,

'-but that will be *The Chariot* twisting things again I have no doubt!-'
Marlow turned to Samuel.
'I would take Master to your chambers, but we must all wait for selection to take place.'
Marlow gestured towards the strange contraption Samuel had been studying before he arrived. There was now an even greater buzz of activity around it.
A moment later, there was a loud mechanical whirring coming from the machine. The head on show in the cutaway segment disappeared, and a succession of different heads flashed past in a blur.
'They are choosing the cleaner for this term-' explained Marlow,
'-the person in charge of tidying up everywhere. Could be any of us, although I don't expect it will be you Master… not since you're the King!'
'But… you are a ghost ar-aren't you?' stammered Jack.
'Well, well, yes, but I am still a pupil here. When I was like you, I failed my exams, so they sent me back to re-sit. They said I was the first person to ever fail… a disgrace to Longwhey and my family… I wasn't even close to passing. Master and Master's friend will do a lot better than me, I have no doubt.'
'So you weren't a ghost back then?'
'No, no… I was not then, but during my re-sit year… well… I set my room alight by accident… and that was that. I was done for! My parents asked for my image to remain here… I'm just a memory now, you know-'
Marlow looked sad for just a moment.
'Just like an Oro-fice?' piped up Jack.
'Just like that, yes, just like that.'
Marlow's clouded face did not remain that way for long. He went on to explain how he had been given the role of butler here, and how much he enjoyed serving others. This was his fifty ninth year as a ghost…and he was living it up as much as he could!
Samuel felt sure Marlow could have gone on for an awful lot longer, but he was interrupted by a loud 'pop' which was issued by the machine. Everyone went silent and peered forward to find out who had been selected. At first there was a bit of confusion as no one could see clearly… but then it became apparent.
'Marlow… it's you!' breathed Jack.
'Oh no! Wretched school!-'
He turned to Samuel,
'-it's not that I mind doing it, or anything, but being a ghost… well Master can imagine, it takes a lot of concentration to stop your hands going through everything when you try to clean it. And Dame Leria gets so impatient. Last time I had to do it was about ten years ago. It took weeks and I had to get Sylvania from the kitchens to help me-'
He smiled to himself,
'-Not that her company was any bad thing though.'
The selection process was over and people were starting to filter away from the hall. Marlow hovered, deep in thought, for a few moments, before he turned to address Samuel.
'I had better take you to the Royal Chambers, Master.'
'But what about Jack -'
Enquired Samuel,
'–Where will he go?'
Marlow gestured to Jack,
'You go that way, up to the dormitory with the rest of the boys.'
Marlow was pointing to a spiral staircase in the distance up which a procession of boys was ambling.

'We go this way, Master-'

Said Marlow, gliding off across the hall, towards a set of stairs which led underground,

'Come on master…this way, this way!'

Samuel trailed along behind him, as Marlow cut through a corner and joined Samuel at the bottom of the stairs. Marlow bounded on ahead, pulling a picture from its hook on the wall in his antics, and consequentially having to replace it once again. That Marlow was clumsy was quite evident to Samuel, and the thought of his company here was…well, at least a little disappointing. That said, his offer of service and friendship seemed genuine, even if he lacked a little in capacity.

The Royal Chambers turned out to be a bit less grand than Samuel might have anticipated, but then after the Royal Palace everything was going to be a bit of a let down. Samuel dropped his bags onto his bed, and turned to find Marlow. It seemed he had disappeared from the room for a while. Exhausted by the early start Samuel was glad to rest a while.

There was a timid knock at the door and it pulled Samuel out of his slumber. Cautiously He made towards the door which had closed behind him when he had entered. He opened the door half expecting to see Marlow, but to his surprise it was a young girl. Her face turned bright red when she saw him. She started to speak, stammering and looking as though she wished the floor would open up beneath her.

'Oh-hu-I'm so-s sorry to have disturbed you. I'm
r-rather lost and trying to find my way b-back to the g-girl's dor-dormatory.'

She looked very shamed faced and was about to hurry away when Samuel stopped her.

'Not at all. I needed to be woken up anyway! My nurse Martharnia would be quite angry with my sleeping during the day.'

The girl smiled nervously back at him.

'What is your name?' enquired Samuel.

'*My* name?-'

She looked quite shocked he had asked this question,

'–Bertis Beavitch…Yes I'm Bertis.'

'And you already know who I am?'

She swallowed hard and nodded.

'Do you want to come in?' Enquired Samuel.

'Oh no…I'm sure you've got plenty to do. I wouldn't want to disturb you.'

'Oh no it's fine; I'm quite bored at the moment actually. Marlow (that's my Butler) has disappeared somewhere. He might be a fifty year old ghost, but I expect he has still managed to get himself lost here.'

Bertis laughed at this, saying she would come in if he insisted. They sat together, chatting for a couple of minutes. Bertis told Samuel about her family, especially her father who was a warrior of Grat and away on a mission at the moment, so she said. They stayed there until Marlow arrived back, hooting his way through the wall carrying a letter. It seemed that a ghost could move solid objects in remarkable ways. The wall didn't seem to mind the letter moving through it much anyway, a slight dent the only mark of its passage.

'Sorry Master to interrupt your company, but I come bearing a gift for you from some unknown benefactor.'

'Well…thank you Marlow. Perhaps you can see my companion to the girl's dormitories. I understand she was lost when she found herself here.'

'Most certainly, Master; if you will step this way young Miss… but before I go I should tell you that everyone is making their way to The Schackler for their first lesson, and I would certainly advise Master to attend.'

Marlow ushered Bertis out through the door and left Samuel holding his package. He scrabbled to open it and untie the thick cord that bound it all together. Samuel found a small note. It read as follows:

My Dear King Samuel,

It is scarcely a couple of hours since your departure that I find myself writing this letter. I need not say how much I am missing you already, but I must content myself with the knowledge that you are acquiring the skills to become a King, and even if this drags you away from me, it must be a pain that I have to endure. I will see you again at Winterville so make sure you come out on time. I will see that the Royal Palace is well prepared for your return: but alas you will not stay longer than the break. In the name of Grat and all that this great city stands for, I do declare that there is no other mother who is so proud of her son! Keep safe!

Your ever loving mother, Saffie

XXX

After reading the note again, Samuel made his way out of the Royal Chambers. It was only as he entered the hall, from the underground stairs, that he realised he had set off for 'The Schackler' without the faintest idea of what it was or where it was supposed to be. Relief flooded through him at the sight of Jack up ahead.

A motley crew of bewildered first years littered the area by the selection machine, and Samuel soon turned to the issue of 'The Schackler'.

'So where are we going then Jack? Marlow mentioned-'

'The Schackler?'

'Yup! So what is it then?'

'Well, I understand The Schackler to be a ship…or, to be more exact, a ship *wreck.*'

'But I could only see an island with a castle on top from Moonside?'

'Ah, but the wreck can't be seen from that side of the lake. You will find the wreck around the back of the island, facing out into the centre of The Deeps.'

'And how did it come to get ship wrecked?'

'I don't know exactly, but I don't think it happened that long ago. Longwhey needed extra capacity so they just did a bit of construction and turned The Schackler into extra teaching rooms.'

The pair started to shuffle off in the same direction as everyone else. They headed through a low archway and along a twisting corridor before it turned sharply to the right and began to slope down steeply. The group directly in front of them stopped abruptly causing Samuel and Jack to slam into their backs. The group in front divided around a girl struggling to collect her fallen possessions amid the human stampede. Only as she finally stood up did Samuel recognise her as Bertis. They made conversation as they continued down the long descent. Eventually the tunnel walls became wooden and Samuel could feel cold air entering through thin gaps in the boards of which it consisted. This wooden construction opened into a dark room, which Samuel took to be the interior of the ship. There were plenty of desks in rows and Samuel scrambled to get one next to Jack, allowing Bertis to join them on his right.

They were not kept waiting long; within half a minute a door at the front slammed open and Mr. Harbury entered. He stared to the back wall, waiting for silence. Then, without directly looking at anyone, he began to speak.

'Longwhey prides itself upon the quality of its teaching. As such this is only valuable depending upon the value of the students. We will weed out any that need to be weeded out, prune what needs to be pruned and cauterize any element of any student that is not fitting for an institute of our prestige.

Here at the *Longwhey Institute* we teach of magical arts infinitely finer than those of temperamental Wandlore. You are the chosen few upon whom we will bestow, through the very best education, the most delicate and select of skills that are the speciality of this school and this great city. It is a city which is famous and envied throughout all worlds for its mastery of these select skills.

Professor Rector will teach you the secrets of Anacamora, the skill of divine protection and undetection. It can provide a cloak of complete physical invisibility that can only be cast by the sharpest minds. It is the centrepiece of all modern security protection used in this world and almost all other civilised ones.

Elsewhere you will learn from Professor Shirballis about Prophetical Hexing, the most powerful attack and defence method ever devised, again using nothing more than the power of your talented minds. Finally the third area of study will be the Eddisa Paradox and how to control it. This is the part of the course which I teach. It is the most complex of all the manipulation skills we teach and the one most students fail to complete. These three elements will combine to form your study of Timelore during the three years you spend with us. We shall complete each of the three areas of study at a higher level with every year that passes. This year we shall master the basics of each.'

Samuel gave Jack a glance. He seemed a bit awestruck to be in his first class at Longwhey. Samuel felt less overawed. Perhaps it was his concerns over this Mr. Harbury which clouded his potential excitement.

'Now that I have given you a short introduction I have no intention to waste this valuable time which we have together. I want to shatter your preconceptions about the Eddisa Paradox, for only then can you really begin to learn about it. Now to start, can anyone tell of the great Gratian who discovered it?'

A few hands were raised tentatively into the air by the students present. Mr. Harbury didn't seem too pleased by those who were so willing to volunteer information. He nodded jerkily to Bertis, who took a moment before answering.

'Eddisa Beavitch I believe.'

Samuel squinted at her rather surprised. It must be odd to have a relation who had made what sounded like such a significant discovery. It also showed something else; that Bertis was a decedent of one of the old Gratian families which he had not heard of before. It made him feel even warmer towards her. There were quite a few old families like the Flints. Mr. Harbury looked ready to speak again.

'Ah, yes, the great Eddisa Beavitch. It was she who discovered the paradox when she was conducting her own Timelore studies here at Longwhey. Her paradox consisted of a core thesis with two subsidiaries. Can anyone state them?'

Another hand shot up.

'The core thesis sir, *Time is a continuate finite stream which eddies at a complex.*'

'Correct, and the subsidiaries?'

'*A complex can cause an echo in certain circumstances.*'

'Correct again, and finally...?'

'*An echo of the stream at a certain complex can be positive and negative.*'

'Good good. The rest of you are expected to look this up in the library later and learn it in your own time. I hope those who have not spoken were aware of these basic facts. Our friend here outlined the theses clearly. Now do you see the paradox?'

There was a general muttering of disagreement among the students.

'Come on now,' he said with an abrupt cold laugh,

'This is rather basic. A stream cannot have a negative inflection by our first premise since it is a *continuate finite stream.* Yet if our two subsidiaries are true, an echo of the stream can be negative.'

A hand was raised in the front row.

'But sir, is it not just as impossible for an echo to be positive?'

'You mean to say is it not impossible for an echo to exist? Of course not, that is a simple elementary error. You just have to consider everyday how each and every action we undertake creates a consequence. That is a positive echo of a continuate finite time stream eddying at a complex.'

The student at the front of the class looked ready to argue back but Mr. Harbury raised his arm for silence and the debate was over as quickly as it had the potential to arise.

'We can approach the Edissa Paradox from a different angle. I hadn't intended discussing this issue with first year students because I know it is an area you will focus on in your final year. My area of research here at Longwhey is 'The Brothership.' No one knows exactly what it is or how it operates. It is a cross world phenomenon which lends support to the existence of the Eddisa Paradox because it is thought to be an example of positive and negative echo. Enough on that for now I think. We shall content ourselves with working from the core thesis and its subsidiaries.

As they sat in this odd seminar Samuel could feel the whole room move a little as a gust of wind rocked the old wreck from the position in which it was lodged. It was rather disconcerting. Samuel glanced at Jack to see if he was still listening. It seemed that all this talk of 'theses' wasn't really of much interest to him. Jack was fiddling with a lump on his desk; probably some unfortunate practical experiment that had melted into the desk in an unsightly fashion.

Samuel felt alarm bells ringing before anything happened. Mr. Harbury might be new to Longwhey but he certainly wasn't new to teaching. His piercing black eyes were lingering on Jack for a few seconds too long for him to pass unnoticed. Alas it was Jack and not Mr. Harbury that brought attention to himself. Feverishly working to relieve the desk of its lump he was applying too much pressure to its fragile foldaway structure. With an alarming creak it gave up the last of its integrity and collapsed unhappy into Jack's lap before it slid dramatically onto the floor in front of him with an almighty clatter.

'Get out.'

It was a simple statement, not a question.

'But Sir...'

'Out,' said Mr. Harbury pointing.

Jack reluctantly gathered himself together and made to leave via the door through which all the students had entered the room.

'The exit is that way Mr. Sorrow.'

Mr. Harbury had pointed to a second door opposite the one which Jack was heading for. He faltered and changed his direction looking pleased at the prospect of leaving the lesson early. Jack wrenched open the door to which he had been directed quite viciously. Samuel doubted that anything could have prepared Jack for what happened.

As the door was pulled open it was as if all the blustery gales which had been hammering at the exterior of The Shackler had burst inside it at once. At the back of the teaching room a pile of manuscripts leapt into the air and tumbled around students like confetti. The force of the wind nearly knocked Jack off his feet as he wrestled with the door in a vain attempted to close it again. The students were all shouting by now, clutching what belongings they had brought in with them for fear of damage to them. Beyond the sound of the gales was something more tumultuous which Samuel soon realised must be waves pounding at the foot of the wreck. Jack, still attempting to shut the door was hit full in the face by the spray of a wave crashing on unseen rocks below. Thankfully Mr. Harbury had made his way to the door by now and pulling a soaked Jack aside he shut the door and locked out the elements once more. Then he turned to address the rest of the students.

'If anyone else wishes to leave my classes early they too will leave by that door. They say swimming in The Deeps can be quite refreshing so if you fancy trying it, go on, I'm not going to stop you. Maybe try and avoid the rocks below as you jump in. No actually, what the hell, just jump in with them, they love it.'

A ripple of disturbed nervous laughter went through the students who were pulling scraps of paper from their hair and off their desks.

Nothing else in that teaching session seemed to match the earlier drama. Jack sat demurely at his semi-resurrected desk which it seemed to Samuel he was holding up underneath for fear of a second imminent collapse, which thankfully never occurred.

The students were dismissed not long after and Samuel took a pleasant dinner with Jack and Bertis in an area reserved for student dining near the piano-like selecting machine. If he had known that Marlow had prepared for him one of the worst meals of his life in the Royal Chambers, Samuel would have been even more grateful for the unremarkable but stable food he was having now.

Bertis presently said her goodbyes and headed off to the Library to do some reading. Samuel sat with Jack chatting for a while then headed to his chamber. There were to be no more teaching sessions today but, according to a notice pinned up in the dining area, tomorrow would bring with it a double introductory session with Professor Rector and Professor Shirballis on Prophetical Hexing and the secrets of Anacamora. If they were anything like Mr. Harbury it was going to be thrilling.

After a night of fitful sleep Samuel arose to go to the early morning double session which he would rather have not attended. He was suffering from the after effects of the meal Marlow had prepared for him; some indiscernible grey pulp, the contents of which he had not dared to enquire about. The room set aside for the double session was between his Royal Chambers and the dining area, so he knew it wouldn't take long to get there or be difficult to find.

Outside the room, bleary eyed students had gathered, less well dressed than the day before, perhaps the product of little sleep and first night excitement. Professor Rector was already in the room when first tentative student decided it would be impolite to wait outside any longer. The Professor barked at them to sit quickly. The lesson didn't progress far without Samuel making characteristically quick observations. Rector was a squat fat old man with a tendency to point and shout. He seemed to believe that audible volume was the only route to a student's attention. He lacked the calm graceful power of Mr. Harbury who could hold a class rapt due to his unpredictability. Rector was perfectly predictable, just an angry man. When he felt students were failing to grasp the point he was making, his face would turn from a pale freckled complexion to a vein-taught purple which looked incredibly bad for his blood pressure and general health.

This shouting accompanied by occasional rages would come to be the broad pattern which all of Samuel's lessons with Professor Rector would follow during his first term at Longwhey. The subject matter of the secrets of Anacamora had the potential to be riveting but in the hands of such a dictatorial teacher it was bled of all such interest inspiring substance.

Samuel would always remember one important teaching session which illustrated just how important Anacamora was. Someone had asked for examples of it at work in other worlds and Rector, never a fan of impromptu interruptions (or any interruptions at all to be precise), had thoughtfully replied as follows:

'In another world a worldwide sporting event was taking place. One team was taken hostage by a volatile terrorist group. An attempt to free the hostages cost nine of their lives and five of the terrorist and an intermediatery were also killed. The next time the event was held, a country called 'Canada' were to host the same games. What no ordinary people knew was that Canada had been selected as the next host because it alone employed our security packages which use Anacamora to conceal guards strategically. Anacamora has been providing cutting edge security at the same event, every time it has been held since, to this very date. Several terror attacks have been thus foiled and of course concealed from the public eye. There is nothing like a bit of terrorism to ruin a public spectacle politically. In our world, Ling will soon be hosting what it calls the International Levish Championships and once again Anacamora provides the vital component in the security.'

It was evident to Samuel from statements like this that Anacamora was vitally important.

Back at the introductory double session, Rector handed over to dumpy Professor Shirballis, notable for the way she carried her right arm limply by her side; the weakness was a sign of fatigue from years of refining Prophetical Hexing. She was an excellent practical teacher and from her very first lesson put every student through their paces, teaching the ways to channel the mind to produce the most ferocious attack.

By the time Winterville approached it was still early days, but the students had collectively managed to make Professor Shirballis' left arm as limp as her right from the ferocity of their test attacks on her. With the Winterville break only a day ahead and the prospect of a lowered drawbridge bringing with it meetings with much missed friends and relations, the mood was understandably electric. Samuel had largely enjoyed his first term but was equally looking forward to a break. Any initial worries he had entertained about Mr. Harbury had been set aside at least, if not disproved. The man didn't seem to have it in for Samuel, or at least this was what he thought.

There was to be a formal address given in the main round hall and Samuel was expected to resume his position in the Royal Box, which he had taken at the start of term. Samuel had been heading up there with Bertis and Jack who had been given permission to sit with him (he didn't really hanker after another audience with Dame Leria). Who should be gliding down the stairs towards them but Marlow. The cheerful trio were ever pleased to see him and have a chat.

It was a real effort to make their own excitement rub off on their ghostly friend. He was full of complaints about his cleaning duties. Frightful they were he said, and Dame Leria was the worst cleaner in the world apparently. Marlow was especially annoyed with Mr. Harbury of all people.

'Master knows I do not often complain, but I really think that asking me to sweep up bird's mess and mouse droppings from the Royal Box is too much. Must be a nest in there or something. I mean, do I look to you like it's a task I deserve to undertake. Basic cleaning yes, but nothing more I say!'

Samuel agreed with Marlow, laughing.

'Master, what I find most annoying is the way Mr. Harbury speaks to me. You should have heard him in the Royal Box just now. 'Inspecting' he said he was. Should go and inspect old Dame L, that's where he'll find things wanting, not with me. I left him to it. Said my pan was full.'

Marlow gestured to them with the dustpan he was struggling to hold and in the process sprayed a dozen lumps of droppings and dirt onto the floor. He apologized and encouraged the trio to make their way up to the Royal Box while he cleared up the fresh mess he had made.

Ahead of Samuel, Bertis bounded up the stairs and onto the landing outside the Royal Box.

'So glad I'm friends with Royalty,' she giggled.

'How else would I get to sit in a Royal Box of all things?'

Samuel pointed to the rusty door which led to the Royal Box. It stood slightly ajar. Bertis pushed it open. The first point at which Samuel realised something was terribly wrong was when Bertis clutched at her face and let out a terrible shriek. As the door continued to open a bucket balanced atop it emptied its contents on her face and all over her clothes. If Samuel and Jack had at first thought this to be a practical joke it would have taken seconds for them to come to their senses. Bertis was clutching at her face screaming in pain. The contents must have been boiling hot. It was scalding her face and continuing to penetrate, eating its way suspiciously through her clothes and her outer layers of skin.

Jack bolted to get help and Professor Shirballis was soon on the scene. Samuel hadn't known what to do. In her agony, Bertis hadn't seemed up for talking, so he had stood by rather pathetically waiting for the help Jack had summoned to arrive. Professor Shirballis was thankfully no shrinker from the odd physical injury, even of this severity, her years of Prophetical Hexing having caused her to witness the full effects of its misguided use.

When Professor Rector appeared at the incident he ushered Samuel and Jack out of the way with the usual pomp, despite their weak protestations. They both felt that their teachers could provide Bertis with the best help for her injuries. They waited at the foot of the stairs for some time and eventually Professor Rector came down, looking bemused to find them still there.

'Boys, boys Simione has the situation quite under control. The girl has been quite fortunate and we are awaiting a carpet to arrive later to take her to Grat for further treatment. It has been agreed that she can go straight to her family when this is done. For us however the show must go on.'

He pointed the boys in the direction which led to the main round hall.

'Samuel, Your Majesty, you must sit with the others today. I'm sure Mr. Harbury will have very little to say if his last formal address was anything to go by.'

In his taught pompous face Samuel thought he detected the flicker of a weak joke. Sighing he headed with Jack into the main hall. He felt terribly guilty at the moment. This was an awful way to end the term. It should have been him that received those dreadful scalds from that awful substance. Someone had laid a trap for him and he knew just who it was now. All his old concerns about Mr. Harbury had returned. Marlow had let it slip, Harbury had been in the Royal Box poking his nose around, using an 'inspection' as an excuse for setting up a death trap. How surprised he would be to see Samuel in the crowd now. Samuel fumed.

As he entered the circular hall he could hear a ripple of whispers shooting around the room. It was always like this on the rare occasions he met second or third years. He was angry enough to ignore it and kept his eyes focused on the empty chair he was heading towards. It was completely wooded, with no visible cushion on it, and the legs were carved to look like hooves. Eventually he reached the chair, and found, to his great surprise, that it was very well cushioned indeed. An invisible layer of padding covered the base and back of the chair, so it appeared that he was sitting slightly above the base of the seat, hovering in mid air. Samuel could see that Jack was fiddling with a knob at the side of the seat. He was trying to turn it, but he appeared to be straining because it was stiff. Then, with one almighty yank, it came loose, and the invisible cushion deflated instantly. Jack fell onto the unpadded wooden structure of the seat with such a smack that a ripple of laughter reached around the students who were seated around them. One of the older boys behind Samuel leant forward,

'You need to let it down gently, you little jerk!'

The group of boys behind continued to snigger for a couple of minutes. It was evident to Samuel from the red look on Jack's face that he had heard what they said. There was no time for Samuel to speak to him because Mr. Harbury had arrived out of the floor just as he did at the start of term. The entry looked pathetic rather than theatrical to Samuel now. Mr.

Harbury must be a good liar he thought. He made no mention of what had happened to Bertis, just thanked everyone for their hard work during the term and wished everyone a great Winterville.

'Well Bertis won't be having one – thanks to you!' He thought bitterly.

As they rose to begin leaving the hall, Samuel saw a wrinkled old woman, bent double and dressed in her usual black robes that identified her as Dame Leria. She was busy organising the stacking of the chairs. The boys behind Samuel had already headed for the doorway, without making the slightest attempt to deflate their cushions. Dame Leria muttered something under her breath, and out of her claw like hand shot several golden ropes, which flew across the room, grabbed the boys by the ankles and dragged them off their feet and back across the floor towards their chairs and the irritable old Dame.

'What goin' on 'ere, boys? Chairs to be stacked, so deflate 'em like the others!'

Everyone around raised a smile to see the boys recalled, and Jack looked especially delighted.

It would take more than this to raise Samuel's mood of course. He left the hall by himself as quickly as he could determined to do something he had been meaning to since he had arrived. He had only been to the Library at Longwhey twice since he had arrived. Like Jack, he preferred to work and read elsewhere, and then only when absolutely necessary.

All he needed to know now was where the old newspapers were kept. He was sure it was just by the entrance and sure enough, when he reached it, copies of The Chariot over the last twenty years were arranged chronologically in boxes by the door. He skipped to the year when he knew he had arrived in Grat and started leafing through the various stories. Three papers in, he spotted something that caught his interest. Despite his lifetime subscription to The Chariot these old copies could be temperamental in repeating archived news. A smart burly man rose out of the open paper talking of the coronation of a new King.

'Of course the arrival of the new monarch in Grat has been marred with controversy. The murder of an elderly dwarf on the Dark Train which brought His Majesty into this world is thought by many to have been an attempt on the young King's life. Following the evacuation of the Dark Train by Cresta officials there were some reports of an unexplained explosion which badly damaged the Dark Train. This has been strenuously denied by Cresta officials although they have offered no explanation for suspension of Dark Train services. There have been some unconfirmed reports of repairs to the Dark Train running to ten thousand peks. It is common knowledge that of the two Dark Trains ever built, only one has remained operational for the last two hundred years.

One person, the honourable Lady Flint, wife of the Royal Physician has been particularly vocal in her condemnation of senior Cresta officials. And how they handled the murder of the dwarf.'

The man returned into a globule and transformed into the Lady Flint that Samuel remembered well. She looked quiet a bit younger and less frail than the last time he had seen her.

'The incident in the Dark Train completely stinks I am ashamed to say. I feel sorry to be a Gratian today. Mr. Harbury has a lot on his conscience.'

The words froze in Samuel's mind. He knew enough. He largely ignored the rest of what the newspaper went on to say; the burly man reappearing to clear the paper of any allegations against Mr. Harbury, who had been cleared of any misconduct a year later.

As he packed his things to leave, all that Samuel could see in his mind were those piercing black eyes. Mr. Harbury. That man was a murderer!

-- CHAPTER SEVEN --

The Ling Crisis

Samuel was sleeping heavily, exhausted from the excitement of returning to the Royal Palace and relieved to have put his first term at the Longwhey Institute behind him. For several hours he had remained oblivious to a steady tapping on a large window pane in his bedchamber. If he had gone to the window he would have found an impatient black bird perched on the window sill, with a note attached to its leg. He might have taken the bird as mundane and rather unmemorable but the invitation which it was carrying was to change dramatically the course of history.

This was no ordinary bird, despite its black and unremarkable appearance. It had flown on swift and silent wings through moonlit pastures, over great dikes and soared through forest glades where the light rebounded from the glistening pearls of water tumbling from rolling mountains high above. On, it had flown, through hamlets, villages and all manner of tiny outposts. Past huts where country folk lit lights in every window, casting patterns of glowing light into the waning dark of night. It had flown above vast plains, knowing the feeling of great thermals catching its wings in those many miles of nothingness, and scoured the sun baked deserts found at the eastern edge of the world. Yet its instruction, this morning, brought it here to where King Samuel was asleep.

Samuel awoke later on with no knowledge of his dawn visitor until his mother came into his bedchamber smiling.

'News, news has arrived! Good news! A nice present for Winterville!'

'What is it?'

'Ling have invited Your Majesty to attend their International Levish Championships as a guest of honour next week. We had been wondering if they might; Lord Ruffus seemed almost positive but Adviser Jacoby was more uncertain. But his opinion was of no consequence, and you are going anyway! Samuel, I'm so pleased!'

'Are you coming, mum?'

She smiled at him and winked,

'Some things are best left to a young King I think and his best friend perhaps? Take Jack with you Samuel; I'm sure he'll need a bit of a lift after a term at Longwhey. It will be his scene more than mine.'

'Wow, thanks mum, he'll be ecstatic! You know he's always been going on about Ling since his sister...'

'Yes, I do... and his mother will have a fit at the thought of him going all that way! If it wasn't with you I'm sure she'd never allow it.'

The pair laughed in mutual understanding of Mrs. Sorrow's sensitivities. Jack was of course thrilled by the prospect of attending the event and even more pleased at the travel arrangements. Ling was sending a contingent of helpers to bring Gratian Royalty and selected guests to the event in the only way they knew how – by air, or rather by carpet to be exact. As Jack had often mentioned to Samuel, Ling was a country renowned throughout all worlds for making flying carpets of the finest quality. People said that once you bought a Lingian carpet it would last for generations. Levish was the art of carpet flying at a professional level and Ling had spawned many champions in the past. Known for its speed and brutality, the championship was a knock out arrangement where the winner was the last man standing or flying at least.

Whilst Samuel's mother was quite relaxed about his attending the event, she was absolutely clear that officials at the Palace must speak to him before he left. He might be a King in terms of Royalty, but as of now he was not yet a practical King in charge of affairs of state. If Samuel was to attend the International Levish Championships in a capacity representing Grat, he had to know what he was doing.

The meeting took place a few days later with Adviser Jacoby. Samuel's mother had arranged for it to take place in a comfortable side room which was near to the Royal bedchambers. Samuel had seen Adviser Jacoby around the Royal Palace before. He was a short man with balding black hair and he always wore a set of thickly rimmed spectacles. He was the sort of man who was so unremarkable in his appearance that he just existed. His appearance could not then be used as an indicator of the sharp mind which he possessed and which had enabled him to reach the very highest level of service for the Gratian Cresta. His success as an Adviser no doubt rested firmly upon his scrupulous approach to all matters in life, for he left no stone unturned and was very aware of the importance of image and how public appearance could be divisive, especially to Royalty. Perhaps this was the reason he chose to dress in a way that made him as exciting as a magnolia coloured room or an office carpet. It was most disarming.

'Your Majesty, they might have filled your head with all manner of interesting ideas at the Longwhey Institute, but as of today you have no practical experience of the politics of this world. Your geographical knowledge is strictly limited to the boundary of the city and your understanding of the fine tuned relationship this city has with its three neighbours is, I think we can assume, virtually nil?'

'Well, I have a little knowledge of Ling. At Longwhey they said it was ruled by an emperor called Visril Chang. Telfon is led by a board of men and Davish; well, we never really talked about it.'

'Davish has a Queen. They call her the sleeping Queen. She sits all day and night upon her throne and never leaves it. Claws at her bony wrists until the paper thin skin rips and her pale whiteness is called to blood. Her minions travel for miles just to catch a glimpse of her unblinking ivory face. And the remainder of her counsel that are still alive spend their days waiting for her fleeting words, her nods when they come. Davish has been a quiet country for many years under the rule of Queen Nashia. The trouble with a country like that is you never know when it might speak up, or quite what it is capable of.'

'How about Telfon?'

'The poorest country by far but not without power. Its sheer size, which is double that of the others, gives it clout. We share with Ling and Telfon the gold mines between Grat and the boundary of their countries. They lie in the middle of the plain which separates us. No city in any of the three countries has natural protection like ours. I don't want to turn this into a history lecture, I trust you had quite enough of those at Longwhey, but I'm sure you know that Grat once ruled all of the three countries including the gold mines in the desert. "He who holds the mines holds the world" as the saying goes. There are naturally sensitivities with regard to Gratian rule and any mention of our historical role in any of the three countries. I strongly counsel against bringing up the subject, and if it does arise then you must take care with what you say because a few unwise words can do a lot of damage.'

'What is the relationship like between the countries themselves?'

'Well Davish does very little internationally with Queen Nashia, and I have already mentioned the danger of that. Ling and Telfon communicate because they must with regard to the gold mines. And that is the same reason they communicate with us. For Ling, trade with us is important and visa versa. For all that Ling can do with carpets, Grat can do with its knowledge. Longwhey teaches fine skills that no other world possesses and our understanding, particularly of the mechanics of time, is unsurpassed.'

'When is the Lingian transport to arrive? And where am I to meet it?'

'It has been arranged for the Lingian contingent to land in the Royal Gardens. They prefer to take you at night because it is generally safer to use carpets over plains then. The heat of the day causes too many changes in air pressure as the warm air rises skyward. As with all international events there are several other things you should be aware of. Grat cannot provide its own security for your Royal person because it would be impolite and diplomatically difficult to appear that we do not trust the Lingian security.'

'Do we?'

'Well, we have to really. There has been no indication of any Lingian conspiracy so there are no real grounds for being suspicious. If they arrive late to pick you up, I shouldn't be worried either. The I.L.C. is such a huge event that the security teams have to journey to all sorts of different worlds to bring in those who wish to attend and to compete. It is easy for them to be overstretched.'

'When was the last I.L.C. held?'

'Ling hosts it every few years; twenty years ago I think. It was a bit awkward for a while because it costs them so much to host, but in the long term Ling usually profits from extra business.'

Samuel was pleased with the advice Adviser Jacoby had given him and he passed the majority of what had been said on to Jack Sorrow.

On the evening of their departure Jack arrived at the Royal Palace with many hours to spare so the pair had a delicious meal together, for which Samuel's mother joined them. They took it in one of the several hundred dining rooms on the lower ground floor. They had been designed for entertaining huge numbers of Royal guests and visitors.

'Haven't used most of them in years,' sighed Samuel's mother. They cost so much to keep running that many have been mothballed away and no one ever goes into them. They are from the time when Grat was one of the most powerful and influential capital cities of any world. Gratians had money and resources in almost limitless amounts. How are you boys enjoying this meal? It will be the last Gratian food you will have before you get back from Ling.'

'Very nice, thank you,' Jack mouthed through a full mouth of wild boar and purple unclasped pericoles. Samuel could see his mother stifling a laugh at Jack's lack of table manners. Adviser Jacoby would no doubt have left the table with embarrassment.

Samuel's mother decided not to wait up with them for the Lingians to arrive. They had better wait on the lawn outside and she didn't fancy getting cold very much. She kissed Samuel goodbye and told him to be careful and spared Jack a hug before she headed off upstairs. Servants began to clear the tables of food and ushered the pair outside where several bags had already been packed. Samuel and Jack had been expecting to be kept waiting bit so were surprised when a shadow came to their mutual attention, high in the sky, towards the eastern mountain range. It flew towards the Royal Palace at a fearsome speed and made a graceful and precise landing. It was more like a flying four-poster bed Samuel thought to himself. The exterior was lit by several flaming torches that showed a richly patterned hanging stretching across the box-like structure which was secured on the hovering carpet. A flap in the hanging was pushed open and a dark figure stepped forward. In the torchlight Samuel could see his burnished bronzy skin which was very different from the paler Gratian complexion. The man held a scroll in his hand and called out in a deeply accented voice,

'The King of Grat, if he be present, plis, you will plis step this way, bring your company plis behind you cearful and plis you will seek the name as you pass I on the way to inside.' He motioned to the flap from which he had emerged and now stood beside.

Samuel looked at Jack behind him and winked. Then he stepped forward towards the man and after announcing himself as the requested Royalty, proceeded forward upon the man's nod, stepped up onto the carpet and pulled the flap aside on his way. Immediately his nostrils were hit by the strong smell of exotic spices which excited his nostrils. There were many ornate lanterns lit inside and by their light Samuel could see a clutch of persons at the back of the structure, sitting on the floor. He made his way towards them, suddenly aware of the smoky atmosphere inside that accompanied the strong scents.

Samuel could feel the carpet working beneath his feet to address the redistribution of his weight and Jack's behind him. The men in front of Samuel made to get up to greet him but he motioned to them to be seated. There were three of them in total with some bags beside them that he had original mistaken for a fourth.

'Your Majesty! At last we meet! Greetings from Telfon!'

All three men smiled at Samuel and seemed to him to be both genuine and friendly. Samuel motioned to Jack as he made to sit down,

'My friend, Jack Sorrow, son of William Sorrow.'

'Ah yes Mr. Sorrow, just like your father, welcome to you too. If our Lingian driver speeds up we might just be on our way to Ling together in a minute.'

The three men went on to introduce themselves individually although to Samuel they all seemed fairly alike. They all claimed to be on the Telfon board of rulers and said a little of their individual roles. Telfon sounded to Samuel like a very civilised country but he was mindful to keep remarks of this nature to himself, aware that they might suggest he had previously suspected otherwise. As they were talking together they could feel the carpet ripple under them as it lifted up into the night, lanterns swinging and disturbed. Samuel asked the men how many times they had been to Ling. It varied amongst them with one saying he was regularly there on diplomatic assignments and another saying this was only his third trip.

'It's the food I have to watch,' he said in a quiet voice, 'all so spicy that it violently disagrees with me.'

Jack sniggered beside Samuel and said 'And I heard that their hygiene isn't exactly great,' which earned him a sharp nudge and glare from Samuel. The Telfonian delegates laughed politely but Samuel could tell the comment had made them uneasy.

The ride on the carpet was fairly smooth but there were a few sudden bumps as the height of the carpet decreased quickly. Samuel could not help but wonder what the journey would have been like if they were making it during the daytime with the variations in pressure that the heat of the sun would bring about over the plains that must be below them now. It was a relief to Jack that he couldn't see how far off the ground they were, but the sensation of flying wasn't one which he was too keen on anyway and he spent much of the flight very quietly beside Samuel. Samuel was glad if it prevented him the opportunity to cause embarrassment through loose language.

The Telfonian delegates seemed to be close to dropping off to sleep several times during the journey, which made Samuel wonder just how long it had taken the carpet to fly from Telfon to Grat prior to picking him up. Adviser Jacoby had said how big Telfon was compared to the other countries, so perhaps the capital city was at its very extent to the south. For the time being Samuel could only wonder.

The changes in pressure announcing their decent were soon detected by the eardrums of the occupants of the carpet. They had been carried very fast over many empty miles and now at last below them the first of the great Lingian Palaces passed by without their knowledge. They would never see the vast dusty gardens and whitewashed turrets or the perfect geometry of the white rooftops that hid in the darkness beneath them.

Tiredness was washing over Samuel as they at last lurched to a stop. They could hear the accented man outside announcing their arrival.

'Grat and Telfon arrival plis come out and welcome.'

Samuel made his way forward first followed by the others to the flap through which they had entered. It was pulled out of the way before he could do it himself and he found that he was in a darkened courtyard. There were people standing around in groups, some looking very nervous. The accented man addressed them again before there was time for any questions.

'You plis wait for address by Grand Chang and then we move into the Palace for feast.'

Samuel nodded in response, his stomach groaning inwardly at the thought of more food. He shot a casual glance at Jack and observed that the prospect of more good food in that quarter was entirely agreeable. Before Samuel had any real time to notice, the carpet behind them was off again, whooshing away in reverse and then up and away into the night sky. The wait that presented itself offered an opportunity to look more intently at the courtyard. It wasn't as big as it might have at first appeared. White colonnades supported a shelter which ran around the entire perimeter and, at intervals, lights had been placed in alcoves which punctured the length of the surrounding wall. Music started playing just as Samuel had been expecting it. He couldn't make out quite where it was coming from but he suspected it was from just beyond the perimeter wall, out of sight but perfectly in earshot for the guest's convenience.

The Grand Visril Chang certainly knew how to entertain and he was also not in the habit of keeping others waiting. As a result it was only a short while before the sound of clapping by some of the people in the courtyard heralded his arrival. Samuel wasn't sure initially quite where to expect to see him, but instinctively he felt this was a man who was intending to make a big impression. His suspicions were justly rewarded as Chang appeared on the roof of the shelter, illuminated by a bright red light.

'Thank you, friends for the warmest welcome.'

He spoke with a well educated twang that did not hide the strong Lingian accent that Samuel had observed in the man on the carpet.

'Peoples from many worlds have gathered here tonight. Those in front of me are the chosen few, the Royalty and their closest friends. Ling hopes that for the sake of security you will not object to being kept away from the crowds that are gathering here ready for the International Levish Championships tomorrow. For those of you who have teams competing tomorrow I'm sure that tonight will be all too short with all the fine tuning you have to do, yes?'

A ripple of polite laughter passed through the court yard.

'Many of you have travelled here in secret where your country or your world does not openly admit trade with Ling. We salute you all under whatever circumstances you have come, and wish you all a most enjoyable day tomorrow.'

From across the courtyard applause rang out and Samuel joined Jack in clapping. Jack had been busy looking around while Samuel had been listening intently to Chang. When he spoke, Samuel could hear the awe in his voice.

'They're all here! Anyone who is anyone. Telfon, us, countries from the world where you were born. I just saw the president of their United States talking to the Prime Minister of the United Kingdom and his wife. It's just incredible to be here.'

'Don't be silly Jack, this is where you belong.'

'No, actually, this is where you belong. I'm not the King of Grat. I'm just Jack Sorrow.'

'Well, that's nothing to be ashamed of, is it? You go to the Longwhey Institute and your dad is in the Gratian Cresta. You saw how the Telfonian delegates knew of William Sorrow didn't you?'

'Yes I guess. Come, people are starting to head inside and I don't want to miss out on all the food?'

'What happened to your hygiene concerns earlier?'

Jack shrugged, 'It's just food isn't it? And it was mainly my mum who said about the hygiene not being up to scratch.'

Samuel laughed but he did notice later that Jack was careful to pick around any dishes which appeared undercooked. Evidently Mrs. Sorrow did hold influence over her son whether he accepted it or not.

Despite not being particularly hungry, Samuel did find dinner very interesting. The President of the United States of America was seated opposite and Samuel exchanged pleasantries with the President while Jack chatted to the First Lady as she called herself. Samuel found that the President knew a lot about Grat and its history. He was careful to avoid discussing the tensions with surrounding countries in too much detail.

'You should see the problems in our world,' said the President, laughing a little sadly.

'I've got half the Middle East up in arms at the moment. Nightmare. But you have to beat the buggers, Your Majesty, can't let them win. We need their oil, like you need your gold.'

Samuel laughed a bit uneasily, glad to move on to discuss sport. Levish didn't hold the President's attention like 'baseball' apparently, but he did admit Levish was damn exciting to watch. Better than motorsport anyway.

Samuel would have gladly enjoyed talking further, but the Prime Minister of the United Kingdom had wandered over.

'We have baseball in our country too, Your Majesty. It's just that we call it rounders and only girls find it interesting.'

The President looked more than a little offended by this joke but the PM seemed to find it very funny. They wanted to have a chat before tomorrow, so both made their excuses and went away to other Palace rooms with their wives. Jack turned to Samuel for a chat.

'Gosh, well, I don't know about you but I can't eat anymore! I'm stuffed! They were all nice weren't they?'

'Yes they were. Jack, do their countries know that they are here?'

Jack shook his head, 'Their world is one which doesn't acknowledge trade with this one so far as I know. This world is an official secret in most countries. Grat sometimes gives their top people time away from their own world; you know how skilled we are at things like that. But they don't always bother; I think it costs them a lot.'

'What do they do then?'

'Official holidays to remote and beautiful places, but they really come here. I expect that's what it is on this occasion.'

'All come by Dark Trains?'

'Some do, but not all. There are other ways to this world. Just have to look very hard to find them.'

Since they had both finished eating they left the dining area which they had come into from the courtyard and followed behind other guests who were moving towards a large ballroom. There was music in here once again, but with a bit more rhythm, far better for dancing. At the end of the ballroom Samuel could see an open doorway leading onto a veranda. He would have headed out anyway despite the abrupt end to the music and the call to head outside for a 'great display for guests of the Great Visril Chang.'

Jack shivered on the balcony. Ling was supposed to be hot during the day and that was what he had dressed for, but by night the desert climate with cool air off the flat plains made the temperature drop considerably.

Far in front of them there was a blast of flames and a visage of Chang burnt alight with bursts of sparks spraying into the air. There was brisk music playing above the veranda and gasps from guests as yet more plumes of light ascended into the sky. Samuel heard a bearded man say to Jack 'No one does a night display like Ling; you have to hand it to them.'

Samuel regretted not having had more of a chance to speak to different people at the earlier feast. He knew there were some very interesting, powerful and influential beings gathered in this part of the Lingian Royal Palace tonight. Samuel couldn't help but prefer his own Royal Palace in Grat. It was vast like this one of course, but it had an age and a history to it which this white clinical beast of a palace seemed to lack. There was something a bit artificial about the small part of the place he had seen, but then perhaps it suited this climate far better than the heavy and dark halls of home.

The show was over too soon they all agreed, but the calls for more were not answered. Samuel agreed that Ling could not only pull off great entertainment but also they were the perfect host. As soon as the display was over Palace servants were swarming among the guests calling out names to show them to bedchambers that had been prepared. A well spoken dark haired boy came to find the Gratians. On the way to the bedchamber Samuel asked his name.

'Your Majesty can call me Yim,' he said, smiling.

'Should Your Majesty or your company require anything during the night please ring the bell to be found in your room. I have also been told to ask you if either of you will require a guide for tomorrow?'

Samuel looked to Jack, a little hesitant.

'Who do we get? If we do ask for a guide I mean?'

'Me,' replied Yim smiling.

'You are the most well spoken Lingian I have yet come across Yim, so I would certainly enjoy your guidance' said Jack and Samuel nodded.

'Most certainly. And here is your room. It has too separate beds and the highest Royal security which we know you are used to. As I'm sure you know that means I cannot come in it with you, but here is the door, and if you just push it Your Majesty, it should open,' Yim said smiling.

'Thanks Yim, see you tomorrow.'

'I shall wake you in time for a breakfast before the Levish Championship begins,' and with that, Yim walked away from them down the corridor. Samuel pushed the door and it opened as promised. Pleased with their beds, the tired pair made for them straight away and slept through an uneventful night.

Neither Samuel nor Jack would have woken up if Yim had not knocked the door hard. Jack shot out of bed, excitement at being in Ling flooding through him. Samuel was a bit less ecstatic but still managed to pull himself together quickly and left the room only a short while later, dressed and ready for breakfast.

'We leave the room for good now,' explained Yim, 'breakfast for you both, and then on to the Championships straight away. They always start early and then finish late.'

Breakfast was taken like the feast the night before, in the large dining room. The seating arrangements had been altered to allow new people to meet. Unlike last nights company those seated opposite from Samuel were not exactly friendly. The couple looked barely human, hairy and dressed in black with badly cracked skin all over. They either didn't understand Samuel and Jack or didn't want to. Eventually they gave up trying to make conversation. Yim was waiting to one side for them to finish breakfast and Samuel was glad to leave. As he got up having finished the last dregs of the spicy juice that had been provided he managed to get a look at the name plate beside the couple. It read 'Vugari.' An unfriendly name for unfriendly people.

Yim led Samuel and Jack quickly out of the dining room and onto a long concourse.

'How far Yim to the race site?'

'Not far into the desert, Your Majesty. We take carpet or walk, however you please?'

'Walk,' replied Samuel firmly. He knew Jack had had quite enough of carpets after yesterday.

Yim led them out of the main Palace building and they began to join other groups of Royalty and delegates who were beginning the slow and winding walk out into the desert to where the Championship was to be held.

'I think it's going to be hot today Yim,' said Jack

'You are quite right. See how the sky is that hazy blue, it's already beginning to heat up. It glows a yellow white when it gets really hot. And not to worry so much about the heat, I have with me a parasol. Guides must ensure at all times the comfort of Lingian guests.'

'Yim! How can we ever thank you enough for being so resourceful! Samuel is going to have to adopt you!'

Yim grinned at Jack, pleased at his gratitude.

'Well I could sure make use of you at Longwhey Yim, you are a darn sight better than Marlow ever has been, but alas I don't want to hurt his sensitive feelings.'

Yim laughed completely oblivious to Marlow's disastrous reputation but sensing it all the same. As they were walking they passed sparse and drought riddled trees and although the well tended path under foot remained safely flat, the surrounding land began to buck and pucker into dune like structures.

'Your Majesty, the land flattens soon you see, perfect for Levish down by the grandstands.'

'How many people will be at the grandstands Yim?'

'Several thousand. The Royal area is of course restricted so there will be the same number there as at the feast - several hundred.'

'And what sort of security have they put in place around the grandstand?'

'There is a team of expert Lingian defence troops with a large number of emergency carpets on standby to get Royalty away from the grandstand at the first sign of trouble. Our reputation rests upon the safety of our guests especially the very important ones.'

Samuel could now make out the end of the path. It led all the way up to the back of the grandstand. From the back it looked a bit ugly despite being as white as all other Lingian structures seemed to be. He judged it to be about a hundred rows high on the front. Yim took the pair to a porter who was waiting at an entrance. Yim spoke to him very fast in a language which Samuel was not at all familiar. They seemed to have passed trackside security as Yim led them forwards into a tunnel made through the grandstand supports which towered upwards above them.

They emerged into hot bright sunlight to which the eyes took some time to adjust. Before them was a vast plain which shimmered in the heat haze. A white line was drawn on top of the sand and stretched away from the grandstand for several miles. Assembled along it were hundreds of teams who were standing beside and working on hovering carpets of all sizes, colours and designs. Some were more open than others, whilst the rest made use of some sort of cover or canopy.

Yim had begun to climb the stairs that ran up to the top section of the grandstand and to the specific area reserved for Royalty. The seats beside the stairs had not yet been filled in order to allow Royal guests to make their way to their seats without interruption. Jack said he needed to go to the toilet before he went up to sit down and he had spotted a sign back where they had entered the grandstand so Samuel nodded him away and went up the stairs to join Yim. As they neared the top of the stairs Yim pointed to two seats that were labelled 'King Deksis of Grat' and 'Guest of former.' Samuel began to head to his seat when he noticed Yim drawing away from him.

'They don't give you a seat here do they Yim?'

'No, Your Majesty, I am just a guide today for you.'

'Look, Jack has gone to the toilet a minute, take his seat until he gets back. Good to be able to talk for a bit.'

Yim looked very hesitant.

'I am not supposed to join you because I am not your guest, Your Majesty.'

'Yim, be my guest for now,' said Samuel pointing at the generic name plate on Jack's seat.

Yim smiled and awkwardly sat down. Samuel began to look more intently out at the white start line and the different teams making their final preparations. Some of the competing teams were semi-visible and it was apparent to Samuel that their partial visibility was no trick of the desert heat. As the thought passed through his head, Samuel subconsciously lifted his arm to wipe the sweat that had formed on his brow.

'A little higher Your Majesty? I hold the parasol a bit more higher?'

'No thanks Yim, just keep it there if you will.' Yim nodded in a characteristically over enthusiastic fashion but at least he always gave a friendly response.

'I'm surprised by how many teams there are, Yim. See that one over there,' he pointed to an entry about fiftieth away from the grandstand and about a tenth of the way across the entire line. It was scarcely possible to make out the end of the line of entries. The team to which he had pointed was on the verge of clear visibility, 'Looks like giant frogs in charge of that!'

'Your Majesty, hush, you must not be heard to be calling them such a derogatory name. They come from an entirely different world to any either of us have been to. I'm sure where they come from they look quite normal. Besides, one of their delegates is just to your right and I don't think we want to upset him.'

Samuel stared to his right and focused on a squat little fellow who sat by himself under a monstrous black hat. He seemed to be quite alone, perhaps having rejected the offer of a Lingian guide which Samuel had readily accepted.

'Yim, how do all these people get here, from all these different worlds I mean?'

'To be totally honest I don't know; I'm just Yim, junior servant to the Great Visril Chang, so I get told very little about anything.'

'Do you have any family, Yim?'

Yim looked away at this question and Samuel knew he had touched a delicate topic.

'I used to. What more do you wish to know about Levish?'

'Umm, well what about the other delegates that get sent here, I don't see Queen Nashia of Telfon anywhere.'

At this Yim let out a low laugh, 'Queen Nashia hasn't attended here for many years, she is a sleeping Queen as I expect you know.'

'I thought perhaps some of her servants might bring her here? I thought they did everything for her?'

'Well, so far as I know they do, but it depends on whether she wants to come here doesn't it, and so far as I know none of her fleeting words have expressed the desire.'

Since they had been sitting there Samuel had been looking both out across the desert and around the rows of previously empty seats which he now observed to be filling up.

'It just seems extraordinary to me, Yim, that the single country of Ling can attract so much attention and get so many teams to compete.'

'Ling does a roaring trade far beyond this world, Your Majesty. We Lingians are taken to allowing our greatest trading partners a chance to compete in the Levish Championships. They are more inter-world than international competitions. By the different countries it's generally considered good for their image here which is especially useful if they do significant trade with us. Take the world in which you were born, for example. If you look out there on the plain you can see the United States of America besides an Arabian entry and further along there is the Lingian entry itself beside what should be Great Britain.'

As yet, the entry for Great Britain was not on site. Samuel could not help but wonder where it was at the moment. All the other teams seemed to be getting ready to start racing. His eyes fixed on what Yim had said to be the entry by the USA. It was as sleek a design as one could imagine a flying carpet to be, decked out in stars and stripes on the carpet and with an arching balustrade attached to the front and tapering gradually down each side. Samuel could easily imagine that the rider would take a position near the front of the carpet, gripping the handrail for support as he would make tiny changes in balance to guide its progress.

'How many riders are allowed on each carpet Yim, is it just one?'

'Maximum of four, Your Majesty. Some teams only have two people during the race. It depends on the dynamics of the carpet.'

'Does Grat have a team, Yim?'

'Yes Your Majesty, although you seem not to be aware of it. It is three away from the USA.'

Samuel could see it quite clearly. A brilliant golden affair that shone perhaps more brightly than any other entry.

'It seems that our main tactic is to blind the other competitors,' said Samuel dryly. He felt a little ashamed that he had not personally been aware that Grat had a team. Jack was bound to know of course. He might even have had a poster of them up in his room back at Longwhey come to think of it. Jack reappeared almost as he was thinking of it and Samuel, thanking Yim for his time and taking the parasol to hold himself, motioned for Jack to take Yim's place. He looked nervous with excitement.

'You should have told me there was a Gratian team, Jack.'

'Your Majesty! I have told you many times while we were at Longwhey but you didn't look very interested. I soon got the message and so I gave up talking to you about it.'

Samuel smiled, knowing what Jack was saying to be completely true. The seating was now almost completely full. Samuel could see some of the teams were sending their non-riding members away now that the final checks had been carried out. Jack was starting to relax and his nervous excited fidgeting was less frequent.

There was suddenly a loud popping sound accompanied by an almost unseen flash and somewhere in Samuel's mind a memory shifted towards the surface but it did not quite make it to the level of conscious accessibility.

What laughter and chatter there had been in the grandstand had abruptly stopped. To his left Samuel felt the heat of the sun on his shoulder that was outside the shade of the parasol give way to a shadow and when he looked he saw its source. There were four bearers holding a wooden chair upon which was seated the most ghostly white woman Samuel had ever seen. She was sitting stock still and unblinking in the blistering hot sunlight. Samuel knew at once who it was. There were gasps from amongst the Royal guests. Several porters came dashing up the stairs and guests were nervously fidgeting in their seats.

While Samuel did not understand a word of the angry conversation that was taking place beside him he could gather the content of it. Queen Nashia had arrived completely out of the blue. She had just appeared without an invite and without a seat reserved for her in the Royal area. The conversation was entirely between porters and chair bearers. They seemed unable to reach an arrangement. Samuel was growing a little tired of the scene that was being made. He motioned to Jack to move out of his way so he could slip past where he spoke to the porters to get their attention.

'Excuse me, why don't you take our seats? We can stand or sit on the steps here perfectly well.'

'The Queen does not move from her chair,' said one of the bearers with distain in his voice. One of the porters spoke up.

'Could we not hover the chair on a carpet, over the seats? There should be just enough room and it could be gently lowered down?'

The bearers were already dismissing the suggestion when they were halted by a sudden nod from the ashen queen on the chair. The bearers immediately concurred with the idea and Jack moved reluctantly to stand beside Samuel and vacate his seat.

'Do you know what you are doing Samuel?'

'Of course, we can stand or sit here on the steps unless chairs become available.'

A porter turned to speak to the pair.

'We have another pair of vacant Royal seats a few rows up, so Your Majesty can go there in a moment. The Vugari Royals decided they wanted to go home. The bearers are calling for immediate rest so we had better put Her Majesty in Your place.'

A carpet was rushed up the stairs to hold the chair in position and to relieve the bearers of their burden. The arrangement, whilst distinctly temporary, seemed acceptable.

The porter gracefully showed Jack and Samuel to the vacant seats a few rows up. When Samuel turned to look at Jack he was almost as white as Queen Nashia herself, to the extent that he almost laughed out loud.

'Something is going on Samuel, I can tell. That never happens. She never comes.'

'Yeah,' said Samuel casually, 'Yim was saying she's not too keen on Levish'

Jack looked at Samuel disapprovingly, 'Exactly. If she has decided to come, it must be for a reason. Something important is going to happen here today.'

Samuel passed off Jack's paranoia fairly easily. It was possible that he was right of course, but it seemed far more likely that Queen Nashia had just decided to come.

Attention turned back to the spectacle that they had all come to witness. Out on the start line all the teams looked ready, apart from Great Britain. Off to the far right of the grandstand there was a sudden increase in chatter. From the side of the grandstand, where it must have been sitting out of sight, there pulled forward what was easily the most comical entry to the championship. It consisted of a shabby grey carpet with the structure of a colourful caravan strapped onto it. Atop the caravan, on what looked suspiciously like a modified bicycle, was a man with grey wispy hair and thick purple ear protectors. The grey carpet lurched forward towards the British position at the start line where it was to set off beside the Lingian entry. The Lingian carpet was, in Samuel's opinion, the most beautiful of all the entries. It consisted of a crisp cream carpet and a structure of the four poster variety which was open, apart from several elegant satin throws which adorned the structure overhead. A four-man bronze skinned team was in charge of it, each member taking a corner and adopting an athletic pose.

Jack discussed the structure and was certain that it was indeed a 'caravan.'

'The British go on holiday in that,' he said.

'Crazy,' replied Samuel.

'Not as much as the Americans; a lot of them live in those permanently.'

As the British 'caravan' pulled into position, its rough handling caused it to slide into the Lingian entry making it spin sideways. Although well out of earshot, Samuel could see the Lingian crew gesture angrily to the man astride the bicycle. He didn't appear to notice, his face trained intently forwards as he stared down the start of the track. Samuel wondered if he was nervous. And whether he was expecting the British contraption to go fast. It appeared that he did, judging from the earmuffs which he was wearing. Either that or he was just very over cautious. The ramshackle affair looked to Samuel like it might easily tear apart if it went at any speed. He wondered if it was just a one man British team. It was possible that there were others inside the caravan itself. He could just make out an open hatch behind the bicycle on the top which allowed access to the interior.

'Converted skylight,' muttered Jack beside him, wondering the very same thing.

Samuel could see a porter step out onto the edge of the track. At the same time there was a crackling noise and a booming announcement was made in the grandstand.

'Guests, we are now at the exciting time we have all been waiting for. The International Levish Championships are about to begin.'

After the announcement things began to happen very quickly. From several rows in front of Samuel there was a mighty blast and flash. The grandstand shook violently beneath them and a hot wave of gas passed over the crowd. Samuel felt splinters hit his cheeks and he saw great clumps of wood shooting overhead and into the crowds above.

The sound was like a thunderclap that echoed around the grandstand and the start line. At first Samuel thought Queen Nashia might just have disappeared again by the same means she had arrived, but surely no such transition would have been this violent.

The emergency operation was swinging into action almost immediately. A hundred carpets shot overhead and were professionally brought to a stop at intervals along each row. Samuel was half pulled, half thrown onto one which lurched off before he managed to get anything of a good hold.

Meanwhile, at the start line, things were getting out of hand. At the sound of the explosion the nervous British carpet had shot forwards almost automatically, with the man astride the bicycle struggling to bring its forward motion under control. He teetered towards control for a few moments with the carpet hovering and making sweeping circular motions before it seemed to take upon a life of its own as his expertise were completely overwhelmed. It lurched sharply sideways and then went shooting upwards into the sky. Samuel was, at this point, in the air, clinging to the emergency carpet with what strength he had. The expert rider, who was controlling it, allowed no time at all for Samuel to adjust his grip to a better position.

The surging British 'caravan' swam into Samuel's view very suddenly. He instinctively knew it was going to hit the underside of the carpet at any second. His reflexes took over and he let go of the carpet in a bid to protect his head and face. The carpet flew from under him almost instantly and this sent him reeling backwards, smacking into the roof the caravan just as its ascent was thankfully beginning to slow. He was winded beyond shouting out. The caravan surged forwards, wildly out of control once again, and Samuel rolled backwards, falling headoverheels through the open converted skylight and into the caravans interior. Mercifully, the floor of the caravan had been removed so that he fell into the cushion of the carpet itself. It knocked all the remaining wind out of him, but it was not nearly as painful as when he hit the caravan roof.

Samuel in his sickened and shocked state was thrown around violently as the carpet continued on its torturous route. He could see that there was no one else in here, much to his surprise. Just as he was starting to recover, the caravan swung violently to the right and turned completely upside down. What was happening to the poor man on the bicycle at this moment, Samuel dreaded to think.

A whooshing sound outside the caravan heralded the arrival in the air of an emergency team. Samuel felt the caravan begin to be righted and he rolled inelegantly around the side of the caravan and back onto the carpet. The ground rose up to meet the descending carpet and the emergency team did a good job of putting it down gently.

Samuel lay still inside the caravan. His sides were heaving from pain and shock. Dizziness overcame him in waves and he was feeling very groggy when hands pulled him to his feet. The side of the caravan had been forced open and he could hear several voices. As faces swam into view he looked for one he could recognise. Yim was nowhere to be seen, hardly surprising given that he was not a member of the emergency team. He found himself focused on a knot of people just beside the caravan talking angrily. Staggering forwards, as those surrounding him urged restraint, he could recognise the British rider talking in fitful apologetic bursts. He looked up as he caught sight of Samuel, and disintegrated into tears. How comical he looked, still wearing the oversized purple ear protectors.

The emergency team were keen to remove Samuel from the crash site as soon as they ascertained that he had not suffered any serious injuries. Demurely, Samuel took secure hold this time, of the carpet to which he was directed, and the expert rider glided him gently into the air and away from the grandstands. Below, the crowds seemed to be under control, although the Royal seating was empty, presumably fully evacuated. The rows where the explosion had taken placed looked damaged, although it was hard to say how badly from above. There was no sign of Queen Nashia.

Samuel was taken to a ‘secure’ building in some distant Lingian suburb. The carpet had descended into a narrow alley way, quiet but filled with evidence of merchant activity. The narrow alley provided shade from all but directly overhead sunshine and Samuel was grateful for this. It had been reasonably cool flying on the carpet, but now he was down, the shade was very welcome. The expert rider, who had brought him, directed him through a doorway amid the jumble of pots and caskets that littered the area. Inside, Samuel could make out one of the Telfonian delegates. He smiled when he saw Samuel although it was clearly apparent that he was ill at ease.

‘Your Majesty, so glad to see you are relatively unharmed. That is fortuitous indeed!’

‘Thank you and the same to you of course.’

Samuel turned to the rider who had brought him here.

‘What are we to do now? Wait to be taken home?’

‘I believe that the I.L.C. will go ahead later but that Royalty will not be able to attend on this occasion. Queen Nashia of Davish was certainly hurt, but mercifully not killed, in the vicious explosion. The grandstands shall all be rechecked, of course, to ensure no other explosives can be found, but assuming they are clear, as we expect, then the teams will get to race. Ling has spent too much money hosting this event to cancel it now. Royalty will wait securely, and then be returned home tonight. These are the wishes of the Great Visril Chang.’

‘Where is Jack Sorrow? What have you done with him?’

‘He is being held securely, there is no need to worry. He will be returned to Grat tonight, but separately. The emergency team will assist him as required.’

Good, thought Samuel, at least Jack is ok. The expert rider had been instructed to stay with guests at the secure building so he waited at the doorway while Samuel passed the rest of the day with the Telfonian delegate inside. At first he had seemed too nervous to talk at length but eventually he seemed to take Samuel into his confidence. Samuel was wary of this but not necessarily suspicious.

'Well, who knows what will happen now. I wonder how Davish will react. Who planted that explosive? There are so many questions. I feel quite wistful that all of this evidently political interference must interfere with a simple Levish Championship.'

'That is always the way, isn't it,' replied Samuel.

They made little more than small talk for the rest of the day. Samuel was the first to be taken home on an enclosed, but far smaller carpet, than that which had first brought him with Jack to Ling. A few hours later he alighted gratefully in the Royal Gardens. In the darkness he could make out Jack and his mother running to greet them. Saffie threw her arms around Samuel, close to being distraught with relief. It transpired that Jack had told her just about everything that had happened. Samuel was longing for bed, but when he expressed such an inclination his mother shook her head.

'This is going to be difficult I know. What has happened today is already changing everything. Adviser Jacoby has told me that the debating chamber must sit in full session throughout the night. This will require Your Majesty to be present and to contribute. Come, I must get you ready.'

Saffie provided new robes for Samuel to wear. She looked very worried, Samuel thought. He hadn't realised that what had happened in Ling, so far away, would have such immediate consequences here in Grat.

'I am informed that Lord Ruffus is sitting today to represent the Cresta. He will be the man with the beard. Usually he is quite coherent for a Lord, so I am pleased it will be him you shall deal with this first time you sit officially in the debating chamber.'

'Will Adviser Jacoby be present?'

'Yes Samuel, he will represent the Advisers to Your Royal person. Advisory work is auxiliary to the Cresta but essentially separate. Jacoby was one of the many who began their career politically in the Cresta and then specialised to become an Adviser. How glad I am that I had the foresight to introduce you to each other before you left for Ling!'

Samuel's mother gave him a warm hug, worry etched into her face. She fussed over the robes which he had been given to wear in such a rush. It was evident that this was not happening in the way she had intended. In her mind it was too soon for him to begin sitting in the debating chamber at the Royal Palace. As she ushered him to the Royal entrance he could hear her breathing become more regular as she steeled her nerves, for his good anyway.

'Enter here and you will find a golden throne inside. Be seated when you enter and the debate will then be in full session. It ends when you rise and exit the chamber, not before, remember.'

Samuel nodded and looked towards the door which his mother was reaching to hold open. It seemed that seeing him inside was something she wished to do, rather than leaving it to some servant or official. He drew in his own breath and braced himself, then took the plunge. As the doors swung open, he entered. The sound of people rising to their feet was immediately audible. The golden throne was as his mother had described, raised on a pedestal and looking into the other two thirds of the structure. The debating chamber itself was best described as the internal shape of an egg. The throne was at the base in one third of that area. The other two thirds were divided by knee height walls, providing for wooden seats occupied by Adviser Jacoby and Lord Ruffus respectively. Above this base area there rose seven or so balcony levels above each debate participant, each level being more constricted, thus creating the egg-like void. The whole building was faced in black marble which had only the faintest veins of other hues buried in it. Each of the three balconies on each floor had a golden handrail behind which officials stood. Above Lord Ruffus they were all members of the Gratian Cresta, representing the civil service of the capital. Above

Adviser Jacoby were further Advisers. And Above Samuel, standing nervously in a shadow so that she would not be seen, was Saffie Deksis.

To Samuel, the arrangement of the chamber was a perfect reflection of the divide of power between Royalty and people in Grat. The Cresta was a semi-autonomous political affair which was said to be rarely impartial, but this was balanced by Advisors to his Royal person who represented his wider interests, and the third component in this trinity was himself, the King of Grat, who held ultimate power over all things. Nothing could be done without his Royal approval. How grateful Samuel was now for the things he had picked up during his time at Longwhey. It had been filled with young, ambitious people desirous of reaching high offices in the Gratian Cresta. He was far from ready for this baptism by fire, but at least he had a chance of holding it together.

Having taken this all in, Samuel was at last seated and all those who had risen to their feet in the chamber could follow his lead, and make themselves comfortable. The exceptions to this were Lord Ruffus and Adviser Jacoby, who had to remain standing at all times in the official presence of the Monarch.

As his mother had instructed Samuel remained silent and waited for Lord Ruffus to open. As he spoke, his words resonated in the strange space, giving each word the tone of officialdom.

'We convene at the twentieth hour of the one hundredth and twenty seventh day of this year the first Full Session in Grat. This Session has been called in accordance with the Opate Declaration which states at subsection fifty that when Advisors and Lords call upon the Monarch to sit in Full Session it will be so for as many hours as are necessary, less the unreasonable discomfort of the Monarch. I open the debate with the issue of the events which have occurred earlier this day in the country of Ling. At the eleventh hour of the morning an explosive device in the Royal stands at the International Levish Championships was detonated, causing severe injury to our ally, Queen Nashia of the country of Davish. In response to this attack the Great Visril Chang of the country of Ling has issued an official statement communicating his belief that the said explosion was the work of the country of Telfon. This was, in the words of Chang, 'A vexatious and inhumane attempt at political assassination with the sole aim of sabotaging the International Levish Championships to the detriment of (his) country, politically and economically.' In response to this, (one may wish to see it in the light of retaliation which essentially it is) Ling is to take sole control of the two Gold Mines, Rafe and Jeten which it owned and ran jointly with Telfon. This will have immediate effect and force will be used if the action meets with any resistance. Ling may be willing to negotiate a handover to Telfon at a later date but will require several concessions. Adviser Jacoby, I pass on this issue for you to speak.'

'Your Majesty, we shall address the issue which Lord Ruffus has honourably brought to the attention of Grat in the manner which it deserves, for it should be treated with the uttermost seriousness. Grat holds the Eloth Gold Mines jointly with Telfon and Ling. We presume for the time being that they have no immediate intention of taking control of them by force. They are a vital resource for this city and must not be disrupted. We are currently awaiting a communiqué by Telfon giving their response to the Ling decision. Lord Ruffus?'

'I have just been passed down by the Cresta a document which I shall read: 'Following the irrational and hasty decision by the country of Ling to remove from our control the jointly owned Gold Mines of Rafe and Jeten, which we condemn outright, Telfon will be placing a blockade on all Lingian exports to our country. We call upon all other countries to take similar action until the unlawful seizure of our Gold Mines is reversed. Telfon expresses its disbelief at the events which occurred earlier today and in no way condoned or contributed to this abhorrent action.' Strong words from the Telfonian board there, as expected. We must now decide what our response will be, even if that is to be to do nothing.'

Adviser Jacoby was listening intently to what had been said and glanced to several of the officials on a balcony above him. One mouthed something back. Jacoby turned to speak again.

'Your Majesty, we must consider our response carefully. We understand that your Royal person was hurt today due to inadequate emergency evacuation arrangements; a factor which I advise should be used to our advantage. It is a huge diplomatic disaster for Ling with their security being so under prepared; such an embarrassment for a proud nation.

If Grat wishes to support Telfon in renouncing the Lingian seizure and Ling then threatens Grat, perhaps with particular reference to the Eloth Gold Mines, we can retort with threats to capitalise on their security failings. This could also strengthen our economy, given that security is our specialist sector.

If, on the other hand, Grat wishes to support Ling, we must have some grounds for doing so. What evidence, other than the Lingian reflex to blame Telfon, can be produced to show Telfonian involvement in some kind of plot?'

Samuel felt confused. He was essentially being faced with three possible courses of action. He had to speak.

'Advisor Jacoby, umm, what to, to do nothing. How would that be effective?'

Samuel could feel his body trembling as he spoke from the throne. Speaking to Jacoby in person had been intimidating enough, but doing it in front of all these people was quite another thing, especially in this great chamber. Advisor Jacoby was ready to respond quickly.

'To do nothing carries its own risks. It will show restraint, but Grat will look politically weak. We may seem to condone the Lingian action and Telfon will undoubtedly harden its useful, friendly relationship.'

Lord Ruffus cleared his throat, indicating a desire to speak. Jacoby gave way.

'There is another option which must be considered and that involves making use of Davish. If we were to respond either way in unison with that country, it would strengthen our position...'

Jacoby did not look upon this suggestion favourably. 'No friends! We cannot wait upon the word of Queen Nashia. She is a compromised monarch and a tyranny for her kingdom which sits on its riches. Our political association with that dreadful country should be kept to a minimum. It is a political wart!'

Samuel was confident Jacoby could have gone on further but he was interrupted by a call of 'Advisor' from a balcony three floors above. A note was passed down to him.

'By this note we should all observe the fluidity of the situation. Ling declared that it intends to take the Eloth Gold Mines under its sole control if Grat will not put the strongest political pressure on Telfon to accept responsibility for the explosion and accept any conditions attached to the return of the Gold Mines, Rafe and Jeten, to joint ownership.'

The chamber was immediately filled with loud mutterings from the floors above. Everyone seemed unsettled, even panicky. Jacoby was the first to speak.

'I call upon the Opate Declaration which states at subsection twenty that the King may be given personal counsel in circumstances of national emergency.'

There were a few cries of disbelief from above. It seemed this was quite an unprecedented step to take.

'In accord with this, I call upon the Gratian Cresta to withdraw from this chamber until further notice.'

Cries were turning angry now. Lord Ruffus flushed just a little, and bowed.

'As you wish.'

Lord Ruffus left his area of the debating chamber and headed out of his door. There was a scraping of chairs from above as officials began to take their forced retirement from the chamber. When they had gone Jacoby turned to his own juniors above and asked them to leave quietly. He wanted to talk to Samuel alone.

'Your Majesty. Ling threatens and Grat must respond, I urge you.'

'Why have you dismissed everyone?'

'In order to, to put to you a proposal.'

'A proposal of what sort, precisely?'

'Gratian troops must be deployed in the region between Ling and ourselves. They should protect our interest in the Eloth Gold Mines and send out a signal to Ling that we will not be bullied into making any sort of declaration. It will be a peace keeping mission, simply putting troops on duty near our Gold Mines.

I think that we can negotiate an occupancy agreement with Telfon. We threaten Ling in respect of the poor security provided to your Royal person. They will hand over the Jeten Gold Mine for us to control if we push hard enough; it is a very small scale operation compared to Rafe. Then we can bargain with Telfon. We will run Jeten, giving half of its output to Ling, as is usual, and dividing the other half between Grat and Telfon. In effect Telfon will be paying towards our troops being kept in the region. I believe this is the best course of action we can take. '

Samuel was feeling exhausted. All he wanted was for all this to be over so he could go to bed.

'If I agree to this, what must I personally do?'

'Simply declare it is your intention to place Gratian troops near the Eloth Gold Mines. The rest can be left to politics, in which Your Majesty need take no part. I will influence the Cresta to take the necessary steps and we shall place Grat in the strongest position possible.'

Samuel nodded. It seemed reasonable enough to him. When the Cresta were recalled and Lord Ruffus assumed his position once more, Samuel declared his intention and, despite the very troubled look on Lord Ruffus' face, he nodded at the end of the instruction and declared that he considered the issue closed. He would put the Gratian Cresta to work as soon as possible. Samuel thought this was the end of the debate and was on the verge of rising to leave, when Lord Ruffus spoke again.

'One final matter of trifling importance, Your Majesty. It simply seems a pity to close this session without ascertaining your decision on it. We have a madman in this city who claims that he has Kingship over it. His dress is as shabby as his talk, and if we didn't know otherwise this issue would be dismissed as an instance of overconsumption of Old Brine. He has a few people who are willing to listen to the claim he is making on your throne. I shall give way to Adviser Jacoby for his views.'

'Yes, Your Majesty, for the time being I think Lord Ruffus would agree that this man poses no threat to Grat. He seems to be one of those delusionals who exist in all societies. This issue would never have raised itself if the story had not been raised and proved popular in 'The Chariot,' but there you have it.'

Samuel nodded and replied as best he could; keen to leave and nervous still of speaking in this great space.

'Umm, well yes, I agree with what has been said. If, if that is all, we shall let that matter rest and, um, call it at an end for tonight.'

Relief flooded through Samuel as he left the debating chamber. It was such a release. His mother was soon with him, smiling wide with pride. He had done very well, she said, despite the mess of a situation that was unfolding. Samuel managed to smile back through his tiredness before heading straight to his bedchamber for well earned rest.

The next few weeks were very politically turbulent. Gratian troops took their position at the Eloth Gold Mines and details of the occupation agreement with Telfon were hammered out. Winterville was certainly overshadowed by regular Full Sessions in the debating chamber. Advisor Jacoby explained to Samuel that despite his mother's protestations it was felt better that he should not return to Longwhey for the new term. He was needed at the Royal Palace to continue the Full Sessions that needed to be held. The occupancy agreement had been drawn up, but a term insisted on by both Ling, Telfon and even supported by Davish, was that this should be a temporary agreement, subject to review at a Summit. Lord Ruffus pushed for a Summit particularly, as a way to resolve the situation properly, and bring all of the different parties together. Adviser Jacoby looked more irritated than anything else. It was agreed for the Summit to be held on the neutral territory of Davish; neutral in the sense that it held no interest in any Gold Mines. Queen Nashia seemed remarkably compliant with this given the supposed lack of communication from her. Samuel wondered if the explosion had livened her up a bit.

The upshot of all this was that Samuel had no hope of returning to Longwhey before the Summit was held in two months time. It was with sadness then, that he counted down the days until his friends Jack and Bertis returned there. Jack seemed to have recovered well from the Ling incident and put it all down to experience. Mrs. Sorrow was still very fretful about the whole episode but Saffie spoke with her at length and they seemed to come to an understanding regarding the matter.

Bertis hadn't seen Samuel since the awful affair at Longwhey at the end of the first term, but he received notice that she intended to call at the Royal Palace to visit him the day before she returned to Longwhey.

'I'm quite healed,' were the first words she spoke, smiling, when they met.

'I spent the Winterville with mum and dad at the village where they live. It's called Aborglacias, nestled in the mountains around Grat where the air is nice and clean and three tributaries of Moonwater meet.'

Samuel felt very awkward. He knew he had to tell Bertis of his suspicions regarding Mr. Harbury. He was so certain Mr. Harbury wanted him dead. Cautiously he broached the subject.

'Back at Longwhey, before what happened to you, we were heading to the Royal Box. Don't you think the awful prank was intended for me, not for you? Wasn't I the one who was supposed to be in there? Do you remember what Marlow said to us before we went up? Mr. Harbury had been in the Royal Box with him inspecting it. I think he set it up quickly after Marlow left and held us up on the stairs.'

'Do you mean Marlow had something to do with it?'

'No, of course not, but Mr. Harbury did. I'm certain of it.'

A troubled shadow passed over Bertis' healed face.

'I might have been inclined to think your suspicions were correct if I hadn't read 'The Chariot' this morning.'

The Chariot, what had they been saying, Samuel wondered.

'Yesterday a body was found on the rocks in The Deeps near Longwhey. Dame Leria found it and made contact with Moonside. Some Cresta officials went over to investigate and they found the body of Mr. Harbury.'

'Oh no! How did he die?'

'According to The Chariot it was an accident. But I know it wasn't, Samuel. I know the truth.'

'You do Bertis? How? Tell me everything.'

So Bertis Beavitch began to tell the full story of her Winterville, which was essentially the story of another; Mr. Harbury.

After the incident at Longwhey, Bertis had been treated and told she had been very lucky that most of the substance had landed on the floor and not on her. Her face was scarred but it would heal, so long as she rested and applied ointment for the next few weeks.

Her family then brought her home to Aborglacias. She had to rest quite a bit while her face healed and she spend many days in her bedroom there, sleeping. One afternoon she had heard a commotion in the cottage next door to hers. There was a knocking and crashing sound, and someone shouting. She had called her parents and her father, Alfred, listened to her account of what she had heard. Sensible girl as she was he was equally concerned. The cottage next door had been empty for some time, so far as he knew. Alfred Beavitch was quite persuaded to go in straight away and find out what had happened, but Bertis' mother urged caution.

Some time later, Mr. Beavitch entered the property and who should he find in there, bound and gagged, but Mr. Harbury. The pair were vaguely acquainted from the days when Mr. Harbury worked in the Gratian Cresta.

Alfred brought Mr. Harbury into his own cottage and Mrs. Beavitch provided food to the withered acquaintance. Even Bertis had forgotten the tiredness associated with her slow recovery enough to meet him. He looked famished, she had thought, as he ravenously tucked in to what food was provided for him. After food, Alfred had thought it acceptable for Mr. Harbury to tell his story.

At the end of term he had left Longwhey for Winterville, leaving behind Dame Leria as usual. His customary residence out of term time was to be near Moonside but when he heard about events in Ling at the I.L.C. he decided to journey, with all haste, to that country to conduct several investigations and attempt to confirm his early suspicions. To him, this attack had all the hallmarks of 'The Brothership.' As this was his specialist interest, he felt under a duty to investigate what had occurred. The trip to Ling might have proved quite fruitless if it were not for a chance encounter with a freelance flight merchant. He had been asked to bring a woman to Ling in advance of the championships along with a small wooden crate. On her finger he had observed a distinctive emerald ring. What should be found at the site of the explosion, but the very same ring! Earnestly, details were obtained of the address from which the merchant had collected the woman and her lethal cargo. It led to the empty cottage here in Aborglacias, next door to this property. He had entered nervously, been hit violently over the head and knocked out. When he came round he was bound and gagged awkwardly, gradually able to kick up the commotion which had been heard in the Beavitch property. He had only heard two voices whilst inside the cottage next door, as he came round, and those present made good their escape before he was in a state to recognise either.

Alfred entreated Mr. Harbury to stay as long as he liked. Mr. Harbury was eager to be going, however, and as soon as he felt well again, he thanked the Beavitch family for their kindness and left. He was as keen as ever to get back to his research into 'The Brothership'. The final thing he said was that he was close to proving that 'The Brothership' had killed Harold Deksis.

What do you make of it Samuel?'

'It looks to me like 'The Brothership' finally caught up with Mr. Harbury.'

'I have to agree,' replied Bertis miserably.

'Mum and dad are going to be terribly upset when they hear about Mr. Harbury's death. They will feel they should have done so much more. They left it up to Mr. Harbury to sort out what had happened. It was his business, wasn't it?'

Bertis seemed to be looking for reassurance and Samuel provided it delicately.

'They will have to put someone else in charge at Longwhey now,' Samuel mused.

'The Chariot expects one of the current Professors to be promoted.'

Samuel had no desire to detain Bertis any longer than necessary. Longwhey beckoned for her in a way which it did not for him. He also had a lot which he needed to give thought to. It seemed he must have been wrong about Mr. Harbury. Yet how could this be the case when it was only he that had the opportunity to set the awful trap at Longwhey. These questions seemed likely to remain unanswered for the time being, at least.

Samuel met Lord Ruffus on the stairs as he wandered the Royal Palace. After enquiring about the latest news regarding the 'Ling Crisis' as it had been titled, he broached a different vexation.

'If I wanted to find out a lot about my father, how could I best accomplish it? The Chariot archives hardly seem a suitable source for the truth.'

Lord Ruffus let out a low laugh, and looked pleased to offer a solution.

'Your Majesty should consult your father's Oro-fice. It is there for such a purpose after all. Start on the fiftieth-floor galleries; I think it is somewhere around there.'

Samuel nodded his thanks and only a little while later headed to the part of the Royal Palace to which he had been directed.

The first of the fiftieth-floor galleries was a cold, stony affair. The first Oro-fice alcove was blackened, as though it had been burnt out, so Samuel avoided it and looked to the next. A candle was alight inside so that it seemed an ordinary enough affair, and a sensible place to start. Samuel pushed his head into the alcove and waited for something to happen. He had watched various people doing this from time to time, both officials from the Cresta and Royal Advisers. Despite this, he could not remember ever having done so himself. Out of the flame erupted a twisted face. Samuel braced himself from an inclination to recoil and focussed on the face. The eyebrows where black and bushy, the jaw line strong and determined.

'Who are you?' he breathed. The face twitched and as the mouth moved in reply small flames burst through it, quite harmless to Samuel, but visually fascinating.

'The late Sir Bertin Flint, father of Lady Flint.'

In his voice Samuel could detect the same tone of finesse which graced the accent of Lady Flint and her family. In the recesses of his mind he could hear her daughter, Rose, talking; the tone was melodic and soothing.

'I am sorry to bother you. I was looking for my father, Harold Deksis? Do you know?'

'The last time I saw the great King, His Majesty was giving council in the debating chamber. It was as he spoke that my heart at last gave way. Ah blissful relief! At least I gave of my final breath in the presence of Harold.'

Samuel nodded and withdrew without ending the conversation. It was urgent to move on. The open doorway leading on to the next gallery beckoned to Samuel. He assumed his father had died some time after Bertin Flint, so it would make sense to go on.

A total of ten Oro-ficese were cut into this wall. Samuel took his chance and took the fifth one along. The flame was transformed again, this time into the face of a woman. She spoke with a gasping flaming breath like the last Oro-fice occupant he had met.

'Eddisa Beavitch, discoverer of the Eddisa Paradox. How may I help?'

Well at least she sounds enthusiastic, thought Samuel.

'Do you know of Harold Deksis?'

'Why yes! I went to Longwhey with His Majesty! And what a great man he was! So much fun. It was sad to leave like I had to. I would have enjoyed the rest of his reign, I think. My illness was sadly unavoidable and I died like my mother before me. Many have wondered why the ones we love always seem to die first. I did too. Until I realised that they do not die first. It is just that they are the ones we notice first. They tear at our hearts when they depart and take a little something of us with them. It never comes back. Be careful Samuel, for you have many to loose. Harold will be in the next gallery, third along. How is that for a paradox?'

Sadly Samuel withdrew, smiling. He felt some connection with Eddisa which was both terrifying and comforting.

The third gallery was grander and larger than its predecessors. Samuel knew just what to do. The third Oro-fice came quickly to life.

Harold Deksis looked after death as he had in life; a noble and attractive man of strength and integrity. His voice was deep but tremored ever so slightly as he spoke.

'My son? Yes it is. And I am Harold Deksis.'

'Umm, hello. I am glad to meet you at last.'

'One day I intend to speak to my son properly again, but for now this must suffice. How may I be of service to you Samuel?'

'What, how much exactly, do you know of The Brothership?'

Harold's brow glowed and sparked alight. The sparking seemed almost to be an expression of worry.

'I know almost as little of The Brothership as any man alive. Eddisa Beavitch believes it exists but even she knows no more. It has always been moving, chasing; like some deathly leach which we pull along with us as the days pass. It is the weight upon the shoulder and the drag in the leg. Maybe it is a part of the heart and, like the dark side of a moon, better left undisturbed. It stalks somewhere in the dusty corners of our minds. It is a wonder, then, of irony that the truth should be thus; the way this day your feet have been led amounts to what can save our head.'

Samuel had not heard Saffie approach while his attention was consumed with his father's Oro-fice. As he at last withdrew, he was more than a little startled to find her there. She looked terribly sad he thought, and a little depressed.

'It was nice to see you talking to him Samuel.'

'Can he really hear me?'

Saffie paused and clenched her jaw as she gently shook her head.

'No Samuel. An Oro-fice is not a person, as I told you once, long ago. They are just memories, reflections only, of the great people who have chosen to leave these reminders here so that, even after death, they may influence events in this City as they once did in life. They have no knowledge of what comes after them. An Oro-fice has no sense of feelings and that is why you must be careful in acting upon what it says. They serve no ones interest but their own. This is a castle of Kings, not of men, Samuel. You are a King, not a man and so you must act as such; blameless in the sight of your subjects for any decisions you make, whatever an Oro-fice or a newspaper might tell you. Make your own decisions and do not follow the wishes of the deceased or the media or anyone else.'

Upon this rather ominous note, Saffie Deksis turned to leave Samuel to his own devices. For many hours he pondered his father's words, resolving to follow his mother's advice and never personally use an Oro-fice again. He had been led today by a route of inquisition, so that must be the meaning of the riddle his father had spoken. Be inquisitive. It didn't seem to make much sense. And then The Brothership. Well that remained as out of reach as ever.

-- CHAPTER EIGHT --

Mysteries of Mother

Samuel had led awake in his bedchamber for hours. This was not the first night he had done so recently but it was one of the worst. A great weight seemed to press down upon him as soon as he began to relax. Perhaps it was his conscience he thought. Since the Ling Crisis nothing seemed to have made complete sense to him. Were they doing the right thing by playing such an artful game of politics? Was it right to play politics with land and lives? His Advisers and all of the Lords seemed adamant that Grat was to rise once again as a great city, to take back its kingdom and reclaim the lands which had been lost over time. Equally, as the Lamp-maker had prophesied long ago, Samuel, the king from under the mountain, was to be at the apex of this restoration. With the mines under its control, Grat would be rich like it had once been; rich as it could now only dare to dream about. The Borrow-Ways would boom with trade and prosperity. But at what cost was this still worthwhile? They were to take terrible risks to make such gains. Samuel knew he was risking the lives of his people and could only hope that they would reap the rewards in the future.

It was the early hours of the morning when Samuel was first made aware of it. He heard some shuffling which sounded distant, and not in itself alarming, as the inhabitants of the Royal Palace often moved around late at night and servants would often enter the Royal quarters to clean and work. What was unusual was the sound which followed. A violent retching noise which, whilst muffled, was distinct enough to grab his attention. Samuel pulled himself into more of an upright position and heard the noise once again. It sounded as though the person was winded and terribly ill. He was ready to get out of bed and investigate himself when there was a sharp rap on his door. Blearily he forced himself out of bed and threw on a thick gown. The person at the door rapped sharply once gain. Samuel opened the door to find a pale faced woman whom he recognised as one of the night servants who was more usually to be found cleaning downstairs at this hour. She would not normally dare to even look at him; few staff would. As he stood there, blinking in the hallway, she bowed quickly without speaking, but the speed with which she started to talk betrayed her urgency.

'Your Majesty, your mother has been taken ill tonight, and the Royal Physician is currently on his way. She did not wish you to be woken and alarmed but it was determined to be unavoidable.'

Samuel nodded, taking it all in as quickly as he could. He did not feel frantic with worry. His mother was, as far as he knew, in good health, although he had seen little of her in recent months as he had been kept occupied with endless meetings and debates about affairs of state. He asked to see his mother, but the servant advised him to refrain as it was apparently against his mother's wishes. Samuel could see little point in returning to bed and took it upon himself to go and wait outside her chambers until the doctor arrived.

He waited as patiently as he could and the servants brought him some blankets for warmth as the stone passages were not well heated at night. The Royal Physician was currently a Dr. Cass. The days of Dr. Flint from Samuel's childhood seemed so very distant. Dr. Flint had taken quite early retirement from the post but he had been dearly missed, especially by Samuel's mother. Samuel also could not summon up a similar affection for the succession of physicians which had taken Dr. Flint's place.

Dr. Cass eventually arrived; dressed in a smart dark blue gown. He bowed to Samuel before entering to tend to his patient. Several servants had gathered outside the chamber equally anxious to hear news. Despite not doubting the genuine sincerity of their intentions they grated on his nerves somewhat at this time of night and he eventually sent them away, mainly so he could listen at the door in silence, hoping to hear something of the conversation taking place inside. As with all such snooping, it proved fairly counterproductive as the words which Samuel could gather were pretty disjointed and confusing at best. Eventually he gave up listening, resolving to wait until the Royal Physician emerged.

After what felt like an eternity Samuel could hear the voices in the chamber rising, signalling the end of the examination. Sure enough, the door soon opened and Dr. Cass emerged.

'Your Majesty, I have conducted a full examination but I cannot at this stage determine the cause of the discomfort. In the morning I shall return to make some more enquiries and attempt to reach some further conclusions.'

'Is it serious?' enquired Samuel.

'The severity is also hard to determine at this stage as the symptoms are not of themselves conclusive, so we shall simply have to wait and see. I did not wish to issue any medication which could obscure the root of the problem.'

Samuel thanked Dr. Cass for his response and returned uneasily to his own bedchamber. He was concerned. Perhaps the kitchen standards had not been adequate lately. There would be severe punishments if he found that to be the case. He had felt a little queer himself after that froge cake the other day, perhaps it was that. Such thoughts dragged him into sullied dreams of giant fish and bountiful meals which turned into spiky creatures just as soon as you swallowed them.

Samuel awoke in the morning to torrential rain which pounded the large windows around the room. The sky was a dull and depressing grey which did little to lift his mood. Breakfast was brought to him as usual, although it was a little late which he snapped about and in response received the customary humble apology which did little to pacify his difficult mood.

A series of meetings awaited him as usual, the first of which was to take place in the debating chamber with Lord Ruffus and Adviser Jocoby. It was a 'review of policy and public reception', the grand title afforded to a debate about the contents of 'The Chariot' this week. Its usual brand of patriotism was masking some underlying tendencies to question Royal decisions which had alarmed Lord Ruffus considerably.

Lord Ruffus was a gruff old man. Bearded and loud he seemed to get through the day's work on his bottle of Old Brine which he kept with him everywhere, and consumption of which was indicated by his reddened faced and heightened temper. Samuel was always impressed by the restraint he showed in his Royal presence which it was always evident was achieved with great effort. The same grace, courtesy and deference were not to be found in the relationship between Ruffus and Jacoby. Ruffus made little attempt to mask his dislike of Advisers and heatedly argued against any suggestions to pacify the media in the face of greater concerns of office.

Having discussed concerns over speculation on the continued deployment of Gratian troops in the region between Ling and the City of Grat they turned to discuss the main story which 'The Chariot' had been carrying. Lord Ruffus opened a copy of the paper in front of him and prodded it into life. 'The Chariot' seemed to dislike the wet weather as much as

Samuel did, for it was distinctly slow in relaying the various news items. A shabby looking man rose up from the page and spoke these words:

'My time is coming. A time when those who abide in the shadows will have to step forward into the light to be counted. Current wrongs shall be put right, the dead shall be revenged and power will be restored to me.'

It was that man again, the one who had been discussed in the very first debate that Samuel had attended in this chamber after the Ling Crisis. This time Samuel was actually ready to say something. Gone were his stuttering inhibitions of old; this was a new found confidence that pronounced itself with a confident, fluent airing of views.

'These are the words of a delusional madman. Typical of The Chariot to publish something like this and treat it as valid propaganda. I trust you will not reproach me, Lord Ruffus, for this outburst, but my birthright is this throne and it has always been. Jacoby, you too, I'm sure, can see that it cannot be denounced by some fool who wanders the streets spreading messages like this. I pity those who listen for their deafness. They should set me as the centre of their universe and if not me, then why not themselves. That has always seemed the perfect recipe for contentment to me, even for those who should care to rebel against Royalty. Do not then set up another 'king' to rule over them. For who can then check his subjective actions?'

Adviser Jacoby was quick to lend his support, which Samuel was pleased to observe in such clear terms.

'Your Majesty, I quite agree, quite agree with you. It seems clear that this man is nothing but a trouble stirrer. We have ignored him before and he has gone away for a while. We should ignore him again and again. And then we should find a way to keep him quiet for his own good.'

Lord Ruffus was quick to interject as usual.

'Far be it for me to be seen to dissent to Your Majesty's will, but we must let the man say as he chooses, that is his right is it not?'

Adviser Jacoby was quick with his response.

'For those who fail to sing from the same hymn sheet as everyone else, life can be made awfully difficult, short of punishing a man. For example, who would wish to marry a man who could not carry gold? His value would be worthless.'

Ruffus was quick to retort.

'I think, Your Majesty, that Adviser Jocoby is quite wild here in his suggestion that any such measure would affect this man or change his message. From what we know he lives as a hermit! I think being an unattractive wedding prospect would be to aid, not restrict, such a person.'

Samuel was ready to conclude this pointless debate and to do so he said,

'We must indeed wait and see what happens. Only then can we determine the correct course of action.'

Lord Ruffus was pushing his calm and polite exterior this morning as he angrily muttered, 'which is not to stop him speaking.'

Samuel let the comment go. Lord Ruffus was always defensive over issues such as controlling free speech and free will. Adviser Jacoby on the other hand saw the matter as different shades of grey, an approach which for the present time suited Samuel.

Over the next few days the debate about keeping Gratian troops outside the city was to rumble on. Telfon sent a delegation of negotiators to alleviate the situation which of course had the opposite effect, with Ling claiming the proposal for talks stank of double handed actions. Little seemed likely to change. The mines were working at half capacity as before, with the majority of the produce passing to Ling, but some was retained under the occupancy agreement that had been negotiated with Telfon. At least that continued to function and alleviate the rising unease at the cost of keeping large numbers of Gratian troops ready for war. Time and time again Samuel stressed the peace keeping role of the troops in the region. It was not war, but the protection of the city and the worldwide economy. The more Samuel said it, the less he found himself believing the mantra, but there was little he could do to advance the position except to issue the usual reassurances which Adviser Jacoby was ever keen to enforce, and 'The Chariot' ever keen to bash.

There had been some news regarding his mother's health or rather the lack of it. She was still unwell and Dr. Cass seemed to have reached a complete blank as to the cause. Samuel, in his exasperation, decided to get in contact personally with Dr. Flint and ask the great man to return to the Royal Palace for the first time in years to give a second, and Samuel hoped more conclusive, diagnosis. Samuel was going to have a message sent directly to the Flints but a letter reached him first informing him that Roseilia Flint begged a meeting with His Majesty in a few days. Samuel hadn't seen Rose in ages. Lady Flint had, herself, seen deteriorating health, part of the reason for Dr. Flint's early retirement. Its acceleration had detained Rose for longer and longer periods of time until her visits to the Royal Palace had stopped altogether and her correspondence had become very infrequent. Such a letter from Rose thus caught Samuel's attention and he could not help but wonder as to the purpose of the meeting.

The date set arrived pretty quickly and as soon as Samuel was relived from his arduous duties in the debating chamber, where that morning they had been trying to discern the safest way to deal with a new Davish blockade on all carpets of Lingian origin, he hurried down the huge staircase to one of the quieter corridors in the Royal Palace where he hoped to find an empty room in which to meet. He found a servant and told her to fetch up Rose when she arrived. Samuel found a majestic room which he did not think he had been in before with a grand fireplace and large tapestry as the perfect setting in which to host this informal meeting. More servants hurried in to set the fire alight and soon it really was a roaring affair. Just the tonic to lift and dispel the feeling of lingering depression which the continued wet weather provided.

Rose arrived with characteristic shy smile and the warm room seemed to Samuel a little warmer with her in it. After enquiring as to the health of Mrs. Flint and hearing that it was as good as could be expected, Samuel spoke of his own concerns for his mother, Rose nodding with concern at the difficult diagnosis. She kindly informed Samuel that Dr. Flint would be only too glad to make a visit, only too pleased for a break from caring for his wife. This was a duty which, according to Rose, could prove rather tiresome given Lady Flint's temperament. Rose then began to tell of the true reason for her visit. It was about Dixi, the recent incarnation of their wood elf who was apparently grating on Lady Flint's tender nerves too greatly and even Rose was finding that she was getting under foot. Rose was wondering if Samuel would admit her to the Royal Palace staff. Samuel said he would be delighted to make this exception in the circumstances. They didn't really need any new staff at the Royal Palace but he felt that an extra hand would not be unwelcome, and Dixi was apparently a little more skilled than previously. No doubt an impatient Lady Flint had seen to that. The pair ended their informal meeting on good terms, Rose promising that she would give her father the message and that he would attend as soon as possible.

Rose was as good as her word and that evening Dr. Flint was to be found attending Samuel's mother. He emerged from her chamber late in the evening and Samuel anxiously met with him in a quiet upper room at the Royal Palace. He looked grey as he entered Samuel thought, tired at best. Evidently the burden of providing constant care to his wife was heavy. Samuel made a note to offer greater Royal assistance to the family, although he knew that such an offer would never be accepted.

Samuel was not used to hearing his mother referred to by her first name so he jarred a little each time Dr. Flint used it.

'Your Majesty, I have worked hard to examine your mother, Saffie, thoroughly and believe I now have a diagnosis of her condition.'

'Condition, Dr. Flint?'

'Yes Your Majesty, I believe it is a condition because I have found several abnormalities.'

'And what condition, pray?'

'I believe that Saffie is suffering from a form of extenuated delifus.'

Samuel could not really be sure how to react to this because he had no real comprehension of what it meant, which appeared to become evident to Dr. Flint who nodded and reached into his pocket, from which he produced an aged booklet.

'This is not the most up-to-date I'm afraid, but I don't think the content has changed much anyway. It is what I used to issue in these circumstances. Provides an explanation of the treatments available for delifus.'

Samuel began to leaf through the booklet. It was arranged alphabetically by the prefix attached to 'delifus.' Samuel flicked past anoxis-delifus, treated very successfully with a large dose of quells and deterior-delifus which was accompanied with a helpful diagram of what looked like a horrific procedure.

'Your Majesty...'

As Samuel raised his hand he continued to look at the booklet, causing Dr. Flint to halt against his better judgement. Samuel then came across it.

''Extenuated-delifus,' no successful cure known. Life extended by hermodgony. Effect varies.'

Samuel looked up slowly and Dr. Flint looked ready to drop his calm professionalism, but only for a moment. He managed a smile.

'It doesn't look very good does it?'

Samuel just stared at him.

'I have started Saffie on a course of hermodgony which Dr. Cass will continue. It is not an easy treatment, Your Majesty, but Saffie is keen to try.'

Samuel wanted Dr. Flint to leave. He rose from his seat and showed him to the door without saying much beyond a gruff goodbye. Dr. Flint seemed to understand his coldness and hastened away. Samuel then turned and strolled to his mother's chambers. The journey there seemed to take an unexpectedly long time but he was glad to have a chance to think. How much had he missed being so busy fighting diplomatic wars with other countries? The signs of severity must have been there before, but he must have been bind to them. This time he would look upon his mother with opened eyes, seeing what he had not before. He knocked her door and it gently swung open. He headed in. He could see her lying on a white four poster; the ivory drapes a similar colour to her face. She did look sick, thin he thought. And her smile looked forced in a way it had never done before.

'Water?' she mouthed at him, smiling gently.

Samuel looked around for a glass and upon finding one proceeded to fill it from a tap at a nearby basin. When he turned back to her she was still smiling but it was more of a grimace which displayed a wave of temporary discomfort. Samuel reached for her hand and she gave it to him. He prayed inwardly for her, that she would have the strength to carry on fighting this. The water was gratefully received and Samuel could tell from the beads of sweat which ran from her forehead that she would need to drink often.

Dr. Flint did not return to the Royal Palace but Rose did periodically. They would sit each side of Samuel's mother's bed while she slept, which she did increasingly as the pain increased. Rose was also marvellous when she was sick as she often was and Samuel couldn't bear it himself. The servants were pretty good on the whole but as time went by their attention seemed distracted. They seemed to sense a deterioration which Samuel was not willing to accept. Dr. Cass eventually called Samuel to a meeting with his Mother. They sat by her bed as Dr. Cass explained the situation. Hermodgony was no longer providing much of a remedy and he was keen to stop it as soon as possible since it was causing more harm than good. Saffie would thus stop taking half of the medication she was on and Dr. Cass would do what he could to control the pain. Saffie nodded calmly at the news for it was as she had expected. Samuel followed her lead and thanked Dr. Cass for all that he had done.

In the days that followed things did get worse. Affairs of state were neglected and Samuel left Lord Ruffus and Adviser Jacoby to argue it out over the different strategies to be adopted. Samuel wished he had left the pair to it earlier and made the best of his mothers company while she had been in better health. He was comforted by the fact that even if this would have been better health, it would still have been tainted by illness.

As she became weaker Samuel spent more time beside her, taking his meals in her bedchamber as and when the servants brought them up. Days and nights began to melt into an all consuming insomnia which showed no sign of abating. Food too was neglected by a body which had no concept of meal times. Samuel toiled hard, fetching drinks and tending to various other needs. Dr Cass popped in periodically and was increasingly bringing with him a contingent of helpers as Saffie's condition became worse.

It was the dead of night in Saffie's bedchamber and the first time Samuel's wearied body had been at rest for many hours. The gentle sound of rain hitting the windows of the Royal Palace provided a steady rhythm like a heartbeat. He had pulled back the curtains earlier so they could both enjoy the majestic view out over the city as night approached. The misty rain-lashed sprawl simmered in a glow that seemed magnified by the rain that hit the panes. He looked at his mother. The fragile candle light softened her pale, papery skin. Her face was so gaunt; her skull pulled tight by her skin and her thinning hair no longer summoned memories of the days when it was long and shiny. He looked towards her beautify eyes, long stripped of their eyelashes. They no longer sparkled as they once did, now appearing sunken and retracted. Samuel slid back in the seat beside her bed and allowed his head to roll backwards to rest, looking upwards, like his mother's on the bed. They were each staring skywards, and Samuel was quite sure they were looking beyond the grey ceiling and the swirling clouds that must be above it, penetrating right into the depths of the heavens. In his mind Samuel tried to look up even further. He was awed by the fragility of life and the vastness of space, thinking of how all the people he had ever met would fit into just a tiny patch of that sky in his mind.

Samuel felt for her hand. He knew that she couldn't feel him. But it didn't matter. He was there for her as he had promised he would be. He lived in that moment truly for the first time in years, and prayed it would last forever. But it could not.

Saffie Deksis died during the night when her rough and heavy breathing gradually gave way to silence. She never saw the mournful sunrise of the morning.

Dr. Cass had been in the room several times during the night, although Samuel could not remember quite how many, and certainly had no real perception of the time at which the visits occurred. The servants probably did not dare enter in the morning which was the reason Dr. Cass called Samuel to leave the room for breakfast. Samuel knew he did not want to eat. But he knew that he needed to do something. He was reluctant to leave, but there was nothing to be gained from staying. His mother was gone. As simple as that. Waiting around wasn't going to bring her back.

Breakfast was horrible and tasteless. Samuel could not remember managing more than a few mouthfuls. He had remained more or less composed in front of Dr. Cass; not intentionally, but it was hard to feel emotional in front of a calm physician. His composure was not to last however, shattered by the arrival of a highly emotional Rose. They left breakfast to head down to the Orangery, perhaps thinking that somewhere green would remind them of life when all that consumed their thoughts was death.

Samuel felt his eyes streaming as Rose hugged him, covered in a wave of emotion which gripped at her heart. Samuel felt like he was bound mercilessly, praying and kneeling before some great alter, hands grasped, stomach retching violently with his wails. It was cold in the Orangery but he could feel sweat pouring from his face. He wished to make himself as small and unnoticeable as the dust on the Orangery floor. What shame he felt. No shame like this before, never, shame, shame, absolute shame. Terror, blinding terror, flashes of white and black and red, pure terror. His blood was alive and boiling, cursing through his brain, building up like some great internal precipitate and breaking forth in the form of effervescence through his scalp. Pain, such pain. Long pale windows and a great stone floor. Samuel felt himself sinking onto it with Rose. His hands were touching those stones. He could feel the coldness and lifelessness in them, and wished to be just like them, to become as cold and as inanimate. He wished with all his heart that life itself would leave him. There was no desire to go on, to go forward, and to know or get to know anyone. He wanted to be all consumed by himself and his personal grief.

He felt that he had lost everything that was worth having and wanted to hit that floor hard despite the preposterous irrationality. But still, it would be worth it. Just to hit it so hard to drain him of emotion. He wanted to do the most irrational thing, because to him there was nothing rational left. Everything, he had lost everything. There was absolutely nothing left. Except him. And what made him think he was so down right important.

So he knelt there and the pressure in his head was released in the form of fresh tears, splashing down onto his cheeks. The cold grip of the stone flowed within him so that he was powerless to move.

Rose whispered hoarsely in his ear, 'The most beautiful and brave always die first. They face death without fear but instead with optimism and anticipation. This is what you will find at their heart. Such people die a beautiful death.'

It didn't stop their sobbing but it did order their emotions for which Samuel was grateful, and when eventually they left, they did so feeling considerably better than they had done earlier. Samuel wasn't sure where he was going. He headed to the debating chamber and sat down. It was empty; void of its usual charisma and power. It seemed such a fruitless and pointless place. As Samuel walked out of the room he caught sight of Lord Ruffus who, in turn, caught sight of Samuel only moments later. Samuel was surprised to see his usually stiff and hardened eyes red and swollen. Lord Ruffus bowed and turned away, apparently uncomfortable at being seen publicly in this state.

Lord Ruffus was the start of a wave of emotion within and outside the Palace. From the vast window pane in his bedchamber Samuel could see an assortment of thousands of creatures and humans gathered outside the gates of the Royal Palace. They stood there taking part in an emotional vigil. Inside the Royal Palace Samuel was greeted with an endless stream of condolences from staff and foreign envoys. Both Davish and Telfon sent messages of condolence while only Ling remained silent. The wave of patriotism in the city was reflected by the headlines in 'The Chariot' which ran with titles like 'Remorseless Ling Shows its True Colours' and 'Obscene Insolence.' Ling eventually bowed to the pressure and issued a statement expressing belated condolences which it put down to 'internal division' which, whilst potentially true, were unlikely to be reflective of the true division of opinion between the top and bottom of Lingian society.

Samuel for his part was utterly exhausted by the whole process. While his own private world was falling apart the last thing he wished was for the outside world and his public life to fall apart too. He had, as a most pressing concern, to sort out the funeral arrangements. Lord Ruffus was especially helpful here and took the King through the usual procedure in the circumstances.

'Normally there will be a procession with the coffin in the Royal Carriage, through the streets and it will make the long journey by road to Lappings End. There, the Borrow-Ways give way to a faster flowing river which eventually collapses deep underground beneath the sandy desert below.'

'How long does the journey normally take?'

'I would put it at a couple of days, given the speed of the Royal Carriage and the amount of public interest which is sure to slow down its progress.'

Samuel was dreading the journey. He was to follow behind the Royal Carriage partly on foot and partly on horse back. Rose came to visit him the day before he was due to make the trip. Samuel was so full of nerves he had just been physically sick himself. Rose was, as expected, very concerned. It was she who came up with the suggestion first. What if, instead of following behind the coffin, he made his own way down to Lappings End in private? If no one knew, no one could follow and bother him. Samuel called up Lord Ruffus to discuss the possibility with Rose.

'The only way in which this would work is if Your Majesty will be prepared to take an unlikely craft. If it is too conspicuous you will be trailed and followed by half the city.'

Samuel thought to himself and the perfect plan formed in his mind. He could travel with Mole and Mr. Shabbers on their vessel, for none could be so unlikely a Royal craft. It was an idea which he put to Jack Sorrow when he came to visit, and Jack immediately leapt at the idea. Originally they discussed the possibility of Jack coming too by boat but it was eventually decided that the vessel was really only large enough to carry three people comfortably. Jack promised to follow the Royal Carriage by road. Samuel was a bit nervous of travelling with two traders of which he knew little, but Jack always spoke so highly of them both and he had been so taken with them, especially Mole when he had met him years ago that his anxiety was eased considerably.

Early the next morning, just as the City was awakening, Jack met Samuel in the Palace grounds and they slipped out by a side entrance. The crowds at the front were still immense, but around the side things were as quiet as could be expected. Jack had provided Samuel with some old clothes to make him less noticeable and presumably this was why they managed to pass through a group of mourning wood elves that were holding hands by the roadside. Samuel wondered if Dixi was among them; it was impossible to tell.

'Must have come down with their families' said Jack, 'The good and the great families of Grat all out for your mother's funeral.'

Samuel smiled. He liked Jack's relaxed attitute. It had a calming and pacifying effect on his worries in this most awful of circumstances. Jack managed to lead Samuel down a series of alley ways, keeping away from Moon-Water Lake which was sure to be crawling with people. Eventually they made it to the Borrow-Ways and a narrow path through the wetlands led them to a secluded mooring spot.

'I always know where to find them, you just have to know where to look,' said Jack gamily.

Samuel nodded in response. The small vessel came into view just as Samuel remembered it. It was piled possibly even higher than it had been before with the oddest cargo. Mole leaped from it onto the bank as he heard them approaching, still wearing his green waistcoat and bowing dramatically low to the ground.

'Your Majesty it is ours greatest pleasure to be havings you riding on 'The Shanty' downriver with us. We is very heartily honoured.'

Samuel managed a weak smile. He wasn't really in the mood for Mole and his amusing approach to mundane language but even now, when his heart felt as heavy as this, it could not help but cheer him a little. Mr. Shabbers was as quiet as usual while Samuel made his way on board. Mole scrabbled to pull various goods out of the way to create a clear path to the vessel's interior, nearly knocking himself overboard in the process as a massive bear head came free from its coupling and bowled down onto the main deck.

Inside, the vessel was just as messy and Samuel had to agree that it would never be guessed a King was going to travel like this. He liked the unconventional aspect of the decision to journey in this way.

The goodbye to Jack was brief as he was keen to set off to join his family. Samuel settled down inside the vessel with a lantern wobbling light down on him from overhead and the shafts of light from the covering casting an uneven pattern through the dusty air. It was a little damp down here and Samuel felt sure he could smell rotting fish. He didn't mind smelling it, so long as he didn't have to eat it. Mole joined Samuel inside for the first part of the journey while Mr. Shabbers punted. Mole was pretty silent for a change, filled with a sombre reverence which Samuel did not think became him.

After several hours in the cramped conditions Samuel was itching to go out on deck to stretch his legs but he was told to stay in the berth for fear of being recognised on deck. It would be alright, Mole said, once they made it further down the river, maybe by evening. Inside the vessel it was getting quite warm. Samuel had been surprised by the change in the weather, from the wet and cold of the past few weeks to this warmth and clear skies. The weather in Grat was never very predictable, except perhaps in the summer.

As evening approached, Samuel still didn't feel at all hungry. Mole offered him some bread which he tried to eat, but it tasted like cardboard; dull and unappetising. Eventually Mr. Shabbers called Mole up on deck, and he soon returned to say they had finished travelling for the day and it was safe to come outside.

Samuel was surprised to find just how wobbly his legs were as he stood up, unsure of whether it was due to his own upset or being on the water. He stumbled out onto the deck, the sunset hitting him square in the eyes and blinding him momentarily. Mole grabbed him to steady him and prevent him falling over. Samuel returned inside the vessel for a short while to avoid the brightness of the light making him feel more nauseous and unwell. He emerged onto the deck once again a little later; finding it more comfortable now that the sun was on the verge of bowing below the horizon.

They gathered on deck; Mole, Mr. Shabbers and Samuel. Samuel was sitting between the pair and all three were trailing their legs in the amber sun-brushed waters, with Mole perched necessarily further forward for his shorter dark feet to brush the silky surface. Samuel made the most of this time, aware that the lingering warmth and light was to be enjoyed before the swift arrival of night. The calm evening air rested, as though a little weary, upon the cheeks, its days work almost at an end and the endless rushing and busyness behind it. The waters were still, rippling only loosely as the trio swung their feet in them.

'Mole, ask King Samuel if he wants some Old Brine!'

Mole cursed fondly, 'Yous can sure as gets it yourself Shabbers, but you knows I'll run along if I must.'

Mole hastened lazily away into the ramshackle barge, leaving Samuel and Mr. Shabbers alone. Samuel could see for once just how old he was. His trousers were rolled up above two sturdy knees. A well worn face framed broad shoulders but the face told of the years and the broadness could not mask a mark of youthful strength that was very much in decline. The face itself was sheltered beneath a whiskery unshaven exterior.

As Samuel turned away from Mr. Shabbers he stared out complacently into the reeds that they were gently approaching. Mr. Shabbers lit a pipe which he had produced from his pocket and began slowly smoking and swaying, causing the vessel to rise and fall rhythmically in the current, a rhythm which he followed in song:

'As the days grow old and the nights draw in,
Alone we sit on the brink of something.
And we wait in the rushes till the wild wind hushes,
Aware of something we were not before.'

Mr. Shabbers paused for a hearty puff on his pipe and a plume of satisfied smoke was dispelled to loiter in the air.

'It seems we grow older but never the wiser,
We all know the truth but it never grows kinder,
All look for love but never to find her.
So better alone we wait by the shore.'

Samuel thought he might be ready to stop, as words of such length and poetic quality from a man as shy as Mr. Shabbers was rare indeed.

'The moon it was rising, the soft silver gliding,
Across twilight waters, the night that I saw her.
Sweet mistress I knew her by the soft winds that blew her,
And that's when I knew her from somewhere before.'

He paused again and continued,

'I'd oft heard her crying, occasionally sighing,
But never had noticed it there all along.
And when at last I saw her, I fell down before her,
And bid her draw near before she was gone.'

Mr. Shabbers continued to hum as the darkening waters gently lapped and the barge murmured back in reply. Samuel caught a glimpse of it first as a darker black, darker than the inky waters dredged of sunlight now and running cooler beneath his feet. With majestic grace she broke the surface, quiet and controlled, purposely leaning towards the barge, just as Mr Shabbers leant forwards. It was an Otter, although difficult to make out now in the sudden dusk. She touched Mr. Shabbers on the nose affectionately before shooting quickly and playfully away to hide beneath the surface as quickly as she had arisen.

'You see now why I like the river Your Majesty. And evenings like this.'

'You know her?' enquired Samuel.

'Hmm, many years. We never speak but we often meet. I think she likes me to sing.'

Mr. Shabbers hummed again to himself deep in thought, a man that was hard to understand, and least of all through words.

Mole returned shortly later and handed round the Old Brine as promised. Samuel drank in the taste of it. A little bitter but meaningful. A bit like life.

The next day was uneventful and mainly spent inside the vessel as they entered an area of greater trading activity and thus an area with the greater inherent danger of being recognised. Both nights in the vessel were better than Samuel would have imagined they would be, the gentle rocking of the boat providing a sort of paternalistic comfort. This did nothing however to meet his third day anxieties.

They were to meet the Royal Carriage at a slipway in the early evening. From there the coffin would be floated out into the river and Samuel was to join the waders in guiding the coffin through the shallow but unstoppable waters. Samuel longed to pace on deck in his anxiety, but managed to quell the urge until it overwhelmed him. He still felt a little uneasy on his feet still, although he had found his sea legs the longer he had been on board. Emerging on deck Samuel found the surrounding waters to be pretty void of other vessels, but his main obstacle was the lack of space to pace. He had to content himself with leaning against a side rail and tapping his arm against it. It gave him some small relief at least. He could feel his heart beating fast and his palms were damp and moist. At times his right leg would tremble uncontrollably until he forced himself to remain still.

Mole was punting at one end of the boat and Mr. Shabbers was smoking once again at the other. Neither seemed to have noticed him so Samuel was happy to stay out in the open. An uneasy breeze furled at the water, causing it to eddy around the boat. Gone was the calmness of the evenings which Samuel had enjoyed before. The water seemed to understand the way in which Samuel was feeling.

The banks on either side began to widen and Samuel was certain they were leaving the Borrow-Ways behind them. There were fewer reeds at the sides of the water, a far less suitable waterscape for trading on boats.

There were a few vessels which passed theirs on the other side of the boat but Samuel kept his head down, caring little whether he was or wasn't recognised. He felt a strong sombre mood settle upon him, where time and space drifted out of focus completely. He was dragged out of it by a call from Mole. They had reached the landing slipway before the Royal Carriage. Samuel was glad not to have to face it and the coffin straight away.

He disembarked the boat and made his way onto land for the first time in three long days. It felt perhaps more unsteady beneath his legs than the vessel did at present.

The arrival of the carriage was preceded by the sound of marching and baying. A herd of stallions, their flanks heaving in the afternoon sunlight galloped ahead of the rest of the procession which was mainly behind the carriage itself. Behind them a group of centaurs rode in equal splendour. The two groups came to halt some way from the water and bowed their heads to Samuel. He thought for a moment that the whites of the stallion's eyes looked red, as though they had been crying, but he shook off the idea. A centaur stepped forward from the group slowly, head still downcast.

'Your Majesty, we await your Royal instruction and shall follow it in obedience.'

Samuel smiled. This was a beautiful creature, no mistake about it. So willing to submit when the slightest ripple of a single muscle could so easily amount to disobedience if he willed it. Samuel motioned to the side of the road where a grassy area opened up before dense woodland took its place.

'We shall wait in this area for the Royal Carriage to arrive.'

It took some time for the Royal Carriage to come into view. Before the coffin was anything like visible Samuel could make out the stream of creatures and people that followed for several miles behind it. It would take a few hours for them all to arrive he noted, and their number was easily greater than that which could be accommodated on the grassy area by the slipway. They would have to spread out amongst the surrounding trees.

'Stallion,' Samuel called out nervously.

'Can it be seen to that the forest will be accessible for those on two legs?'

'Hurrumph, Gladd at your Royal service, it will be done.'

The stallion made away and set off with the rest of the four legged beasts to clear corridors through the thick forests. The Royal Carriage was now coming into view, pulled by two silvery horses whose skin rippled unnaturally as they walked. They did not appear to be alive as the stallions and centaurs whose breath he had felt on his cheeks. Samuel could make out the white coffin now, through the carriage windows. It looked pure and brilliant, adorned with white lilies which he knew grew in the gardens of the Royal Palace.

With the arrival of the Royal Carriage came the first wave of mourners from behind it. Jack sorrow was beside his father William Sorrow, Rose was there with Dr. Flint and she ran towards him upon arrival, throwing her arms awkwardly around his waist and looking immediately as though she regretted such a show of public affection.

A tent was erected in the grassy area, and Samuel made his way inside with Rose and Jack. He didn't remember much of what happened in there. They must have made small talk, on nothing terribly significant. Samuel was waiting instinctively for the moment the coffin would descend into the water. Dr. Flint eventually came to stand puffing in the tent entrance, calling Samuel forwards. The centaurs and stallions had formed a semi circle around the carriage and the shore, holding back the mourners which were now hundreds deep. From this point of view it turned out to be easier than he expected. There were to be several bearers; Mr. Shabbers, Dr. Flint, Dr. Cess, Jack Sorrow and William Sorrow and Samuel himself as the sixth. Dr. Flint and Dr. Cess moved the coffin from the Royal Carriage so that it hovered in mid air upon a beautiful white carpet. The bearers took position three each side and took a silvery handle, the carpet itself bearing most of the weight. Their differing heights would be less of a problem once the coffin was afloat in the water.

They strode forwards towards the water at Dr. Flint's command as the sun was setting. Dusk arrived just as the coffin touched the water which received it upon the carpet very gently, sending out ripples which sparkled. Samuel stumbled under foot at one point and he heard the crowds behind him gasp. When all the bearers were submerged it was evident that the water was deep only up to the shoulders. At this depth it was easier to half swim than walk. So this is just what the bearers did in a rather awkward arrangement which was correct simply because it worked. As they waded further from the bank, the current began to drag the carpet from under the coffin. Samuel felt it go limp, its work done. Although it was quiet, beyond the sound of the lapping water, Samuel could hear crying. As his eyes became used to the dark, and his body less concerned with the chill of the water, he could make out each bank of the river, lined with colourful glowing lanterns and torches. The differing heights of the creatures there was evident from the differing height at which lanterns were held.

Samuel felt something catch his arm and brushed it away. It responded with a quiet yelp. Moments later a small flair ignited and Samuel could see a mouse in a tiny coracle looking intently at him. When the flare burnt out the mouse replaced it with another and was gradually joined by a whole fleet of other tiny coracles, some bearing real minute lanterns. By their light Samuel could make out that the waters around the coffin were filled with a flotilla of small and larger creatures. Samuel caught sight of Mole diving alongside him, and a flutter against his leg revealed another occupant of the water.

'water fairies,' gulped Mole, before he dived under water once again.

It was certainly a suitable name for the delicate creatures which swam through the surface water issuing an iridescent glow rather like a glow worm. Samuel caught a closer look at one which was perched on a coracle looking intently at the coffin and wiping its eyes occasionally. It was a tiny delicate creature, a feminine body structure, lacy wings with a glowing region placed near the small of its back. After a few moments it fluttered away into the water beneath the coracle and Samuel was sorry to see it go. He had been enjoying its silent companionship.

Samuel could feel the water tugging harder now and the bearers around him seemed to have eased off in their guidance. Jack came swimming behind the coffin and splashed his way up to Samuel, sending a trail of water fairies shooting out of his way.

'Nearly there', he panted, 'the others have let go now. You're on your own.'

Samuel gulped, a mistake given the increased depth of the water which was given a reason to gush into his mouth. He felt Jack grab him and guide the coffin at the same time. For the first time Samuel could hear a mighty distant roar which he assumed was the falls where all this water disappeared under ground. He knew that it would not be possible to safely continue much further. After spluttering a little, Samuel edged back from the handle which he had been guiding and took control of the coffin from behind. Jack swam along beside him but let him guide it alone. The water dragged insatiably at the coffin now, and it was evident that it was on a one way journey without a return ticket.

'When the coffin starts to glow you must let it go,' panted Jack. Moments later the glowing began, until a hazy light illuminated the water all around the coffin. The tiny coracles that had followed the coffin down the river were starting to move off towards the respective shores. Samuel did not want to let go.

'Your Majesty, you must leave it now...'

With these words Samuel felt his feet hit an invisible dip in the river bed and he dropped momentarily under the surface, inhaling a substantial amount of the river water. In his panic his grasp on the back of the coffin was weakened and it tugged itself out of his reach. Jack dragged Samuel from under the water, and in his state of dazed confusion Samuel felt himself being pulled by several hands to the side of the river. He was shivering quite violently and uncontrollably. Once they reached the bank, eager arms lifted him from the water, and blankets were quickly brought forward for him. As he turned to look back at the river he could see a black beyond the inky depths of the river that must be the rocky edge of its path. The roar from where he was standing was distinct and loud. The coffin was glowing even more brightly in the water than he remembered and slowly he saw it glide closer to the edge. The falls quickly claimed his mother and the coffin fell from sight beneath the waters. Samuel felt his gut wrench. At last they had reached Lappings End.

Samuel was almost too tired to cry. There were too many people around him and he was too dazed to recognise anyone for quite some time. His shivering soon subsided beneath the thick blankets which he tugged even more tightly around him. Some time later he observed Mr. Shabbers beside him. He leant towards him in his usual gruff manner and picked Samuel up within the blankets, an act testament to his strength which still remained.

Although uncertain of the exact direction of the route Mr. Shabbers was taking within the woodland Samuel could tell from the increased roar of the falls at Lappings End that they were getting nearer. Presently the woodland gave way to an open rocky outcrop which was bathed in moonlight from above. Mr. Shabbers found somewhere comfortable for Samuel and placed him down. Samuel was aware of something snuggle up to him on his left side and from the snuffling he took it that it was Mole. Exhausted, they both drifted asleep for several hours while Mr. Shabbers stood looking out over the darkened plane which was spread out before them, bathed in moonlight but still barely visible.

When Samuel awoke it was still very dark and he could feel Mole stirring beside him. The air on his face was cold and fresh and he felt stiff. His garments were still a little damp beneath the blankets. To his right he felt Mr. Shabbers grunt acknowledgment that he had stirred. Samuel blinked sleep from his eyes and stared out into the darkness. Ahead, on the horizon, where the firmament met the sky there stood in insidious defiance the shadow of a distant city. It was many miles away but in the grey light that precedes dawn it was quite clear. Samuel blinked once in case he had imagined seeing something but he then saw it again. A green tinge that rippled across the sky repeatedly. He jumped violently as Mr. Shabbers uttered his first words.

'That place is an enchanted city to the North East. They say that on a warm summer's night you can watch the western lights of the Solaris as they blaze out in all their glory from here but I find that at winter you have just as good a chance of seeing it if you are patient. We have not witnessed that but instead a rupture where the city emerges into this world. We have seen a sight tonight that will not be witnessed again for a thousand years. It will be there on the plane between Grat and Davish for a hundred years. That is the length of time the sinister city of Zu-Sahn spends in this world at one time. Then it will vanish to be lost from time until it is due to reappear nine hundred years later.'

'I have never heard of it,' murmured Samuel, taken by surprise at the hoarseness of his own voice.

'Some things are known better by tradesmen than academics at the Longwhey Institute. The truth is out here on the ground. You just have to spend enough time out here in order to find it.'

'Where does it go to when it's not here?'

'No one knows. The inhabitants never return with the city when it reappears.'

Samuel must have shortly drifted back off to sleep for the next time he awoke it was light and Mr. Shabbers was hovering around them looking keen to make a move. Dragging himself to his feet, Mr. Shabbers took the blankets from him and Mole likewise sprang to his senses or at least what senses he had. The trio began to wander through a forest pathway, deserted now where last night it had been teeming. It was quite a long and sobering walk along the wooded river bank to the slip way where they had entered the water with the coffin and where the vessel, The Shanty, upon which they had arrived here, had brought them. When they arrived Samuel was surprised to see the tent still standing in the deserted grassy area and before long the emergence of a sleeping Jack Sorrow. He smiled weakly at Samuel and pointed to the track. Where the Royal Carriage had yesterday halted there was a more ordinary cart and donkey.

'Ours, dad's,' muttered Jack semi-incoherently. His intention was clear as William Sorrow emerged from the tent behind his son. It disassembled itself behind him as he walked towards them then rolled itself along the ground to curl up in front of where he came to stand by the group.

'Home, I think, Your Majesty is best reached by our old cart. Snuffy is slow but reliable. Shabbers, thanks for your help yesterday.'

Mr. Shabbers gruffly declined the thanks and looked uneasy. Samuel thanked him and Mole who was more taken to be appreciative of gratitude. The pair then made their way to the vessel leaving Samuel with Jack and William.

The journey by cart was not quick, or for that matter comfortable, but Samuel slept through as much of it as he could. They arrived at the side of the Royal Palace as noon approached, and Samuel was glad to escape the confines of the cart for the space of the gardens. He made to his bed chamber as soon as he could, the sleep he had so far achieved inadequate still beside the deficit provided by late, sleepless nights while caring for his mother. He was not sure whether he would have awoken if it were not for a soft knock on the door of the bed chamber which at first he tried to ignore, but became more receptive to when he heard the call of a familiar voice. He gathered himself together and made for the door. Pulling it open, he saw there a welcome sight. Martharnia in all her bushy glory stood there, all business like but kindness itself beneath. She looked older than he had remembered, and distinctly more grey. But she still looked pleasantly familiar. He hugged her as he longed to do and she did not resist. Neither was crying but they understood exactly how the other felt. There followed the usual exchange of pleasantries followed by a proposition.

The Lampmaker had sent her. He wanted to see Samuel and the only way was for Samuel to make the journey to him deep in the caves beneath the Warren Kitchens.

Samuel was unsure as to what reaction he was supposed to give. He had no idea why the Lampmaker should summon him on the death of his mother. It was a mystery that would only be answered by a visit. He nodded in deaf agreement to Martharnia's proposal that he should come straight away. It was, she said, the only opportunity since he would continue to be relieved from affairs of state for the rest of the week but thereafter would resume them in full. She said they didn't need to hurry away, but that they must leave before the city gates closed for the night. She would give him enough time to get ready, get food and make the other necessary domestic arrangements. Then they really had to be off.

Samuel met Martharnia in the Orangery with a satchel over his shoulder filled with some food that the servants had made up. It had been brought to him by a small wood elf who looked strangely familiar. She declared herself to be Dixi when he enquired and nervously smiled before she dashed away. Samuel felt pleased to know he had been able to help out the Flints.

'But Martharnia, I thought it wasn't very safe for me to make journeys alone and without protection?'

She smiled at Samuel, replying that she had of course arranged cover, but most of it would not be visible. Samuel trusted her, but felt sure Adviser Jacoby would not approve. He was in two minds as to whether he should contact him before he left, but decided against it, given the urgency to get away before the city gates closed for the night.

There is not much to be said about the journey up to the Warren Kitchens. To Samuel it might as well have been the first time he had ever made it, for he still couldn't personally recall the journey in by cart years ago that he had been told of so often. It was as good as a pleasant childhood tale, abstract and removed from reality.

Once they entered the tunnel to the Warren kitchens Martharnia pulled a lantern from the bag on her back and it started to glow and light up the way forwards. The Warren Kitchen itself was in near darkness when the pair arrived there, lit only by some dim lamps dotted around the rooms. Business had been bad recently according to Martharnia. When there was fear of war and more fighting business was never good. They only opened once a week now, and that wasn't today. Once Martharnia got the door open with her keys she took off her bag and took Samuel through several caverns of seating and into a back room. She went over to what looked from the outside like a mere storage cupboard. It opened to show an oval hole cut into its back, the entrance to a narrow tunnel.

'It spirals down from here, Your Majesty, no need for any lifts to the Lampmaker's Cottage.'

'You're not coming any further?' enquired Samuel.

Martharnia shook her head while Samuel frowned. He had expected her to come all the way to the Cottage. The narrow rounded tunnel ahead looked dark, dirty and uninviting. It suited the Warren Kitchens of course, being rounded and shaped just like it had been burrowed out of the ground, which of course it had.

'Ok then, I'm going down. Wish me luck...'

'Of course, Your Majesty; take my lantern. I hope that whatever the Lampmaker has to say it will be good news.' She smiled and took a few steps backwards into the Warren Kitchens and then whipped around and scampered away, with her bushy tail bounding along behind her.

Samuel held Martharnia's lantern gingerly in front of him and took tentative steps forward. At times he reached out with his hand and touched the damp earthen walls of the passage. He was sure he could feel roots binding the soil together in places. The tunnel wound on endlessly downwards, just as Martharnia had promised it would. At times it narrowed but never uncomfortably so. It was always curving to his right to create a continuous spiral. Samuel almost didn't notice the tunnel floor turn into steps, but was glad he did given that they made the tunnel descend steeply, and he wouldn't fancy falling down them. The tunnel was descending now at the rate of a spiral staircase.

A door arrived at the end of the tunnel sooner than Samuel had expected, and he could tell it went into the cottage from the glowing light which was flowing through the crack around it. He knocked and a few moments later it opened by itself. The Lampmaker was slumped in a chair by one of the many hearths in the 'cottage'. His eyes flew open as Samuel walked in, and he grunted through his wild fiery red beard.

'Thank you, thank you, my King, my Sovereign. It is good of you to come, very good, take a seat.'

Samuel took one of the comfy chairs by the hearth and turned to look at the Lampmaker, waiting for him to speak again.

'I heard the news from your dear Martharnia. So good of her to tell me, although I knew it would be soon. Your mother, Saffie, was a good person and it is sad to see her go.'

Samuel nodded, wondering if passing on condolences was the purpose this meeting.

'You don't remember me much do you, Your Majesty?'

Samuel shook his head.

'I remember the first time I saw you. They brought you to me through the front entrance that time. You looked very scared of me, I recall.'

'I know of you, Sir, only what I have been told; you are the Lampmaker who many years ago predicted that the first king of the city of Grat who came from under the mountains would unite it to its lost lands and make it the capital city of a kingdom once again.'

'Why yes, that is very true, so I did. But was I right? Only time will tell.'

He let out a rasping hearty chuckle which winded him.

'How would it be if I told you that you remember so much more of your life before you came here than you realise?'

'Well, I do have flashbacks. My Dr., a Dr. Flint, told me that this would happen sometimes.'

'And have you had any? If so, tell?'

'Once, a few years ago when I was younger, just before I started my studies at Longwhey I had a flash back to one of my lecturers, Mr. Harbury.'

'Yes, yes you did, and do you know why?'

'Not for sure. But I think I might know. I thought I did anyway.'

'You made use of the Orifice of your father didn't you?'

'Yes Sir, I did, and others. But it was 'The Chariot' in the Royal Library archives which confirmed it. The article cast a lot of doubt on Mr. Harbury and suggested he...'

'...Had tried to kill you before you arrived here,' continued the Lampmaker, finishing Samuel's sentence for him. 'And at Longwhey he seemed to dislike you a lot, yes? So he seemed to have the motivation? But what makes you think you are wrong?'

'Mr. Harbury was murdered just after my first Winterville at Longwhey. His body was found on the rocks in The Deeps.'

'Perhaps someone was worried he might try to kill you again?'

Samuel shrugged his shoulders. He had no idea what had been going on and wasn't inclined to pretend. His mind wandered back to Bertis, Jack and the mysterious Brothership which they had discovered. The more he thought about it, the more he felt this was the right time to bring it up.

'The Brothership, do you know anything about it?'

The Lampmaker gazed at Samuel with an expression which was next to impossible to read. Samuel swallowed, aware that he had gone out on a limb here.

'The Brothership is one of the most mysterious organisations in this world, in fact in any world. You may recall that Mr. Harbury was an expert on the topic. Wouldn't you have thought that he could have told you far more about it that I can?'

'I suppose,' murmured Samuel.

'Your Majesty, I didn't call you here today to talk about the Brothership.'

'No?'

'No. I called you here to talk about your mother. There are a few characters I need to bring out of your memory. They will feel vaguely familiar first, but the harder you think about them the more familiar they will feel. They are all a part of the society and world in which you lived before you were brought here to the city of Grat. Back in those days you lived in a large house in the village of Little Tunlings with a man called Albert Hawkins. He was your legal guardian and you took his surname for many years. There was also a housekeeper you knew called Marion Monroe. Do you remember anything?'

'Not much... those around me talked sometimes of my life outside the city before I arrived but it has never felt real to me. I can't recall much at all.'

'I need to tell you more about this Albert Hawkins and a conversation you had with him some time before you moved out of his house. He told you that your mother had been married to him, but had left him some years later. Previously she had been married to a man called Harold Deksis. Albert had been very interested in the Deksis family and had read as much about their history as possible. He discovered there was a link between them and another world, that world being this one. He was desperate to know more. When your mother, Saffie, went missing for several years without a trace along with Harold, Albert immediately suspected that they had come here. He had no idea where Grat was or how to get to it but was quite determined to find out. He quietly waited as the years passed, finding out as much about Grat as he could.

Your mother was found one winter morning with a small child. She was disturbed and in no state to look after the baby, so it was taken away. They say that the first word your mother spoke again was 'Jonoway' and this is how the orphanage named your brother. The baby died in the orphanage and was buried in a place called Pebble Lane under the name of Jonoway Deksis. It is the only place in that world where an heir to the throne of Grat is buried and also one of the most cursed places there. Those who venture near its shadow when the curse is at its strongest, every Christmas Eve, have paid dearly for doing so, be they animals or children.'

Samuel felt himself sicken, and the room around him dissolved; it was a flashback to a fireplace in an apricot room with a silver haired man by the fire. It was gone as quickly as it had arrived and the Lampmaker swam back into view. He was silent for a minute before he began to speak again.

'It's there somewhere, all of this, isn't it?'

Samuel nodded slowly in response.

'Perhaps you can fill in the rest, Your Majesty?'

Samuel strained his mind but found nothing.

'It doesn't really seem to work like that; apart from the flashbacks I don't really get anything.'

'Not to worry, I shall continue. You were told by Albert Hawkins that he took in your mother and cared for her. He discovered Saffie was pregnant with you and supported her when she gave birth to you, Samuel. Eventually, he said, she gave in to his advances and they were married, but more for his research than for love. He thought that through marriage he might break a seal and have access to her memories of the missing years which he believed she spent in Grat with your father. Albert claimed that he was successful in this. He also told you, and this was the worst bit, that your mother left you because she hated the sight of you, that you reminded her of her first husband and the reason why she had been pressured to enter this second, miserable marriage. She had left you with him and had run away.'

'That is a terrible story, heartbreaking.'

'It is, or at least it would be if it were all true.'

'Albert Hawkins lied to me?' questioned Samuel?

'Well, at first it might look as though he did, but that isn't actually the case.'

'What do you mean?'

'Well, Saffie's story is more or less correct at the start as Albert told it. Your brother was buried in Pebble Lane and Albert Hawkins did pounce on your mother in her weak state.'

'Where had my mother really been in those years where Albert waited for her?' wondered Samuel aloud.

'Look, Your Majesty. That is your mother's story and not your own. You may be told it one day, but not today. Today is about you and her.'

'Oh, ok,' replied Samuel, a little exasperated. 'Did they marry at least, Albert and my mother?'

'Ah, no, they did not. You will probably be pleased to know that your mother was never Mrs. Hawkins. Never!' The Lampmaker spoke the last word louder for emphasis.

'Saffie made use of the situation with Mr. Hawkin's advances on her, for reasons which may not seem entirely clear. What you have to remember about Saffie is that she was a Gratian, born and bred. A powerful woman. After she gave birth to you, she was getting stronger. She knew that she had just given birth to a future king outside of Grat. This could be the king who would bring about the restoration of Grat, just as I had predicted. Saffie knew not only of that part of my prediction, but also the second; that the life of such a king was in grave danger. One day Albert showed Saffie the secret of his bookcase. If know just where to press it, it swings open, giving access to a hidden passage and, from that, a hidden room which backed onto yours. Your mother pounced, and used all of her abilities to convince Albert that he had been married to her, but that she had left him, that she had told him all he desired to know, and that his bookcase was just an ordinary bookcase, but one which he should never let anyone touch'

Samuel felt the sickness touch him again before anything happened. Then a red book shot into his mind, just for a flash, leaving him shaky and breathless.

'Again, Your Majesty?'

'Yes, a red book.'

'No doubt your mind is recalling the way in which Albert was so defensive of his bookcase. He never let anyone near it. Your mother had no idea just how brilliantly she had protected her hiding place.'

'Hiding place?'

'Why yes, you didn't really think she would leave you do you? Of course Saffie wouldn't. No. She chose a hiding place from which she could both watch you and protect you.'

This time sickness did not provide any warning, and the flash was more violent, pulling Samuel out of the chair and down to the floor in a fit of convulsion. The image which he could see for a few moments was the most pronounced despite its darkness. There was a sour woman with terribly dim eyes staring at him quite wickedly. As it passed the Lampmaker seemed concerned, anxious not to push Samuel too far.

'A few moments longer my King. That is all I need to put you through tonight. What did you see?'

'A dark, terrible woman.'

'Ah, the painting in your bedroom. Maybe you subconsciously suspected it too then?'

'What?'

'Saffie spent every night watching over you through it, peering through the eye holes of that painting into the room. Such a fortunate hiding place for her. What is it, my King; you look strange Your Majesty?'

'Yes, yes, I have just remembered something without a violent flashback. Albert, Mr. Hawkins, he said that there was a strange protection over me, and that he could not kill me. Something magical.'

The Lampmaker let out a genuine chortle of laugher at this before he replied.

'Mr. Hawkins was very much a man of his world. Despite all the ancient books he read, despite the way in which he presented himself as an academic he was far too reliant on popular fiction than the real substance of the different worlds which do exist. A child with a special protection over them might sell novels but even a woman as talented as Saffie knew when to be subtle. If Albert hurt you, he woke up to find one of his precious books missing, or a parchment defaced. In the early hours of the morning your mother often ventured out of her hiding place to get food from your kitchen and while out she would do those deeds. It convinced Mr. Hawkins in the supernatural anyway, worked a treat!'

'The food bills, always over budget!'

'But of course, Your Majesty! See how things are starting to return to you!'

Samuel nodded feeling better than he had at any other point in this meeting.

'Is this over now, please may I go?'

'Of course, Your Majesty, that is enough. The mysteries of Saffie Deksis are beginning to unravel, eh?'

Samuel smiled in response. He had asked to leave with an unexpected desperation. He was glad memories were beginning to return, he really was, but there was only so much he could take at once.

Samuel made his way up the steps he had descended earlier deep in thought. His head was spinning with all that he had been told and that had returned to him. Albert and even the house keeper, Mrs. Monroe seemed real in his mind. How much had she known about his mother? He hadn't thought to ask the Lamp-maker that, Samuel pondered as he led awake in a room of the Warren Kitchens, beside the dying embers of a fire which Martharnia had stoked up for him when he had returned. She hadn't asked him what had been said and Samuel didn't feel like saying anything. How that man knew so much about everything, Samuel just couldn't fathom. But he certainly knew a lot. Even about looking into his father's Oro-fice. Perhaps Saffie had told him about that? It seemed unlikely, but so far as he knew she was the only person who knew about that.

The next day, the pair returned to the Royal Palace by late afternoon and Samuel spent the next few days resting up, ready to resume all his usual duties. He had a feeling of unease about him. If his mother had kept so much secret from him for so long, how many more things might there be which she hadn't made clear?

-- CHAPTER NINE --

A Surprising Summit

The date which the occupancy agreement with Telfon had set for the Summit seemed to have drawn closer at an alarming rate. To Samuel, it seemed hard to believe that it was really two months since the occupancy agreement had been drawn up, and only slightly longer since the I.L.C., the catalyst for the Ling Crisis, had occurred. Advisor Jacoby had decided to abstain from making the trip to the neutral site for the Summit selected in Davish. His already damp enthusiasm for the event seemed to have continued unabated. No doubt he felt that any issues discussed at the Summit could be more easily resolved by a single Full Session in the debating chamber.

Lord Ruffus, a key architect of the Summit was obviously making the trip, despite difficulties posed to his aging health. Ruffus was a man who was not easily perturbed by anything. The loss of Jacoby as Advisor on the trip was to be remedied by the attendance of several junior Advisors; very much a token gesture rather than a real aid to the King, in Samuel's opinion. Still, Samuel felt in safe hands with Lord Ruffus anyway. The interests of Grat would, no doubt, get the representation they deserved.

Several modes of transport to the Summit had been discussed and rejected, usually due to concerns raised by Lord Ruffus. His desired transportation was slow and reliable, so it was finally decided that Grat would send a Royal consignment on horseback. The finest stallions agreed to the task, so thirty or so bore Lord Ruffus, Samuel and their entourage through the winding mountain pass and onto the plains that separated Grat and Davish. Samuel was grateful that the desert area through which they had to pass was not as vast as that which they would have had to traverse in order to reach Ling. The plains around them soon became fertile and a smattering of shrubbery and scrub penetrated the thickening soil. To their right the freshly arisen empty city of Su-Zahn occupied the horizon. Samuel could see that the city was walled protectively around its circumference, and rose to a towering pinnacle in its dense centre. The empty scrub land over which they were riding served to emphasise the desolate surroundings of the strange city. Lord Ruffus was directly alongside Samuel at this point, exclaiming with delight at the views which were afforded of the country of Davish up ahead. Despite the stallion doing all the work beneath him, Ruffus still sounded out of breath as he shouted over the sound of thundering hoofs.

'I trust that Your Majesty can see why Davish has never had much interest in Goldmines. Their country is so rich in different natural resources that it has been impossible for them to find they are wanting in almost anything. The woodlands here are the envy of many worlds. I hope we will get to see some of my favourite parts on this trip. The Summit site was selected by Queen Nashia, and frankly I could not have made a better choice myself. Verades is a beautiful woodland retreat backed by stunning cascades and waterfalls that descend over rich, mossy rock faces and into a splendid pool. At this time of year the lake should be full of water lilies in bloom. You will soon see why Moonwater can never live up to the beauty of Davish, for all its grandeur.'

Lord Ruffus subsided, allowing Samuel to follow his line of sight to the undulated woodlands which billowed out of the ground ahead of them. The stallions pressed on all afternoon, as thick woodland rose up on either sides of a well worn track. The Royal party began to pass other daytime travellers who were also making their way to and from Davish by foot. A small wagon painted in beautiful bright colours caught Samuel's attention, as did the tiny man pulling it. Startled at the noise and pace of the stallions, he summoned his young family to stick their heads out of the wagon cover and take a peep at the strange Royalty passing by. Later on, a group of wandering souls had formed a woodland settlement in a forest glade to one side of the track, and Samuel enjoyed the sweet music which they made there, the tuneful jingles spilling out amongst the great trunks and twisting branches of the surrounding woodland.

Day was turning to night as they arrived at the woodland retreat of Verades which Ruffus had spoken of so highly. The structure in which delegates would be staying was a magnificent tiered wooden affair which was raised out of the forest just enough to give a view of the lake in front of it. The lake itself was alive at this time with fluttering lights, both on top and under the water.

'Those will be the dainty water fairies, Your Majesty. For all the ones you can find visiting Grat, not one of them ever stays. This lake is their natural home, and it is to here that they always return.'

'I wish that Gratian wood elves were half as beautiful,' murmured Samuel.

'Ah, your majesty, beauty and even brains are not all they are made out to be. In this world, substance of character matters just as much. That is what I believe anyway.'

As night drew in completely, Samuel joined other delegates from Telfon at the side of the lake. Everyone was marvelling at the water fairies that were darting around in the water, creating an enchanting glowing cobweb of patterns.

'It is good to have Grat ready to talk, Your Majesty. We do hope this summit can help us resolve the difficult situation that has arisen since the events that occurred in Ling.'

'So do I. Grat is very hopeful of a peaceful resolution which can be to the benefit of all the parties involved. Do you know whether Queen Nashia will be present at the Summit tomorrow? Back in Grat people were divided and sceptical. It is thought there that she is not very fond of negotiating and debating.'

'The last indications back in Telfon were just as mixed, but having spoken to our Davish hosts it does seem that Queen Nashia intends to be around tomorrow. They say that she wants to put a Royal claim on the city of Su-Zahn which has arisen.'

'And on what basis does she advance for such a claim? If she has any chance of success then there must be substance to it?'

'Telfon is under the impression that she claims the city should be under Davishian control because it is located closer to its jurisdiction than that of any other country. We believe Su-Zahn is likely to become the focus, or at least the main contention of these talks. Goldmines, it seems, may have to take a back seat.'

'From Grat's point of view it would be very disappointing if this opportunity to resolve disputes in respect of Goldmines was missed or forsaken in search of bigger political points.'

'Well yes, Your Majesty, for Grat that may be true. The Eloth Goldmines are so important to your economy. Speaking for Telfon, we do not need our shares in Rafe and Jeten to the same extent. Telfon is a large, diverse and resilient country.'

Samuel knew he could say more. Lord Ruffus had painted a picture of a country which was vast and, certainly in places, impoverished. Telfon seemed to be calling Grat's bluff on the issue.

'Speaking for Grat, the main division of our economy is in the security sector and its subsidiaries. I should not be placing Eloth above the importance it deserves.'

'Of course, Your Majesty. And Telfon is equally keen to see the return of our full half share in Jeten from you, a withdrawal of Gratian troops from the region and even Rafe returned to joint ownership between Telfon and Ling. All these things are possible and desirable to us.'

Samuel nodded quietly in response.

'We shall have to wait and see what happens tomorrow. A lot rests on the way Ling and Davish decide to play the game.'

The night for Samuel proved to be fitful, as most were of late. His mind wandered to thoughts of Gratian troops trapped in impossible circumstances and then when he drifted into consciousness and from it again he could see Rose and Martharnia. They were both shouting at him and looked distressed, but he could never hear the words they were saying despite trying to listen to the pair and shout back as hard as he could. The image was repetitive and raw. It gave a sense of foreboding to what the future might bring.

The official three week Summit was to start over breakfast and today's itinerary would continue until dinner time in the evening. Lunch would be served as part of the main session. However pleasant the Davishian hosts would prove to be, it seemed to Samuel that they would have trampled on many of the delegates sensibilities by insisting on such a lengthy itinerary without any break for lunch.

Samuel entered the large oval room set aside for the Summit. At the head of the long table, Queen Nashia was sitting, waiting silent and unmoving, for everyone else to arrive. She was flanked at her end of the table by her own advisers but it certainly looked as if she intended to make all the moves today.

Lord Ruffus assumed the seat at Samuel's side. The pair had a good view of Queen Nashia from here. Samuel half expected her to acknowledge their presence, but she maintained her stiff, corpse like demeanour, even now. Other delegates shuffled in and took their places. The junior Gratian Advisors which Advisor Jacoby had sent on his behalf looked weak and nervous in the presence of such high ranking officials.

The Grand Visril Chang of Ling was dressed in a suitably show-off attire, consisting of a bright gold jacket, purple and orange blouse and a glistening silver over-gown. Breakfast bowls were brought around before any serious talking started, and once the interruption was out of the way one of the Telfonians stood up.

'Despite the difficult circumstances which bring us altogether, Telfon is glad that a Summit of discussion is thought to be the way forward.'

There was a general muttering of assent around the table at this.

'Telfon would like to thank Davish for maintaining its neutral stance in these circumstances and enabling this Summit to take place under its jurisdiction. Thank you, Your Majesty, Queen Nashia.'

All Telfonians present politely bowed their heads to the unblinking Queen at the head of the table. The Grand Visril Chang rose next to speak for Ling.

'Ling is glad also for this meeting. It would be good to resolve the problems of ownership over Rafe and Jeten at this Summit.'

Lord Ruffus rose next to speak for Grat.

'It is only by discussion of this sort that Grat believes real progress can be made. I would like to open the Summit here today with a proposal. If Telfon were to take some public responsibility for the events at the I.L.C. upon the understanding that its half share in Rafe will be returned to it by Ling and that Grat will withdraw from running Jeten, thus restoring joint ownership between Ling and Telfon, would this be acceptable to all parties? If Telfon has an understanding that in taking responsibility for the attack it can fear no retribution and that the return of its Goldmines will be without problematic sanctions, would this not be an acceptable outcome for all?'

The Grand Visril Chang rose slowly to his feet to speak again.

'For Ling these terms seem quite acceptable. The perpetrator of the attack at the I.L.C. must stand up and take responsibility. The damage to our reputation has been severe although far from fatal.'

For many hours the bargaining continued. At first Telfon was very reluctant to accept responsibility for an attack which it believed it did not commit. As the hours passed the Telfonian resolution seemed to crumble. The feeling was that so long as there would be no sanctions imposed on them by Ling or Grat, taking public responsibility was reasonably acceptable if it meant the Telfonian shares in Rafe and Jeten could be restored.

Just when real progress seemed to be being made, a snagging point was hit. Ling was very unhappy with Grat keeping troops around the Eloth Goldmines. As Adviser Jacoby had intended, they read this as a sign of Gratian aggression and mistrust. They proposed two solutions. Either Grat would withdraw all forces from the region or Ling would have to put into own forces into place around Rafe and Jeten. Lord Ruffus was very unhappy with Grat withdrawing all forces from the area at a time of such turbulence as the present. In a final attempt to broker a deal, one of the junior Advisors suggested Grat should pull its troops back from the Eloth Goldmines, towards Grat, but not out of the region entirely. This seemed to meet with general agreement. Samuel rose to give his Royal assent, Ling agreed in return and Telfon accepted responsibility for what had happened at the I.L.C. over two months ago. In many ways all this bartering seemed so awkward to Samuel. This was politics, he guessed; a world where taking responsibility for something you knew you had not done could be a powerful tool.

The day seemed to be drawing to a close when Queen Nashia began to speak. Unlike everyone else present she did not bother to stand. Around her mouth, her paper white skin cracked in thin lines with the effort of speaking. Her voice was so quiet that absolute silence and attention was required in order for anyone present to understand her meaning.

'Davish wishes to discuss the city of Su-Zahn. It has arrived, empty, near our land once again, and I, Queen Nashia of Davish, intend to take it under the stewardship of my country.'

The silence which followed this quiet declaration was stony. Chang rose to his feet.

'Ling considers it rather presumptuous of Her Majesty to make such a statement. Ling has a vested interest in the city and will fight to maintain it.'

A Telfonian delegate wished to add his opinion to the debate:

'For Telfon it is accepted that we cannot make any claim upon this new city based upon its geographical proximity to our own. However, the understanding between the three countries of Ling, Telfon, Davish and the city of Grat has always been that resources in the plains which divide us are to be shared. That is why Ling, Telfon and Grat all have interests in the Goldmines found there. If we apply this principle to the city of Su-Zahn, then it should fall under joint occupancy, rather than the single sovereignty of Davish.'

Queen Nashia gave an uncharacteristically sharp reply.

'Davish has never had any interest in Goldmines in any part of this world. Our interest now is only in the city of Su-Zahn. Many years ago Davish lost a huge proportion of its population when the city disappeared. It is now time for Davish to unravel that part of its history by taking control of the city once again. In one month I shall give the orders for my armies to march on the city and claim it for Davish. You have until then to decide your individual responses.'

The Summit was over for today. Tomorrow there would be more details to thrash out in the morning regarding the deal that had been struck concerning the Goldmines. Samuel would largely be able to leave all this to Lord Ruffus and the junior Advisors present, so he intended to spend a large part of the day enjoying the beautiful area of Verades. The rest of the three week summit had been assigned to other minor discussions which Samuel was required to attend but was unlikely to speak at.

With dinner finished he had headed down the lake once again to watch the water fairies playing in the water again. They comforted him as they had done at his mother's funeral. As he stared out over the glowing waters he felt a tear slip from his eye. Gusts of emotion could ever provide a sudden threat, and he was glad to have found a spot by the lake well away from the other delegates. Pulling himself together, Samuel was about to walk away from the lake when he heard a shuffling noise emanating from the thicket by his side. Looking towards it he could see a woman pushing her way through the dense undergrowth. It was Rose Flint.

'Samuel? Oh I'm glad it's you. I hope I'm not interrupting?'

'What are you doing here in Davish?'

'I'm sorry, don't be angry. I wanted to come and speak to you.'

'I'm not angry.'

'Well you sounded it to me. There's no need to snap.'

'I'm sorry Rose; I didn't mean to be awkward. It has been a long and difficult Summit today and I really wasn't expecting to see you. I thought you were busy helping your father look after Lady Flint?'

'Oh Samuel,' her fragile face fell at his words.

'Lady Flint, mum, died just a few hours after you left for Davish yesterday. I didn't know what to do, so I used the old carpet we have to fly here tonight.'

'Rose... I'm so sorry. I didn't realise.'

Rose sobbed gratefully against Samuel's chest. He really felt for her at that moment.

'Mum was buried this morning. I wanted you there, Samuel. That is why I had to come and find you now.'

It really upset him to see her in this state. When her sobbing eventually subsided the pair sat close together, looking out over the glimmering lake which lapped around the bank where they were sitting.

Samuel caught a fleeting glimpse of Rose's slender face that caused him to stare in rapture for far longer than he had intended. He tried to quell the tremor that swept through him, but to no avail. Profusely he sweated, quite alone and yet, paradoxically, comforted. Her lucid, dark thick hair that slid gracefully and without effort down each side of her face, framed her rosy cheeks, which beckoned him ever closer with urgency. She looked more beautiful, more fertile, more elegant than ever before, and her moist lips, below her penetratingly black eyes, were more pronounced and burningly determined than usual, beyond the natural strength of the forceless fading light. In his eyes they were beacons of burnished hope, beacons of change, as he leant forward to kiss her.

She smiled intently as they moved closer together, blinking away the tears that still lingered in her eyes, and in the light of the fire flies that floated around them in ecstasy, they kissed. They kissed slowly at first and then more vigorously with a young, desperate passion. It was passion of the type that is hard to sustain; so much more than lust and far more frail because it dies gradually in the first slender shafts of a faint morning light, cutting through the cover of darkness. It was silent in its desperation, quiet and patient in its expression, but yet so terribly meaningful. It had a raw power all of its own, that captured and set Samuel in a trance.

They were close together for the first time and alone. That was all that mattered, her perfect face close to his, her perfect, astonishing eyes, each containing an entire galaxy, full of a billion possibilities, intent and focused entirely upon him. The sounds of the evening quickly drifted away like smoke on a midnight breeze as they walked together back to the main wooden structure and into the Royal apartments that had been set aside for the Verades guests. Before they knew it, they were beneath the covers clutching each other close, intent in a matter of love for which they both cared so deeply, where they indulged in each other and it was nothing but goodness, fruitful and passionate desire, being fulfilled like never before.

This was love, raw and unregulated in its burning passion, bright in sight and so strong and lingering in scent. Samuel had never seen a sight so beautiful, so close to flawlessness as Rose; she was his choice for eternity, and an unquestionable source of love and comfort. This was. This was love.

Morning came as slowly as it could, bringing with it the reality which any dawn must. Rose slept peacefully beside Samuel as he watched the sun rise over the forest glade outside. Presently, Rose awoke, smiling sleepily up at him.

'I'm going to marry you, Samuel Deksis.'

She breathed the words like magic, Samuel thought.

He smiled back at her and nodded.

'It needs to be soon I think, but don't marry me because you are upset about Lady Flint.'

'Don't worry about that. I am upset of course, but I've intended to marry you for a long time. Until now, I just wasn't sure when would be right. Let's do it here in Verades! Can you be excused from the Summit for one day?'

'Errm, well that is very quick! I think... I think it shouldn't be a problem. I will be here for the rest of the three weeks so I should have thought there would be time. We both need a chance to think things through; a quick marriage is one thing but a hasty marriage quite another. I will need to speak to Lord Ruffus about it.'

'Of course, go and speak to him in an hour or so. Then come back and tell me what he said.'

This is exactly what Samuel did. Lord Ruffus had looked more than a little concerned at the speed of the proposed wedding. Samuel did his best to allay him of his fears.

'Does Rose not wish for her father to be present? It would be sad to see Dr. Flint hurt. She should be with him in his grief at this time. I shall only be persuaded of this plan, and cover for you on the last day of the Summit if he can be brought here by Rose and will consent to the arrangement.'

Rose had beamed at Samuel when he told her the news. She would fly back to Grat straight away as she knew she must. Dr. Flint would, she was certain, be delighted by the turn of events. She would return on the last day of the Summit in the late afternoon, as the heat over the plains subsided. Samuel waved her warmly away from Verades after he put in a personal request. Martharnia, Jack Sorrow and Bertis Beavitch deserved to be here on that evening if they were able to make it at short notice. Life seemed so much more than it had yesterday, all of a sudden.

Lord Ruffus was soon informed of Rose's departure and word of the news spread quickly through the delegates present at the Summit. Congratulations were forthcoming from all quarters in the oval room where Samuel was persuaded to join assembled representatives.

The Grand Visril Chang was the first to propose that the Summit should be suspended late afternoon on the final day to leave the rest of the day free for the wedding. No one present saw fit to object and Lord Ruffus positively beamed at all the delegates present. Samuel noticed that even Queen Nashia broke into an awkward smile. She had a raw terrible beauty, he noticed; the sort most people overlooked.

Samuel spent much of the next few weeks outdoors and away from the conference table. Most days he would be present in the morning and then leave as tedious details were discussed regarding matters of trade and commerce. Samuel was quite certain about the wedding. He was ready to marry Rose.

Chang was insistent that he should help the Gratian Advisors to make arrangements for the special evening. It was his way, he said later to Samuel, of saying sorry for the deficiencies in Royal security at the I.L.C. which had placed Samuel in such a dangerous situation.

When the final evening of the Summit came at last, everyone gathered around the lake at Verades to await the arrival of the bride. Jack Sorrow had arrived earlier with his family including his sister Kleveris and his father William. Then Bertis Beavitch and her parents had appeared, each congratulating Samuel warmly upon the happy news that they had received. They had flown in dear old Martharnia with them who, despite her protestations about the dangers of flying on Lingian carpets, had been quite beside herself at the prospect of missing the wedding. She hugged Samuel, so full in her bushiness as always.

Samuel did not see Rose or Dr. Flint arrive which was presumably the intention. The first sight he caught of her was a movement in the water at the far end of the lake. The water fairies were swarming more densely down there, giving the ripples the impression that they pulsed with electricity. Then she came, gliding upon a snow white swan towards Samuel across the lake. The bird was as beautiful as the woman that rode it, he thought, both as beautiful as anything here in the fine country of Davish. Dr. Flint stepped out of the darkness in front of Samuel to help Rose off the serene swan that had taken her on her last journey as his daughter.

The crowds on the banks held their breath as the couple stood before each other. Dr. Flint spoke, his voice shaking with emotion.

'I give to Your Majesty, Samuel Deksis, King of the city of Grat, the hand of my daughter, Miss Roseilia Flint, in marriage if you will accept it?'

'I do Rose, I do.'

'And I take Your Majesty, Samuel Deksis, King of the city of Grat as my husband.'

The crowd gasped and applauded as the couple kissed. It was not the Gratian custom to exchange rings or to have any sort of extended ceremony. A marriage was sealed with a kiss and with sincerity, as had just occurred. Despite this, Chang had instructed his advisors to set up nothing short of a spectacular Lingian display over the lake at Verades, and the exploding glittering lights high in the sky above the forest glade were reflected many times over in the shimmering waters of the lake.

When eventually it was over and the happy crowds began to disperse, Samuel and Rose returned to the quiet spot they had sat at on the evening they had first kissed. Rose was to return to Grat with her father in a few hours and would leave Samuel to accompany Lord Ruffus home. It had been a very surprising Summit, pondered Samuel. It had started out with such political aspirations but seemed to have ended in such personal ones. Life would never be the same again now that Rose was his wife.

-- CHAPTER TEN --

Gold Rush

Samuel was glad to return from the Summit in Davish. The country there had seemed strangely less beautiful after Rose had left it, and the few days which the newly married couple had been forced to spend apart had seemed unbearable.

The Royal Palace had been done up beautifully for his arrival by the servants and Palace staff, who were ever ready for a cause to celebrate. For several days Rose and Samuel Deksis were treated to lavish meals in the exquisite banqueting halls that were rarely used, at the base of the Palace. It was quite a sadness that business of Grat beckoned in a way that broke with all this merriment. The debating chamber was sitting in Full Session again and the King was required to be present.

The debating chamber had echoed more coldly than ever on the day Samuel returned to his position there. Several matters requiring urgent attention were itemised by Adviser Jacoby. Since Samuel had been away, Jacoby had seen fit to arrest the man who seemed unable to keep out of debates when Samuel was present. It was that man again, the one who claimed a right to the throne in Grat. Today the man was to be brought before the chamber for sentencing. To do so he had to be present in the chamber behind Lord Ruffus. Samuel would ultimately sit in judgement upon the matter. He had done something similar in the past, since he had assumed the position as a practical monarch. Only the most concerning cases were brought to him for judgement to be pronounced, other sectors of the Gratian Cresta doing the rest of the work in this area.

Lord Ruffus called forward prisoner two five three into the chamber. The darkness of the area behind him did not afford Samuel a clear sight of the man's face. The charge was read out: 'treason'. The man had been plotting against the King and was duly brought for sentencing before him. Jacoby elaborated on the details.

'Your Majesty, it is my belief that this deluded man presents a severe threat to your authority and has a gravely unsettling effect upon Your subjects. The sentence for such treason is noted at section twenty of the much celebrated penal declaration, which His Majesty Harold Deksis put in place before his death, to be life imprisonment at Your Majesty's pleasure. Your Majesty should be aware that the detention complex at Porthnarth is customarily used in such a high security case. I now defer to Lord Ruffus.'

'Ah, yes, Advisor Jacoby, I thank you for enlightening me to some of the details of what has occurred during my absence. Can you produce any evidence for this accusation to treason? What plot has been uncovered? And after you have provided this, prisoner two five three, who is present behind me, must be afforded the chance to speak in his defence.'

'Of course, Lord Ruffus: I call upon a man by the name of Larkin to enter the chamber.'

Dimly Samuel could recall this name, and further, the man who entered. He had been at Lady Flint's just after he had arrived in Grat. Since Samuel's last meeting with the Lampmaker, he had been able to recall at least some of the details of his arrival in Grat, although much was still foggy.

Larkin entered behind Advisor Jacoby. He lumbered forward and assumed a position just behind him.

'Larkin Lea will provide an account of how he overheard a conversation which revealed the plot.'

'Well, well, yes Advisor Jacoby. I remember being in my, my usual drinking place and hearing this chap behind me. He were talking about how he was King of Grat, the real King he said. One day everyone would see, he was going to show them. He wanted people to follow him, so that he could show them the light, or something like that.'

'I'm sure everyone present in the chamber today will thank Larkin for his brave account of what he heard and thank him for coming forward so courageously. The evidence seems quite conclusive to me; now is a fine opportunity to take this dangerous man off the streets.'

Larkin shuffled out of the chamber, his work done. From the dim recollection Samuel was making of him, the man was a drunk. How much of a state he was in to hear anything accurately was definitely a moot point. And what to the substance of what had been said? This was not treason of which he had spoken, merely an unaccountable desire to assume the position of Kingship. Jacoby's idea of evidence was nothing more than farce.

Lord Ruffus looked weary as he called on the prisoner to make any representations that he wished on his behalf. The man held his silence, as though he feared mockery more than anything else. Samuel felt certain derision would have been forthcoming from Adviser Jacoby's direction if anything had been said. Lord Ruffus turned to face Samuel and spoke thoughtfully.

'Your Majesty, I am far from convinced by the evidence that has been presented here today that this man should be imprisoned for life. If we had more time in this chamber I would very much like to hear more about the man. At the time of making judgement, Your Majesty will know him to be nothing more than a number; would it not be desirable to at least know his name? Alas, time will not permit further discussion, since we must be detained by other vital matters following the outcome of the recent Summit in Davish. Perhaps on this occasion, Your Majesty, we should place faith in the work of Adviser Jacoby who, since it was he that was present at the time of the arrest, must be far better informed than we are. Therefore I hand this issue to Your Majesty for judgement with the recommendation of a life sentence to be served at Porthnarth.'

Samuel felt in quite a predicament. Like Lord Ruffus he was far from convinced by the evidence that Adviser Jacoby had provided, but he shared the desire to move on to other topics. This irritating man would never have to be dealt with again if he was consigned to Porthnarth forever. Samuel could recall looking at Porthnarth from Longwhey. It was built on a separate craggy rock in Moonwater, much nearer to the Borrow Ways. Each time he had stared at the place, whether it was during winter squalls or warm sunshine, it was a sight which had seemed to drain the life out of him and filled him with a silent dread. Sending an innocent man to be incarcerated there was a dreadful thing, but looking across at Advisor Jacoby and the way his countenance was set in expectance of the full sentence, he knew this was a risk he was going to have to take. Standing, he pronounced the sentence; in the void of the debating chamber it sounded nothing other than calculating and cold.

Prisoner two five three was silently herded out of the debating chamber by Cresta officials. Lord Ruffus rose to state the next issue for the Full Session to deal with. Ling had recently issued a statement which a Cresta official had passed to Ruffus in order for him to read in full.

'The country of Ling wishes to issue a declaration on behalf of the Grand Visril Chang indicating its intended action in the event that the country of Davish sees fit to take the new city of Su-Zahn under its control and jurisdiction. Should this occur, as Her Majesty, Queen Nashia of Davish pronounced at the recent Summit at Verades, Ling intends to take the immediate action of bringing all the Goldmines Eloth, Rafe and Jared under its complete control.'

'Friends, this is without doubt one of the gravest threats Grat has faced in many years. The first thought on all our minds will no doubt be the troops that are stationed but some twenty miles from our Eloth Goldmines. The heavens are truly worthy of thanks for the foresight of our sovereign who had the wisdom to keep these troops ready so that they may defend our interest at little more than a few moments notice. If Queen Nashia keeps to her word, then there are only twenty days until she intends to take Su-Zahn. We must make firm decisions today about how we are to react if this occurs. Perhaps the time has come to position our troops around Eloth once again. I defer now to Adviser Jacoby on this issue.'

'Thank you for your words which were equally full of wisdom, Lord Ruffus, if I might say so. I concur strongly with the idea of reinstating the protection around Eloth, but I want to suggest to Your Majesty an even bolder strategy which I have prepared for a circumstance, the like of which has arisen today. Grat is as much of an imperial power as any of the countries which surround us, and it has long been my personal belief that Grat is to play a major part in the future development of this world. Why should we wait for Davish to make the first move? The new city of Su-Zahn is there for the taking. Anyone can have her if they are willing to take her and defend her. This would be my advice to Your Majesty: take a firm stance on this issue.'

'Advisor Jacoby, would it really be wise for His Majesty to make such a move? Speaking for the Gratian Cresta, we have grave concerns over the city of Su-Zahn. Only a short while ago at the Summit which I attended with His Majesty, Queen Nashia mentioned the losses her country sustained in the past through taking control of Su-Zahn. It is my opinion that the site is not stable, and thus it is not good for our taking. This is companioned with the additional burden which protecting the city will create. Can we really afford to protect so many objectives?'

'I respond to your points as follows. Su-Zahn is certainly stable for the time being and the risk of taking it is negligible. As to our forces, Your Majesty can be quite certain that we have a force to reckon with. All we need is the courage to be bold. I recommend to Your Majesty all the steps that I have advised.'

The tension in the debating chamber was almost audible now. So much rested on Samuel's decision. He nodded, slowly, thinking it all over. Perhaps it was now time for Grat to take action. He had to think about the long term. Su-Zahn was an interesting, if dangerous, place and taking it would avert any action from Ling. Yes. He would agree to all that Advisor Jacoby had suggested.

Later that night, when Samuel was thinking over the decision he had made in his Royal Bedchamber he was still certain he had made the right choice. Now was the time for being bold. The decision which he doubted far more was the one he had taken with respect to prisoner two five three. Samuel absentmindedly fingered the dusty golden picture frame that he had kept for as long as he could remember by his bedside. He could dimly recall that it was a gift which he had received in the years before he came to Grat. His eye was drawn to the empty hang-mans noose. At least he hadn't sent the prisoner to a fate like that. Would a lifetime spent at Porthnarth be worse than death? It wasn't something Samuel ever intended finding out.

Over the next few days the Full Sessions in the debating chamber were tense. Every day would bring fresh news of developments. Initially none of the countries responded, much to everyone's relief. Queen Nashia remained silent, and it was a silence which no other country seemed willing to break. Then Ling sent out a new communication which was customarily read out by Lord Ruffus:

'In response to the Gratian aggression in protecting its Goldmines and taking the city of Su-Zahn as its own, the country of Ling, under the orders of the Grand Visril Chang will be placing its own troops in the area surrounding the Goldmines of Rafe and Jared.'

No one was stunned by this news, but it was worrying. Grat could ill afford a major standoff with Ling at the moment. Advisor Jacoby became more worried by the day.

'What Your Majesty must understand is that if Chang places any more troops in the region then he will have our own forces outnumbered almost two to one. This simply cannot be allowed.'

The show of force by Ling continued daily, and Lord Ruffus joined Adviser Jacoby in calling for something to be done.

'Your Majesty must issue a decree that if Ling insists on bringing any more troops into the region, our own forces will attack them and claim temporal control over the Goldmines of Rafe and Jeten.'

Samuel issued a decree in almost identical terms. Ling did not even bother to respond on paper. The continued increase in its troops surrounding Rafe and Jeten was enough evidence of its continued defiance.

The day when things came to a real head had started like any other. Adviser Jacoby had been issuing an update on troop numbers in the region when there was a commotion on one of the balconies above Lord Ruffus. A message was passed down.

'At the tenth hour of this morning a Lingian battalion attacked a portion of the most forward Gratian troops who had been defending our Eloth Goldmines. So far our troops have defended their position, but it is understood that some of the fighting has been quite fierce.'

The atmosphere in the chamber was more solemn and nervous than Samuel could ever remember it being. Adviser Jacoby seemed to take longer than usual to rise to his feet and begin talking.

'Your Majesty, it seems that Ling has decided to make the first move in this giant game of political chess. At the very least, we must vigorously defend our Eloth Goldmines. On the other hand, now may be the time to stay true to the warning we issued Ling. They have defied our demands to stop increasing troops in the region with an utter disregard for the consequences. I would therefore urge Your Majesty to consider ordering our troops to take the Goldmines of Rafe and Jeten under Gratian control.'

The discussion on this issue continued for several hours and became very heated at times. Samuel decided to retire for the day without making a decision. In his mind the risk of taking such a military stretch was etched out as a warning against making a rash decision. At the end of the Full Session, Adviser Jacoby requested that Samuel would wait behind so that he could speak to him alone. His footsteps echoed loudly as he paced about his area of the debating chamber.

'Your Majesty did not have the usual nerves of steel today?'

'I have never had nerves of steel Adviser Jacoby, any more than I have a heart of stone.'

'Has Your Majesty forgotten the prophecy the Lampmaker made many years ago? The first king who was born outside this world and brought into it via the route under the mountain would unite the city of Grat with the countries it once ruled. Perhaps the time is coming soon Your Majesty. Taking control of all the Goldmines is just the start.'

'Are you not assuming that the prediction the Lampmaker made is correct?'

'What evidence do you have that he is a liar?'

The discussion was going nowhere, but Samuel got the point that was being made. He thought it over at length all evening and, by the next day, he was ready to make a decision on committing troops to take the Goldmines.

'In line with the advise Adviser Jacoby issues yesterday, I command Gratian troops to both defend the Eloth Goldmines and also to take the Goldmines of Rafe and Jeten, meeting any resistance they find there with force.'

There were gasps from the balconies all around, but the decision was made. For the next few days all they could do was wait. Lord Ruffus took to bringing a copy of The Chariot into the debating chamber with him. He would then prod it into life and everyone present could pour over the scenes of fighting.

'Your Majesty, a brave centaur by the name of Corvus is providing the main strategy for the Gratian attack and defence. He is working closely with senior Cresta officials to bring about a coordinated action. Having said this, The Chariot provides probably the most up to date view of the fighting. They have filled the battle lines with reporters. Corvus has frequently complained that they get in the way, but at least they relay the news to us quickly.'

Lord Ruffus always spoke his thoughts out loud as he viewed the seething battlefield that rose out of the newspaper in front of him. Samuel could see a mixture of humans and animals fighting on the Gratian side. In the front were beautiful centaurs, closely followed by sleek silvery stallions. Behind them a mixture of Dwarfs, Fawns and Humans were fighting, carrying an assortment of weapons and armour. The Lingian troops that were gathered around Rafe and Jeten were mainly highly skilled human fighters. They lacked the speed of the Gratian forward troops but had an advantage of acrobatic agility. Time and time again Samuel witnessed them push back the Gratian charges as they made towards Rafe and Jeten. Sometimes the centaurs would be forced to veer off to one side in order to avoid clashing with Lingian forces head on. A volley of Gratian arrows would inflict some harm on the Lingians, but more of them missed than hit their targets. Ling started making effective use of mortars against the Gratian attacks and some of the battles which Samuel was witnessing were becoming too gruesome to watch. He had spoken to both Lord Ruffus and Advisor Jacoby about pulling back, but both had sadly but vigorously shaken their heads.

'To pull out now is to loose the Eloth Goldmines. Ling is very angry with Grat, and we cannot expect them to leave us alone. They may even try and attack the city, although that would be madness. Ling has a good army but it is not big enough for that.'

The other discussion which had played out in the debating chamber recently was whether Queen Nashia could be approached to join Grat in defending the Goldmines in return for Su-Zahn. The date which Queen Nashia had set for taking the city had come and gone without any sign of movement on the part of Davish. Advisor Jacoby was vehement in supporting a stance of no contact with Davish:

'Nashia remains a compromised monarch, too unpredictable for us to rely on at a time like this. We should have nothing to do with the woman. Grat must fight this battle and win it alone. Telfon have already expressed their stance as being that they have no interest in becoming involved in this war at this stage. They are waiting to see who takes all the Goldmines and will then decide how they wish to bargain with the winner in order to take back some control over the Goldmines.'

With everyone's mind set in such a manner, Samuel could see no option other than to press ahead. His determination was soon to be tested when the effects of distant bloody battles was brought uncomfortably close to home.

Samuel had been sitting in a Full Session at the debating chamber when Rose had a message passed down to him. Martharnia had called at the Royal Palace and wished to speak to him. He hoped she would not entice him to make another trip to visit the Lampmaker. He had experience quite enough of him already. When he greeted her later near the grand staircase he was surprised to see she had dispensed with the usual maids pinafore that she wore. It was replaced with a much plainer overall, rather like a uniform.

'Your Majesty, Samuel, I had to come and say goodbye!'

'Martharnia! Where are you going?'

'I am joining a group of nurses heading out on assignment to treat the Gratian wounded at the Gratian front. You must have heard of the terrible injuries that have been inflicted upon our troops?'

'Martharnia, I forbid you, for the sake of Grat from putting yourself in perfectly avoidable danger like this! You must not go! Stay here in Grat where you will be safe!'

Beneath her bushy exterior, Martharnia bristled with hurt.

'Samuel, Your Majesty! I am truly shocked that you would tell me to disobey my own conscience. I have many friends who are sacrificing their lives to support our country! The least I must do is attend to the wounded. My heart tells me I should have joined my friends in the fight against Ling long ago!'

Samuel could see that arguing would be completely pointless. He knew Martharnia well enough to know that when her heart was set on something she could be obstinate to the end, even against the will of her Sovereign. In many ways, it was this quality in her which he had always admired the most. It showed a robustness of character which Samuel often wished he possessed more himself. With sadness he hugged her goodbye. She, in turn, promised to return to Grat as soon as her work would permit. Never would she allow Samuel to be without the nurse of his childhood; Martharnia would always be there for him.

During the weeks which followed the fighting continued to intensify with heavy losses for both Grat and Ling. Samuel had an opportunity to spend a few fleeting minutes between fraught, heated sessions in the debating chamber reading a letter from Jack Sorrow and Bertis Beavitch. They both mentioned that their fathers had been called up as reinforcements in the Gratian forces. They were taking the place of others who had fallen in the front line near the Eloth Goldmines. Samuel was just glad that Jack and Bertis were safe at Longwhey, continuing their studies in Timelore. All academic aspirations seemed terribly removed from reality for Samuel now. The only battle he had to face was to stop the city of Grat falling apart. Gradually the daily news provided in the debating chamber improved as the traditional Summer Retreat threatened its arrival. Heat out on the plains had threatened any intentions of continued warfare by either Ling or Grat, but gradually the Lingian troops had been pushed back. It was with great relief, but heavy losses, that Lord Ruffus announced that the Goldmines of Rafe and Jeten had been taken under Gratian control at last. The Lingian troops had not been entirely defeated, but had decided to pull back into Ling completely. The region which had for months been a battlefield was left in a peaceful, sombre silence as the disheartened remnants of the Gratian troops half-heartedly guarded the Goldmines which they had fought so hard to gain.

Adviser Jacoby had been more than pleased that events had eventually turned out as he had planned. The same could not be said for Lord Ruffus. Samuel thought he looked like a ghost of the man he had once been. This seemed to have been a battle too far for him. Whether it was old age, exhaustion or sensitivity, Samuel could not say. Lord Ruffus caught him quiet by surprise outside the debating chamber when everyone had exited.

'Lord Ruffus?'

'Your Majesty, I'm sorry to make you jump. I wanted to have a private word with you.'

'Oh yes, great news about Grat pulling through?'

'With respect, I did not wish to congratulate Your Majesty on any military victories. Perhaps, in fact, it was quiet the opposite. For months you and I have graced the debating chamber with our presence and pursued a policy of aggression and warfare.'

'Justifiably so, wouldn't you say?'

'Perhaps, it is not the justification which concerns me at present. Here, look at this paper.'

He pulled out a copy of The Chariot, and spread it in his arms. A male figure rose out of the paper and spoke aloud:

'Today at the Gratian front the Goldmines of Rafe and Jeten were finally taken by Grat. We now look back at the terrible losses that have been inflicted upon the citizens of Grat who have sacrificed themselves for our city. Only yesterday, a large nursing station was caught in the crossfire, and less than a tenth of the one hundred strong nursing team escaped the Lingian attack. The site where this occurred was just beyond the Eloth Goldmines where some of the worst of the wounded were being tended...'

Ruffus shut the paper at this point and looked at Samuel with concern.

'Your nurse, Martharnia, she joined a nursing station I believe...'

The words had barely left his tongue before Samuel caught his meaning.

'I didn't show Your Majesty this with the intention of frightening you. Instead, I simply wanted to show how much the battle which has been fought has cost the people of Grat. They fought in your name. The least you owe them is to visit the site where they fell? Oh, I know Jacoby, Your Adviser, would not council in favour of the idea. He prefers wars and battles fought in the clinical calm of a marble lined debating chamber with thought only of the political effects and without any thought of the consequences on the life of our citizens. For every being that has fallen in your battles, think of all the family that remain behind here in Grat, now lacking the relatives they loved. At least when Saffie died you had a chance to say goodbye. Many of these relatives won't even have a body to bury. You saw what the fighting was like; it was awful by any standards.'

Samuel was taken aback by the strength of what Lord Ruffus was saying.

'But Lord Ruffus, every war brings its casualties doesn't it?'

Ruffus almost spat his answer in reply:

'In the eyes of many, the day that a Monarch stops valuing every single life that is sacrificed for the sake of a cause which he has instigated, He is no longer fit to govern. That King will find that the respect of His people for Him is destroyed. They may not expect to see their King openly weeping and distraught at the losses sustained, but there is something far deeper, something subliminal. People treat you differently when they know that somewhere behind the shiny laughter is buried great pain. Your Majesty should remember that this Royal Palace, this castle was built for Kings, not mere men. Leaders are required to be something more than human. They must respond to the usual lusts and desires of the mortal condition differently if they are to truly deserve their title. You, King Samuel Deksis, must prove yourself in the same way in my eyes.'

Samuel nodded slowly, waiting for Lord Ruffus to continue. He sensed there was something more to this outburst.

'Tomorrow I will set off to visit the plains between Grat and Ling where so many of our people have fallen. I entreat Your Majesty to join me if you will. Two of the remaining centaurs have agreed to carry us out there. You have tonight to make your decision. We leave early at the break of dawn.'

Samuel spent a sleepless night beside Rose in their Royal Bedchamber. Before dawn his mind was made up. He owed it to Martharnia if nothing else to see whether she was still alive. If she was, she would still be near the Eloth Goldmines for sure. If she was injured he may be able to get her the help she needed. He kissed a sleepy Rose goodbye, confirming that he would head out to the front line, as he had been considering with her last night.

Lord Ruffus was waiting for Samuel in the Royal Gardens. He introduced Samuel's steed as Corvus. He could remember the name distinctly as the main strategist of the recent battle with Ling. Samuel mounted and waited for Lord Ruffus to ready himself. Gruffly the centaur beneath Samuel started speaking.

'We will be riding out of Grat today with a group of other centaurs that are to assume key replacement roles in the Gratian forces spread out in the plains towards Ling.'

'How many will there be, Corvus?'

'I'm sorry to say there will only be eight including myself and Equuleus. We are the only ones who remain alive in this world.'

Samuel swallowed hard. News like this seemed to make the losses that had been sustained a lot more real. Corvus and his companion did not seemed inclined to dwell in depression and were soon riding with beautiful rhythm and precision through the centre of the city of Grat, towards Aborglacias and the gates that were situated just beyond there.

A city which had once sparkled with life seemed little more than a ghost town today. It was stripped of all signs of affluence. Ripped papers and boxes littered many of the streets and parts were mired by severe squalor. It was evident to Samuel that in his confinement to the Royal Palace he had been blinded from the plight of many of his people. As the city blocks gave way to a less metropolitan environment different centaurs began to join them. When eventually they were riding past the attractive cottages of Aborglacias a total of six had joined them, bring the number of centaurs to eight as Corvus had anticipated.

Lord Ruffus called up the command for the city gates beyond Aborglacias to be opened and, without delay, the centaurs thundered through and into the narrow mountain pass that lay beyond it. It was far narrower and rockier than the one he had used the last time he rode with Lord Ruffus to the Summit in Davish. This one would bring them out directly onto the plains between Grat and Ling. Quite unexpectedly the centaurs surrounding Samuel and Lord Ruffus broke into a low, deep song that rolled around the craggy pass like a force of nature; strong, beautiful and sincere. Its intonation and rhythm matched the melancholy beat of their slender hoofs on the stony ground.

'Out, out to battle we solemnly ride,
Ready to die from a sword in our side,
Ready to give our sprinkling of blood,
Ready to show our King of our love.'

The singing subsided momentarily, allowing the deep tune to be entirely replaced by the rise and fall of hooves. Behind him, Samuel heard Lord Ruffus breathe a sigh and exclaim aloud:

'The war chant of the centaurs of Grat, nothing quite like it! It moves the very essence of the soul.'

The chant continued to flow easily into a second verse.

'Defenders of honour, defenders of light,
We steadily gallop with all of our might.
Watching the stars as we charge through the dawn,
Remembering all of the friends that we mourn.'

Faintly, and with a vague sense of irritation, Samuel felt the thread of a tear prickle at the corner of his eye. He could not allow his calm integrity to disintegrate at this stage. The song led on, with Samuel battling to ignore the words.

'Today we will roam far from our home,
Giving our lives to the cause of our throne.
The lands are unknown but the purpose the same,
We fight for the King and die by the mane.

Without tears in our eyes we will watch on our sunset,
Ready to give all at the close of the day.
The last of our strength, reserves we have kept,
All shall be spent 'till death forces its way.

Stars above, are awake, and look down so kindly,

Etching the very seams of the sky.
As our hoofs keep on pounding by the centaurs surrounding,
We pray that we see them last as we die.'

The thunder of hooves continued the mournful song as its last strains dissipated. The pass was widening and Samuel could make out the plains in front. The dark shadow of the craggy pass gave way to the unbearable glare of the near desert. They passed from an environment of claustrophobic rocky walls to one which, for mile upon empty mile, lay unobstructed. Some way into the scrub land where the vegetation gave way to more dusty, dry looking land Samuel could make out the settlement which surrounded Grat's Eloth Goldmines. It was situated directly on top of a rocky ridge which rose distinctly out of the empty land in that area and consisted of a variety of distant huts and tents surrounding a pit head, the only visible workings of the Goldmines beneath the ground.

Beyond this settlement, the ground returned to dusty sand before the Goldmines of Rafe and Jeten rose up on the horizon nearer to Ling, which from here was still out of sight in the scorching heat haze.

The centaurs charged on with no visible sign of heavy exertion. Samuel's eyes were drawn to the space between Eloth and the two distant mines. From here he could see what looked like small crops of rock lying in the desert. He stared until his eyes burned, surveying the vast distance over which these clumps were spread.

'Your Majesty can see even from here the size of the battlefield?'

'Where, where am I supposed to be looking, Lord Ruffus?'

'The fallen bodies are spread all the way between Eloth and the other mines, Your Majesty. If you think it looks bad from here, just wait until we get up-close.'

In little over an hour Samuel would realise the truth in these words. The centaurs had at last slowed as they skirted the Eloth Goldmines and headed into the area where the battle had raged for the last few weeks. Corvus halted, and asked the King to dismount.

Samuel was surrounded by a sea of utter desolation. The burning heat of the desert climate here had evidently chased all remnants of survivors of the battle far from the scene. Sandy hummocks were piled high with the charred and tortured remnants of those who had sacrificed their lives fighting for Grat. It was impossible not to be moved by the abhorrent scene. The whole area was filled with the heavy, unforgettable stench of death and it was terribly silent. The only audible noise was the buzz issued by the flies who were feasting on the festering corpses. The eight centaurs which had ridden with them were moving off to one side, passing reverently the different corpses, looking for friends who had fallen.

'Aye, Your Majesty, these are the spoils of your war.'

Samuel felt himself choke, unable to reply. Just a few metres to the right of where he was standing, something bushy was lying stiffly, half buried in the ground.

'Is it...'

'If Your Majesty will wait, I will look. All nurses on the battle field carried papers with them.'

Lord Ruffus moved over to the remains with the gentle calmness which was the blessed quality he could so often find. Samuel looked away. He could hear Lord Ruffus gingerly shifting the body to search for the papers. He returned in silence, clutching them. Samuel looked grimly at them. There must have been many Squirrels who had both fought and fallen in this battle. There was no reason why it should be her. The paper unfolded in front of him so that he could read the details inscribed:

'Race: Squirrel
Gender: Female
Position: Nurse
Common Name: Martharnia...'

The cold hand of realisation twisted and wrenched at his heart. Whether it was the heat or the shock, Samuel would forever be uncertain, but at that moment he let the documents fall to the ground and sank to it himself, heaving sickly.

Some time passed before he felt well enough to stand again. Lord Ruffus stood beside him, greatly concerned. The sight of the old man made Samuel feel sick once again.

'Look what I've done! Look what I've done. All around me, this sea, this tide of destruction is my work and in my name! WHY, why didn't you stop me!'

'Your Majesty... I have always tried my best to, to guide you. But that really is the job of Advisor Jacoby...'

'I have a Royal Advisor who cannot even be bothered to make a trip to a battle field where half of the world lie dead...'

Samuel dissolved into heavy, fitful sobs. Lord Ruffus stood awkwardly to one side, wringing his hands as he surveyed both his King and the surrounding horrors.

'I think, Your Majesty, it is time that Corvus took you back to Grat.'

'You can clear off back to Grat if you want to Ruffus, go and join Jacoby and debate everything that has happened. Go on, I don't ever want to see your face again. And don't ever bother washing your filthy hands while you're back in Grat!'

'Why is that, Your Majesty?'

'Because there's blood on them that'll never wash off!'

Lord Ruffus seemed to think it best not to provide any reply to this. Samuel was sitting on the ground, mentally quite disturbed and tortured. He remained in that position for over an hour. Eventually Lord Ruffus spoke quietly.

'Can I entreat with all my might and being that Your Majesty now rides back to Grat. I will be coming with you so that you won't be alone. You must dismiss the six centaurs that joined us so that they can ride on to Rafe and take up their posts there.'

'Centaurs, be gone, all of you. Ruffus, you can go back with the other two centaurs to Grat.'

'Your Majesty, you cannot be left in this boiling desert any longer. I cannot leave you here.'

'Today I stopped taking advice or guidance from either you or Jacoby. Go on, clear off to Grat. I don't intend to ever see you again.'

'Your Majesty... for my own health I have to retreat back to the edge of the mountains to find shade. I will go no further. When the heat of the desert is relieved I shall return to get you. If you will not leave by then I will have the centaurs bind You and drag You back against Your will.'

Samuel did not respond to this and Lord Ruffus soon left, taking the remaining two centaurs with him. All around, the heat of the desert seemed to intensify, and the smells and sounds were magnified. If the scalding heat was making him delirious Samuel certainly didn't feel it. He had no hope, no sense of feeling left in him. Perhaps this was what being dead would feel like. He wished he was. Like dear, dear Martharnia he would be away from it all. How she must blame him for all that had happened! If he stayed sitting here like this maybe he would die before Lord Ruffus came back to collect him. He looked around for something, anything that he might use to hasten the process.

In the distance, amid some of the bodies, something moved. It would have made Samuel jump if he hadn't been stuck in a state of hazy delirious paralysis. Something small and mouse-like was stumbling across the barren sands towards him. As it approached, Samuel could see that it was indeed a mouse; clutching a miniature bottle of Old Brine as it weaved and struggled forward. On its head was a battered hat.

'I'ss a mouse, I'ss a mouse... three bottles of brine, ten for a dime, four for a Grat, five for my hat! You want??'

'No, I don't. Who, what are you?'

'Me? You do not know me, sirrr? Why, I am most, most offended; yes indeed, offended in the highest state. I sirrr am a star!'

'A star?'

'Yes sirrr, I was a huge star, all the world they new me,' he stopped to take a deep swig from the bottle of Old Brine which he carried and, finishing it, discarded it in the sand beside him. Unsteadily he began speaking again.

'My name, it is, it is, Pinochet, the most famous mouse that ever lived in the city of Grat! Pinochet is my stage name. I use it only when I perform. Which is all, all days.'

'What did you do to be so well known?'

'Why sirrr, I fronted The Chariot newspapers, I was the star. You may have seen me at my prime. With every salutation you will think it rather nice and, and in Elvish and the other, other one too...'

Dimly, very dimly, Samuel could recall something from the time he had spent with Lady Flint when he arrived in Grat. Before he had a subscription to The Chariot arranged, a very loud and brash mouse had appeared, trying to entice Samuel to join. Gone now was the neat jaunty hat. The thing this mouse wore on its head looked old and dirty. Yet there was still just a hint of the old sparkle, the old showbiz sentiment that could have made this petulant beast into a celebrity.

'What sirrr, brings you here amongst this sleepy audience? Do you want an autography? I might, if you wanted...'

'I just want to be left alone.'

'Alone eh? Who are you exactly to make yer so high and mighty?'

Samuel Swallowed,

'I am, I was the King of Grat.'

'Samuel Deksis? Didn't expect to see him here. Thought Royalty only stayed in their Royal Palaces while honest hard working folk like me lose their jobs and join up to fight.'

'I don't want to be a King any more. I hate it.'

'Can't say I blame you sirrr. I hate Royalty. Load of rich posh heads who talented folk, the likes of myself, work to keep. Pinochet says no to anything of the sort.'

By Samuel's side a second creature fluttered. It was a tiny green bird. He ignored it and turned back to the mouse.

'I am wishing that I never existed. That I was never allowed to be born. That my father never lived and that there were never any Kings in the city of Grat.'

'Here, here, Majesty, I raise an empty bottle to you, look.'

The mouse strode to the bottle which he had allowed to roll away from him earlier and drank the final drips that remained in it.

'We are brothers, Sirrr. An end to all Kings is our aim. Look, even that bird agrees. Do you want to join our Brothership, little thing?'

The bird which had been sitting beside Samuel flapped its wings and landed on the palm he stretched out.

'You like to hate kings do you? Little bird. Then salute our cause! Death to royalty!'

As the bird steadied itself on Samuel's hand, the mouse, Pinochet, toppled slowly over in the sand, driven to sleep by overconsumption and the heat.

The bird flew off, back onto the ground.

'You're going to leave me now as well are you, bird? Leave me all alone.'

As Samuel spoke, the bird flapped its wings onto the ground and started to grow. Slowly it expanded in the bright sunlight, morphing into something quite different. The change in mass was sizable and as the mass began to form into something coherent, Samuel could tell that it was human. Moreover, it was female. In only a few more seconds the transformation was entirely complete.

The woman standing before him was fully clothed and wearing a green feathered hat.

'Do I know you? You look familiar.'

'I'm not sure, Your Majesty, do you often frequent with strange green birds?'

'I can't say that I do.'

'Well in that case it would seem unlikely?'

'I heard all that You said to Pinochet and I concur with Your sentiment. We shall work together to annihilate all of the kings of Grat. No more will they terrorise this world...'

The scene before Samuel misted over completely and faded away. He collapsed there in the desert heat, completely exhausted. From many miles away, the precise sight of the centaur Corvus picked out the slumped form and rode out to collect the dishevelled King. Lord Ruffus rode with the unconscious body back into Grat.

When Samuel started to come round the first thing he noticed was that he had no movement in his arms. They seemed to be stuck behind him and, try as he might, they would not be released. Before him the dark, cold outline of the debating chamber swam into view. Something seemed strange and for a while he could not work out what it was. The view was different. He was looking at his own throne across the room. And there was a man. A man was sitting in that golden chair of authority. It was Advisor Jacoby. He rose to speak as he had done many times before.

'We bring to account before this chamber today, Mr. Samuel Deksis and Lord Ruffus former head of the Gratian Cresta. These two humans were the architects of the Gratian offensive that secured the Goldmines of Rafe and Jeten at a bloody and unnecessary cost. All of the nations that surround us have risen in unison against Grat and over the past days have pressed the remnants of our forces back to a position some way behind the Eloth Goldmines. Grat has lost everything it gained under the direction of the two people we see before us. The people of Grat who remain alive have elected me, Adviser Jacoby, to lead their country from now on. This chamber must today sit in judgment upon these souls and determine the punishment which they shall be given.'

There were shouts from above them and Samuel strained to see a collection of creatures and humans shouting in an uncouth manner into the chamber.

'Let them die like my brother and my father. They sacrificed so much of ours; let them now sacrifice their lives!'

These were the much lauded cries that were issued into the chamber at volume.

'Do the prisoners have anything to say in their defence? I think that's what I'm supposed to ask isn't it Lord Ruffus?'

Beside Samuel Lord Ruffus rose shakily to his feet.

'Nothing, except that we do not recognise the authority of this Full Session which you hold. What part of the Opate Declaration makes its existence lawful? No section which I have read gives an Advisor the authority to hold council.'

'Look around you Ruffus, the evidence is everywhere! I am speaking and you are listening. I am mightier and you are weaker. I am in control and you are not. The people of Grat wanted change and that is exactly what they got. Under my leadership, justice is administered simply and quickly. The people of Grat shall get what they desire. Shall we lock them up in Porthnarth for life, or hang them both?'

The replies came back loud and mixed. Samuel watched Adviser Jacoby's face crack into a wicked smirk.

'I think we'll give them a bit of both. A week in Porthnarth and then a public hanging. Guards, lead them out immediately. The citizens of this city have seen quiet enough of their faces!'

The pair were dragged at force through the labyrinthine streets of Grat. Samuel had found his hands bound and chained behind him when he had been pushed out of the debating chamber. He had frantically looked for Rose as he left the Royal Palace but could see no trace of her. The streets outside were quite empty, but a few of the poorest, sickest people were slumped in the darker narrower streets of the dirty city centre. One old man called out to Samuel and the guards that were pushing him stopped.

'I've moved all my belongings down to the end of the room in here, look!'

He shuffled down towards an amassed pile of objects including books and coats and other daily possessions before looking up at his former Sovereign, sadly.

'They closed down the city gates for the last time yesterday. I took my last walk through them knowing it would be the last time I would ever make that journey. I've reached the end of my hoarded resources too. I finished the last of the canned foods at the break of light this morning while I was looking out at the deserted city streets which used to teem with life. Now the life that remains just crawls along with the silent desperation of the forgotten. You could hear the sounds of mortars from the front line last night for the first time too. War is coming here to the City of Grat. I believe that this is the end Your Majesty. The end of the world has arrived in my lifetime.

As it is written, the great armies peer through a cleft in the hill, and the first specs of dust settle on the muddy fields of war. The world will sink into the last great battle which will herald the complete annihilation of everything we've loved and known. That time is definitely coming. We know it will bring about the end of this world. The question is, is it now? Are the sounds of the footsteps of the forces the same drums that will sound the death knoll of the hidden worlds?'

The guards led Samuel on past the man.

Things really were desperate in the city. Lord Ruffus stumbled along behind Samuel. As they approached the short bridge to Porthnarth several humans lined up to spit in their faces. Samuel got the impression that this was the treatment most of those entering Porthnarth received.

Once inside they were both untied and handed filthy prison uniforms to wear. They bore the respective numbers of the cells to which they would be assigned. In Samuel's case he received the number two five two. He was dragged off first and did not bother resisting.

The room in which he was dumped was windowless and dirty. There was no bed, no chair; it was really no more than a cupboard. During all his years as King of this country Samuel had never realised anyone was kept in conditions like these. The metal door clanged shut as the guards left him. Samuel sat in a dejected huddle for many hours.

Sleep must have taken him at some point because he found a morsel of food had been pushed into the cell. He could also hear fresh noises in the cell to his left. Samuel crept forwards to the bars of his cell and tried to hear the words spoken. He did not recognise the accent, but the words were indistinguishable anyway at the volume which they were being spoken. Samuel called out several times to see if the prisoner there would respond. Nothing was forthcoming from the direction of that cell, but to his right a familiar voice did cry out.

'Samuel, is that you?'

'Lord Ruffus, are you there?'

'Yes, yes I'm quite alright. I am so glad that you have come around at least, even if it had to be at a sentencing by Advisor Jacoby.'

He went on to tell Samuel how he had brought him back to Grat but found himself arrested at the city gates. Whilst they had been away Ling, Davish and Telfon had all declared war on the city of Grat, and Adviser Jacoby had appointed himself the leader of the city in their absence. The population was angry at the number that had been killed in the battle for Rafe and Jeten. The thirst for gold seemed to have been valued more highly than life itself.

'Jacoby blamed Your Majesty and myself for this error and whilst we must share some of the blame for what happened, the picture which he has been painting is an entire fabrication. For now he seems to have had his way, but I have hope. Rose escaped from the Royal Palace and I am sure will intercede on our behalves. We just have to wait here until she can reach us. That wife of yours is very brave and strong as I'm sure you well know. With her working for us there can be no failure. What happened to you out on the desert without me? You seemed to be suffering sunstroke from what I could see. Holding council with people that weren't there?'

'I imagine the reason why it appeared like that was because they were so small. I might have been somewhat delirious but I'm sure they were real. It is a strange, an odd thing, that now I have been locked up here at Porthnarth I have the freedom, for the first time in my life, to really understand everything that has happened to me.'

Samuel went on to explain all that had occurred with the mouse and the bird.

'Do you see what was formed out there Lord Ruffus?'

'No I'm not sure I do.'

'The Brothership has been following me all my life. It killed my father before me according to the late Mr. Harbury. He paid with his life for finding out where the bird and the mouse were hiding out; in an empty cottage in Aborglacias.'

'I am aware, Your Majesty, that The Brothership is thought to provide evidence of the Eddisa Paradox.'

'Exactly, the deadly pact to kill all Kings of Grat has had consequences backwards and forwards in time. The woman that the bird became looked strangely familiar to me. It was only a few hours ago that I realised who it was. I knew her in my life before entering this world as Marion Monroe. She was a housekeeper for the man, Albert who I lived with. The first time she affected my life was earlier than I realised. I was sent to spend each Christmas, the equivalent of Winterville, with a woman called Aunt Mulltasch and I recall dimly a day when she was attacked. She thought it was a thug dressed as a cowboy who mugged her, but I don't think so. In the darkness of the alley way Marion's green feathered hat could easily be mistaken for a garish costume.'

'Your Majesty speaks of many things with which I am not especially familiar but it seems plausible. A prison cell can be a dangerous place to think though, for it makes the wildest ideas seem sane. Perhaps we had better not reach any firm judgements until we are freed.'

Samuel sat in silence for many more hours. There followed after this a mixture of sleeping, thinking and talking. Most of it Samuel would not remember. Days must have been passing and the impending hanging nearing fast. The faith which Lord Ruffus placed in Rose was impossibly firm. It almost annoyed Samuel. Of course she was very brave. It didn't mean she could get them out of this mess. For Samuel each passing moment gained a new sense of empty desperation. He did not want to die now as he had out on the plain, but if death was forced upon him, then he did not want to be seen to cower in the face of it.

A passing guard called out a number.

'Prisoner two five one, you are to be hooded in preparation for the hanging later today. You will either put the hood on yourself or it will be forced on you. Which do you prefer?'

Samuel did not hear Lord Ruffus reply and truthfully did not want to know what he had said. He knew it would be his turn next.

'Prisoner two five two, you are to be hooded now so that you are ready for the hanging later today. You will either tie the hood over yourself or it will be forced on you. Which do you choose?'

'Go hang yourselves.'

'Guards, enter the cell of prisoner two five two.'

It was not a pretty scene. Samuel did struggle. It was not pleasant to have your entire face covered by a thick, leathery bag. The guards tied the cords so tightly around his neck that he started to choke and writhed on the floor, to their amusement. He heard the barred door slam closed behind them as they left and cursed each one of them under his breath. He knew that sound was going to be his only companion now that the sense of sight had deserted him. The hood was still tight and it was completely black inside. The material of the hood had been chosen without any thought of human dignity.

The minutes were ticking away. Prisoner two five three had been hooded next door and Samuel heard the guards laughing as they walked from the cell. That was all he heard. It seemed only three people would go to their deaths today.

A bolt on the door to his cell was shot open and Samuel knew the time had come. There was the sound of the door creaking open and a guard entering. Samuel felt what he thought was a hand clutch as his face and he lashed out with his foot in front of him. He heard the guard fall surprisingly easily and lightly. The voice which whispered near his ear was like music to his soul.

'Samuel, it's me, Rose. I've come to get you out.'

'Rose! Rose! Is it really you? How did you get in?'

'Shush, yes, Adviser Jacoby sent me. He has pardoned your life.'

'Why the shush then? I'm a free man?'

'Jacoby has had to pardon you in secret. He could not do so publicly because you are hated so much in the city that it would have caused a riot. I am to get you out of here in the change of clothes he provided. We're going to go to the apartment my mother lived in, you might remember it. It's been empty for some time but it should serve as a safe place for a while.'

Samuel allowed Rose to gently untie the brutal cords of the wretched hood which had nearly suffocated him. At last here was hope. Lord Ruffus had been right again. Rose did come.

-- CHAPTER ELEVEN --

Days of Flight

'Has Lord Ruffus been pardoned too, Rose?'

'Yes he has, and a separate team are working to free him at the moment. I was only sent to bring you out. It is urgent that we leave quickly and without being seen. I used Marlow from Longwhey to distract the guards near the entrance to this forsaken hell hole. Now come on, change into these clothes....'

The pair dashed through the open barred door and down the dark corridor. Samuel did not have a chance to look in on Lord Ruffus because Rose was in such a hurry to get away. Thankfully the route that she had chosen to take out of the complex was uneventful and clear. You could always rely on Marlow to distract guards well, thought Samuel with a wry smile.

Across the bridge they ran and onto Moonside. The streets around seemed totally void of life.

'Can you hear that sound of thunder Samuel?'

He could

'The fighting is getting very close to Grat now. Some of the Lingian troops managed to break through a poorly guarded pass this morning. They say that a lot of damage has been done to the Borrow Ways.'

'Damage, what sort of damage?'

'Poisons and stuff like that I understand. We might see something of what has happened when we pass there?'

'Strange route to take isn't it Rose?'

'Well in case we get followed, and I thought it best to use quieter routes.'

Samuel was starting to get quite out of breath now and a mean stitch pain was developing in his chest. Still Rose kept on pounding ahead down the streets in front of her. She didn't slow down at all until she came to a narrow pathway that led along a grassy bank.

'You, huh, might, huh, not recognise this path, but the Borrow Ways will soon be on our right. In fact look, you can see them over there.'

Tall grasses by the side of the path had given way to a view over what had in years gone by been a teeming site of water trade. Today the waters ran thick with oil. Where this had not coated everything the water which was visible was a putrid green hue that stood testament to the Lingian sabotage earlier in the day. It would take years for the waterways to recover from this, Samuel thought. He could see different boats had been smashed and half sunk. Some lay completely upturned in the water.

'Rose, can you see that boat over there?'

'Do you mean the wide upturned one by the reeds?'

'Yeah, can you read the name of the vessel? I can see it dimly above the waterline, but it's hard to read in this light.'

'Is that an S? Sh, Shan, Shanty – The Shanty? I think?'

'Oh no, I do hope not!'

'Is it theirs?'

‘Yes, that would be Mole and Mr. Shabbers’ boat then. I wonder what has happened to them.’

‘The Chariot said that a group of traders mounted a valiant effort to stop the Lingians advancing further into Grat. None of them survived but they enabled the rest of our troops to cut them off. I expect it was them.’

Samuel was sure she was right. He was bitterly sorry that he had been forced to let them go without saying goodbye. He would never get to see them again. Pausing longer was never an option as Rose spurred Samuel to complete the rest of the journey quickly. They arrived quite exhausted at the relative safety of Lady Flint’s apartment just over an hour later.

‘We can sit down for a chat now but then I need you to change your clothes again.’

‘Again, why again?’

‘Because if all goes to plan you will soon leave Grat altogether. It is the only safe option for you.

‘Am I going to return to the world that I came here from? Without you?’

‘Yes, and of course not. I can’t come straight away but it is so urgent that you leave that you must go on ahead without me. I will come and join you as soon as I can I promise. Now use the time we have here wisely. Talk only of important things.’

Samuel went on tell Rose what had happened out in the desert. She listened intently, especially when Samuel told her about Marion Monroe. Rose knew as much of Samuel’s life before he came to Grat as he could recall and for this reason she was the best person to help him to piece everything together.

‘I think I can see something that you may have missed Samuel. We know that while you were with Albert Hawkins your mother watched over you and protected you. She made sure that you were sent away to Aunt Mulltasch at Christmas every year because it was safer there for you. You knew how Marion complained about food going missing while your mother had hidden herself away, you noticed the remark yourself. How long would it have taken Marion to figure out that your mother was around? I don’t think anyone intended to kill Albert Hawkins that night as you have long suspected; they intended to kill your mother. Albert Hawkins was small fry, a simple stupid man who thought himself something of an intellectual.’

‘Rose, Rose you’re right. I remember a cup left out by the fireplace. Marion must have hoped my mother would drink it when she came looking for food and drink in the night. Instead, and I remember now distinctly that I heard someone going into the main room during the night. Albert must have been thirsty and decided to drink what was left out. No wonder Marion was so keen to make all the funeral arrangements. There is one thing I don’t understand though Rose. While I was with the McGills, why did Marion come and tell me about the journey into Grat and the Lampmaker’s prophecy?’

‘Well from what details you gave me, Samuel, she never actually showed you her face.’

‘No I agree. She said she had come in disguise with a scarf wrapped around most of her head so that she would not be recognised. It wasn’t much of a disguise if you ask me. She still wore the feathered hat...’

‘Samuel, how would it seem if the disguise which she wore was intended only to fool you?’

‘How’d you mean?’

‘Well I don’t think Marion Monroe ever went to the McGills. I think that was your mother. She wanted to be the one to tell you about Grat. After you left Albert Hawkins I think the next time you encountered Marion Monroe was in the Dark Train.’

‘But she wasn’t there! I didn’t see her at all!’

‘Are you sure? There wasn’t a small green bird hiding in a corner of the train?’

‘Rose, Rose you’re right! I do remember a boy with a small green bird in his hands. But why was Gredric attacked and not me?’

‘A mistake perhaps?’

‘Oh Yes! That makes sense. The boy cupped the bird in his hands. It could not see that I swapped seats. And Rose, dear Rose it’s all making sense now. When Bertis was burnt in that awful prank at Longwhey Marlow had said there were bird dropping in the Royal Box. It must have been her again!’

‘I think I can help you out with the Ling crisis. That has to be the easiest mystery of them all to solve. From what you have told me of it you swapped places with Queen Nashia. It was you who was intended to be blown up. You told me that Mr. Harbury identified the traveller from the green ring she dropped. I note that green is the same colour as the bird, but can you connect Marion Monroe with a peculiar green ring?’

Samuel strained his mind as hard as he could but nothing leapt out at him. Perhaps it would come back to him later. So many mysteries had been resolved that it seemed a pity to stop now. Alas Rose called time and made Samuel change. It was night outside as they flew together on the carpet she had prepared to take them out of Grat and up the entrance to the Warren Kitchens.

Rose had mastered the art of flying to a precise degree and very capably brought them down at the entrance to the Warren Kitchen’s tunnel. The door to it opened at her grasp. Rose had brought with them the old lamp which the Lampmaker had given Samuel years ago when he arrived in the city of Grat and she held it aloft as they quickly raced to the Warren Kitchens themselves.

‘I found this lamp under your bed in the Royal Bedchambers before I left the Royal Palace. You must have left it there for safe keeping for many years. I thought I had better take it with me. I wanted to leave as little as possible behind for Adviser Jacoby to get his hands on. It is imperative now for all of us that you get out quickly. The Lampmaker’s Cottage will be empty tonight because the Lampmaker has been called away to a meeting. From the Warren Kitchens you must take the secret passage which Martharnia showed you down to his Cottage. The stairs come out two chambers from the end of the line for the Dark Train which will be at your right. The external door to his Cottage has been left unlocked so you can let yourself out and quickly find the start of the line. Follow it to the place between worlds and cautiously make your way across. Don’t forget to blindfold yourself with your jumper. Once you are through, follow the line and keep walking until you eventually get to the village outside. When I leave Grat I will meet you there.’

They had reached the Warren Kitchens now and it was evident that there was no need to bother with a key. The site had been ransacked and ruined, the door kicked in and the collection of glass panes smashed beyond recognition. Samuel led the way to the room that contained the cupboard that concealed the entrance to the passage. It seemed to be one of the only things that had been left untouched by the looters.

‘I would be much happier if you were coming with me Rose!’

‘So would I, but some things cannot be left undone. I will come and join you as soon as I can I promise. Have your lamp and take care.’

Rose and Samuel exchanged a quick farewell and Samuel hoped with all his heart that they would be reunited again soon. Leaving Rose behind with a simple lamp of her own, Samuel began the arduous trek down the stairs that eventually led to the Lampmaker’s cottage. Breathless and exhausted, he arrived there after what seemed like an eternity. The place was open and empty. The fires which usually burned with splendour might never have existed. Samuel followed Rose’s advice and walked through the two chambers to his right. The external door, through which he had entered years ago, was open and he passed through the exit as quickly as he could.

Samuel pulled the door to the Lampmaker’s cottage shut. If he hadn’t been in such a hurry he might have lingered for a while outside, glad to have passed through it without having to meet the Lampmaker. Samuel couldn't help but wonder where the Lampmaker was. Rose had said that he had been called away to a meeting, but the thought of the huge, disproportioned Lampmaker going anywhere beyond his 'Cottage' was difficult to entertain; it must be a very important meeting indeed. The external green door complete with knocker, which he could recall from his very first encounter with the Lampmaker, stirred old memories as it glowed in the light of the lamp which he had been given as a present on that occasion.

Instead Samuel focused on the two large buffers, which marked the end of the railway line, so that he could follow it out of this cavern and towards the place between worlds. From what he could remember it was about a half hour walk from here. The track had not glinted as he might have been expecting it to in the light of his lamp and, as he started to follow it, the reason became clear. The track was rusting and grimy in the damp condition which the tunnel was now in. It didn't look to Samuel as though any Dark Trains had run along the track in a while. He wondered to himself where a Dark Train might be kept? There didn't seem to be any sidings around that would offer an explanation.

Eventually the track ran up to the metal doors which separated the place between worlds from this side of the tunnel. As Rose had instructed, Samuel began searching for the wheel which would secure their release.

Samuel was still in the middle of searching when, to his amazement, the doors swung open quickly of their own accord. From inside there was a shimmering light which even his magnificent lamp could not compete with. Rose's insistence that he should wear a blindfold as he passed through this area melted away to something which seemed to be of no consequence. Without hesitation he strode into the beckoning light.

Something seemed to hit him in the eyes and everything became completely white and blank. It was as though a thick and seamless white skin had grown over his eyes. The skin was alight, burning over its entirety without causing him pain. When he had strode into the light, despite his lack of trepidation, Samuel had expected something apocalyptic beyond the doors, but instead what he had found was strangely beautiful. It wasn't even an empty whiteness, for as his eyes settled a little, something swam out of the whiteness towards him. It moved closer little by little, rather like an image seen while in a dream.

The image shimmered like one viewed over a fire and Samuel could at last make out that it was a stone cottage. His line of sight glided towards a doorway, first passing a sign hanging from the thatched eaves which read:

The Gate House at The Last Post

He had passed through the doorway now and into the quaint insides. Out of the darkness Samuel could make out a well known figure. It was Martharnia. Her usual apron was on and as she stared in Samuel's direction she raised a finger to her furry lips. She looked furtive as though she should not be acknowledging his presence. Samuel could see her mouth moving, but her words did not seem to carry to him. Instead they seemed to ring out softly in his head.

'The Master of the Gate House cannot see you at the moment because he is in a meeting with the Lampmaker.'

'Who's the Master, Martharnia?'

'He said that you knew his son, who you sat in judgement over, as he will one day sit in judgment over you.'

Martharnia looked down at a book which was lying on a table in front of her before she spoke again. She seemed to be checking something.

'You have work left to do in two worlds. Be then divided and execute. Fable's Passage must be closed. Board the last Dark Train quickly. And I need your lamp...'

Her words rang out in Samuel's head as the image of Martharnia and the whiteness of his surroundings melted away into near darkness.

Samuel found that his lamp was gone from his person, but the doors of the place between worlds were slightly open behind him so as to let enough light through to show up the hulk of a Dark Train. He must now be on the other side of the place between worlds. The Dark Train was waiting with a door in an open position. There was no time to think about what to do. Samuel would have to merely 'execute' and take Martharnia at her word.

As Samuel clambered aboard, the door closed behind him and the whole train began to move. He was thrown against the far wall of the interior while the great candelabras flickered dimly overhead. From somewhere outside there was a thunderous explosion which was dreadfully loud even inside the protected interior of the Dark Train. Samuel managed to crawl towards the middle of the train, eventually reaching its front end. There was no light inside now, but sensation was rawer than ever. Samuel could feel the Dark Train being propelled forwards by the blast and gathering tremendous speed as it accelerated away. The train was shaking and shuddering, jolting as it shot over the rusty track joints beneath it. It started screaming with a shrill piercing sound, as though it were a wild creature in agonising pain. Through mile upon mile of tunnel the Dark Train made its escape from the excavations which he could hear collapsing behind it.

Samuel remained crouched inside the Dark Train until he felt it roll to a halt. The interior had been plunged into near darkness when the huge blast had occurred, so it was with some difficulty that he edged towards the door. Feeling for the handle carefully, he managed to find it, and the side door crept open in slow reluctance.

Emerging onto the side of the track, the rear of the Dark Train came into his view. No wonder it had been screaming as it was dragged along the railway track, for it was now no more than a twisted hulk of metal and splintered wood at its rear. It was an awful sight to see this beautiful, faithful train that had borne so many individuals safely between worlds in such a state that it would never move again. In was nothing short of a miracle that Samuel had survived its last journey in a section which had remained in one piece. The front end had not de-railed, but had simply been thrust along its normal path until it had reached its final resting place, which was not more than a hundred metres from Little Tunlings railway station.

Memories were pouring back to Samuel with a greater coherence than ever before. He remembered from years ago catching the Dark Train after he left the McGill's. What had happened to them? Would they still be at the farm? With memories came questions, but not answers. It was time to get going. Leaving what remained of the Dark Train behind him, Samuel limped his way along the track. Dawn was starting to grace the night sky with her first grey plumes signalling daybreak but they were not yet, by any stretch of the imagination, sufficient for good visibility. In the distance at the far end of a platform Samuel could make out a light. As he edged closer it became clearer, and he could make out a lit window cut into a small hut, presumably wooden, which had been erected on the platform. Samuel couldn't work out why it was so difficult to walk along the track, which he had assumed would be clear. Instead, long weeds seemed to bind around his ankles, reaching out to pull him down.

The answer was not to be long in its discovery. Samuel hauled himself onto the station platform and, panting, surveyed the view. Even in the musky light of the hour and in the light from the window it was evident that the station had not been used for years. The concrete slabs underfoot were uneven and in some cases missing entirely. Elsewhere, they had been lifted and broken by nature as shrubs and bushes pushed through the cracks. It was a far cry from the neat station quiet Mr. Potts had once kept, from which Samuel used to catch the train to go and stay with Aunt Mulltasch. How he could remember her now! Funny thing that she had been! Once Rose joined him, Samuel was keen to find out more about her. Perhaps there was family of hers in this world which he had never known about years ago. He felt there was a lot to thank the queer Germanic woman for.

Samuel had been pondering the future when he heard the sound of a door creaking open. From the direction of the shed, fresh light issued forth, accompanied with the sound of a rifle being cocked.

'Hands up phantom, and step where I can see ye!'

Now did not seem like a good time to argue. Forwards from the shed there limped a man that Samuel could not say he recognised at all. The limp was severe, and every time the man moved there was the sound of a wooden 'clunk'. The rifle which he held out looked ancient but dangerously menacing.

'Sir, I mean no harm. Please put the gun down!'

'I've had enough of the ghosties, phantom! Look at the state of you! Bearded and dressed in rags! From which grave did you rise, phantom? What member of the undead are you?'

'Sir I am neither! I used to live in this village of Little Tunlings. I used to catch the train from this very station in the days when it was run by Mr. Potts.'

The man drew closer, rifle still trained on Samuel. He was getting so near that Samuel could hear the man's rasping breath.

'Mr. Potts ye say? You don't seem like no ghost, phantom, when you are able to speak my name. If it is from the next world that you come, how is my wife, Geraldine? Does she ask after me? Has she sent you to get me?'

He seemed to be getting more nervous, and fumbled loosely with the rifle.

'Mr. Potts, I am Samuel. Samuel Deksis. Do you remember me?'

Thinking a moment, the man shook his head gruffly.

'I remember a Samuel Hawkins, Albert's boy, when he was alive. Went missing they say, after he moved to stay with the McGill's. Must 'ave been fifty years ago or so now.'

'I am Samuel Hawkins, yes sir, I am.'

'Then you are a ghost, phantom; a ghost with a name. And you're about twenty years old now I should say; how does a phantom come to age?'

'Sir, Mr. Potts, if you will but answer a few questions then I will leave you and trouble you no longer.'

'Ye will I have no doubt, for if not I'll shoot with this gun. Ask quickly then, and after be gone!'

'Are the McGill's still at the farm? Mirabella and Henry?'

'Not for many years, phantom. Both are buried in the graveyard at St. Quains besides their children, Eraill and Daniel. I go up there to see Geraldine's grave. You remember Mrs. Potts, yes? Died of a heart attack twenty years back. I couldn't bear the post office in the village after that. The sweets section reminded me of 'er too much. After I fell onto the line and lost my leg; it was too much for me to do anyway. I can move, but only slowly. She's buried next to our little blighter who died before he ever had a chance to live. Cursed they were, all the children round 'ere. Ye know of Pebble Lane? Somat bad about the place. Never set eyes on it myself, but the McGill's boys did. Killed all of them too. Hawkins House lies in ruins up by the trees. The McGill's farm is a pile of rubble too, although one of them barns is still nearly standin' right. There's no people left in Tunlings now, phantom, save me and old Reverend Knock. And if life there be in those veins of yours, St. Quains is the place to go. The Reverend there will give ye shelter. Now pray, phantom, if phantom you be, be gone! Or shoot I will!'

The distraught old man gestured to a gap in the dilapidated fence at the edge of the platform. Reluctantly Samuel moved off. It seemed like St. Quains would be the place to head. From what Samuel remembered of Little Tunlings it was near the McGills farm. He had a dim recollection of the view from one of the upper fields. From there you could see down the valley to St. Quains, waiting at the end of a rough track as a bleak obelisk to religious control.

Samuel could see how his appearance might appear phantom like. The clothes which Rose had given him to wear had been torn and ripped in the scramble to leave Grat quickly.

Inside the Dark Train after the blast, the air had been thick with dust and soot. He made an effort now to make himself more presentable, hoping to receive better treatment from the Reverend Knock than he had from Mr. Potts. Whether an ancient clergyman would be any less superstitious than a fretful one legged man was debatable.

It felt too early to wake the Reverend when Samuel arrived so he found a dry and sheltered corner of the graveyard and slept there.

Brushing off the dead leaves which again added to his wild visage, Samuel headed to the main hall of St. Quains. This was the only way to reach the Reverends quarters it seemed. The graveyard was overgrown but there were signs of life here and there. Some of the grass had been roughly cut, apparently with the scythe which lay abandoned by the path. The gravestones caught his attention as he passed them.

'In loving memory of Geraldine Potts and child.'

'Phyllis Monroe, much loved and missed.'

'Albert Hawkins buried in the village he loved.'

'Henry and Mirabella McGill, united at last.'

'Here Lie Eraill McGill, Daniel McGill, who were called away too soon.'

They were all here, he thought. All of the people he remembered.

As Samuel had been observing the inscriptions he heard a twig snap behind him. It was the elderly Reverend Knock.

Gone was the youthful being that had waited in vain to take that ill-fated Christmas Day service on the dreadful day all the children of the village died. Knock had kept St. Quains open with the assistance of the older members of Little Tunlings society. Stalwarts such as old Phyllis Monroe had been determined that services should continue when her health permitted it. There had been others who had helped, most of whom were now buried here in the graveyard.

Knock had only known Albert Hawkins through word of mouth. Mr. Hawkins had not been much of a church man, too consumed with his books and parchments. Samuel Hawkins was only a vague memory of a name to him. Yet the name of Samuel Deksis, as Samuel introduced himself, was as well known to the old Reverend as his own son. Reverend Knock had grown to believe he knew of Samuel, Saffie and Harold Deksis as if they were his own family.

It had all started for Knock when he read through the scruffy notes providing details about church services which he had been given upon assuming his role as vicar in Little Tunlings. After the information about church service times was a lifetime of records made by the late Reverend Hector Grey, former vicar of Little Tunlings.

A lesser man than Knock might have burnt the papers, taking them to be the confused ramblings of a deranged old Reverend. Knock was no such person. Although the handwriting was frequently difficult to read, perhaps even madly so, there was a coherence to the witness borne out in the records and musings which quite caught his mind and imagination.

As the frequency of church services and visitors plummeted to zero, except for old Mr. Potts who staggered up to St. Quains in only the best of weather, Knock had found the time to work through the confused jumble of information. No story more fantastical had he ever read! The rest of his life he had dedicated to writing up the account. It was a story of love and desperation, the toils of Saffie and Harold Deksis and everything that had happened to them. In his imagination the history of Grat, Ling, Telfon and Davish had been played out more vividly than any motion picture film. This was real and earthy, something he understood.

'Mr. Deksis, Your Majesty, I had been hoping so much to meet you. I feel quite overcome!'

'You had?'

'Oh yes, I have read so much about your family, although I know very little of your own story. Perhaps I could persuade you to tell it over a mug of hot cocoa?'

And that is exactly what they did. Samuel told his story right from the very beginning and Knock listened, interrupting little, entranced until it had played out to its dreadful end. How glad he was that Samuel had at last been freed.

When he finished, they sat in silence as Knock pondered all that he had been told. He, of course, had never been to Grat, but all that Samuel told him of the great city and its neighbours tallied with the notes he had deciphered. Hector Grey, it seemed, had known almost as much about Grat as Samuel.

'Rose promised that she would meet me here in Little Tunlings. But that was before the way between was closed. The Dark Train is in ruins as I told you, fit only to rust away. How will Rose find me now?'

'I do not doubt the sincerity of her promise and neither should you. This 'Brothership' is something which fascinates me, Your Majesty. Do you understand the only way in which the Eddisa paradox can be explained?'

'I can't say that I do, Reverend.'

'This is mere conjecture on my part, and you must forgive the witterings of an old fool. I believe that in order for 'The Brothership' to penetrate time, both forwards and backwards, it must have a beginning somewhere. In the case of 'The Brothership,' you created the deadly pact with Marion Monroe and Pinochet that they would seek to obliterate your own existence from reality. Neither Marion nor Pinochet are going to live forever, or have lived forever. There is a point in time when their existence begins at their birth and ends at their death.

But The Brothership penetrates further back than this, though. Your own father, if you knew the full story... Hector recorded it so well. In time I shall tell you everything.

I believe that the existence of Marion and Pinochet begins with The Brothership and works backwards. In effect you created them with the power of your imagination. You said how desperately low you were when they befriended you. It is as though they were monsters in the dark corners of your minds that stepped, blinking, into reality. I might be wrong; it is just a thought.'

'Reverend, there is something I am very confused about, or rather someone. 'The Lampmaker' made a prophecy that the first King of Grat to come from another world would unite all of the countries around under its control once again. When I left Grat the city was surrounded by the armies of its neighbouring countries. It was under siege and only a matter of time before they won. Grat will be obliterated, not strengthened under my rule. How did he get this so wrong? And another thing, he seemed to know so much about my mother and I daresay The Brothership too, even if he didn't let on very much.'

'Ah yes, I wondered something similar when you told your story, Your Majesty. I would have continued entirely perplexed if it were not for an idea that old Hector seems to have had. In his notes he suggested that The Lampmaker, as he is known, goes by different names in different worlds. In some, he is just a mere reference in folk law, in others a fully accessible, solid being. In this world, Hector believed he went by the name 'Old Man Time.' Daft as this sounds, it would make sense. If The Lampmaker is a part of time itself then it would explain why he knows so much. I also have another reason for this belief, based upon the gifts which the McGills gave you on the Christmas day before you left. Mrs. McGill told me after you left Little Tunlings that The Lampmaker calved the wooden picture frame you were give. With it, it seems to me that he warned you of your potential fate; it is almost as if he was trying to prevent you from being hanged. It seems he succeeded.

We could talk at length for longer, but I would like to take you outside, Your Majesty. Will you come with me to the place called Pebble Lane? Now that you are here I believe the time is right.'

'What about the curse? Will it happen again when someone goes near that place?'

'I have been fearful that it might, but Christmas Eve is a long way off, and that is when the curse is at its strongest.'

'The Lampmaker confirmed that my older brother Jonoway is buried there. I have long wondered why the ground where he is buried should be cursed. Do you know Reverend?'

'In short, I do not, Your Majesty. But I do know that there is something very odd about the place. Hector believed that the curse had much in common with The Brothership, in fact he was certain it ran backwards and forwards in time in just the same way. A short visit together may tell us much more.'

In no time at all, it seemed, they were off together. The overgrown graveyard of St. Quains was left behind and Knock led Samuel through fields and gaps in hedges. Samuel saw the remains of the McGill's farmhouse as they passed it. The stone walls had quickly collapsed, it seemed. As Knock had said, only a distant barn was standing complete.

A copse of thick trees came into view, and the ground became boggier under foot. A stream was spilling into the field and draining away into the ground. Samuel had to be careful not to slip on loose, muddy rocks as Knock led the way up the stream. The undergrowth was thick and knotted, very difficult to penetrate if it were not for the stream cutting a path.

Presently it opened up onto an overgrown pathway. Despite the great trees overhead, a multitude of weeds had seeded successfully between the awkward cobbles which gave the ancient lane its name. An angular hulk of stone stood erect, not more than a few metres down the lane from here, and Knock was already heading towards it. Upon approaching, he knelt down at the clearest face. Samuel followed suit and joined him. Together they read the words engraved there:

HERE IS THE FINAL RESTING PLACE OF JONOWAY DEKSIS
BESIDE HIS BROTHER, SAMUEL DEKSIS
Eternally a fallen prince among the pale ghosts of Pebble Lane

For all his knowledge of fantastical things and other worlds, Reverend Knock let out an audible gasp. Of all the things he had expected from a visit to the forbidden domain of Pebble Lane it had not been this.

'It seems that Mr. Potts was right; I am a phantom!'

Knock gave Samuel a look as though considering this a real possibility for a moment.

'Seem more like flesh and blood to me.'

'Mr. Potts said he thought Samuel Hawkins to be dead; perhaps the carving was a reference to that misunderstanding.'

Knock was not a man taken to giving withering looks, but his expression was certainly akin to such a thing. No small minded villager from Tunlings would have dared go near Pebble Lane, let alone deface the accursed stone that was erect there.

There was nothing more to be said. Reverend knock was locked in thought as the pair made their retreat from the forsaken lane. Samuel felt as bewildered as ever. As soon as it seemed things were beginning to unravel they became even more complicated. The carving had looked ancient; it seemed he was supposed to have been dead a long time.

The McGills farmhouse passed by and the fields led closer to St. Quains. Samuel could not say for certain when he noticed it, for it was sight, and not smell, that alerted him to the distant fire. The wind was blowing gustily away from them so that plumes of grey smoke ebbed and waned above the horizon. Anxiety became more etched in Reverend Knock's countenance as the final approach to St. Quains brought the building into view.

The church roof was fiercely alight, and from the way the fire seemed to have a hold on the structure, it must have started quite a while earlier. Knock began running onwards and Samuel ran hard to keep up.

'The notes! My book! Your Majesty, my life's work is – huhh – in there and – huhh – I have to get it out!'

They were dashing through the graveyard now, Samuel finding it hopeless to warn Knock of the dangers. The man was not to be persuaded against entering.

The roof was burning up fast and crackling dangerously as the dry wood that was not alight already kindled and combusted. Knock lived in a part of the church structure accessible only from the main hall. Samuel dared not enter the building beyond the porch as Knock dashed on. A minute passed. And another. Where was Knock?

At last Samuel could see him emerging from a doorway into the hall and staggering forwards carrying a hefty brief case and a mountain of bundled sheets in his arms.

'I've got them,' he managed to pant, just audible over the sound of the fire.

Almost as he spoke there was a cracking noise from overhead. Several wooden beams supporting the main hall roof collapsed, one of which landed on top of Knock. The debris which fell with the beams was burning fast and the heat was fierce.

Samuel tried to enter the hall and manoeuvre between the burning beams. It was quite hopeless and even from here he could feel his face burning and his palms stinging. The smoke was increasing too and he was soon starting to choke.

'Reverend?' he managed to cry out.

The only answer was the crackling rage of the inferno.

With tears streaming down his soot coated face, Samuel had left St. Quains. The only place he could think to head was to the old barn that remained standing on the McGill's farm. He could wait there until nightfall at least and nurse his burns and blisters. He knew it was imperative to stay near Little Tunlings. Rose had promised him she would join him and it was a promise which Samuel knew she hadn't made lightly. How she would come he didn't know, but come he knew she would.

Samuel found the barn with ease and, having forced the brittle door open, he sank in exhaustion onto several abandoned bales of hay. The barn was heavily musty but dry enough; the reason why the ancient straw had been preserved. He slept fitfully until nightfall and beyond, not finding the energy to rise until late morning.

When Samuel at last rose from slumber he could hear the sound of muffled scuffling. At first he thought it was coming from outside the barn, but after a time he became more certain that it actually emanated from inside. He would have supposed it was rats if the sounds of scuffling didn't seem to be getting louder and louder, nearer and nearer. Samuel went to open the barn doors and let the daylight come streaming in upon the mess of hay bundles and straw tufts that were strewn in disorder around the place. He was glad of light, glad to let it warm the musty barn air.

Then, right before his eyes, he saw something move. It was in an open area of the barn. Something black and a little shiny, but not too much. It was there for an instant and then it was gone. Then back again, and little more pronounced, repeatedly coming and going until it bore up through the very dirt floor of the barn.

And then, with a mighty heave, snuffling and wheezing in the light, Samuel saw with the greatest surprise none other than Mole himself, blinking and twitching in his filthy waistcoat which was even more torn and shabby than usual. Mole gave a shriek of pure wheezy delight and launched himself with all his remaining strength at Samuel so that he hugged his legs tightly around the knees. Caught quite off balance and unprepared, Samuel toppled backwards without being able to help himself and landed neatly in a strewn bail of hay with mole still clinging to his legs in a sort of rugby tackle.

It took quite a while for Samuel to persuade a tearful Mole to part with his legs, and when he eventually did so, Mole still seemed quite uncontrollable, snuffling and sniffling like he was never going to stop. He eventually started to make sense, and snuggling next to Samuel on the bail of hay, the creature finally reached a state of calm coherent speech.

'I was shearching for Your Majeshty, not shent to find you… I come under my own orders and strengths, but Rose did suggestuns I might praps find you near 'ere.'

Samuel looked at Mole rather aghast.

'You didn't… you didn't come all the way here underground did you?'

'The passage is sealed. You can't come outs that way now King Samuel, not since you escapsied.'

'– But I didn't think you could just dig your way through? Well, I suppose that must have been what happened the first time Fable's Passage was opened?'

'As usual Master is quite correcting in 'is answers. It's not just a matter of digging alone; it's a matter of digging and wanting. I wanted very much earnestly to be finding. Look –' he said pointing with his rough claw to the hole from which he had emerged, '– I was within a few metres of you. My father would be very much proud of my diggings.'

Samuel hugged Mole, who sat there in beady eyed pride at his own work.

'I, I thought you were dead Mole? I saw the Borrow Ways turned to waste as I left. They had sullied and poisoned the water, killed many if not most of the traders, destroyed boats and moorings. It was terrible. And I thought I saw your boat, The Shanty, upside down and half sunk. I am so glad I was mistaken.'

Mole let out a mournful wail.

'Master is not wrong 'ere. Our boat is gone, and Mr. Shabbers, poor poor Mr. Shabbers, they got 'im with their vilest poisonous poisons, Mole pulledsied 'im off the boat as they advanced with nasties like axes and 'ammers to break 'em all up. I dragsed 'im through the waters but it was all in vain. I watched 'im die coughing on the river back as they tore our boat apart and plundered alls our goods.'

'Oh Mole. I'm so, so sorry.'

'Mole is not 'ere for your pities. I am 'ere to telluns you what has 'appened since you left.'

Samuel felt like he hardly dared to ask. He swallowed.

'Tell me about Rose, Mole. Tell me about her. What happened? Is she coming to join me?'

Mole answered in his queer little way which, for the sake of clarity, has been simplified.

'When you were divided between this world and ours, the part of you there, whose story I now tell, returned to find none other than Rose. She met you in the city somewhere and she brought you down to see us, me and Mr. Shabbers both. And she told us all what was happening. The centaurs were loosing in the final battle; even they, the last great believers were failing to hold firm to orders to be fighting. It wasn't about greed any more, just about surviving. The city of Grat would fall in this battle to the armies of Ling if we did not pull out our last reserves. If we did that then we might just defeat them, enough to maintain our soverignty and keep charge of the city.'

'Mole, tell me, what did we do then? What happened?'

'She told us of her plan. A last and final charge with the remainder of the forces of Grat. She would be leading with you beside her. The Royal figure heads leading the way. No more would the people call you traitor, call you greedy, or try to be hanging you.'

'But Mole! Why, that would be suicide! For me and for her against those forces. The charge might stop them but we could never hope to survive.'

'Master, we told her the same as did you, but she was not to be persuaded. She knew what she was doing. She'd made her mind up she said. She would go by herself if no one would go with her. And you said if she was going then you would go too. And we begged you both to let us fight, but Rose was quite insistent, told us something plain, we would watch the charge, but then after haste away. Then as we got a bit more ready, she spoke to me alone. Quietly told me once the charge was over to get out of there and be finding your world as quickly as possible just as soon as Mr. Shabbers was safe, and to do so by any means I could. Dig, dig dig she said, until I found you.'

'Oh Mole, this is all so awful! Did the final charge go ahead?'

'You both passed our forces as you walked slowly to the hill crest beyond Aborglacias. At the first trumpety trump sounding you both pulled off your disguises and mounted a centaur each as Rose had prepared. On the battle field below, beyond the carnage and the ravages, you could be seeing the opposing armies assemblied. They all thought Grat would fall that day, but the trump called again and you both began to gallop, side by side straight towards the armies of Ling, Telfon and Davish ahead. And though the centaurs felt too tired to follow and the stallions behind them felt just the same, and the dwarfs and fawns behind them were quite exhausted too, they could all be seeing you. A couple riding out alone, quite brave, quite unprotected, without fear. And they could not watch with apathy.

How they would curse that they ever doubted you. They could be seeing you then for the true King, not the one they thought they hung earlier, but the one that loved his people until death, supported by his bride, his wife, the bravest wife that ever had lived. I was watching you both ride alone into the distance. And yes… I watched… watched as you both fell under the volley of nasties of arrows and mortars. And our armies roared their anger and swarmed forward after you. It was they who launched the ferocious attack. Never in the history of anywhere has there been a fight like that one. We thought no more than tens walked away from the thousands that joined you in the last stand. We won, but this time it wasn't like before. We were winning for the right things.'

Samuel saw it then in an instant. Rose. Her urgency the last time they had met. There had been no pardon. She had switched the places of the king with someone else. He felt like cursing her. She had lied. What innocent man had she led to death to save him?

'It were you friend, Master. Jack Shorrow. It was he that tooksied your place in Porthnarth. Not Rose's ideauns, Master. It was actually 'is.'

Samuel wept bitterly. It was all he could do. Jack had been his best friend. They had known each other for years. How he must have loved Grat and loved his King to have done that. As brave as his father before him, maybe even braver. And Rose too, his brave, his beautiful wife. How she loved everyone. And died in the filth and dirt of a battle field, so unbefitting, to save the world and peoples that she loved to serve. It was tragedy upon tragedy, death upon death and waste upon waste. The prophecy of the Lampmaker was correct in a terrible way. Grat had conquered but at a dreadful cost. So Jack Sorrow was the hero buried under a pseudonym in Pebble Lane; for the real Samuel Deksis to live, Jack had died.

When Jack took Samuel's place at Porthnarth he had pulled on the same hood his Majesty had been released from by Rose. Bertis Beavitch had helped him on with it, waiting only to exchange one final kiss. She was his willing accomplice in this deceit and would shortly exchange places with Lord Ruffus in the cell next door. Prisoner two five two was ready to face the final curtain and prisoner two five one would soon be in the same position. The guards kept Jack hooded in his cell until the call came for hanging. On a mound, between Aborglacias village and the centre of Grat, the scaffold had been erected. As Advisor Jacoby had decreed, three prisoners were to be hung at once. Samuel would be in the centre, the mysterious prisoner two five three to his left, and Lord Ruffus to his right. A piece of wood beneath Samuel was inscribed to read 'The King, who killed,' beneath Lord Ruffus a similar token blared 'The Lord, who lied' and beneath the third death bound prisoner 'The man who claimed to be King.' At least if someone was to be hanged they should know their crime. To Adviser Jacoby the signs more than met the requirements of Justice.

Jacoby was present to watch the end of all three prisoners. None of them required any last words. Officials opened the wooden traps, and the three bodies dropped. All around the valley a thundering blast rent the air while the ground tremored and shook like this was the end of days. When at last it settled all three were dead. In the Royal Palace the debating chamber had crumbled as the ground beneath it was cleft in two. Royalty seemed to have been wrenched from government and authority, its reputation in tatters. There were many in Grat who had felt little discomfort in this.

Influenced by The Brothership, Advisor Jacoby saw to it that Samuel's supposed body was taken and buried in Pebble Lane and, using the lamp which the Lamp Maker had provided years ago, Samuel was buried at the hands of Marion Monroe, both in reality and in time, backwards and forwards. Stretching through eternity, the ground there would bear the mark of its content; if any ventured near, all their kind in the village of Little Tunlings would die, furthering The Brothership's aim of slaying Samuel Deksis and wiping him from existence. The curse would fester in the way that all such things do, rising to be its most dangerous on Christmas Eve every year. For that was the cursed day when Samuel had started to make the journey into Grat to become its king.

Mole was sniffing once again as he snuffled against Samuel's side, his story fully told and explained.

'You go now, Master. Leave this godforsaken area. Be findings something better.'

'I've been told I have work left to do in this world, but I don't know yet what it will be. Will it be to do with Grat? Am I still the king of that hidden city in the other world?'

'Master, I would not really like to say. But I wouldn't be putting it down as unlikely.'

'And you Mole, you will come with me? For you must go back too one day.'

'Master. Mole knows he is not goings back. And nor will Mole be stayings 'ere. I'm old like my grime riddled waistycoat, and in needs of a bit of a wash. Let me gouns now and I'll be findings shomewhere quiet. Shettle down amongst shome leaves shomewhere; find shomethings a little shnugly to beuns by. And then I'll moveuns on and leave my waisty coat far behind. Take careuns Your Majeshty. Until we meetuns again on the last days. And you'll be knowings me then, 'cause I'll be lookuns a little whiter.'

And these were the last words of Mole. Samuel had to let him scrabble away out of barn and into the world. And then Samuel too decided to follow. It was time to move away from here. This chapter had ended.

THE END

Forthcoming Titles by the Author:

For Younger Children:
The Magic of Mr. Mordaine

For more details visit **www.samueldeksis.com**

Postscript

Dear reader, I hope that you gained as much enjoyment from reading this novel as I did from writing it. Despite the fact it nearly drove me to a nervous breakdown several times, I think the final out come is a first novel to be proud of. Pride must not, of course, obscure the truth that this is very much a work by an author who is new to his art. In years to come I hope to write better and bigger novels – and do not worry, I am certainly not short of ideas.

I now wish to thank those who have had a specific influence on this book. I include only those that have given specific inspiration and encouragement along the way. The first has to be Celia Thomas of Rhydypenau Primary School, because it was in her class room that I first dreamed up the city of Grat for my SATs English examination.

Then a huge debt of gratitude is due to the late Valerie Ruth Roberts, my mother, who proof read very early drafts of this novel. Sadly she never had the opportunity to meet Samuel Deksis and the rest of the gang. The only remaining character which has lasted all this time has been the ever amusing Marlow. It is said that out of great storms come a silver lining, and that is very much the way I view this novel.

My cousin Sophie deserves my thanks for the initial writing which she did in exploring ways to take this novel forwards. Although none of them have been used directly, the faith you put in me was much appreciated as has been your recent support.

Joanne Hopkins of Cardiff High School deserves my thanks for her assurance that I would one day finish this novel off. The legendary Jude Brigley, also of Cardiff High School, deserves my thanks for ensuring my enthusiasm for writing will last for the rest of my life. Anthony Toye of Cardiff High School was an enthusiastic supporter of my intention to get a novel of my own written. Zoe Brigley read a very early copy of the first chapter a few years ago, and the knowledge that she had it made me determined to make it a lot better. Her excellent creative writing course was a great inspiration to me and still aids me with setting and character work. Ben Poole of Cardiff High School was a general influence on my writing, and his helpful feedback during my A-Levels has improved my writing considerably.

Rhys Andrews and Gregory Lines became early supporters of my work and Greg has been particularly supportive of my bid to finish the novel completely. I know he is itching to read it. Michael Hodge has been an enthusiastic supporter of my work in Cardiff, and his promise to read this novel once it was finished spurred me on several times.

At University College London I wish to thank all of my friends, but particularly Stuart Goosey, Samuel Brewer, Jack Davies and Sonia Namutebi since without their enthusiasm I don't believe this novel would have ever been finished.

Thanks are due to Jane Austin for her novel 'Emma' which finally enabled me to grasp how to write detailed interactions without making them seem stilted. I am still in awe of the set pieces in her work.

My final thanks to my father, Richard Hugh Roberts for his encouragement and the hours that went in to proof reading the final manuscript.

Now I must hand things over to you. I am relying on my friends and contacts entirely at the moment. Please become another link in the chain to making this novel a success after my eight years of hard work and sleepless nights. Encourage all of your friends to make a purchase.

James Richard Roberts
University College London
October 2008

www.ingramcontent.com/pod-product-compliance
Ingram Content Group UK Ltd.
Pitfield, Milton Keynes, MK11 3LW, UK
UKHW020257250726
13967UKWH00004B/1723